HAUNT ME, THEN

A Queer Occult Horror Novel

LARAMIE DEAN

HORRORSMITH PUBLISHING

To my parents

PROLOGUE

December 1988

1

I came back to the homeplace without sending word. No notice. Didn't tell nobody. Just showed up. In the night. In the dark and the cold.

It spread out below me like I remembered it from old pictures. I hadn't been there since childhood.

Or maybe I had never been there.

Memory plays tricks, don't you know.

Heath called it the "Heights." He would smile when he said it. Not a pleasant smile; Heath didn't do pleasantness. He smiled because the house was placed low and not high. Tucked down. There was no height about it. The house sat at the base of a hill, see, and the entire ranch— what was a ranch, I guess, but isn't anymore, not so much—it was all lowland.

You got to the homeplace by traveling down old Highway 201, which wasn't paved, and then you made a right onto a road that was even less of road than *that*. Really, not even much of a road, but is almost—but not quite—two simple ruts cutting through all that yeller grass. They lead you down and down and down, and so you go, and there's the house.

Big, used to be white-painted with red trim, if the pictures told you the truth, if you can trust a photo or a story. Three high gables, big front door, and a smaller one to the side. A path made of flat, brown rocks collected from the creek, which snaked its way through the prairie out there. And so, you followed the rocks, and they took you to one of the doors. Two doors on opposite sides of the house to bring you inside. Into its belly.

Into the Heights.

I followed them rocks; I trusted them. Couldn't help myself.

Snow coming down. I remember that. I had forgotten about the snow out here. The wind. Christ, I forgot it all. Fucking, *fucking* Montana. In the winter. Biting at me. It chews on you. Like a goblin. Cackling and chewing like a goddamn goblin. But I wore my gloves because I am not an idiot, no matter what you think or what they say.

I had my thick leather gloves, a big ol' black duster my great-grandpa Linden had handed down to me, and one of them funny hats you never saw people wear anywhere outside the country. Huge wooly earflaps and a single black—or red or blue or white—pom in the direct center of the crown of your head. I also rode my horse, a savage black witch named Sasha. Should have been in my truck, but I was staying at my grandparents' farm four miles down the road, and I had been so cocksure I would make it back before the storm hit.

The homeplace—the Heights, if that is what you want—was closest, and the snow was thick and growing thicker, mean growing meaner. I was cold. Hungry.

The homeplace seemed like the wiser choice.

And Heath didn't scare me.

I told myself he didn't scare me.

Dark by the time I made it down the road. A mile or so. Hard to see in the snow; impossible to see if they had the porchlight off. That night, it glowed up at me through all the skeins of snow like a yeller—like a *yellow* eye.

Why would I go out on a day like today anyway, taking a horse instead of a truck, before a storm like the one spreading its big black wings over the horizon, sinking into black? Gramma had asked me. "You don't wanna die out there," she had said. "It's happened before. I told you." She had. "People go, and the country swallows them. Then they ain't never seen again. It's happened before. I told you. Trust me, baby boy, you don't want it to happen to *you*."

Montana is bigger than you think. If you live here, plains or cities or towns or mountains or valleys...Hell, maybe *you* got a grasp on the size. But I only say "maybe." I left for years and came back, and I thought I knew all about it, but I forgot. I forgot about how really big the prairie is and how it spreads sweet and slow or hard and slow. Or how it *goes* and it doesn't pay any attention to you, no matter how hard you pick at its hide, where you build your house, how big you build your house, how big you think it is, or where. Winds come and scour it all away eventually anyway.

Most of them homesteader cabins sit empty now, full of junk, useless papers and photos and keepsakes, even a pair of shoes I saw at the old Barnes place, real old-fashioned like—like from the eighteen hundreds—propped up in an empty room that used to be the kitchen, I guess. Next to a canceled check from ol' Irving Barnes to the Bank o' Burke. Dated 1963.

Burke was the closest town to the Heights. I been there a time or two. Nothing left now of that man but his check and his shoes. Poor ol' Irving. Who was still here who remembered him? Who could have picked him out of a crowd if they had to?

Nothing left of any of them people who settled out here. Might as well be as if they had never come at all. Ask the land. It will tell you.

Maybe they never wanted to live forever. Whoever asked?

Dark by the time me and Sasha had made it down the long road to the Heights. Heath would laugh about it, if I ever seen Heath laugh. If *anyone* ever seen a miracle like that. Wind screaming like an old woman with her throat choked but still full of feeling. And that feeling was all misery and cold and white death.

I had seen the lights from up at 201. Just barely through the ropes of snow, flickering by. I forgot how damn fast the sun set this far east, so close to the North Dakota border. It was there for a breath or two, making everything all stark and white by day and faded and bluish about three, three-thirty. And then there it goes. Down. And gone. Leaving just ashes. Then dark.

Sasha was snorting and fidgeting. I did my best to soothe her. Whispered compliments. Told her how pretty she was. She would toss her head and glare at me, but I wouldn't stop. Pat, pat, pat; pet, pet, pet. Shush, pretty girl. You hush now, beautiful.

And there was the house, rearing at us out of the dark, like a skeleton. The bones of something huge. Only the eyes lived. The windows, I mean. Glowing with warmth. I breathed a sigh that turned into a flood of moths out of my mouth, but they were torn away by the grasping fingers of the wind.

So, Heath was home. With his wife, Annabelle. And the hired man, if the hired man had stayed up t'the house and not gone to his quarters —an old shanty shack several yards away.

I whispered to Sasha while I tied her up at the jerry-rigged fence Heath had built. Not such a good job. "My cousin Earnest," Grandpa would say, clucking his tongue, "Ol' Earnest wouldn't have approved." I never met my cousin Earnest, though. Heath must have torn the old man's fence down after he died and put up *this* one. Piss poor. Posts nothing but driftwood sticking out of the snow, laced with rusty barbed wire. It snarled at me but hardly did its job. Sinking and falling off its slats. The gate was a piece of discarded pallet wood held in place by a horseshoe.

Clever, Heath.

Patted Sasha one more time. Slipped through the gate like a wraith. She whinnied, all uneasy, but the wind grabbed the sound, held it, and then ran off with it into the dark. She was a good old girl, my Sasha, and didn't deserve cold like this. Wind like this. Sharp snow, like bits of shattered glass, dancing at her out of the sky.

Must have been nearly five o'clock. What a fool I was. Heath would let me stay the night, though. Tie up Sasha with his horses. Gramma had said he still kept horses. Gramma had said he still worked.

"He'll work 'til he's dead," she claimed.

I wondered about that.

3

Someone up there, watching. Spooked the living hell out of me, though I guess it shouldn't have. Heath, hulking up against the kitchen window, light from the living room behind him making him nothing but a silhouette. I shook my head. The neighborly thing—the *family* thing—would have been to go right to the door and open it up. Shout a few words of welcome into the storm before it grew worse. Not Heath, though.

The old bastard.

I started toward the door. A voice, then, stopped me cold. Calling. Man's voice or a boy's?

"Hello?" I called back, like an idiot.

Above the house, a hill swelled up, and atop the hill rested the homesteader cabin Great-Gramma and Great-Grandpa Lyon built between the two of them back during the summer of 1872. Fresh off the wagon from Minnesota, homesteader land at a premium. Arrived in the earliest part of the summer so the heat didn't seem too bad. The creek, a red ribbon cutting through the grass, making it look lush, had helped some with that.

There was water for bathing, swimming, and boiling before they had finished the well, but the well, to hear Heath tell it, always smelled sour, like shit and minerals. There was row after row of trees, an orchard Great-Gramma and Great-Grandpa Lyon planted the year after they moved from the east. They were all dead. Just bones. The trees, I mean. Sentinel skeletons keeping watch, marching up and down the east side of the hill. Like they would begin to move every time you look away, so you can almost catch them. Almost.

The voice came from there.

"Hello?" I called again, uncertain-like, and took a few steps in the direction of the grove.

Behind me, Sasha whickered and snorted, stomped her heavy feet in the snow. I did my best to ignore her.

That voice. A man's voice, for sure, though it had sounded like it trembled on the border of manhood. A teenager. Someone lost in the snow, maybe? A neighbor wandered too far afield, as I had?

Across the plains, about a mile or so, there waited the old Reardon farm, a house just about as big as the Heights, maybe a room or two smaller. Reardons were long gone, but these were nice people. A young couple, from what I had gathered. Couple of brats.

No, this had been the voice of someone almost a man or newly a man. Maybe my age. A year or two on either side.

"Help me," the voice said, clear as a church bell. "I'm so cold."

"Where are you?" I called back. "Can't see you!"

"Help me," the voice said. "Help me, please. I'm cold. So cold."

"I'm trying!" I hollered, but the wind kept its filthy habit of snatching the words from my mouth and laughing away, replacing them with its own particular bite and flecks of snow to burn the cheek and gullet.

I saw it—the figure of the boy. Flickering about in the trees. Moving here and there. White. So white.

I froze. It couldn't have been real, I decided. A trick of the blizzard. Moving about, moving about. Did it raise arms high to the sky? Did it beg and entreat, imploring me for help? Hands, I thought. I swear I saw fingers. Long and bony.

Then there was no boy at all, but an animal instead, running at me, baying, huge. A hound, but white as the snow, eyes yellow as piss, teeth the same. Sabers. Foam flew from its massive jaws in freshets.

I screamed, turned, and tried to run. Then it was on me.

4

"Damn fool," he growled in my ear. "Goddamn, goddamn fool. *Fool.*"

My arm throbbed. I was being dragged, bump, bump, bump, upward. Steps, maybe? I tried to see, but the sudden flood of light, buttery and warm, blinded me. Somewhere, too close for my comfort, that giant animal bayed its fury and loss. Snowflakes floated, circled, and landed on my lashes, where they neglected to melt.

"I'm just visiting," I said through a throat full of slush. My tongue had frozen in rills against my traitorous teeth, which chattered even though I insisted they stop. "I'm j-just a p-passing c-c-cousin—"

"*Fucking* goddamn fool." The old man's breath was sour and yellow when it flitted across my face.

I winced. Heath. Just as I had remembered him from our most recent family gathering. The Christmas before last.

"L-Linden." I choked. "L-L-Lockwood Linden." I yelped when he released his grip on my shoulders and my head struck the floor.

"Don't make no difference to me," Heath said, my cousin. "A fool is a fool. Goddamn fool."

"The day got away from me." I sat up, wincing, and rubbed the back of my head.

I lay in the hallway of the big house. The lights from above stabbed down at me. I grumbled and tried to stand. Cowboy boots, work boots, and overshoes, all clotted with dried hunks of mud, lay in a scatter on a rubber mat beside my head.

Heath watched me, expressionless, while I crawled to my knees, planted a hand against the wall, filthy with grime and fingerprints, and hauled myself to my feet. His hair was nearly white but still streaked with thick black slashes. It had receded far back on his forehead, which was lined and angry. His eyebrows had grown into bushy white caterpillars he refused to maintain. Dark purple circles ringed his black eyes, where I could, as always, find no pupils. Only chips of coal flecked with gold if they caught the light right. Like a dog's eyes.

I thought of the beast that had attacked me outside and shuddered.

"I seen you before," said the old man.

"I'm your cousin. Lock. Lockwood."

"That ain't any kinda name." He sneered at me, revealing yellow, pitted teeth.

I didn't argue. What would you say to a man with no last name, no middle initial?

"Listen. The storm is pretty bad—"

"Getting worse all the time." He didn't stop grinning. His teeth, more and more, looked like stumps to me. Tombstones. My stomach turned over.

"And I know it's only a few miles to Grandma and Grandpa's—"

"You can't stay here. Not tonight."

"You gotta let me." I was dismayed by the whine I heard in my voice, but I couldn't hold it back. He didn't expect me to go back out into the storm, did he? With that monster dog out there and the wind howling like a fiend?

And there was a boy in the trees. You know there was—

"And the boy—"

Heath's grin vanished, as if it had never been. His caterpillar eyebrows drew together into a bar of solid white. "What boy?"

"Someone out there." I gestured in the direction of the trees. "Out in the storm—" *Oh, damn. I just remembered.* "And my horse—"

"Fuck your horse," he muttered, but I didn't really think he heard me.

"Listen," I said. The famous Linden temper reared up inside me, zero to ten, with no warning. "Listen, you can't say things like that. Look, I'm family—"

"There ain't no one out there."

"My horse. And the boy—"

"I'll send Robbie after your horse." His eyes settled on the window that peered out the door and into the storm. They narrowed a bit. He stepped heavily toward it and shuffled aside the curtain with gnarled, jaundiced fingers, pressing his forehead to the glass. "But there ain't no one out there now."

"The dog—"

"That dog won't be back. Not no more." His shoulders slumped. He sounded exhausted.

"Cousin Heath—"

He turned to me, glaring. "There ain't no room for you here.

Robbie will take care o' your horse, and you can warm up for a bit, but then you got to go. I don't put up strangers."

"I told you, I'm not—"

"I don't put up *no one*, then." His corneas gleamed in the light over our heads. His lips, withered, lined, drew back over those teeth, those stumps. He *seethed* at me.

His hatred was something I could feel. It pawed at me, steamed at me. It stank.

I drew a breath.

The wind screamed like a witch.

Outside, I could have sworn someone was moving. Someone came out of the trees, whiter than the snow, and approached the steps, reaching—

"Okay," I said, turning to face him. "If that's how you want it."

5

His wife basked in the soft golden light from the lamp on the table beside her easy chair. Her face was hard and white as porcelain but unlined, except for one long slash above the bridge of her nose, as if someone had carved at her, slicing her with the blade of a particularly nasty knife.

Annabelle Thrush she had been, and Annabelle Thrush she remained. For Heath, as I said, had no last name. They had been married for almost thirty years, according to Grandma. At her side, leaning against the back of her chair and glaring at me with eyes as yellow and sullen as his father's, was their son, Hare. Big sonofabitch too, bigger than Heath. Shoulders like twin mattresses. Thick snarl of coal-black hair. Handsome, though, like his father.

But I wasn't paying any attention to that.

"It's me," I said, cheerful as I could. "Your cousin Lock. Remember me?"

Annabelle shifted in her chair. She wore a pantsuit of polyester and solid pink, pink as the Pepto Bismol Grandma Linden always kept on hand. Annabelle's hair, white or blond—I couldn't tell—was pulled back behind her head so it fell onto one of her shoulders in ringlets, coiled and tight as bedsprings.

She held the remote control to a thyroidal television. I saw it when I glanced over my shoulder, lying behind me, shoved up against the far wall. Enormous, ancient, but modern enough that a remote would work, I guessed. I wasn't sure if Cousin Annabelle saw me or saw through me, or if she aimed the remote at me like a pistol.

"Cousin Annabelle," I said. "Cousin Hare."

Hare's lips peeled back from his teeth. A wave of dark stink struck me, and it took all the control I had left not to grimace: a stench like onions, unwashed bodies, ancient shit that clung forever and could not —would not—be wiped away.

"The fuck you want?" Hare said clearly, almost sweetly.

I blinked. His voice carried easily to me across the vast living room they had filled with furniture. Dark, old, and mismatched. Heavy-framed photographs and some paintings of horses and cows, even a stat-uette or two. Graceful young men with their arms raised over their heads, nary a stitch of clothing to be found about them. Little cocks everywhere.

I blushed seeing them. Who decorated like this? And *had* I ever been to the Heights before? My head swam. Nothing pieced together. Memory had tattered and twisted itself. Maybe as a child...

"The fuck you want?" Hare said again. No sweetness now.

I had been wrong about that. Wrong about a lot of things that night, I guess.

"I got caught," I said stupidly. My hands balled into fists.

Christ, but the whole house stank. Paint peeled on the living room walls. Black spots—must have been mold, Jesus—spreading from the ceiling and down the peeling walls, like big stinking flowers. The floor beneath my feet was hardwood, but splintered, destroyed, worn trails in some spots, a hundred years of treading.

"Caught in the snowstorm."

"Fucking retard," Hare said and spat.

"You watch your mouth." Annabelle's voice was lifeless, thin, and dull. Her eyes floated somewhere over my shoulder. Perhaps at the TV screen I blocked. "You watch it," she said. "Don't be spitting on my floor. Don't be talking like no hired man."

From somewhere outside, farther up the hill, maybe toward that original homesteader cabin, I heard the baying of that big damned dog. I shivered.

They exchanged glances. I know they did.

"You heard it too," I said without thinking.

"You shut your goddamn head." Annabelle stood. The remote fell onto the floor with a clatter. Her eyes, dusty marbles, locked on mine. The effect was terrible.

My will sapped, draining out of me. She shuffled forward, a dusty mummy set free from its tomb of millennia. Jesus, she *was* an old woman. Unblinking, hands twisted with arthritis, but that ageless, unlined face didn't move. Maybe *couldn't* move.

"Mama," Hare said.

She stopped. Looked at him. Shook her head. Glared back in my direction. I realized she was toothless. Only pink gums gnashed wetly at me.

"There ain't nothing out there," she said.

"I already told him that."

Heath, framed in the doorway leading from the living room to the kitchen. The lights in the room we currently occupied were dim, nearly dying. The light in the kitchen, however, streamed at us. It was white, bright, cold. Still, a more welcoming room than this one, I thought.

"There's a dog," I insisted. "It attacked me."

"Robbie put your horse away. Storm's worse." Heath grinned at me. "Guess you'll stay tonight."

"Oh, maybe...I mean, I don't—"

"You can't get that horse back up to 201, back to your grandaddy's farm. Not tonight. Maybe not tomorrow neither. No way in heaven or hell, son."

Hare scowled.

I shifted my weight from foot to foot. My feet ached in their boots. I wasn't used to wearing cowboy boots, not anymore. And these were Granddad's old pair, a little too small for me. I was a college boy, went and got myself educated. Learned the wages of sin and all that nonsense my friends and family from Burke, Lambert, and Circle all mocked me endlessly for. Not one of them anymore. Too good for them, maybe. Thought myself real high and mighty. And maybe I did.

The smell of shit, onions, and vinegary sweat flooded into my nostrils again. Maybe I was, at that.

"Okay," I said at last.

"You can sleep with Hare."

"Fuck that!" the other man bellowed. Man? He was my age, maybe a year or two older, his size be damned.

"I'll use a chair in this room," I said hastily. "Honest, Cousin, it'll be fine."

"You can sleep in the barn," Hare growled. "You can bed down with the pigs, for all I care."

"He'll freeze to death," Annabelle whispered. "No one needs to freeze to death tonight." Her eyes widened, focused on one of them big black flowers spreading on the ceiling above her head. "No one needs to freeze *here*."

"You can nestle down in their *shit*."

"Honest, a chair, one of those easy chairs, will be just—"

"Show him to your room, Hare," Heath said, grinning. "Strange bedfellows." He snickered and shook his enormous head. "Oh, yes. Yes, yes. Strange, strange bedfellows indeed."

6

Annabelle pulled a shoestring attached to six small silver beads, summoning the dull, yellowish light of an ancient bulb to life, and then shuffled down the cluttered hallway of the attic. At the hallway's end, she opened a door and turned to stare at me, her mouth slack, hanging slightly open. I had to duck my head to enter; I didn't make six feet, but the doorway came to just below where my nose and mouth met.

"No one needs to know I took you to this room," Annabelle said.

"I won't tell." I felt childishly frightened. Afraid of the dark. Of this woman. Of the room before me.

"You keep your mouth shut. That's all." Her unblinking eyes were toad-like. I wondered if, once, she had been beautiful.

What is beautiful out here?

Stupid question.

She fluttered before me, weaving in and out of herself, her shadow, her age. For a moment, she was young and if not beautiful, then beguiling, maybe, with her long blond hair and eyes that had, as of that long ago moment, not yet gone toadish. Maybe I had seen photos of her— Grandma had boxes full of old, faded Polaroids—or a family picture, framed and hung somewhere where we all could bear witness to the way of life at the Heights. Life with Heath, life under the relentless wind, which tore at the prairie grasses, and the sun that yellowed and grayed it while cracking the skin of anyone who tried to work these desolate places...

"You don't know nothin'," she muttered, her face a hag's scrawl, a porcelain mask, then a delighted young woman with wide, eloquent eyes. She lowered her head and heaved a sigh.

How had she married Heath; how had Heath married *her*? I thought of a girl named Jenny, a stranger to me now. Or maybe I was a stranger to her, or we were strange to each other. I thought of that girl, that Jenny, back at my college in Garden City, educating the masses at the far west of the state. And I remembered others—unnamable, indescribable others it was unsafe to dwell on, especially here, especially under this terrible roof.

Would my strange Jenny be like this woman someday? Would I do that to her? Wear her down? Or should I preserve her and keep her safe in a town or a big city, somewhere on the coast, away from these people and the ways they did things out on the plains? These rural people and the things they did, their *rituals*...Should I?

"Heath's gone to bed," Annabelle muttered. She moved away from me, gesturing with some irritation in the direction of the room.

I stuck my head into the darkness within, squinting. Another shoestring, another bare light bulb. I pulled the string, and the light bloomed but dimly, soft gold, a dying firefly.

"He won't have to know you was ever in this room."

"Thank you, Cousin."

"You don't got to call me that."

"But it's what we are."

"No one cares. Not out here. No one *cares*." Her eyes had welled up, I saw with some alarm, and her lower lip, what there was of it, trembled. "No one is *family* anymore," she whispered, covering her face with her hand.

I reached out to pat her shoulder, clumsily, stupidly, and she swatted me away, as I might have expected, hissing like a cat. Her toothless mouth became a square of fury, and her eyes slitted and glared.

"I don't need you," she snarled. "I don't need *no* one. You understand me, boy?"

"I understand."

She nodded. Good enough. Turned away. Shuffled back down that endless hallway, past two other rooms with doors she hadn't even acknowledged, back down the attic steps leading to the hallway and the front door Heath had dragged me through.

I pulled the light string behind me and entered the room that was to be mine for the night. Why did Heath care so much? It was probably Heath being Heath: old, crotchety, mean.

The room was small, maybe ten feet by fifteen, with a low, sloping ceiling. A single bed—no blanket, only a top sheet, and no pillow either —had been shoved haphazardly against a window, its glass rimed with frost both inside and out. I shivered. It was only six thirty. Maybe, I told myself, maybe I can sleep for a few hours, try for midnight, see if the storm has passed, sneak out of the house, find Sasha, and ride her back to Grandma and Grandpa's. Get the hell out of this freak palace.

A hand tapped on the glass.

I started. I *gaped*.

A hand tapped on the glass *outside*.

A hand tapped on the glass outside, *three stories off the ground*.

I recoiled with a cry and clapped a hand—my own hand, thank God —over my mouth.

But I could see it. I saw it still. A white hand with long fingers.

Out there in the dark.

It struck the glass.

Again.

"No," I whispered. No one could hear me. No one, let alone Heath, God forbid, needed to know where I was.

The hand struck the glass *again*.

I caught a glimpse of eyes in that darkness. Just beyond the glass.

Wide eyes. Yellow as coins.

Staring.

In.

At me.

7

I gripped a handful of the shirt he wore—white with blue stripes, pearl snaps, like every other damned cowboy in this world, but left half-unbuttoned— and dragged him up from his pillow. Heath blinked at me blearily. Pig-drunk, I thought, baring my teeth at him as he would have at me, the coyote, the wolf, the *dog*. But I saw light flash into those eyes and sense, and he shoved me back with more strength than I had thought possible for a man his age.

Heath was out of the bed in an instant, snarling at me and waving his fists, which were cinder blocks and ate up the world. I thought it tremendously likely he would kill me.

His room stank. Worse than the rest of the house. The poor Heights, Lord Christ how it stank. What had they *done* to it, these terrible people?

"Get out of my room, boy," he roared. Hair, crisped white and coiled like clock springs, leaped out of his wrinkled, ancient shirt. Still in his jeans. Feet bare. He seemed both vulnerable and insane, a raging torrent about to hit me until I died.

"You tell me," I said. My voice was calm but deadly. I had never heard myself sound like that before. I felt like a snake. Like I could strike *him.* I wanted to. I would have. "You tell me now, you sonofabitch. Who is he?"

He froze. His eyes slitted. Heath looked more like an animal than ever. Some beast of the field or plain.

"What the fuck are you talking about?" he whispered.

I wanted to grab ahold of his shirt again, pull him up, slam him down, and slap him across his broad and hideous face.

"Tell me who he is," I said, reasonable as hell. "The boy. The man. The dog. The *snow,* for all I know. Tell me who the fuck he is."

"*Was,*" Heath whispered. His eyes never left mine.

The wind hummed and chuckled outside Heath's window. I refused to look.

"Where did you see him?" Heath asked. All malice had evaporated, but his fists continued to dance on the air between us.

"Outside my window."

"No."

"He was. He was *there.*" Now I *did* seize him. I clenched my fingers into the folds of his shirt and wished, *wished,* it was his throat. "*He told me things, and it is impossible that I saw him, and he said his name, and now you tell me who he was and what you did to him*!" I shook him once for good measure.

Heath allowed this...somehow.

I released him. He stumbled away. Heath sat on the bed and stared at the floor. His mouth moved, but no words came out. I watched him.

Finally: "You were there."

"Yes," I said.

"You were in that room."

"Yes."

"*Our* room."

I froze.

"Our room," Heath repeated. Light flickered in his eyes, and his mouth quirked into a half-smile. A cruel one. A crazy one. Maybe a loving one. "*Our* room, yes. Cat's...and mine."

"Who is Cat?"

But Heath only laughed.

"*Who is Cat?*"

"The curse," Heath whispered, and the laughter dammed up inside him again, as if it had never been. He drew together, a thundercloud in the shape of man, and stood.

I winced, though I told myself not to. But I wouldn't allow myself to fully recoil. *He'll kill me now.*

"You're nuts," I said. "No such thing as curses."

But I had seen those yellow eyes, hadn't I?

I had felt the mouth of that dog, hadn't I?

Hadn't I?

"Take any form," Heath whispered and laughed and laughed, then ran a giant hand over his giant face. His shoulders trembled. His entire body tried to shake itself apart. "Take any form!" he howled. "*Take any form!*"

"What are you talking about?" I cried. "Tell me!"

But Heath only laughed.

"Tell me about the curse! Tell me about the *boy!*"

Laughing and laughing.

That hand had broken through the glass of the window. That hand had seized me by the *wrist.* That hand had been cold as *death.*

Heath kept laughing. Laughing...Oh, how he laughed.

Until he screamed.

Then he began his story.

This one.

PART ONE

One

Spring 1948

1

The older man closed the door of the pickup truck and hurried around the front. The boy on the passenger seat watched him but sat perfectly still, frozen, a little animal who might bolt or curl itself into a ball. He didn't blink; he barely breathed.

When the passenger-side door was opened, the smell of the country flooded the boy's nostrils: grass, carried by the warm breath of wind, and the scent of wetness. The boy had lived next to a river all his life. He knew water when he smelled it. This was different. It was sweet, but something dark lay beneath it. Something sour, maybe. Something that stank a bit. The boy thought of black mud running after him, reaching for him.

The man smiled kindly. He always smiled, it seemed. "Time to go," said the man.

The boy shrank back against the seat. The pickup was new. He had never been in a new vehicle before. In fact, he had barely been in a vehicle at all.

"Home," the man said.

The boy looked again at the house before him, outside the window of the truck. He had been staring at it ever since they turned off the big dirt road onto another dirt road—slimmer, a brown snake slithering through the green grass. The *endless* green grass. Nothing out here but hills and wave after wave of grass. The boy had never seen anything like it.

The house: big and white. Sparkling in the hand of the sun. Three gables—though he didn't know the word for them, not yet—painted red and arched, like wicked eyebrows above three big windows. Below them, there were six more.

Like the eyes of a spider, the boy thought, *watching me*. Hungry, evil spider.

A door bisected those six windows, and below that door, a deck of stained wood reachable by four stout steps. To the far right was second set of steps and another door. He had never seen a house with two front doors before. Who needed that many?

On the hill above the house, there waited what appeared to be a cabin. A shack, maybe. Black, covered in tar paper, three windows looking down. Smoke curled like a seductive little finger from the chimney. The sun flashed off the window-glass.

It was springtime, the boy thought, confused. Spring and *warm*. Why was smoke coming from the chimney?

"Don't you worry about *her*," the kind man said, following the boy's gaze up the hill. "You won't even meet her for a while now. But the big house. That's *your* house now."

The boy considered this.

Then he slid off the seat on his back, quick as an eel, past the kind man, who watched him with wide, shocked eyes. The boy dashed back down the road they had just traveled and darted off to the right, into the great green masses of the waving, swallowing prairie grass.

2

The boy came out eventually, on his own. The man didn't have to find him or drag him. He merely waited patiently by the side of his pickup. The boy hunkered low in the grass, but only for a moment or two. The smell was familiar, but it wasn't like home, where the lawns had been dead and dry, where blades of grass, gone gray, crunched under his bare feet and between his fingertips.

The creek, a great red thing winding its way through the endless sheaves, in an even more serpentine fashion than the road, fed the grass, obviously. It smelled of iron and the mud that so scared the boy, and it was, he saw, black and thick after all, like liquid shit beside the water. But the water itself appeared red to the boy. A family of ducks swam in its center, watching him coolly, all of them, before lifting their heads high and sailing off around the bend, out of his sight.

He couldn't stay in the grass by the creek's side forever. The boy had already acknowledged to himself that this unknown place was, as the kind man had told him, home. It seemed foolish to run and hide. He wasn't accustomed to it, so why do it now?

The house...He emerged from his hidey-hole and made his way back up the road, the way he had come. It had to be the house. It was the biggest he had ever seen, for one, so clean and well put together. He couldn't imagine stepping inside it. Touching the door. Peering out the windows. It would lick at him and find him wanting. It would spit him out into the grass, and this time, he wouldn't be able to return. Shame smote him. He was a fool. A stupid little boy.

His eyes burned, and his nose dripped.

The man saw him and straightened. "See any rattlers?" he asked cheerfully. "There's big 'uns out there. And bull snakes too. Never liked a rattler, but a bull snake keeps the packrat population in check. We got a lot of those."

The boy considered this, shook his head.

The man laughed heartily.

Extended a hand that threatened to swallow the boy.

"Heath," the man said. "Come inside."

3

. . .

The house found him, centered, breathed upon him. The carpet beneath his feet was new, a luscious blue the color of the sky in high summer, and wound through with twisting green lines that were, on closer inspection, vines lined with the tiniest, most delicate leaves.

That isn't my name, he said. Only he didn't. He didn't speak at all. He didn't dare.

The man had given him food. Had found him in the ruins of the house—the shack, really, smoking and blackened. The man had asked about his family. Heath had shaken his head. The man had asked if Heath understood his words. The boy had nodded. His eyes had flashed out at the man, black, like a snake's, but the man had smiled his by-now familiar grin and asked Heath his name.

The boy had only looked away.

He had not cried. Heath did not know if he could.

"That hair," the man had said, his voice soft and measuring. "May I?"

The boy had only watched him warily. Smiled.

The man had touched Heath's hair, which hung down near his shoulders, so black it swallowed the sun and gave back pure blue night. The man had made a small sound.

"So soft," he had whispered. "You might have been my very own."

The boy had only watched the man. He didn't mind being touched. His mother had liked to touch his hair like this.

"She died in the fire," he said to the man, and the man, blinking, had shaken his head, smiled his smile, and stroked the boy's hair until Heath came close to him.

Closer. Wrapped his arms around the man's waist. The man, surprised, allowed this.

"She died." The boy sighed and buried his face in the man's stomach. "Died, died, died," he whispered.

"There was a fire," the man said.

The boy did not remove his face.

"Is there anyone? Anyone for you?"

Aunties, he wanted to reply, *only my aunties*. But he didn't. Heath kept his mouth shut, his face pressed against the man. He closed his eyes and imagined a great sky over his head, one peppered with blazing stars. It was the sky he knew, out here, where even the lights of town couldn't dull the cold flecks of the stars overhead.

But in his mind it was a living thing, breathing and watching and aware. It knew him. Wiped away his name. Wiped away the past Heath didn't care about. The hunger and the waiting. The men, his mother's men, and maybe his brothers...Maybe they were wiped away too. The fire was hot, and the stars were cold, and there were no more men and no more brothers and no Mama.

Heath closed his eyes so tightly. He asked the sky to take him away with it. The sky said, Yes. The sky said, Come along now. The sky opened, and it was really the door of the truck, and the man said, "I'll take you, if you want me to." The boy had nodded without hesitation.

The door had closed behind him, and Heath nestled against the back of the seat, which was softer and more comfortable than anything he had ever known.

The man joined him and asked, "Are you sure, Heath?"

The boy said, "Mama died, sir. The fire ate her up. Who's Heath?"

You are, the sky said. The stars whispered. The lightning racing in rapid wrath across it all screamed out at him, *You are Heath; you are Heath.*

"Heath was my little boy," the man had said. "I have two other boys. Heath was the last. And he died. His lungs weren't developed enough, and so, he couldn't breathe. He died. In my arms. We buried him in the cemetery in town, not the one way out back of our house. You must never go there. Or try to find it. But the house, son. It's a grand house. A big one. You'll like it. You'll like being Heath. Won't you? Won't you, son?"

4

The house came down all around him with a whisper and a gasp and something like muffled laughter. Heath was sure there was laughter. He didn't say, *That isn't my name, sir.* He simply took it all in.

The house was cool despite the heat of the day outside. A woman rushed down the hall toward them, and the man closed the door.

Broad shoulders. Square jaw, like the kind man. Same eyes. Twinkling. Hers were darker. A slight fuzz of hair lay over her upper lip. Heath smiled to see it. His aunties had had hair like that, some of them. He thought, *I'll never see my aunties again.*

"Oh, Earnest," said the woman when her eyes fell on the boy at his side, clutching onto him once more. "Oh, Earnest, you didn't."

"The boy has no one. Not in all this world."

"You left this morning. You've only been gone since this *morning*."

"He needs somebody, Lucy."

Lucy. Earnest. The boy—Heath, now—said, *Remember.*

The woman laid her hands on her hips. She scowled. Her face grew ugly under that scowl, like the underside of a mushroom. "What will Lee say?"

"Lee will say what I want him to."

The woman rolled her eyes. "We know how that turns out. Don't we?"

The house smelled nice, Heath decided. Like sugar. Cinnamon. Someone had been baking. He stole a few feet down the hall. To his left, a door led into a kitchen, where the good smells emanated from. Heath pressed against the wall, palms flat, through the door and inside.

The floor was white and blue alternating tile. The walls, likewise, were painted a sparkling white, with a sky-blue trim. Over the big sink, a window looked toward a sprawling corral and two large wooden granaries. Before Heath, another window gazed out onto the road the kind man—*Earnest, Earnest*—had driven them both down in that new pickup truck. The road where the boy, Heath, had fled down to the redwater creek, to hide near the slicks of mud and the waving green grasses.

"Shaw won't be home for another month," the woman in the hallway was saying, but Heath didn't pay much attention.

A plate of cookies waited enticingly at the center of a round wooden table, gussied up with a blue tablecloth that matched the trim. Heath snatched a cookie without hesitation and crammed it into his mouth. Crumbs fell onto the tile. He stared at them. Smiled. It wasn't all so nice, was it? It could be made *un*nice, if he wanted...

Terrible boy. Wicked, evil wolf.

Yes. Yes, he was all those things.

He chewed on the cookie. It was overdone. Cooked too long. Heath knew an overdone cookie when he chewed it.

"Take this," the woman said at his side.

He jumped a little, finished chewing, swallowed. Glared at her. She scowled back down at him. Thrust a strong wooden broom into his hands.

"You make a mess; you clean up your mess. That's how we do things here at the Heights."

"The Heights."

"It's a joke. Not much of a joke. Because we're so lowdown, you see. We Lyons. Ask them in the town."

"Lowdown."

"You just repeat the things I say?" She sounded exasperated, but her eyes sparkled, like those of the kind man.

"No," Heath said, sullen. He swept the crumbs into a little pile. "Now what?"

"Surly little thing, ain't you? You use this dustpan, braintrust."

"What's braintrust?"

"Nothing, nothing." The woman sighed. "I'm your Auntie Lucy. And you're my little Heath."

"I'm no one's."

"No. You're mine. Mine."

"I don't belong to *no one*."

Heath swept the crumbs into the pan and handed it to her. She handed it back and pointed to the sink.

"Garbage can's under there. Unless you want to eat the crumbs."

"I ate worse."

She snorted horsey laughter. "I'll bet," she said, scrubbing fondly at his thick mop of hair. "I'll just bet you have."

5

"Faggot. *Nigger faggot.*"

Heath's fist was a bright flaming streak through the air that the other boy caught before it could reach his chin. The boy sneered. His face was thin like a rat's, white as cheese, and his eyes, which were dreadfully far apart, gleamed with slyness and hate.

Heath cried out when the other boy twisted his arm around his back. He wished immediately that he hadn't made any kind of sound. But the pain was real and red and furious, and anyway, the other boy had surprised him.

Lee: Wesley Lyon, Earnest Lyon's son. Tall and thin, but muscular too. Giant jug-ears. Red cheeks that stood out against the paleness of his skin. Freckles. Ugly, like a starving hound. Heath had had the acquaintance of many starving dogs at the old place, in the town where he had been born, before Mama and the others had burnt up in their fire.

"Let me go," Heath said. It came out a wheeze.

Heath wanted to sound strong. He urged his body to become a storm cloud, wished to rain hail and fire down on the terrible other boy. But Lee only tightened his grip. Heath's body was stubborn and retained his ordinary shape. His shoulder screamed. White flames danced up and down the length of his arm.

"I'll break it." Lee panted in his ear. "See if I don't."

"Let me *go.*"

The pain increased.

Heath bit back a scream.

"Who are you, huh?" Lee slobbered in his ear. "Who are you, even? You can't come here." He twisted again.

Again, white-hot agony. Heath was certain he had heard a tiny cracking sound.

"You can't come to *my* house. You can't come *here* without my permission."

"Fuck...your...permission." Heath growled and bit back another scream. A white-flame sheet blazed up and down his entire right side.

"Can't talk to me like that. Can't say *shit*."

Heath stamped down hard on Lee's foot. At the same time, he swiveled, and Lee released him, shrieking in surprise. Heath sank his teeth into the meat of the boy's upper arm. Lee screeched again, piercing, like a girl's scream, and fell backward. Heath lifted his bare foot to stamp on the other boy's skull.

"No."

Heath froze.

Turned.

Mr. Lyon—Earnest—stood on the front steps of the Heights, watching them both with a face that didn't move and eyes that didn't blink. "You don't want to hurt him back, do you?" Mr. Lyon asked calmly.

"Yes," Heath said. "More than anything."

"We don't need to hurt those who hurt us, do we? The Bible tells us to forgive trespasses."

Lee lay where he had fallen, quietly sobbing. Heath's foot remained poised above his skull. It would be so easy, he thought, to just bring it down. Crush his forehead. Drive Lee's nose back into his face. Stomp on his throat until his larynx gave way and he died, choking on his own blood.

So easy.

"Forgive trespasses, as we pray that others forgive us our own trespasses. Have you trespassed, son?"

Lee sobbed and sobbed. He turned over. His eyes glared up, red with hatred. Like a dog, a goddamn feral goddamn *dog*. His mouth was slick with drool and snot.

"Have you?"

Heath considered.

6

I ran a lot. But I never ran away. I never did that.

I chased cats sometimes out into the tall grass, down the road and by the crick, but I never went too far away because I thought I would get lost and I didn't want to tell anyone I was afraid of anything, especially not Lee. I called him Wesley when we was alone. He hated that name more than fire, maybe even more than he hated me. But I hated him too, and my hate burned deep inside me. Coals that never went out. Sometimes, I thought I had lava in me instead of blood. I knew what lava was.

I started to read books. Wasn't hard. And there was TV at the Heights. Not good, but better than anything I'd had before. Black and white and cut through with snow. With snow. With snow...snow...

I feel the snow on my face now. It comes down and cuts down and falls from the sky, streaking white comets. Oh, how it burns. Cat...Cat... I hear you. That boy said he saw you at his window, yellow-eyed at his *window*. He couldn't see you. He *couldn't*—

The Heights. Come back to the Heights. Safe in that late spring of '48.

I had never counted time before. Auntie Lucy showed me. Clocks with round glass faces and hands like knives. I wanted them to cut at Lee until blood squirted out of him. I thought, I spared you, you sonofapig-fucker, but I would never say anything like that, terrible like that, not where Mr. Lyon could hear me. I called him "Mr. Lyon," even though he asked me over and *over*...He asked me to call him "Father" or "Dad."

"I don't have a father," I would say, and he would shake his head and pet my hair because he was always petting my hair, but he would smile and hum a little. I had never heard a man hum before.

"This is my ranch," he would say. "Heath, this is my ranch that my grandfather made and my father built up and that I'm going to give away someday. I have two sons, Heath, Lee and Shaw. But, no...I guess I'm wrong. I guess I have three sons now because there's you."

"Shaw," I said, but he didn't hear me. "Where is Shaw?"

"Hmmm?"

"Where is Shaw?"

"Oh. He's a special boy, you know, my Shaw."

"Where is he?"

"He's so smart, you see. Smarter than Lee. He isn't meant for life on the ranch. I figured that out long ago. Others wouldn't have done what I did, but"—*chuckle*—"there are so many things I do others wouldn't. Ever. *Lee* is meant for the Heights. Lee rides his horse. Lee works the cows. He's not very good at it, but he wants to. Shaw never did. Shaw won't even wear boots, you know, or jeans. He never would."

"But where is he?"

"At school, Heath. Don't *tug* at me so. He'll be back. Someday. I can't ever keep track. The days, they go and go."

Something moved in the grass below us, down by the creek. I watched it slink along, parting the tall blades in waves. A cat, I thought, bigger than it should have been, bigger than it had any right to be. A cat, a cat.

"A puma," Mr. Lyon said. "A mountain lion, Heath. They show up sometimes, though most of them are far to the west of us, over the mountains. Watch its tail. Isn't that funny! How it lashes back and forth? As if it's going to cut the grass like a scythe?"

"A mountain lion? But there ain't no mountains out here."

"No. You are correct."

"So, it's just...a lion."

"Perhaps."

"A *prairie* lion."

It's just a cat, like our farm cats, only bigger. It'll swallow you whole. You run back to me when you see one, though you might not, you know, not ever again. They're rare. I've only seen one other in my time here. Up at the old homesteader cabin. Your grandmother—"

"My grandmother?"

"—your *grandmother* chased it away with a broom. She's a brave old beast. She doesn't come down much. Not to us. But you'll meet her someday. Yes, that devil cat was just sunning itself on this big chunk of sandstone outside the cabin. Large as life. Big as a cow. Eyes closed. Probably purring, for all I know. Wicked, heathen animal. She *screamed* when she saw it, then took after it with a broom. I never seen an animal run so fast, Heath, you mark me. But it went. Devil cat."

"Devil cat."

"Puma. A beast, Heath, my boy. Swallow you whole."
"Swallow me whole."

I thought about that.

Would it have been so bad if it did? Really? Would it have been so bad?

Two

Summers 1948-1950

1

1948

"You're that boy."

Heath stiffened. Didn't turn, though he wanted to, more than anything. He stared straight ahead instead.

Heath had been sitting at the kitchen table, coloring away at a book Auntie Lucy had given him, with the crayons she had also provided.

"Lee didn't want it," was all she had said.

But Heath did. It was the story of *The Wizard of Oz*. He had never heard of it before. Now, he never wanted anything else. The cover depicted a little girl in a blue dress, with hair as black as his own, only her eyes were blue. She held a little dog that looked like the Scotty dog mascot he had seen the time his mother had borrowed her sister's car and driven him to Glasgow for pizza. She had loved the pizza in Glasgow, and she had said, "You'll love the pizza too."

And he did. She had been right.

The mascot at the high school, she had explained to him. He licked a little at the orange grease lying in pools atop his first pizza slice.

"The mascot there," she had said, "is a Scotty dog. Because Glasgow is a place in Scotland too, not just here."

He hadn't really understood. Heath only remembered the pizza and the time with Mom. But not her face. Her face was really a shimmer for him now, bright colors that danced and swirled.

Heath frowned, doubled down. *Best not to think of her or any of them.* Not his brothers, not the aunties. Just the book. Oz. And the dog the little girl in the coloring book held...It was a dog like the Glasgow Scotty, named Toto, and the girl's name was Dorothy. She had friends too. A handsome scarecrow—*How is it a scarecrow can look handsome?* Heath asked himself, but the answer didn't seem terrifically important, so he shook it away and simply accepted that he *was*—and a man made of tin, and a lion who cried all the time. Heath didn't know lions could cry.

There was a witch too. He recognized her from the Halloween decorations that went up all over town when the wind got too cold and knocked the red and orange leaves off the trees. Heath didn't like the witch, except he guessed he did, a little. She was scary, but that was fine. Sometimes, he thought he liked to be scared.

Her face was green. He wasn't sure why. Was she dead? Did one's face turn green when they died? He would ask Mr. Lyon. A question about rotting old dead people with green skin might make Auntie Lucy upset.

Color, color. Crayon to paper. Press. *Yes, enchantment. Live in that world, the magic one. Don't think of your mom, whoever she was. Or your cousins, your aunties. Not any of them. Not any of them. Live forever in the magic world.*

"You're *that* boy." Behind him. He had said it again.

Heath hesitated. Bowed his head. Added purple to the lion's mane. Cerulean. Bright streaks and flares of emerald.

"That isn't the right color at all. Lions aren't green. Or purple either."

"Mine is."

"What did you say?"

A voice like Lee's. Only not. Higher. Hint of a lisp on the word "say." Almost a girl's voice, Heath thought. He cleared his throat.

"I said, mine is. Mine is green. And purple. And *blue*."

The other boy drew closer. Heath still refused to turn, to look, to even see his face. He thought he might die and turn green if he dared do that. There might be a sun inside him that would flare white-hot and molten and blaze away until he was burned thoroughly and forever into ashes. Heath didn't want that. He told himself he didn't.

"It isn't bad," the other boy said. "You've...huh. You've *shaded*. You've used those crayons to *shade*. Mr. Winterburn would have a heart attack. We aren't allowed crayons, see."

Still wouldn't look. "Who's Mr. Winterburn?" Heath added a deep stroke of blue to the lion's muzzle.

"Hey, that's pretty. He's my art teacher. He's awfully touchy-feely. A super creep. Maybe I won't have to see him again. I don't know really at all, ever at all, if I'll ever even go back to school there. Or anywhere."

Now Heath turned. But carefully. Slowly.

"You have the blackest hair I've ever seen."

The other boy's face was white, but his cheeks glowed, maybe too much. It seemed as if he were blushing, only the blush didn't disappear. His eyes were light blue, almost white. His pupils appeared to float in the whites of his eyes. The effect was eerie.

"And your eyes are black too."

"Yours are white."

"Touché."

"I don't know what that means."

"Doesn't matter. Lee told me about you. Oh, he hates you. Heath? Is that your name?"

Careful nod.

"Dad named you that, didn't he?"

Another careful nod.

"What's your real name?"

Shrug.

The other boy giggled. "You don't know? Really? I don't believe you."

Another shrug.

"I'm Shaw." He seized both of Heath's hands in his own, squeezed them, and shook them, and they were cold.

They shouldn't have been. It was summer. The heat was everywhere, pressing down the prairie grass and leaching all the color away until it was dull and yellow. The house itself swam with heat. So why were Shaw's hands like branches running cold with streams of ice?

Now they looked at each other.

Eye to eye. Black to blue, or white.

Shaw smiled.

The earth shuddered and hitched. The house groaned all around them. Somewhere, Lee screamed like a furious, cheated animal. After an endless moment, Heath smiled too.

And realized Shaw continued to hold his hands.

He didn't let them go.

2

1949

"This will be all mine, someday."

"Hmmm."

"Don't you like this house?"

"Mmmhmm."

"No one ever taught you to talk, did they?"

"Nope."

"You're an ape."

"Yup."

"No. You're some other kind of an animal."

"Who says I'm an animal?"

"*I'm* an animal, then. Guess which kind."

"I know."

"I know you know."

Silence. Thinking.

"I miss summers out here."

"Hm."

"Can't believe it's been a whole year since I was last home. Since I saw you last, even."

"Hmmm."

"Say something, idiot."

"Not an idiot."

"Just teasing."

"I'm *not*."

"If you say so. Don't you think it's pretty?"

"Yes."

"That's better."

Touch of wind, hint of flower.

"I'll take you all around, if you want."

"Okay."

"Maybe deeper in the country, where you haven't ever been. I'd like to see it all again anyway. I forget, sometimes, what things look like. I forget what they *are*."

"There's just what you see."

Playful. "You don't believe that."

Shrug.

"I planted these flowers with Aunt Lucy when I was little. See? They've managed to stay alive. I'm not sure how."

"Hollyhocks."

"Yes! You know!"

"We had them. Before."

"Before?"

"Before *this*."

"Ah. I love them. I make people out of them to play with. Or I *did*, once. Little ladies. Dolls. Lee called me names. But I made them anyway because who cares for Lee. Like this. See?"

"You killed them."

"Not *all* of them. Just...just this one stalk."

"No. You killed it."

"Don't be an idiot, I said. It's fine. It's just a game."

"Okay."

"Don't be like that. Don't be so sullen. It's all all right, I promise. Don't you believe me?"

"I don't know if I do."

"You should. You should always believe me."

"I don't know you."

"Yes, you do."

He did.

"I don't know how you do, but you do. Can't you feel it?"

Nod.

Satisfied. "Yes."

That sibilant S. It didn't bother Heath. He had thought it might bother him after a while. It didn't.

"All mine," Shaw whispered, standing there, there before the enormity of the house. Heath watching, fascinated. Shaw spun in a circle, arms outstretched. "All, all, all, all *mine*," he sang.

3

I dreamed the old woman came down from the hill and saw me. And I saw her, and she was beautiful for a while…until she wasn't.

"Come be my son," she whispered to me. "Come be my husband," she sang. She reached through the glass of the windows, like it wasn't there at all, and put her fingers into my mouth.

I tried to scream, but I couldn't. Her fingers tasted like dirt. She laughed and she sang a little song for me while I tried not to throw up.

This isn't a dream, I tried to say.

"This isn't a dream," she cooed like a bird, with a bird's large yellow eyes and slashing beak. And her fingers were claws crusted with blackness that wasn't dirt at all.

"Be quiet," Shaw said, somehow next to my bed. "Be quiet," he said. "You're screaming. You'll wake up the whole damn house."

"I'm sorry. I was dreaming."

Bad dreams.

The worst dreams.

My bedroom had a window, a big window, looking out into the grove of trees, which were only now beginning to die. It was summer, so most of them had their leaves, but they were all black under the light of the moon. And they moved. They shivered and danced.

"Only the wind," I said.

"What?" Shaw asked.

"Only the wind," I said, and he laughed.

His room was far away from mine.

"Maybe I didn't hear you screaming," he told me. "At first. Maybe I knew something was wrong. You're okay now."

I said I was.

"Cold in here," he said.

"Not too bad."

"Bright too. With all that moonlight."

He went to the window. His body was a white stitch in the darkness of my room. He wore only a pair of shorts. His feet were bare and big. Biggest feet I ever seen. His legs were long—a statue's legs. He moved heavily, like a statue that managed to live and to walk. Shaw put his forehead against the glass.

"Glass is hot," he said. "Summer's here are too goddamn hot. I forgot about that."

"It's not so bad."

"Better than where you came from?" he asked.

I told him I didn't know where I came from. I couldn't remember. He faced the window and didn't turn, so I couldn't see his face, but I thought he might have laughed.

"She's got her light on," he said, and I froze.

My muscles tightened. I couldn't move.

"She's got her light on up there. It's so late. Wonder what she's up to?"

I opened my mouth and closed it because I couldn't make any sounds.

Shaw didn't turn to me. He only looked out the window.

"Old woman. Old witch," he said. Or might have said. He had whispered, so it was hard to tell. "So late to have her light on."

Come here to me, I tried to say. *Please*. But the words wouldn't come.

He didn't look at me, and he didn't look.

Only out the window.

Only out into the dark.

Where the trees moved on their own.

Where the wind didn't blow them, and they moved and swayed until they danced. And the grass. And somewhere, a coyote howled. The saddest sound I had ever heard.

"The saddest sound," Shaw said, turning to me. He was smiling.

I remember how he smiled. I remember his teeth. How white he was, so unnatural. No, not like nature at all.

"Are you a ghost?" I asked, and he laughed.

"I might be a ghost. Maybe I'm a dream. Or a memory. I'm not really me at all," he said.

"How would you know if you weren't you?" I asked. *Get into my bed*, I wanted to say, but I couldn't, goddamn it. And he stood there in the dark so I could watch him and say nothing. What could I say? What would I say? I didn't know.

I still don't know.

"The saddest, the saddest sound," he said.

I'm sure that's what he said. We thought the same things all the time. Why wouldn't he have echoed the words inside my head?

The coyote howled.

The trees swayed and danced and flung their arms into the air. The hot and sucking air.

My room wasn't cold at all.

Shaw stood there and smiled at me. I know he did. I saw his teeth. Perfect little bones.

I heard the animal howling.

I blinked and it was morning. The sun was everywhere, and it was too, too hot. I was alone.

I have always been alone.

For the first time, I felt bad about it.

1950

"You've seen all this already?"

Heath shook his head.

"Goddamn but it's hot." Shaw drew a hand across his forehead. It came away wet.

Heath watched, fascinated. Shaw pulled with an irritated grunt at his T-shirt, jerked it up and over his head, and tossed it into the green-yellow grass. His chest was white as a statue, lightly muscled.

"You're so *white*," Heath said without thinking, but Shaw only laughed.

"There's not much sun in Massachusetts in the springtime," was all he said, still gazing down at the red water. "Not at my school."

The creek lapped at their feet. Mr. Lyon had given Heath both sneakers and cowboy boots. Today he wore sneakers, but he was afraid the mud would suck them from his feet and they would disappear, then he would have to explain where they had gone. He didn't want to—couldn't have, even if it were demanded of him—do that. And Lee would laugh and beat him up. Again. Backhand him, as he had the other day, before Shaw's latest return to the Heights.

"I'll never let him do that to you again," Shaw had sworn after Heath's broken description of the encounter. Shaw's face had been thin with anger, and his hands had bunched into stony fists. "He won't ever dare lay a hand on me. Let him try again, Heath. Just let him."

Heath had believed him.

"We never go outside anyway," Shaw said. He pulled at his own sneakers and dropped them next to his shirt. His feet were, as Heath noticed before, surprisingly large but also pale and defenseless-looking, somehow. White. Nearly blue. Veins slinked along them like water snakes. He dropped into the grass beside the creek and slid his feet into the water, sighing while he did.

Heath watched.

Shaw leaned back and closed his eyes, exulting in the sun. "The sporty kids do. I'm not a sporty kid."

"I guess I'm not either."

Shaw cracked one eye. "Did you ever go to school?"

Shyly, Heath shook his head.

"You've been here...what? Two years now?"

Heath shrugged.

"Lee said it's been forever." Shaw snorted. "What an utter turd."

Heath snickered.

"Oh, you like that?"

He nodded.

Shaw splashed water in his direction. Heath allowed it. It ran in delicious rivers down his cheek and chin and smelled like iron. Like growing things.

They were farther from the house than Heath had yet to go, even after all his time at the Heights. He enjoyed wandering through the house itself, spending time in the attic, the basement, and the rabbit warren of rooms he could never keep straight in his mind—though he enjoyed his perceptions that they moved on their own, doubling, tripling, playing hopscotch with him. Yes, he loved the house.

The country made him more nervous. The creek led them a quarter of a mile, half a mile, then more, out into the openness of the prairie. The sky over their heads was distant, blue, beautiful, bright, and uncaring. Heath had never paid much attention to it before. But out here, with all this wild nothingness, it made him feel like a flea.

I won't be a flea forever, he swore, pulling at his own shirt.

"You're so *dark*," Shaw say breathlessly, flicking at Heath with his T-shirt.

They laughed together.

"Do you like school?" Heath asked.

"No."

"I want to go."

"Do you? Why?"

Words were easier with Shaw somehow, but they still felt like great chunks of broken concrete mixed with shards of rock, exhumed, swallowed, and stuck in his throat.

"Dunno," was all he said.

"Maybe they'd like you...in town. I doubt it."

"Why?"

"You're dark. And angry."

"I'm not always angry."

"You look *wild*. You have a glint." Shaw touched the direct center of Heath's forehead. "Here. You have this *glint*."

"I don't think that's true."

"*I* have a glint."

"*You're* wild."

Grin. Hint of teeth. "I am."

"*You're* a beast." Heath almost pleaded with him: *Don't compare me to an animal. I don't like to be compared to an animal. I'm not a beast. I'm not.* But the words died in his throat.

"Lots of beasts out here." Shaw rolled over onto his back. "I missed all the beasts."

"I have a horse."

"I heard."

"Your dad is teaching me to ride."

"Of course he is."

"He wanted Lee to teach me. But he wouldn't."

Shaw made a derisive sound. Heath looked away and pulled at a little yellow wildflower until it came away from the earth and died between his fingers. He thought, *I feel it passing out of this world, all because of me.*

"Those are edible, you know."

"No shit!"

"Shit."

They laughed.

"Here. Let me show you." Shaw picked one of the yellow petals from the poor dead thing and laid it on his tongue. He chewed it delicately.

Heath snickered.

"They taste okay. Here."

Heath obeyed, imitating Shaw in an exaggerated fashion, and nibbled it like one of the farm dogs of which he was fond—a big white Collie named Boo, who chewed everything at first with his minuscule front teeth. The taste of the flower bloomed on his tongue. It was unpleasant, he decided. Organic, like chewing on grass, only more bitter. Then, when he was about to swallow, sweetness blossomed. He swallowed, the sweetness spread over his tongue, and the little flower was gone.

Shaw watched him avidly, amused. "We have a lot to teach you."

"Horseback riding."

"Flower eating."

"Plato and Socrates."

"The manly art of boxing."

They giggled together and lay back, each lacing his own fingers together to create a support for his head there in the softness of the grass.

"Lunch soon," Shaw said after a time.

"I don't want to go back."

"You want to stay out here? There's nothing out here."

"I know."

"You're an idiot."

"Yeah."

"You're not *really* an idiot. Dad said you taught yourself to read."

Heath said nothing.

"You did, didn't you?"

Heath said nothing.

"That's brilliant."

Something stirred—a bird in Heath's chest made of feathers and fire.

"But we have to go back. We always, always have to go back. The Heights waits."

"I don't like it there." *Lies.*

"'Cause it's haunted."

Lies. Weren't they?

"No, it's not."

"Have you met Granny yet?"

"Not yet."

"How is that possible? Anyway, *she'll* tell you. All about it. Ghosts and witches and werewolves and vampires. All the pretty things her mama brought with her from Minnesota. Before that, Norway."

"She doesn't come down from the hill."

"Oh, yes, she does. She takes off her skin from her bones until she's only bones and *eyes,* and then she comes tip-toeing down the hill—"

"Shaw—"

"—tip-toeing past those trees that are just as bony as she is—"

"Don't."

"—and she'll go past your window, and she'll stop, and she'll look in, and she'll see you, and she'll go *whoooooooooooo—*"

"I said *don't!*" Heath sat up, tucked his legs to his chest, and wrapped his arms around them. His eyes smarted, but he refused to admit there might be tears inside. He thought his tear ducts were imaginary, dusty roads. Barren. Useless.

Shaw said nothing. Somewhere, back at the house, a dog barked. A man's voice—Don, one of the two hired men, probably—rang out a command, and the dog ceased its harangue. The sky continued flawless, with only the slight tatter of a cloud to mar its perfection.

"It isn't just our house, you know."

Heath drew himself tighter, compressed his body until he thought he would grow so small he disappeared into the air, through the air, into darkness, beyond darkness until there was light again and no people, no people at all.

"It's everything out here." Shaw's voice had lost that teasing tone.

Now, Heath realized, he sounded melancholy. Heath released his legs and turned to look at the other boy, who was gazing again at the creek.

Shaw's voice trembled a bit. "Everything has a ghost in it."

"Maybe so."

"It *is* so. I hate coming back here, but I miss it *so* much when I'm at school again."

"Don't go back."

Shaw snorted. Heath's cheeks burned with shame.

I want to understand, he thought to say, but he kept his mouth closed tightly. Heath watched Shaw observing his own reflection caught deep inside the creek.

"*You* should go," Shaw said at last, flickering his eyes to Heath's. He attempted to smile. "Maybe you'd like school."

"I think I have to go."

"Probably."

"Your dad thinks I'm thirteen."

"I'm fourteen."

"So I'd only have to go for a few years."

"Maybe you'll like it."

"Yeah. Maybe."

"Maybe you'll even like *them*." Shaw's face twisted slightly. His eyes grew hooded. "Maybe you'll make friends."

"You don't like them."

Shaw pulled his T-shirt back over his head. His arms were lightly muscled. So was his back, despite what he had said about not indulging in athletics at his fancy school. Heath watched and watched. Didn't care if Shaw noticed. Maybe he wanted him to notice.

"I hardly know them," Shaw said.

"A little."

"A little. Put your shirt back on. We have to go back."

"I don't want to."

"Aunt Lucy will tan your hide."

"Not yours?"

Shaw snickered. "No."

Heath moved like syrup, reluctant, and slid his arms back into his own shirt. Slowly, slowly, he fastened each button. *He's watching too*, he told himself smugly. *It isn't just me. Shaw likes to watch me too.*

"Do you really believe in ghosts?" Heath asked.

Shrug.

"Witches? Werewolves?"

Shrug, shrug. Another derisive sound. "Hurry. We have to *go*."

"Vampires?"

"Vampires *everywhere*. I'll do it myself if you won't."

Heath chimed laughter. "I'm done. See?"

"You did it wrong. Haven't you ever buttoned a shirt before?"

He glanced down at his chest. "Hmmm. I guess I did."

"You're an *idiot*." Fondly.

"I didn't have any life before this one." Heath sighed happily. "No buttons anywhere."

Shaw's fingers flew down the length of Heath's chest and stitched it back up again. Quickly, like fluttering insects. "You're getting fat."

"I eat all the time."

"I never eat."

"You should eat. You should lie out in the sun with me."

"All I want to do is lie out in the sun with you."

Heat bloomed inside Heath.

"But I have to go back."

"*We*."

"Not to the house, dummy. I have to go back to *school*."

Stung. "When?"

"Dad's taking me to the train tomorrow. Or Don is. Or Aunt Lucy. *Someone* will take me to the train. Then it's a three-day trip across the country. Back at Christmas. *Maybe*."

"You just got here."

"It's been a week."

"You just *got* here."

"Don't cry."

"I'm not."

"It's pointless to cry. We don't really know each other, do we? Are we even friends?"

"Yes."

Shaw stood. He blocked the sun, hands on his hips. A tall, lithe warrior. His features were lost in shadow. Heath thought he saw the glimmer of those white-blue eyes, but he couldn't be certain. He couldn't read whatever complicated emotion might lie within them.

"The embryo of friends." Shaw snorted ironically. Then, softer, "But I'm leaving. Leaving this whole place again."

"Write me."

"You can read, after all."

"I'll save your letters."

"Lee will tear them up. I never write *Lee* letters."

"I'll hide them."

"I'll bet you would. You're really good at hiding, aren't you?"

"I don't know what I am."

"Me either."

"Come back."

"I have to."

"Promise me you'll come back."

"You're being exceptionally dramatic."

But Shaw's voice quavered just a bit, Heath thought, and felt smug again.

They were walking through the grass. The house rose before them, white and shining proudly. Over it, looming, was the dark homesteader cabin shimmering in the heat.

"Do you really believe in ghosts?" Heath asked. "I mean it this time."

"I...don't know. Do you?"

"I don't know either. I never seen one."

"You've never seen one."

"Don't correct me."

"Don't sound like one of *them* and I won't."

"One of who?"

"Oh, Christ." Shaw sighed. "Now *I'm* being dramatic. Like Lee. Like Don. One of those idiot men. There are so *many* idiot men out here, and they all speak like that. 'I seen it.' No, you didn't. You *saw* it."

"I *saw* it."

"A ghost."

"I *saw* a ghost. I mean, I never did. I mean, I never *saw* a ghost."

"I just feel them, maybe."

"Everything is haunted."

"Everything," Shaw said with a bitter smile, "is haunted."

"The house, the land—"

"Especially the land. I think it's the wind sometimes. There isn't wind like that in Massachusetts. There isn't wind like ours *anywhere*."

"Sounds like crying. Moaning."

"Or screaming. Wailing, sometimes," Shaw said.

"Ghosts. Dead cowboys. Dead homesteaders. Dead Indians. Dead animals too. Deer and coyotes and lions—"

"I'm sorry, okay? I'm sorry."

"Don't be mad."

"I'm not mad. I'm *sorry*."

"For what?"

Shaw stopped. "For scaring you. Trying to scare you."

Heath dropped his gaze immediately to the grass at their feet. "You didn't scare me."

A hesitation. Heath dared to glance up. Shaw smiled at him wickedly.

Yes, Heath thought, there was that glint. Wildness in his eyes. Animal eyes.

"So, I failed. But I'm sorry I tried."

"Are you?"

"Yeah. Because I ended up scaring myself. A little."

Heath lifted his chin, thrust out his chest. "What do we have to be scared of? We're wild things."

"Beasts."

"Wild and wicked beasts."

"With fangs and claws."

"Teeth and sharp, sharp claws and teeth."

"We'll tear them apart, anyone who stands in our way."

"Tear them into *pieces*."

"Pieces," they said together and laughed together and walked again until they ran. And they ran right into the shadow of the hill and of the two houses, which fell, heavy and silent and complicated, over them both.

5

The smell of the hay was dry and stale, and yet he loved it. He snuffled it greedily through his nostrils, even while he wiped in a fury at the tears streaking his face.

I do not cry, Heath told himself savagely, and it was possible he never had. Until now.

It was a rare cloudy day in the summertime, which leached away the vibrancy of the grass and the shimmer of the creek. Instead, there was only the wind, which gibbered and fretted until Heath thought he would scream. And anyway, Shaw was gone again, and no one paid the least bit of attention to *him* because they had taken Shaw into Wolf Point: Mr. Lyon, Aunt Lucy, Lee, Don, and a passel of ghosts and things with long white limbs and snouts.

Heath had run into the shadows, away from all that noise, that nonsense, until they were good and gone. He had come to the corral, where the horses were and the hay, and he kicked furiously at the weeds, the tall grass, and the gray, splintered posts making up the pen holding their six horses. Heath kicked until his feet hurt and found his legs wouldn't hold him because they were useless, worthless noodles.

He sank into the grass and curled up against one of the big posts. The poisonous flowers tried to bloom in his guts and his chest. He refused to allow it, *refused* to allow it, but they grew stealthily, with long tendrils, vines that grew thorns. They filled his throat, his mouth, his nose, and his eyes, where they stabbed until the tears came. He wasn't proud of that, but he choked back the sobs the vines provoked and swallowed them down deep so he only shook and rocked. Scrubbed angrily at the tears scalding him the way he imagined lava burned the earth.

So Heath stayed there for a time he did not care to keep track of, aware of the low moaning of the wind, which was warm with summer and redolent of the plains, sweetgrass, the iron-tang of the creek, until he felt soothed. The shadows swelled around him, and finally, his stomach complaining, he crawled away from the corral post, out of the tall weeds, and stood to his full height. Heath gazed around.

One of the horses watched him solemnly, smiling, he thought, a bit to herself. Big and ghostly white, she was, with large, expressive eyes, one brown, one a shade of blue lighter even than the sky.

"I do not love you," he told her, but they both knew he lied.

She whickered a bit to let him know she knew.

Heath traced the shape of her jaw with one finger. She allowed this, but her eyes were full of reproach. He stroked her ears. The tips were the softest. They held little tufts of white fur, like cotton down. Her name was Goose, which Heath privately thought was an amazing name for a horse, and she was older than the others, arguably gentler—the mare Mr. Lyon had given to Heath while he taught him to ride.

It was stupid to cry, Heath realized now, glad that his face was dry. Goose nodded her agreement and stomped one foot into the soft earth of the corral. She wanted out; she wanted to run.

"I can't," he whispered. "They're gone. I can't go alone."

She sighed, shook her head, turned away.

There is a train somewhere, Heath thought, *and that train holds Shaw. And that train is taking him all across the country, and it is thousands of miles and thousands of months until he'll be back here. Maybe more.*

"Maybe more," he said.

Goose rolled her eyes and whickered again.

If only he knew what time it was…If only he had ever cared about the passing of time before…

"I just don't know," Heath said, stroking Goose's mane. "They could be back at any moment. And I can't take you out alone. Mr. Lyon —Earnest—he said—"

Do you always do what you're told?

Shaw.

Heath straightened. His throat was a desert filled with a long, white bone. He could swallow around it but barely. His eyes watered. The flesh on his arms gnarled into hard rows of bumps.

"I heard you," he said. Clear as day.

Do you always do what you're told?

Shaw, definitely. Amused. He seemed perpetually amused, except when he was sad or angry, when his eyes narrowed into slits and filled with sparks or tears or both.

"I don't belong here."

Yes, you do.

Somewhere, Heath knew, Shaw leaned his head against the glass of a window. Somewhere, passing over plains even flatter than these, Shaw saw Heath here, in this moment, and spoke these words to him. Heath *knew.*

You belong here as much as I do. You belong here because I say you do. You belong here because you *say you do.*

Goose sang a song to Heath he had never heard before. He cast his eyes over to her uneasily, then back out onto the road and the grass it cut through. The grass made Shaw's shape, his long face, his ironic mouth. Heath licked his lips. Heat burned away the poisoned flowers in his gut and tingled in his fingertips.

"They're all gone," he said at last but carefully, as if trying the words. *You're safe with me.*

"You're gone." Fury, red as blood. Fury filled his veins. Fury clenched his fists. "You *left me.*"

I'm always here. Don't you know that by now?

The wind danced laughingly against his cheek.

Don't you know?

And somehow, a saddle rested upon Goose's back. There was a bit in her mouth, and she smiled around it, showing her long yellow teeth for Heath to admire.

"Beautiful," he sang back to her, and she sang back to him, and they sang together.

He was astride her, and they were trotting. Heath froze and drew the reins up tightly so Goose stopped too, but she wasn't happy about it. She snarled something uncouth at him.

"Look," Heath whispered, "up there."

And they looked together, up *there*, at the top of the hill, where stood a figure on the porch of the homesteader cabin.

Her.

Oh, Shaw said. *Dammit. Her. I forgot all about* her.

Heath made out no features. The figure was tall, thin, and white against the backdrop of the house and the green of the hill. Beyond that, he could tell nothing.

Granny. Ol' Granny Lyon.

Goose whickered softly.

Heath scratched her ears. "'S okay," he murmured. "'S fine."

Keep going. She's not even really there. Just go. *What can she do, after all?*

Heath nudged the horse's ribs lightly, and she began to trot. Down the road. Away from the house, the cabin, and the old woman atop the hill who, Heath knew, continued to watch him while he and Goose left the road and cut through the grass.

They waded through the creek, trotted through a field soft and alive with golden beams of wheat, up and into the hills that grew in great and grand profusions back of the Heights. Goose ran and Heath let her do it. She took him gloriously through the air, and he yelled his joy. It was so much better than the sobs and wails of grief which were, after all, fairly pointless. He felt Shaw's arms around his belly, Shaw's pointed chin resting on his shoulder, Shaw's breath, sweet like the prairie grass, drifting over his face.

"Nothing here is *yours*."

Breath washed over him: onions and shit.

Yeasty. Bread. No. Beer.

He was drunk. Lee was drunk.

Heath lay sprawled on the ground where Lee had surprised him upon returning Goose to the corral, replacing the saddle, the reins, and the bit. He had been gasping, still exhilarated from their galloping, which, of course, had felt like flying, smiling like a great idiot, when Lee's fist came out of the air and collided with Heath's right ear, sending him sprawling.

His ear rang. Bells, he thought. Dazed, bells, bells, bells.

Goose whinnied her anger.

Lee breathed in great, tearing gasps.

Heath smiled up at him.

Lee's boot-clad foot lashed out. Connected with Heath's gut. And again, connected with his jaw.

Blood came out of his nose, mouth. and ears.

"*Faggot*!" shrieked Lee Lyon.

And left Heath there, smiling into the growing darkness.

Goose sang him a few sad songs until he felt strong enough to stand again, weaving drunkenly, grasping at the wooden bars of the corral until his fingers found them, closed over them, and allowed the splinters inside his skin so they became a part of him. Someday, they would dissolve, he thought, or maybe not. Perhaps they would always be inside him, a part of the Heights worked into his blood and the marrow of his bones.

Heath smiled. He liked that.

Weaving, weaving, he ignored Goose's cries behind him. Heath wandered away from the corral and onto the road, turned to gaze up at the house, the orchard marching up the hill, and the homesteader cabin atop it. Lights glared inside. Smoke writhed and twined from the chimney.

He smiled. Heath licked blood from the corner of his mouth and from his teeth, which were all accounted for, thankfully.

From somewhere came the distant echo of sobbing. Shaw, weeping somewhere. For me? How kind. *I'll find you again, or you'll find me. You'll come back here. I know it.* We *know it.*

Dirt streaked his face. Dirt fouled his hair, stained his hands, and sank back deep, deep beneath his fingernails.

Heath showed his teeth. He flashed his bones.

"Yes," he whispered, raising his arms, opening his hands as if to grab, to *seize.* "Yes!" he roared. "*Yes!*"

Now lights were coming on in the house. They wondered where he had gone. Lee would be beaten or sent out to find him, and if that happened, Heath would kill him.

Mine.

Whose voice? Shaw's or his own?

Didn't matter.

Mine, mine.

"Yes, yes."

"One day."

"Oh, one day."

"One day, this."

This.

"Will all be."

Mine.

THREE

Winter, Early 1951

1

Winter was always worse than summer. Heath remembered that from before. Before his life at the Heights, working the cows astride Goose, ignoring Lee's taunts, which came only when Lee was absolutely, *absolutely* certain they were alone.

Mr. Lyon had backhanded Lee when he had seen the damage Lee had done to his adopted son. He had threatened to cast Lee out, and forever, if he ever laid a hand on Heath again. So now Lee had become overly cautious, but he was still vicious when he could be.

Heath was learning to cook alongside Aunt Lucy. He enjoyed baking and had developed some skill, particularly the art of making donuts, which was not nearly as easy as Lucy made it appear. Breads, too, he excelled at, coaxing into existence. And a marble cake, yellow and chocolate, which Mr. Lyon especially enjoyed.

Winter swept over them earlier than was its wont, as Don the hired man said one afternoon in mid-October, smoking his old wooden pipe beside Lee, who smoked cigarettes, and Heath, who had just begun to learn.

"She's a cruel old bitch," Don said mournfully, sucking at his pipe. "She don't care for you, and she don't for me."

"No one cares for me," Lee muttered, but they ignored him.

"You'll see," Don told Heath. "You'll see what the winter does to the ranch now that you're workin' it. That house will stand forever, I know it, but it's a body of work keeping it up. The wind digs at the boards, see, and the snow scours it all like sand in the desert."

"You never been to the desert, you old fool," Lee said, exhaling a claw of smoke and rolling his eyes.

Don narrowed his own and sucked at his lower lip.

He wasn't so old, Heath thought. Probably in his late forties. But he had lost a great many of his teeth, and those that remained were yellow and black by turns.

"Like a sandstorm," Don said reverently, turning away from Lee. "Just eats and eats."

Heath took this all in. He worried occasionally about the house, which did seem so permanent and certain, but he had learned there was no such thing as permanence. People and things were certain until they weren't. But, as Don had said, the big house *did* feel as if it would stand for a million more years, if a million more years were to come.

Heath's room was in the attic, as far from Lee's as possible—*thank God*—since Lee dwelt on the first floor, next to his father. Shaw's room lay ten feet or so from Heath's, at the attic's far end. Small, smaller, Heath thought, than befitted one of the heirs to the Lyon ranch. Shaw hadn't returned since his departure in August, and there had been no word from him at all.

Heath visited Shaw's room when he thought no one would notice and was prone to gazing out the window beside Shaw's little twin bed, seeing what Shaw must have seen as a child: the big hill that rolled up and over like a green wave—or a white one now—the little barn they had built for calving, and of course, the homesteader cabin, where dwelt the old woman Heath still, even after three years, had yet to set eyes on.

That, he decided, was about to change.

Heath set out on a grim morning in late January—a Sunday, since Mr. Lyon insisted, despite holding no allegiance to any particular brand of religion, that Sundays were to be a day of rest for everyone on the ranch. Don attended church in Burke, twenty miles away, but no one else did, not even Aunt Lucy, who was known to wear a simple silver cross around her neck.

Heath stood silently in the entryway, where all the coats were hung and the boots were stored, and donned his red and black checked cap, the one he wore for feeding the cows before the sun rose. He liked it secretly because of the pert pom-pom attached to its top and the earflaps lined with wool. It wasn't wise to admit to liking anything around the men of these parts. Heath had found he could not stand their derision.

He wore his gloves as well. The wind had taken up howling the previous afternoon while he and Mr. Lyon had worked together on an obstinate pickup that refused to start and which they required for passing out chunks of hay to the greedy herd of cows. The wind clawed, bit, and nipped at Heath's exposed nose, but he had doggedly attacked the pickup's innards with wrench and hammer until, finally, unexpectedly, it bloomed into life, roaring, sputtering, and roaring again.

Mr. Lyon had whooped, and Heath had smiled. Together they loaded the bed of the truck high with hay bales and set out for the pasture where the cows waited, lowing impatiently, though their voices were whipped away from them by that bitch of the wind, as Mr. Lyon called it, and sent out into the swirling whiteness obscuring Highway 201 and the rest of the world.

The wind was worse today, Heath thought while he slid like a shadow through the side door and out into the early winter morning. The sun had yet to rise, though it lurked somewhere off to the east, dispelling enough of the darkness that everything took on an eerie bluish cast.

Heath squinted. His eyes were already dry, as were his lips, despite the scarf he had wrapped two times around his neck and mouth. Now they burned, eyes and mouth, but he was resolute. He had woken that morning in the dark and the cold and thought, eyes opening, *Today*.

"Shaw?" he had whispered, but there was no Shaw.

Shaw, who had not returned to the ranch for the holiday, had called on Christmas morning, but Heath had slid away, afraid to hear Shaw's voice or to attempt to mimic any ordinary person who knew, intuitively, how to craft words into sentences, to spin out yards of wit, maybe even *charm*. Heath had no sense of how to do any of that, and so he had slunk away, back to the attic and his own room, ignoring their voices when they called him until, at last, they gave up.

Shaw was gone, but not, Heath knew, *forever*.

Perhaps the old woman on the hill knew when he would be back to the ranch, the house.

The Heights.

Why would you think that?

He didn't know. He just *did*.

Heath had awakened that morning with the knowledge full and shining inside him that he needed to brave the darkness, the cold, and the wolfen winter wind and climb the hill to knock on the old woman's door. How was it possible he had lived at the Heights for three *years* and he had yet to meet her?

He lowered his head and used it to cut through the wind, which was a solid thing shoving at him, like the invisible wing of some furious, mammoth bird. Or bat. Picturing a shrieking bat of impossible size was easier for him. But he endured. The snow was deep, nearly to his knees, and there was no path from the back of the house up the hill. He squinted.

The lights were on up there, and, yes, smoke twined its way from the chimney, which was nothing more than a simple pipe. *How does she live up there?* Heath asked himself, smiling beneath his scarf. *Gonna find out.*

Beside him, the orchard—which was really too pretty of a word, he thought, for the configuration of dead-looking trees marching somnolently up the hillside toward the homesteader cabin—stood resolute, the biggest of the tree trunks only as thick as his arm, the branches twisted and gnarled and all white, blending in with the sheets of snow as they came, relentless and screaming with wind. They danced along with it, urged by its power to sway and swing, and for a moment, Heath stood and simply gawped at them.

Foolish; his eyes burned and teared, and the tears froze. Through the prism of frozen saltwater, Heath saw how the trees waltzed up and down the hill, clasping at each other with their bony limbs, their skeletal appendages, gripping and seizing and heaving and helping, and he laughed. It was so insane, impossible, but there it was. The trees were nothing but distorted skeletons, and they performed their hideous *danse macabre* there on the hillside before Heath's frozen eyes while the sun broke the horizon and dispelled the night's shadows.

Everything was so *white*, everything blazed with brightness, and, yes, the trees marched and danced and weaved and twisted. He heard the cracking of their limbs—*their branches*, he hissed to himself—while they went.

He lowered his head, growled, "Fuck this," and continued to make his way up the hill.

2

She was a young woman at first, or so she seemed: pink of cheek, her eyes cornflower, her lips parted with surprise. Her hair, lustrous gold, curled in a foam all around her shoulders.

"The devil," she said.

It was actively terrifying to hear an old woman's voice come cracking out of the plump, crimson mouth of the youthful creature before him.

Two doors separated them: a screen door that had been patched and then patched again, and a thick door of dark oak she struggled to open. The big house lay below them, only fifteen yards or so away, but Heath had spent years on the hill, he knew, fascinated by the trees that crawled and crept and threw their bony arms into the air. And in that time, he had grown old, white-haired, deaf from the shriek of the wind that refused to die. So perhaps it was only fitting he must appear to be a hideous, aged monster while the woman in the homesteader cabin retained her youth and beauty.

But no. Heath blinked.

She was an old woman after all, lovely, with her white hair twisted into a chignon at the nape of her long, swan's neck and her large blue eyes magnified by the glasses she wore. Still pleasantly plump, smiling at him, she said, "Come in, come in, hurry, come in," and he obeyed, shivering, removing his hat awkwardly and hugging it to his chest. She closed both doors behind him.

The wind, caterwauling without, was at least dampened a bit. Perhaps the walls of the cabin were thicker than he had estimated.

Heath looked around the room amazed. It seemed bigger inside than out. The old woman, slightly stooped, hovered beside a sink where she had obviously been washing dishes when he had come knocking: a small blue teacup with a rose-pink handle and a plate to match, still damp. She held the drying rag in one hand and resumed rubbing at the plate.

"My grandson insisted on running water," she said, smiling prettily, "and electricity. I thought I was fine without it, but here we are."

"Heath," he said foolishly, offering her a stupid smile. "I mean, heat."

"Your name?"

"Heath, yes, ma'am. But I meant *heat*."

"Ah! The stove. Wood. No central heating, not like down *there*." And her face darkened and she sniffed. "I don't go down *there*. Not often."

"I know. I mean, I guessed."

She offered him a half-smile. "You've probably chopped some of it for me."

Heath nodded. Chopping wood had been one of his chores assigned to him by Mr. Lyon, yes.

"Thank you."

Shy, Heath turned away and glanced around.

The ceilings of the cabin were low, perhaps six and a half feet, *maybe*. Off to the left was a small sitting room with a rocker and a little television on a stand. Her bedroom sat to the right. He could just make out the bed, with the homemade quilt fixed neatly over the mattress. A shelf of spices and knickknacks—a pink-cheeked boy and a pink-cheeked girl, both composed of glass and possessing matching yellow hair, were frozen in the act-of skipping. The little girl wore a red cloak, and Heath wondered if she was intended to be Little Red Riding Hood. If so, where was the wolf? Was the boy the wolf? A werewolf eternally poised between transformations? He couldn't bring himself to ask.

Next to the shelf was the smallest stove Heath had ever seen, with two burners, maybe three feet across, if that. The old lady watched him with a sly smile on her face.

"Not much, is it?"

"No," he said, flustered. "It's—"

"But it's home. Suits me to the ground. I have everything I need up here."

"Food?"

"Ah, well. Once upon a time, we went into town for our supplies. Once upon a time, I grew it myself. Once, I did *everything*. But my lovely Earnest comes once a week or so. Sometimes, he sends the boy. I can't remember his name."

"Lee."

"Yes, yes. Not the *other*, though. *Him* I never see. Never, ever."

"Shaw." The name caught in Heath's throat. He tried to clear it, but it wouldn't clear.

"I manage. I suppose I'll die someday, and it will be as if I never existed. I've lived up here for over fifty years, and twenty of those years, I've been alone. We cracked open this land ourselves, you know, me and my husband. Built this house and cracked the land and grew what we needed and grew our children, and they grew their own children and—" Her eyes misted, narrowed behind her spectacles. "But you. You aren't Lee. You aren't t'other one. Who are you?"

"Heath."

"You said that."

"I..." He licked his lips. Immediately, they flared with pain, chapped from the razoring of the wind outside. "I was...found. Mr. Lyon—Earnest—he found me. Brung me—*brought* me here."

"Oh, Earnest." She sighed, and her mouth turned down, but her eyes, Heath observed, sparkled with amusement. "You're a stray."

"I...Yes."

"They told you about me." Now her lips dimpled with her barely contained amusement.

"They...Yes. Ma'am. A little."

"So polite. What did they tell you?"

"Not much. That you live up here. That I wouldn't ever see you."

"They were right. Until now, I mean. Here you are. Was that *all* they said?"

"Shaw—"

"Ah! Yes. That's the one. T'other one." Her lips pursed.

"He—" But he couldn't tell her the terrible thing Shaw had said about her.

"Yes?"

"Nothing. Ma'am."

"Not true. Don't tell lies to me, boy." Her eyes glittered. "He said I was...a witch?"

"No—"

"A devil? A spirit?"

"Not—"

"Fortune-teller? Gypsy?" She laughed musically. For a moment, she was young again, like he had seen her at the door, and the room swam with the scent of roses. A thick, dark scent, cloying. Heath blinked rapidly until she was just an old woman again in a long dress. Red? Yellow? Impossible to tell. "You must be many things to live out here and not die. That's what I learned when we came here from Minnesota. You ever been to Minnesota, boy?"

"No."

"I've never been back. I don't leave if I don't have to. Like to get back here soon as I can. It's been years since I've even been t'town."

"You aren't lonely up here?"

She merely gazed at him through those thick, magnifying spectacles of hers.

"It's nice," he said after an awkward moment. "Cozy."

She moved toward him like a shimmer of light on the surface of water. Her hair, golden once more, floated around her. Her bare white arms reached for him. Her hands glowed with rosy light, her nails painted a delicate, coral pink.

"I occupy myself," she said.

The chiming voice of a young woman vibrated inside Heath's skull, and the vibration grew so intensely it took all his strength to keep his hands at his sides, for they very badly wanted to press against his head until the sensation faded. At last it did.

But she smiled at him coquettishly, young and blond and lovely. "See?"

He nodded foolishly.

She beckoned and he followed her out of the kitchen and down a hallway—and how odd there should be a hallway because the entire cabin could have only been, by his figuring, thirty feet by forty feet, *maybe*. Yet she led him anyway, stopping every once in a while to beckon.

The woman wore a dress of the palest yellow—a party dress, he thought, an old-fashioned kind of party dress, though it hung low on her shoulders and pressed her breasts up so they gleamed at him in the light of the candle she held. She stopped once when they mounted a staircase, a great spiral thing that wound up and up and up—*Not*...He sighed to himself. *Not, not possible, not*, and yet, here they climbed. She examined him and smiled.

"You are perfectly attired, sir, for your first dance. We may be country people, but we know how to throw a party, I must say."

Heath looked down at himself in surprise and found he wore a long, royal-blue frock coat such as he had never seen outside of books—fairy tales, really, and he hadn't even been able to read them until recently—a white shirt, and a blood-red vest. From somewhere above them, music snapped, whistled, cheered, and cavorted, and there was the sound of a fiddle sawing away with hundreds of stomping feet.

His feet were shod in a pair of immaculate, gleaming snakeskin cowboy boots as red as his vest. *Stomp, stomp* went the feet above them, even though Heath knew, he *knew*, the homesteader cabin contained but one floor and three rooms. Yet the music played, and the dancers stomped and hollered while the beautiful young woman in yellow led him up the stairs.

He yearned after her, wished for her to kiss him with those red lips. Heath floated outside his body for the barest flash of a moment and looked down the winding staircase, but he couldn't see the bottom. He thought he could smell the grass of summer, even inside this giant house, and hear the frogs chirruping by the creek. Heath watched himself climbing.

Once, the woman in yellow stopped, took him by the hand, and squeezed it. "You're going to have the loveliest time. I promise you that."

They went on.

They stopped when his calves were beginning to ache and his feet to throb in the foreign, unyielding boots. She dropped his hand and turned the knob on a giant door. It swung open with a burst of light so dazzling it forced Heath to shield his eyes.

The woman at his side giggled prettily and said, "Take your hand away, you fool. It isn't *that* bright," and he did as she bade him.

They stood within a great barn, its ceiling soaring a hundred feet high. The floor was scattered with straw constantly pushed aside by the dancers. Oh, Heath thought, they were grand indeed: the women in their calico and blue and pink dresses, and the men in their blue jeans and boots. They kicked at the floor and stomped and hollered. The women tossed their pretty skirts while they jigged, and the men clapped for them.

A band of four, including a banjo and a fiddle, had established themselves in the far corner of the barn, and they produced furious music for the dancers to appreciate. A few old women, fat as hens, sat in chairs, with their arms folded and disapproving scowls marring their faces.

The woman in yellow laughed merrily to see them, and Heath cracked a smile as well.

"They think it's the Devil's work," his new friend whispered in his ear. "They think that music will call the Devil and lead these poor sinners down the rosy road to damnation."

Through the windows, Heath saw the purple sky at summer sunset, the stars beginning their own dance, sparkling at all the homesteaders.

He couldn't hear the frogs singing, but he knew they were there, with the hum of the mosquitos and the iron-wet tang of the creek water. For a moment, the musicians paused, and the dancers all stopped, clapped, whooped, and bowed to each other.

The woman in yellow tugged at Heath's elbow. "Come *on*. You're *far* too slow."

And, helplessly, he could only follow her.

"I can't dance," he tried to tell her, or he thought he did, but maybe he didn't speak at all.

One hand pressed against her waist, and the other slid into hers, as if one were a glove for the other. They moved swiftly and brightly across the floor, and the other dancers clapped for them, smiled, and whistled.

Heath thought his heart would explode in his chest. It kicked at his insides, like a rabbit with wild, thorny feet. Sweat poured down his forehead, and he tossed his wet hair back. The young woman in yellow shrieked delighted laughter, which the other dancers echoed. The musicians played faster, then faster than that, and Heath whirled the pretty girl around the dance floor.

I only want to do this, he thought dreamily. *I only want this and this and this, forever and ever.*

"Drink, drink," she sang, pressing the tin cup against his lips. It spilled, but only a few drops.

The liquor burned his throat, searing the tender meat within, but it bloomed heat in the pit of his stomach. Flowers burst into bloom behind his eyes, golden and green and the most vivid violet he had ever seen—

"A curse isn't the easiest thing in the world to endure," the old woman said from her place beside the sink.

Heath blinked rapidly and moaned, perfectly harmonizing with the wind wailing at that moment outside the cabin.

"But we do," she continued. "We do endure it. We have to. So do you, if you want to be one of us. Is that what you want, boy? Tell me. Speak up. Is that what you want?"

———

Heath whirled her around, only she wasn't a young woman in yellow any longer. She was *he*—Shaw or, blinking, someone who resembled Shaw closely enough they could be brothers. Purple evening sent lovely shadows over them while they sat together beside the creek. Behind them, the fiddles sang wildly, and a woman's voice chanted, "Dance, brothers! Dance, sisters! Dance, dance!" which was followed by a peal of unsteady laughter.

Heath could hardly see the other's face, but the eyes sparkled in the light of the rising moon, and the voice was familiar, if not identical.

"They'll find us, you know, if we aren't careful." Not as cultured as Shaw's. A little deeper, perhaps. Lacking that sibilant S. But similar. God, *so* similar.

Heath ached. He wanted to groan.

"No one," Heath said. "No one will find us."

"They will. No one can know."

"No, I know it. I understand."

"Do you?"

"I swear."

A breath. "Good." A smile. Turned smirk. Then the other's mouth on his.

Heath nearly withdrew from the shock of it, but there was no shock, he found. He had done this before. *They had* done this before. They had their little history. They kissed like lovers. Their hands wandered and pressed. Their breath passed back and forth. They panted like beasts into each other's mouths.

They lay back together so the tall grass disguised them. At their backs, the dancers in the hall stomped like buffalo. Sparks flared inside Heath's stomach and private parts, which he had never much considered before but which lived and burned now. He found the hand of the other and took it. The other squeezed his, and he squeezed it back. They sighed together, harmonizing.

Harmonizing still with the moan of the wind.

"If you want it..." the old crone said, one eye gummed shut, the other bulging obscenely. A brilliant blue, the whites rippling with crimson veins. "If you *want* any of it, you'll have to fight. Be sneaky. You may even need to kill. And you'll need the curse. Can you handle the curse?"

Heath nodded before he could stop himself.

The old woman seethed. Her hands warred with each other. A cat, yellow as mustard, sat on her lap and glared at Heath with one emerald eye.

"You don't know *anything*," she spat in the voice of winter—

"Dance, lovers, dance!" cried the women, and "Catherine!" Heath cried, for that was her name, the pretty girl with the golden hair and dandelion dress. How could he have ever forgotten it? "Catherine, don't leave me!"

But she fled, laughing wicked laughter, and he ran after her.

Someone tripped him. It was a deliberate trip, he thought as he fell, forever it seemed, until his chin struck the floor. Hay motes filled his nostrils, and he cried out in rage and pain. But the dancers laughed, and the fiddle shrieked, producing only off-key notes now—

"Bring him back to me. That's all I ask," Heath cried.

The old woman sneered at him. "Oh? Oh, is that all? Is that *really* all you ask? You make me ill to my stomach, *boy*."

"He's gone, and he'll stay gone," Heath babbled over the rising shriek of the wind, "unless you do something. Unless you help me!"

Somewhere, deeper within the impossible depths of the house, a door slammed.

Terror such as Heath had never experienced filled him like ice water. He opened his mouth to scream, but his vocal cords were glass.

Footsteps: heavy and dragging, seeking, relentless. They would bring their owner soon to this room, where he sat with the hag, where he bargained with her. Her good eye glowed, and she laughed. The cat opened its mouth and *hissed*—

Blood marred his face, and the man who was Shaw-yet-not-Shaw mopped at it solemnly. "You shouldn't trust *her*. You know that, don't you? Listen to me. Believe *me*. You can't trust Catherine Lyon. She's not *right*."

"They tripped me," Heath said. His lip was split and swelling. It tasted like the iron of the creek.

"Poor baby," Shaw-not-Shaw said, smiling. He leaned in to kiss Heath, even with all that blood staining his mouth—

And the dancers all bore the heads of beasts: fat pigs with beady black eyes and bloodstained tusks, enormous shaggy bear heads too big for their human shoulders, wildcats, pumas and lynxes, dogs with lolling tongues, gray wolves and coyotes. They all pointed at Heath and laughed at him, stomping out of time to the wheezing of the fiddle and the occasional pluck of the banjo. They swayed together. Some of them pressed gaping mouth to gaping mouth, ignoring tusk, fang, and the occasional whisker. Others fucked indiscriminately in the center of the floor.

The lights of the hall blazed blue and dim. Somewhere, thunder crashed and roared. Their eyes glowed with inhuman lights, and together, slobbering and growling, they managed to sing, "Buffalo gals, won't you come out tonight, come out tonight, come out tonight." And of course, some of them wore the ridiculous but terrifying heads of buffalo, eyes the size of dinner plates, brown, full of condemnatory solemnity, hanks of brown fur hanging down to their chests, their hands white and clutching, clutching.

"Animals..." Heath sobbed. "Fiends, *beasts!*"

But they only sang louder to drown him out.

"Help me!" he cried. "Please, please, you can. I know you can—"

They fell on him.

3

"Help...me," Heath whispered, but the words were stolen by the covetous wind and spirited away into the blizzard.

He tried to stand, but his knees refused to support him. The wind licked and sucked at him, drinking all the warmth he produced as soon as he produced it. His fingers clutched at the black-tarred sides of the cabin, trying desperately to keep himself upright, to stop his slow, liquid descent onto the ground, into the snow, into oblivion.

But it might be nice. To let go. Heath didn't feel pain anymore, just a general kind of numbness giving way to warmth. *This is what it must be to freeze to death*, he thought dreamily. His fingers dragged down, down, down along the cabin's side.

One winter long ago, Heath's cousin Desmond, a rambunctious seven-year-old, had run from the house and into the snatching arms of a blizzard, much like this one, during a Christmas party at his auntie's house in the country when Heath was younger. How much younger? Younger than Desmond, but no one had ever really kept track, certainly not with things so silly as birthday parties. Desmond had never come back.

No one had noticed he had gone—except for Heath, who watched him go, called after him, couldn't stop him. No one could stop Desmond if Desmond wanted to *go*. And when Heath tried to tell the adults, no one really listened to him, so he had slunk into a corner. He occupied himself with one of his cousin Rosie's doll-babies she had been given for Christmas until one of his uncles slapped it from his hands and snarled that boys didn't play with dolls. Didn't he know that?

Much later, Desmond's mother called for him and called for him, and he didn't answer. They had searched the house and the outside world, where they found dear Desmond beside a haystack, his face blue and somehow dreamy. Despite all the wailing and shrieking, Desmond never regained consciousness.

All Heath remembered about the funeral was the intense cold and the droning of the minister. No one blamed Heath for Desmond's death. No one except Heath himself, of course, for the others never knew he had watched Desmond run out into the swirling darkness and had failed to bring him back. And he never told anyone. Why would he?

Heath had made it to the ground, where the rocks and pebbles beneath the snowdrift gathered at the cabin door. He tried to stand. It was as if he possessed no legs, as if he had never possessed them. He tried to flex his fingers. Even safe inside his gloves, they refused to obey him. He tried to smile. His cheeks flexed; the muscles beneath the skin twitched. Maybe they would find him like that. Smiling and frozen.

Like Desmond.

No.

"Shhh," he murmured. Heath wanted to sleep.

No, I said.

Wasn't he at a party? A dance? Some kind of old-fashioned, insane barn dance? A witches' sabbat, he thought. The witches gathered. *They danced and whooped it up and wore animal faces, and they ate my face.*

Get up.

"Can't," he said. Best to lie still.

Heath, I know you can hear me.

"That's not my name," he said, but it was. That was the crazy thing. Heath, named for a dead boy. Now he was the dead boy, maybe. That was even stranger. Everything he had been—maybe even the guilt he had carried for allowing cousin Desmond to sprint from the house and into that long-ago blizzard—everything he had been up until the point Mr. Lyon found him in the road, dusty and streaked with dirt, all of *that* was rubbed away. As if someone—Heath himself?—had taken an eraser to it. Like what the storm was doing right now. Whiteness. Brightness. Freezing and beautiful.

He would be beautiful. Forever. Heath forever.

You'll die.

"Yes," he said.

You'll die, and you'll never see me again.

Heath paused.

He tried to say the name. The boy's name. It wouldn't come. His lips wouldn't open. His tongue was a dead blue worm in his mouth.

You'll never see me again, I said.

"But I want to," Heath replied.

Somewhere, a hag was shrieking wicked laughter. Somewhere, a chorus of horrors swayed together, singing, "Buffalo gals, won't you come out tonight, come out tonight—"

"I don't want to die."

Get up.

"Can't."

Try. Harder.

Fingers. Flex.

Fingers flex.

Fingers *dig.*

They dug into the snow. Heath managed to grunt. He thought he could rise.

The wind screamed angrily. Snow ground against his face, scoured his eyes. He closed them. So easy—

No!

Electricity. He clawed at the side of the house, heaved himself up, opened his mouth to scream, but no sound emerged. The wind filled him. Burning but icy. It hurt. Too much hurt.

A hand took his. Warmth filled him. Fingers laced through his. Someone pulling at him, yanking him up, so he groaned a protest.

Up. Up, my Heath.

He tried to pound on the cabin door, but his hand couldn't form a fist.

"—boy—"

A dark figure lurched through the shreds of snow. Hands gripped his shoulder and pulled him close. Someone pounded heavily on the door of the cabin.

"Open up!" screamed Earnest Lyon. "Mama, for the love of God, open the door!"

———

The blanket they wrapped around him did little to help at first, but gradually, feeling restored itself to his extremities and his face. The tips of his fingers and his ears burned, and his limbs pulsed and throbbed.

The woman standing next to Mr. Lyon, clucking her tongue and shaking her head, adjusting her glasses—*At least*, Heath thought, *the glasses are still there*—was not at all the same woman who had answered the door when he came knocking the first time.

The interior of the house was familiar—the Little Red Riding Hood figurine smiled at him, as it had before—but its owner appeared to be a different person: reed-thin, hair cut short in a cloud around her face, which was lined and seamed, like clay that had dried beneath the harshness of the sun, eyes small marbles behind the lenses.

"At least his eyes aren't frozen shut," the old lady said pertly.

Heath shuddered at the rasp of her voice.

"Heath," Mr. Lyon said soothingly. "Heath, what brought you up here? On a day like today? What was going through your mind?"

"Don't talk," the old woman said brusquely.

"Catherine," Heath said.

They exchanged glances over him, Mr. Lyon and the old woman.

"Who did you say?" Mr. Lyon cleared his throat.

"Birdie." The old woman patted her breastbone. "That's what *I* go by. My name is Elizabeth. My mother—"

"Catherine Lyon," Heath said.

"My mother. She died, oh, a long time ago. Forty years or so."

"The curse."

Mr. Lyon's mouth dropped open. Quite simply, he goggled.

"The curse killed her. Didn't it?"

The old woman gasped.

Heath smiled weakly.

. . .

4

"There's no such thing as a curse," is what the old woman said to me, scolded me, sharp tongue, sharp words. Oh, but I scared 'em. Scared 'em both. I could tell. Scared 'em *good*. They kept exchangin' looks, and that old bitch kept clutching her pearls, even though she didn't have no pearls. I went up there robbing once, you know, after she died. I went there to take whatever I could that weren't nailed down, and all her jewelry was just costume jewelry. Fake as fuck. Nothing but paste and cheap beads.

And finally, Mr. Lyon, he said, "Welp, we gotta get back down the hill, Mother. Mother, it's time we went."

And the old lady, she just smiled her simpering little smile and gave him this dry smack on the side of his face with her withered old monkey lips.

She says, "I understand. I know .Now, don't be scared. No reason to be scared."

"Not scared," says Mr. Lyon.

But, oh, I think that he *was*. I think he was scared *plenty*. And not just 'cause I almost froze to death outside that awful little house that was bigger on the inside than it was out.

He didn't say a word to me on the way down—well, how could he, with the wind and the snow tearin' away like they was?—but I knew he was disappointed in me. Maybe not even angry. Just that dog-sad disappointment in his big eyes, lookin' at me.

Don't look at me like that, I tried to say, but the words didn't come out. Or maybe they did. He didn't say nothing back if he heard me.

Shame pounded in me like a wild horse. My eyes burned. Hands clenched into fists. I wanted to hit something. I wanted to hit something so damned *hard*.

Back in the house, with its walls folding down all around me, Aunt Lucy clucking and pecking at me, they put me in a steaming bath, and I didn't even care that I was naked. First I couldn't feel the heat. Then I did. It burned me. I screamed. Aunt Lucy only laughed.

After a while, I laughed with her.

"I love you," I told her. Only, just like on the hill, I don't think the words came out.

Maybe the words would never come out again. Maybe they never had in the first place. I didn't have no name; I didn't have no memories of a time before this place. I thought about this while the water cooled around me, and I sucked up all that heat into myself.

Aunt Lucy washed my hair. "You're a handsome boy," she told me, matter of fact, splashing water in my face so soap didn't get in my eyes. She used a special shampoo, she told me, that she kept just for herself. It smelled like flowers.

I liked the smell of flowers. Reminded me of Shaw.

"I heard Shaw's voice up there," I said, and I musta really said the words because she looked at me all wide-eyed, like a frightened deer.

"Oh, sure. Of course," like she was pretending not to believe me, but deep down, I knew she did.

"He saved me," I said. "He told me to get up. Told me not to fall asleep. Told me to keep going."

"That sounds like Shaw," Aunt Lucy said. Scrub, scrub. "He thinks about other people. When he's not thinking about himself."

"Everyone thinks about themselves."

"Some people do it more than most." Scrub, scrub.

"He's good to me."

"That's good."

"He *is*."

"I believe you, my Heath. You just...You be careful, that's all."

"I'm careful."

"Sometimes"—scrub—"Sometimes, I wish my brother wouldn't—"

"You wish he'd left me, don't you?"

"I didn't say that."

"You're thinking it."

"So what if I am?" Scrub. Hurt. Too much. Fingers. Digging. "So what if I think this house is no good sometimes? So what if I think it's like a cage? Or a trap? You ever seen a dog that survived a trap, my Heath?"

I didn't say nothing back. Just closed my eyes and listened.

"It's a sight. We had a Collie—good as could be, smart, white as snow. One blue eye, one brown. Earnest said that meant he could see the wind."

"What's that mean?"

"I've never been sure. But I always liked the sound of it. A dog that could see the wind. And out here, where there's nothing but wind most of the year? What a sight for the eyes of that beautiful dog. That sweet, loving dog. But he roamed. Dogs do that out here."

"I know. I follows them sometimes."

"*I* know because I watch you. I see things, my Heath, and I pay attention. So, this poor beautiful creature runs away from the house every night. Maybe he's following the wind. I don't know. But he returns every morning until one day he doesn't. My brother takes one of the hired men, and they go out looking. My brother always had a heart, just like this one, you know? Even when we were children. He put aside everything to go searching for that dog. And they found him. Eventually. One leg caught in a wire trap.

"No one is supposed to be leaving wire traps on our property. Probably a hunter. Someone who either didn't know or didn't care that this was Lyon land. Oh, I remember just wailing when they brought the poor thing home. The leg was already destroyed. Gangrene. We took him to the vet, and the vet cut off the leg, and that lovely creature was never the same. Could he see the wind to begin with? Could he see it *now*? After all that pain? Lying out there for three days?"

"Did he live?"

"Oh, he lived. But he didn't roam anymore. Stayed near the house. But he was scared, and he'd slink around and growl at you sometimes. Scared of his own shadow. Tied to this place as surely as the rest of us."

"Hobbled."

"What's that?"

"Hobbled. It's called hobbling."

"Oh, you know that word, do you?"

I nodded.

"That's what I mean about the Heights." Rinse, rinse. "If I wish you'd never come here, it isn't because I don't love you. Because I do."

Then, in a rush:

"EventhoughIshouldn'tbut I do."

"Why shouldn't you?"

Nothing.

"Aunt Lucy, why?"

Rinse.

"Here's a towel. Get out of there now and put on some warm clothes. We'll mix us up some pancakes, you and me, because you make them a fine sight better than *me*."

She turned away and let me out of the bath. I dressed in a sweater she handed me. She didn't even have to tell me it was Shaw's—soft, lambswool, colored a green that was almost blue.

We made the pancakes, and everyone ate together, Lee glaring at me, Mr. Lyon avoiding my eye. When I went back to my room, the old lady from before was sitting on my bed, watching me, pert as could be.

"You took your time," she said. Oh, yes, so pert. "You certainly did take your sweet time."

I watched her without moving but gave her my coldest, most measuring look.

A little smile danced on the lines of her mouth.

"See somethin' green?"

"Catherine," I said.

The old woman only giggled. She wore that yellow dress from the party. Obscene on a creature as ancient as she was. Nearly bald, what hair remained on her head like ropes of snow. Eyes like eggs, bulging out of her face. She had lost her glasses, but I wondered if she really needed them. Her eyes were just like Shaw's—so blue they was nearly white.

"Catherine," I said again. "Catherine Lyon. Catherine."

"I never come to this house anymore. I feel safer up *there*. But you brought me down, boy, and maybe I'll stay a spell."

My eyes drifted past her to my window, to the hill behind the house, to where the windows of the homesteader cabin glowed with the living old lady's warmth, even through the snow and panther screams of the blizzard.

"Yes, yes." She giggled. "I built that house. Me. Me and my man. But I did the brunt of the work"

Now she was young again, comely, one leg crossed over the other, revealing the slim, white length of her calf. Her foot bare, the toes painted gold, shining.

"I was strong."

"You *are* strong."

"Oh, you think so?" She simpered at me.

"You have to be. To be here now."

"I think you're right. Doesn't hurt that the Heights is on my side. All of it, my sweet. The hills and the creek and even the roads the men laid with their foolish red rocks. Even those roads are on my side. Though they'll be gone soon enough. The road that leads from the highway to the Heights...That'll go too. Left unattended, the land takes it all back."

Her lovely eyes filled with water.

"But we'll remain," she whispered.

"So maybe I'm not so strong as I thought I was."

"Could be your Aunt Lucy is right. This house *is* a trap. So is the land. It holds us."

"It holds us under its spell."

"Forever."

"Maybe," I said, grinning at her like a fiend. "*Maybe* some of us like the idea of forever. Maybe some of us want to go on and on. Maybe some of us never want to even think of death."

She reflected my smile back at me, tooth for tooth.

"Oh," she purred. "You think so?"

"You know how?"

"Dying here isn't enough," she said.

"I figured."

"You need the curse."

"What is it?" I sounded too eager.

She flinched away from me, my devil's face. My satanic eyes and sharp fox features.

"Tell me!" I begged her. I even sank to my knees and offered her up my fists, clenched together, the fingers locked.

I think she saw the blizzard from the window behind her in the mirrors of my eyes. Maybe she thought it was a part of me. Cold and determined and eternal.

She took my hands. I felt hers. They were warm.

Old lady: "You know what the curse is, boy."

Young Catherine Lyon: "You have it in you already."

Old lady: "When he returns, you'll see."

Young Catherine Lyon: "When he's back at the Heights."

Old lady: "You'll see."

And, grotesquely, they were old *and* young, a hag and a beauty, gasping and chortling and giggling like a schoolgirl. And they said to me, "Your love is the curse, boy."

"Love is not a curse," I said, but even as the words left me, I wondered.

"It can be," they said to me slyly, old and young. "Heaven and hell know love can be a curse more potent than any other. I found out, I found out."

"I found out," young Catherine whispered, tears streaking her face like snow streaking from the black-night sky.

Then she wasn't there anymore, and my room was cold. The wind snarled at me and froze patterns in frost on the inside of my window. They looked like faces whining to get in.

I turned my back on that room.

I turned my back on the whispers of the old lady.

"Go back to your cabin," I told her through gritted teeth. "Go back to your hell. And stay out of mine."

I turned to look back before I switched off the light.

The old lady's cat lounged on my bed, glaring at me with hateful yellow eyes, like lamps.

It opened its mouth to hiss.

I hissed right back at it.

It turned into smoke and twisted itself out and away.

"Good," I told it, leaving my room to its remaining darkness.

FOUR

Summer 1954

1

Shaw finally came back to the homeplace to stay when Mr. Lyon died.

Lee brought a woman to the Heights, married her, and announced his plans to father a child, that the houses and the land were *his* now, a fact Shaw immediately disputed.

"You can stay"—Lee grinned down into Heath's face, taking obvious delight in his clenched teeth and narrowed eyes—"but you can live in the barn. Or in the stables with your horse. I'm giving you that horse, see. Which is really big of me, I think."

"No," Heath said.

Lee's grin widened, threatened to circle around the back of his head. "No?" he said. "*No?*"

"No." Shaw dropped an arm around Heath's shoulders. "Nothing will change. Except that I'm here now. I'll run things. I can do that for poor old Dad, anyway."

The smile faded from Lee's face. "The hell you say."

"The hell *you* say. And Heath stays. *Inside* the house."

"I'm in charge here."

"No," Heath said, surprising them all. "Aunt Lucy—"

"She's no kin to *you*," Lee snarled, moving in.

"Aunt Lucy..." Heath said. He didn't move. Heath drew himself up, earning a smile from Shaw. "Aunt Lucy owns the house and the land and the business. Mr. Lyon left it all to her."

Lee's face turned red until it shone like a fresh apple. Finally, he gnashed his teeth, snarled, "Goddamn *women*," and strode away, out the door and down to the corral, leaving Shaw and Heath to beam at each other.

Later, Shaw enjoyed a long, hot bath—"To wash off the entire country I had to cross to get back here to this house," he said, with a glint of wickedness in his eye, adding, "to *you*," leaving Heath breathless and gaping. After Shaw's bath, they left the house together and walked out into the tall grass.

Shaw stood out starkly from everyone else around them, with his white linen pants rolled to his knees, revealing his long, tanned legs, his billowing shirts of linen in a rainbow array of color, which he habitually left only half-buttoned, exposing, to Heath's greedy eyes, coils of hair at his breastbone so fine they were nearly white. Heath wore what he always wore: the dark Levi jeans, his battered tan boots, his blue and white plaid cotton shirt with the pearl snaps—fully buttoned, of course, just like the other men.

Mosquitos buzzed around them, but none, Heath observed, landed anywhere near Shaw. None dared to pierce his skin and drink his blood. Shaw didn't seem to notice. His eyes had settled somewhere near the horizon.

"Dad is dead," he said at last, though to Heath's ears, it sounded more like a question.

He nodded, but hesitantly.

"Dad is dead."

Heath nodded again.

Shaw crammed both hands into the pockets of his pants. The sun, hovering near the horizon, cast them into a brilliant, fiery light so that, to Heath's eyes, Shaw became a creature of flame. Orange and yellow points glinted in his eyes. His hair a ball of fire. Even his teeth, when he spoke, shone with heat.

"Did I know him?"

Heath considered this.

"No, really. Did I?"

"Did you?"

"Idiot. Throwing my words back to me."

"Not an idiot," Heath growled.

"You're not. I forgot. It's been too long."

"Yup."

"They kicked me out of school, you know."

Heath raised a shaggy eyebrow but said nothing.

"Oh, yes, they did. Sure, they did. A boy like *me*. Why he can't be allowed to—" Shaw stopped, looked away, bared those fiery teeth into the growing darkness. "Hell," he whispered, removed his hands from his pockets, scrubbed at his face.

Heath couldn't bring himself to touch the other boy—the other man. *We're men now*, he wanted to say. *We're eighteen. We will own this place and run this place together, and we'll be happy. No such thing as curses. We'll be* happy. But his mouth was held in place by stitches of the strongest iron, and stitched together it would stay. He burned to lay an arm around Shaw's shoulders; he blazed to pull him in tightly. Against his shoulder. Or his chest.

"Yeah, they kicked me out. Two years ago. Dad knew. He let me stay in Massachusetts. I never should have left. I never should have—" Shaw scrubbed again at his face. When he dropped his hands, Heath saw the way the last rays of the sun caught and were held by the wetness in his palms, so it seemed Shaw wept pure fire. "But I did." He sighed. "Dad didn't want me here. He knew this wasn't the place for me. But I—"

Shaw whirled around and glared into the gloom. Heath followed his gaze, back to the house, where no lights glowed yet, but the windows also captured the sun's final fiery swords. They appeared to be eyes, red and hateful.

"But I missed you!" Shaw cried, shaking his fists at the house. "Goddamn you, I missed you so much!"

"I missed you," Heath whispered, but Shaw didn't seem to hear him.

At last, he dropped his fists. His shoulders hunched. "They kicked me out, those bastards. They finally did. I should have come back here."

"Why did they kick you out?"

Shaw merely sneered.

"Why didn't your father want you here?"

"I don't really know. I teased you one time. Told you our house was haunted, remember?"

Heath nodded grimly. He remembered.

"You've spent more time here than I have. What do you think?"

Buffalo gals, won't you come out tonight, come out tonight, come out—

He shivered.

Shaw's eyes narrowed. "What? You just thought of something. What was it?"

"Nothin'."

"Don't give me that."

"I don't know what a ghost is."

"I guess I don't either."

They looked at each other, nearly identical in height. The sun passed below the horizon, turning their faces blue. Their eyes locked and would not look away from the other.

"I miss him," Shaw whispered.

"Me too," Heath said softly.

"I never really knew him, you know? And he never knew me."

Heath opened his mouth and closed it quickly.

Shaw took a step nearer to Heath. Another. Heath let him. Shaw's chest heaved. He dropped his head onto Heath's shoulder. His body quaked, yet he made no sound. Heath moved to put his arms around Shaw, pulled him close. Scalding wetness on his chest where Shaw's face tortured itself and worked against him. Heath pulled him closer. He held him tightly.

Down by the creek, a curlew piped at them. A light breeze passed playfully over their linked bodies. Shaw made no move to withdraw. Heath only held him. Far away, a coyote called to the sky, maybe to the stars, perhaps an attempt to summon the moon.

A mile or so away, Nathan Reardon and his wife and children lived their own lives, farmed their own land, near to the Heights but an impossible distance away at the same time. Heath saw the lights of their distant farmhouse come alive. One of their dogs began to bark, a hateful, jarring sound. What did the Reardons have to worry about?

Not curses. Certainly not.

Buffalo gals, won't you come out tonight—

Shaw stirred. Stepped away. Wiped at his face. Turned back to Heath and grinned. "Your shirt's all snotty."

"Just tears."

"Tears and *snot*."

Heath smiled weakly.

"Listen to that coyote. He's making the Reardon dog go *crazy*."

Heath tilted his head back and offered up an imitation of the coyote.

"That's pretty good."

Heath howled again, louder this time.

"You're not a coyote, though. You're a wolf."

Heath shook his head. "I'm not. I'm not an animal."

"You sounded like one just now."

"But I'm *not*, though."

"Oh. Right. Lee's been calling you names, I bet."

Heath glared into the darkness.

"Well," Shaw said, laying his head against Heath's chest again. "*I'm* an animal."

"Yes."

"You know."

"Yes. Cat."

"A little on the nose. But yes. You too. You can be a cat too. You're just like me."

"Yeah?"

"All cats are gray in the dark. Haven't you ever heard that before?"

Heath shook his head.

Buffalo gals—

He pulled away. His head buzzed. Somewhere, he thought he caught the hint of a bow dancing against its fiddle, the roar of laughter—

Shaw looked around uneasily. He heard it too, Heath thought. A bubble of fear rose into his chest and burst there.

A single light—too dull to be electricity, and flickering—appeared in the window of the homesteader cabin.

They watched it together, silently.

The lights in the Heights came on.

All at once.

Every light.

All at once.

Impossibly, of course.

Somewhere behind them, in the deeper country, not too far from them, a man laughed. It was a deep, rasping sound, eminently unpleasant. It held no humor.

Also impossible.

"My father," Shaw whispered, "didn't want to die here."

Heath took Shaw's hand and held it tightly.

"He didn't want *me* here either."

The man's laughter rose, becoming something inhuman, impossibly high, a steady gibbering, a mad kind of barking, rising, cut off finally, as if the laugher were choked by strong hands—

They began to run, hand in hand, pelting through the grass, away from the impossible sound, the coyote howling, the dog barking, until they pounded up the road, through the gate, up the path, and onto the steps, up the steps, through the door, until they stood, finally, panting, hands on knees, swallowed by the house and in the first ring of its gut: the front hallway of the Heights.

2

I didn't tell anyone about the Heights at first, once I left them behind. Thousands and thousands of miles away, riding a ribbon across the entire country, and here I am, a country boy who doesn't belong in the country and a city boy who doesn't understand the city. Classic conflict, my roommate said, once I confided in him. Eventually, that is.

He was a rich kid from up Bedford way, but he was smart. Excruciatingly smart. Smarter than me. Which was probably why I poured a pitcher of my piss all over him while he was sleeping one sticky September night. That was the first time I was expelled. They let me come back, though. We had money.

The Lyons *always* had money. Enough to keep me in some kind of line. I told him, my roommate—Rick was his name: silly, lantern-jawed, bespectacled Richard Hawthorne the Fifth—I *pleaded* with him, told him I was sorry, and I meant it. I did! I switched rooms the next week. And again the week after. The curtains proved to be too flammable. So did my roommate's boxer shorts.

That's mostly a joke.

They kept me because of my father's money—which was really my mother's money, but mother was long dead and no one worked the ranch like my father did, so I suppose he deserved it. But they also kept me because I could argue. As in, I was great on the debate team. My dad had his sights set on a law degree for me someday. Maybe that'll happen. It probably won't. Or maybe. I don't know. I think I want to stay at the Heights. For a while, anyway. Or maybe forever. Listen, Dad's body isn't even *cold*.

I used to dream about it. The hills—oh man, those hills, the ones behind the house, reaching up and out and *back*, miles and miles of hills —green and shimmering. Like a dress I saw wrapped around this drag queen at the Fensgate Hotel two years ago.

They let me in because they said, "You got a pretty face." I tried to cut my goddamn pretty face up one time, but my friend Jeanette stopped me. She took the razor out of my hand and threw it out a window. I told her to go get it, but she said no, and I cried until I laughed, and my nose started to bleed, and I threw up.

Shit. The Fensgate. Right.

I saw a drag queen there one night, wearing a dress that just shimmered so and caught the light. It reminded me right off of the hills behind our ranch. The Heights. *My* Heights. Maybe that was when I started to dream about them.

They flooded one year, those hills, or the coulees between them, when I was a wee thing, and Lee threatened to drown me. We had a hell of a snowfall that year—'45 or '46, maybe—and it warmed up. All the snow melted and just right off filled the little coulees between the hills so that the water churned and roared like the big rivers we would see when we would go to Wolf Point or Glasgow, the Missouri River, or the Milk.

I don't remember what I was doing. Probably following Lee all over the house. All I wanted was his attention, his love. He was older than me. Lee was my big brother, and I thought if I could be the biggest and the loudest, he would love me back. I followed him around with a little toy drum Aunt Lucy had given me and eventually took back because I could hit it and hit it night and day and night.

Lee, I thought, *bang*, Lee, *bang*, love me, love me, *bang*, love me, Lee, *bang*, but he didn't. He still doesn't—so that's probably why. He picked me up and held me by the ankles. I screamed, but no one heard me. He finally put me down, but for a while, I thought I would actually die. That Lee would drop me into the water and I would sink like a rock to the bottom of the river that wasn't supposed to be there at all and never came back after the ground drank all its water by spring and early summer.

When I read *Hamlet* as a twelfth birthday present to myself, I pretended to be Ophelia. I read all the Ophelia scenes and memorized every single word she had to say on the subject of the property of flowers.

And drowning.

There are flowers out there too.

I showed them to Heath. Every one I could find.

Heath.

I grew out of Ophelia relatively quickly. I didn't want to die, after all, and I certainly didn't want to die because of a man. If I were Ophelia, I told Jeanette with the confidence of a thirteen-year-old white boy from Montana, if *I* were Ophelia, I would march up to Hamlet and slap him and kiss him and force him to atone for his sins. I would have an entire list of atonements. That's what I would have. And Hamlet would have to be my slave for the rest of our lives.

"I wouldn't mind so much if he killed my brother," I said.

Jeanette laughed and asked me about the atonements I would have for Hamlet. When I told her, *she* slapped *me* and laughed. She told me I had a filthy mind and I should keep it out of the gutter, but I said I wouldn't *ever* and, if I had my way, I would stay in the gutter for the rest of my days.

She said, "You don't mean half the things you say."

"Oh yes, I do."

"You'd never *do* them."

"I would," I said. "You don't know half the things I've done."

She still doesn't. No one does. But I wrote them all down, and someday, I will publish them, and they will be my dirty, sexy memoirs.

Sexy.

Heath. Strong face. Long, thin nose. Full lips. High cheekbones. Arrogant cheekbones. Big, dark eyes. Brown? Black? Green? Slate? They change. I swear they change.

Heath, Heath.

He has grown since last I saw him. Muscles risen under the skin of those arms, muscles on his chest when he stripped off his shirt the night I came home for Dad's funeral and he didn't know I was watching him change, but I was. Little, skimpy, dark blue jockey shorts. Filled those out too.

Heath didn't know I was watching. He doesn't know. Or maybe he does.

Caught my eye in the mirror when I passed by his room. Glided by soundlessly. All those ballet lessons I forced myself to take allow me to glide and be soundless. Gliding by on little cat feet. Did he catch my eye? Did he see me seeing him like...that? So exposed? Vulnerable?

Heath doesn't like to be vulnerable. He is like all the other men out here, and how I despise them. They keep themselves hidden away, tucked away, until they whip you with a casual cruelty. Or sometimes when they shove you or punch you. Protecting themselves. Hiding themselves away. Their true selves. Bastards. But Heath does that, and I don't consider *him* a bastard. Muscled. Cracked.

Where are his parents? He doesn't know. Dead? Could be dead. He doesn't remember anything, he claims, before the time my father found him and brought him back to the Heights.

That jaw. I want to trace it with the tip of my tongue. Would he let me? I think he would. I think he would let me do anything I asked. Anything, anything. That jaw, those lips. My lips on those lips. Crushing them. Soft. I'll bet they are just so soft. Never been used. Not like mine. Not like me.

He can't know. I won't tell him. The things I have done. Where I have been and with whom I have been there. He can't know. I won't tell him. Heath. *I'm* the dirty one. He doesn't know.

I will take him back to the creek, that's what, like I did years and years ago. We were boys. What are we now? Are we men, the way the other men are out here? God, I don't even know anymore. Who they are? Who I am? How I'm supposed to be. Christ, like I give a fuck.

I wear what I want to wear. I won't wear their jeans and their boots, those bright shirts of stiff cotton that button up with pearl snaps. *Fuck* that. I won't. Their boots. Their giant clompy, stompy boots. Too big for their feet. I won't wear those boots. Dad never made me, and I won't do it now. But I'll live out here. I will live at the Heights with my Heath, and I will even tolerate Lee and that abysmal creature he married and dropped directly in the center of our lives. I will even tolerate *that* nonsense.

That jaw. Those lips. I want them. Soft. The press of them. I want. I *want* them.

Jeanette and I went for a walk one night. We had a curfew. I was sixteen, maybe seventeen, so not *too* long ago. We went for a walk. We left the school grounds. I wore my new blue tweed coat, long, came down past my knees, and she wore a dress of daisy yellow. My eyes just blazed, she told me, laughing, while we walked along. After a while we held hands.

Jeanette understood me. She didn't need me to say anything.

"My father is going to die," I told her. "Soon."

"Don't say such things," but she smiled when she said it because I think she knew.

"We're tied to the land, we Lyons, and we're tied to our houses too. We can't ever leave them."

"But you're here," she said.

"My father is dying. How much longer can I stay?"

We went to a bar. I can't remember the name. And Jeanette found a woman whose head she pushed under that daisy yellow skirt, up against the bathroom sink in the men's room, while I danced with a bearded, dark-eyed man whose hair was strained with streaks of iron gray. Oh, Jeanette just *pushed* that woman's head into her center, and that man pushed his tongue into my *mouth,* and we all four of us just *writhed,* heat flowering up and swallowing us. I didn't know Jeanette had it in her. *Ha ha.*

"I don't like to compete," she said later, during our walk back to the school, her face prim and only slightly flushed. "I don't like to compete, Shaw dearest, but I figured I had to show you a thing or two."

And I laughed.

Could I ever bring Heath to a place like that?

Would Heath ever *want* to go to a place like that?

Heath is tied to the Heights now, like I am. And Lee. Even my father. My poor dead father.

Lying in that casket.

How did he die?

Aunt Lucy didn't say.

Is that a part of the curse he never wanted to talk about?

Or is it more like boogedy boogedies and ghosty ghosties?

Lying in that casket. Still handsome. You can say that about the men of the Lyon family. We are handsome to the end. Even Lee.

Okay, maybe not Lee.

"Stop being such a fruit," he told me the night I arrived. He shoved me. "Stop being such a fucking faggot."

I shoved him back. I would have blackened his eye, but the funeral was the next day and think of the scandal. So I kicked him in the jewels instead. He lay on the hardwood floor at my feet, twisting himself into knots, squirming like a bull snake, and I kicked him again.

"I'll be whatever the hell I want," I told him.

He opened his mouth, but no sound came out. I like him better that way, I think.

I am going to miss Boston. People talk about the winters. They are worse here. There is the wind, for one thing. It is the breath of an old woman when it is calm and the roar of some het up young buck at its worst. It moans through the poor dead trees in the orchard on the hill-side, below Grandma's cabin. It moans like an animal in pain or a child. Sometimes, I moan with it. No wind like that in Boston.

Maybe I won't miss it. Maybe I will forget it soon enough. Jeanette and I used to visit the ocean, and there is no ocean here. Not even close. Last year, she took me to the town where she grew up, along the coast. Some small place. All clapboard houses. Faded and gray, rubbed raw by the sea wind. "By Nor'easters," she told me.

The people in that town reminded me of the people in the towns around here: colorless and staring. Eyes that don't blink. Toad eyes. Jeanette laughed when I told her that.

"Let's smoke," she said because she always had fancy cigarettes from Paris.

"Let's smoke weed," I told her, and we did because I always had weed on me.

We smoked in her old bedroom, sitting on her childhood bed. Yellow comforter, the same yellow as her dress, the one she had worn to that nameless bar. We giggled, opened the windows, and fanned out the fragrant smoke so her mother the Puritan wouldn't know or suspect, although I think she probably did. She certainly stared at me with a rigid marble face and slitted eyes when I left early, early the following morning so Jeanette and I wouldn't miss our train back to the city.

I dreamed that night about Heath. I wrote him letter after letter. I never mailed them but kept them instead inside an antique steamer trunk which had belonged to my great-grandmother Catherine when she and my great-grandfather came to eastern Montana and home-steaded. Everything in all the world, my father would say time and again, everything that mattered to Grandma Catherine she kept in that trunk. So I lay beside Jeanette, who was snoring softly, rhythmically, and imag-ined Heath as last I had seen him years ago: that pointed nose, those dark eyes, that pouting mouth. Arrogant cheekbones, like cuts in his face.

I dreamed we ran together in the yellow grass, and we were yellow too, yellow and tawny as mountain lions, our limbs long and unfettered, our arms pumping, heads lowered, running and leaping over rocks and snakes, until we stood at the edge of a cliff. Far below, we could see the

Heights, Lee, my father, Aunt Lucy, and a pathway made of bones leading up and over the hill. Shadowy figures stood along that path like sentinels, but we couldn't see their faces.

"This is all ours now," Heath said, and we were holding hands as if we had always been holding hands. "All of this is ours, and it will be ours forever."

"Oh yes," I said.

Together, we leaped over the edge of the cliff.

Jeanette said, "You were having a nightmare."

"It wasn't a nightmare. It was beautiful."

"Why were you thrashing and groaning? I kicked you in the leg seven or eight times, and it didn't help. You didn't even notice. You just kept thrashing and groaning."

"Not a nightmare," I said and grinned at her.

She rolled her eyes, but she laughed, and when we left, her gargoyle mother glared at me and would have hissed, I think, if she had been any less of a lady.

If there is a curse on my family—and I think there must be—what is it? Do we haunt the house? Do we slink beneath the soil, waiting to plunge our bony arms up, up, up into the night sky, to seize innocent wanderers with skeleton fingers? Or do we even know we are dead? Do we just return and return and return in any way we can?

I will look for my father wherever I go in the house or anywhere in the landscape, maybe in the land, wherever I can look.

But I don't think I will find him.

I will take control of the Heights. I will run the ranch. I will pay Lee to work the cattle, or I will throw him out and away forever. But Heath will be in charge. Lee will work for him. Lee will hate it and want to kill him. And maybe they will fight each other, and Heath will win. And maybe Lee will die. I might not mind that so much.

I will find a way to live in this house forever.

I will find a way to return with another face if I can't perform a simple haunting.

I will tell Heath tonight.

I will come to him tonight.

I will tell him.

"I will always come back to you," I will say.

Who you are doesn't matter to me. Your past doesn't matter to me. Where you come from doesn't matter to me.

"All cats are gray in the dark," I'll say.

"We are cats," I'll say.

I want to stay here forever.

3

"Lee really hates you some, huh?"

Heath looked up from doughnut batter he had been rolling out on the counter. He wasn't surprised to find Lee's wife there, leaning against the doorway to the hall, a smile on her wide face, revealing the gap between her two front teeth he found so aggravating but couldn't articulate why, not even to Shaw.

He looked down. Said nothing.

July, late, and the heat from outside permeated the walls of the house and battled the cold and won, at least in the afternoons. Lee placed fans, ugly metal contraptions that growled like coyotes, throughout the house in as many rooms as possible, but their eternal grinding away at the air did little to trounce the heat and send it back, howling, to the outside world.

Sweat rolled down Heath's forehead. He constantly wiped at the aggravating beadlets with the back of his arm, where he had rolled up the sleeve of his thin cotton button-up, the one Shaw liked best, blue and green plaid. The fabric turned dark and stayed dark with his moisture. He heard the cows lowing outside in the north pasture. One of them bawled furiously. Her calf was probably misbehaving, or one of the farm dogs Lee coaxed and coddled had snuck through the fence and tormented the herd of great ladies and their toddling, wobbling babes until the cows were riled into paroxysms of great vocal exhalations. Like this goddamn bawling.

Heath shook his head. Nearly smiled. Rolled at the dough. Rolled at the dough.

Flora Lyon—Heath refused to call her "Flo," as she had insisted at their first meeting when Lee brought her to the Heights in late May—crossed her arms over her breasts and lowered her head, shot her dart eyes right at Heath. He felt their heat. Hard to ignore. He sighed. Looked up.

"Yeah, Lee sure hates *you*," she said.

"I guess so," was all he replied.

"I can't imagine why," she said airily, fanning herself with a paper plate she had materialized from somewhere. It held ghastly oil stains from whatever had occupied it before Flora had repurposed it. She fanned and fanned away at herself. "You seem all right to me."

"Thanks."

"Don't talk much."

"Nope."

"That's okay. A lot of quiet, that's all. This house is so big."

"Yup."

She laughed, tinkling and merry. "And you're *funny*! Lee doesn't see that."

"I guess not."

Flora sidled up to the counter near to the window overlooking the granaries and the first hint of the orchard slinking up the hillside. "I heard about your doughnuts."

"I like to make 'em, that's all."

"Lucy raved."

Heath said nothing. He rolled. Beside them, on the stovetop, the big pan full of Wesson oil bubbled.

"But it's so *hot*," Flora said. Fan, fan. "I can't believe you're doing that *now*."

"Work to do in the fields later."

"Bailing hay. I know. Lee's out there now."

Which was why Heath wasn't, but he didn't respond.

"I won't offer to help."

"Thanks."

"I'll only be in the way, is the thing."

Rolling, rolling. Cutting out the dough using a glass tumbler from the cupboard. One of Shaw's mother's glasses, Fiesta, with alternating stripes of red and green and orange. Heath hated them for their ugliness. But they cut the doughnut dough.

"I'm usually in the way."

He spared a glance into her shining, amused eyes. Her lips split into a smile and revealed her great gapped teeth. He looked away quickly.

"You sure sweat a lot."

"It's hot."

"What I said!" She hee-hawed explosive laughter.

Heath bore down on the dough with the edge of the glass. But his lips slipped into a smile despite himself.

"Whatcha making for dinner tonight?"

"Lucy is."

That wasn't entirely true. Heath planned to barbecue the short ribs himself. He had prepared his own rub with a variety of spices from an old cookbook he had discovered on a bookshelf in Mr. Lyon's bedroom. It seemed to have belonged to his grandmother. "Catherine Lyon" was printed on the inside leaflet in neat block script. Seeing the name had caused a flash of heat to flare all over his body when he had discovered it after he and Shaw cleaned out the room following Mr. Lyon's funeral.

"Ah," Flora said slyly, leaning in, "but you'll have a hand in it, won'tcha? You have a hand in most of the cookin's done here. Well..." And she tossed her great head of peroxide-blond hair, all done up and teased to highest heaven. "I, for one, appreciate it. Even if Lee don't."

"I don't like to talk about Lee."

"Sorry, sorry. My mouth. My ma used to tell me I'd open it up so far one day I'd just fall right in." Another huge hee-haw of laughter. "Do you mind me spendin' time here while you're s'busy?"

"No." *Yes.*

She leaned in close so he could smell the Juicy Fruit gum she chewed and smacked. Her teeth were pristine and white, despite the gap in them. He found this fairly honorable. Not everyone in the neighborhood or the neighboring towns could say the same about their own. Heath brushed and flossed because he imagined Shaw would want him to. Shaw, naturally, possessed a set of straight, immaculate teeth.

"You *sure*?" she purred.

"Company's okay."

"Where's Shaw?"

Heath stiffened for only a moment and forced himself to relax. Easy, he told himself, easy, easy. "How would I know?"

"Oh," she said, airily once again. "I just figured you would, that's all. Seems like you two spend an awful lot of time together ever since he come back here."

"Not really."

"If you say so." Flora turned so her back pressed against the counter and her elbows supported her. Her breasts, thinly coated in the red and white checked dress she wore, which reminded Heath of a picnic table, jutted out to their best advantage.

She wanted him to look. A part of him wanted to look. He wouldn't allow himself to look.

Until he did.

He caught her eye. Her mouth. She was smirking.

"Hot, hot, hot," she sang and moved, a red streak, across the kitchen to the window that overlooked the front lawn, the path down to the road, the road itself, and, a mile away, up Highway 201. "Someone's comin'," she said. "Don't recognize the truck."

"Hell," Heath growled.

"That damn road. Why are we so far from the highway? This road turns to pig-mud in the spring. Why put this goldarn house so far *away*?"

The house sighed around them. Someone walked around upstairs, their footsteps circling, circling.

Sweat collected above his right eye. *Don't fall*, he prayed, his hands up to the elbows in the doughnut batter. *Don't you dare, don't you* dare.

Drip.

He scowled.

"Lee lets me go wherever I want," Flora said from her place by the window, still watching the slow approach of the vehicle outside. "He don't even ask me where I'm going. I'm that free. I can take walks around the property like it was nothing."

Heath grunted. Dropped a doughnut into the seething oil.

Shoulda kept tracka which one has my sweat. Feed it to Shaw. Make sure he gets that one.

He nearly hee-hawed laughter like Flora's but stopped himself.

What a grotesque thought.

Heath had entertained thoughts like that before, though. Pouring himself into the food he served to the family. His breath. Blood. Even his jizz once. He had thought about it. Wouldn't do it. Wouldn't dare to do it.

Thought about it, though.

"It's that neighbor man," Flora said. "What's-his-name. Starts with an R."

"Reardon," Heath said absently. He flipped the doughnuts. His nostrils filled with the smell of yeast and nutmeg. Good. Good smells. And the oil. Worth it. "Nathan."

"Yeah. He's handsome, ain't he?"

Another grunt.

"You can tell me," Flora said, turning away from the window. "I won't tell nobody. Anyways, I already know."

"Know what?" Heath's muscles twitched under his shirt. His belly ran slick with sweat.

"Lee told me. You know what Lee says about you? What he calls you? What he tells the hired men?"

"You don't need to say because I already know."

"So, I know you can appreciate a handsome man."

"Shut up. Shut your mouth."

Shockingly, she was at his side. Shockingly, her hand drew back, and she slapped him. Spit flew from his mouth. Into the batter. Of course.

He froze. His fists curled. His sweat ran rivers down his face and pattered into the batter like rain.

"Don't you *never* talk to me like that again," Flora Lyon growled. "Don't you *never*. I am the *lady* of this house, and don't you *never* talk to a lady like that. You hear me, boy?"

Heath glowered, drawing himself up to his full height. "I ain't your *boy*," he spat back at her.

She grinned at him humorlessly. Her eyes danced. Her smell overpowered him: a hint of jasmine oil and body odor, a dark smell, and iron. No, not iron. Copper, the smell of blood.

"Boy," she said, inches from his mouth.

Three knocks at the door.

Footsteps circling around and around over their heads. Heath's eyes drifted to the ceiling.

"Answer that," Flora said. Her eyes flickered with the late afternoon July light. She snapped her gum.

Heath looked at the ceiling.

"What are you *staring* at? Someone's *out* there," she whined, and the knocking came again.

Stomp, stomp, stomp.

Someone up there. Making a real ruckus. And awfully near his room.

Stomp.

"Goldarn it," Flora muttered and strode away from the kitchen.

Heath stood panting by the plate of doughnuts. His cheeks smarted from the flat of her palm. Bitch, he wanted to snarl, *bitch.*

Shaw called her worse. Shaw hated her, he said, with the passion of a thousand universes, each holding millions of suns.

He heard the creak of the door opening, Flora's high-pitched, booming hello, and the gentle, familiar murmur of Nathan Reardon.

Heath wiped away the sweat from his forehead with the back of his arm.

"We're just making doughnuts," Flora sang while she led the other man into the kitchen.

Not much older than Heath, Shaw, and Lee, Heath figured. Golden-headed. Receding hairline, though. Round spectacles perched on the pencil snub of his nose. Rounded cheekbones. Great muscular arms. Incongruous with that sensitive face. Chapped hands, scarred.

One of these hands clasped Heath's.

"Heath," Nathan Reardon said, allowing himself the scantest of smiles. The man didn't smile much. His religion, Heath figured, didn't allow for something so human as smiling.

"Nathan," Heath said. "It's been awhile."

"That dance out t'the hall," Nathan said, "if I remember correctly. Last winter. No, fall. Halloween, I think."

Yes, he was correct. And should it come as any surprise that the Hall, the gathering place for all the farmers in this corner of the state for maybe fifty miles around, that the Hall had been, of course, the place of Heath's dream? If, indeed, it had *been* a dream. Where he had skipped up the endless staircase of time and followed Catherine Lyon to a long-ago dance. Where the dancers screamed, hooted, lay with each other, and wore the heads of wild, terrifying animals. Should it?

It was an old barn, smaller than it had seemed in Heath's—well, call it an "experience"—*experience*, but a place where the farmers and their families could gather for parties and dances, where the women would prepare cold meat sandwiches, chocolate cakes, and lemon meringue pies. If it was Halloween, they would festoon it with orange and black crepe, tell ghost stories, and dance, someone on the fiddle, someone on the guitar. Once, it had been Earnest Lyon, and could he ever play you the merriest tune. Now, no one knew who would take his place. Inevitably someone would sing. Heath loved it and was afraid of it. How had it come into his dream? How could he have known about its existence before he had ever even been there?

Nathan was watching him closely. Heath smiled, embarrassed. Flora grinned, enjoying his embarrassment.

"What brings you out here?"

"Long overdue," Nathan said. He held up a long ceramic pan covered in aluminum foil. "The wife sent this. Her lasagna. Famous around these parts, don'tcha know?" He beamed. "Two reasons. We didn't do it when Earnest passed, and I suppose it don't hurt to have extra food around a place big as this. And to welcome Shaw back. Is he here?"

"No," Heath said after a moment. "He went into town."

"Well," Nathan Reardon said brightly, pronouncing the word as *wall*. "You can tell him when he gets back, I suppose. Haven't seen him in a coon's age. Wanted to welcome him back to the homeplace myself."

"Oh. Sure. Yeah, okay. Sure."

"You're, um, involved at the moment." Nathan smiled approvingly at the doughnuts bobbing and browned in the oil behind them. *Woman's work.*

Heath moved swiftly to the stove and rescued them from the pot. Nathan laughed.

"I'll just give this to you, Missus."

"Flo," Flora purred. "No one calls me that. Just Flo."

"Just Flo. Here." He handed her the pan.

"Smells heavenly."

"Lots of garlic. Onion. Tomatoes. From our garden. The wife does it all." Nathan winked at Heath. "Stuff you grow yourself always tastes better." *You a woman, Heath?*

"Yeah," Heath said, staring.

Shuffling upstairs. No one looked.

The walls pressed closer. The glass before him swam. Reflections of faces Heath couldn't identify bobbed up and pressed against the kitchen window and disappeared again.

He wanted to moan.

Faces in the reflection of the oil. Wide eyes. Gaping mouths. Tongues. Faces eaten away, leaving only bone—

"You're busy," Nathan Reardon was saying, and Flo giggled mindlessly.

Footsteps, heavy, on the porch outside.

The door opened.

Shaw stepped into the kitchen. His eyes gleamed. His color was high. His chest heaved. He wore running shorts he had used back in Boston and a pair of bright white sneakers streaked with bits of mud.

Right, Heath recalled. He had gone for a run. Not into town. Something no one on the ranch had ever done. Something no one Heath knew ever did. But Shaw loved it. It had been part of his routine, he had said, back at school in Massachusetts, and he wasn't going to stop now just because this uncivilized country had no paved roads or trails. He liked to run out into the prairie and let it swallow him, he had told Heath the other night while they sat on the hood of Heath's dark green '49 Chevy farm truck, looking at the vast and flawless sky together.

"Just let it take me. That's all I want. Disappear into it. Maybe forever."

"I'd miss you," Heath said, "if you did that."

"I'd miss you too," was all Shaw had said, but he hadn't made eye contact with Heath when he said it, and he hadn't moved to touch him.

Shaw stood there, panting.

"Thirsty," he said to Heath, pointedly ignoring Florence. Then, while he took in the gangly form of Nathan Reardon, his eyes lit up, and he beamed. "You old son of a dog," he said, pulling Nathan into a tight, back-slapping embrace.

Thump, thump, thump. Footsteps descending the attic stairs.

Heath's forehead leaked sweat beads.

Nathan slapped Shaw's back with equal enthusiasm. They parted, staring at each other with delight.

"You should'a come sooner, old sport," Shaw said, just as Nathan said, "You ugly old bastard! The east coast's not good enough for you no more, huh? Had to come snaking back home for good?"

Thump thump. A door opened and closed. The door to the attic.

"You know ol' Nathan," Shaw said, an arm draped around the young farmer's shoulder.

The wife-beater Shaw wore—and what a dreadful name, Heath thought dimly, what a terrible name for such a beautiful article of clothing—clung to his pectorals, streaked with his sweat. So close to the other man, Heath thought, so damned close.

"We go way back."

"I never have a reason to come here anymore," Nathan said, grinning. "'Sides, I'm a busy man."

"Married."

"A father."

"Yes," Shaw said cheerfully, "a father."

They beamed at each other while, behind them, gape-mouthed, a tall, thin figure glided down the hallway. No, it didn't glide. Heath slammed his mouth shut so hard his teeth clicked. He heard the sound its feet made, the same footsteps that had come from above his head not five minutes before.

Shaw and Nathan chattered like idiot apes, but Flora's eyes had widened. Her face had paled, and her lipstick made her mouth appear to be a garish smear of blood.

Their eyes met.

And Heath knew.

She had seen the figure too.

———

"Long time ago," Shaw said later, back on the hood of the old truck parked beside the creek, the westering rays of the sun stabbing red into the water, stretching. The bottle of wine he had spirited from the kitchen lay, empty and defeated, in the grass beside them.

Heath's head buzzed pleasantly. Full of bees, he thought, all full of honey. And stings, stings, stings. For everybody.

"You fucked each other."

Shaw snorted laughter. Heath blinked. He hadn't meant to say that. *Had* he said that, something so coarse and so vile?

"Well," Shaw said at last. "Yeah, I suppose you could say that."

"Did you?"

"More wine."

"Listen. Listen. Did you?"

Shaw fixed Heath with his eyes, crystal and sharp, even through the growing summer gloom hanging over them, with its wet and sticky webbing. "You are filthy. You know that? You never even showered after you came back from the field. You smell like an *ape*." And he giggled.

Heath gritted his teeth. "Yes," he said at last. "Call me names. Bastard. I'm dirty as sin. Dirty as *fuck*. But so are you!"

Somewhere, behind them, frogs sang a delicate paean to the rising moon. The invisible web of a hot night in July, smelling of iron and sweetgrass, drew tighter around them. Can't breathe, Heath thought. *I'm strangling. I'm caught. I can't breathe.*

"I am," Shaw said reflectively. "I am foul and filthy and disgusting. Ask Lee. You know he used to try to watch me shower? The last time I was home, he burst into the bathroom just as I was coming out. He crawled into bed with me one night, whimpering. Begging for me to touch him." His face scrawled under a black wave of hate. "He said he'd kill himself if I didn't."

"No..."

"Oh, yes. Lee is degraded, *far* more than you or I. If there's a curse at the Heights, he suffers from it more than we do."

"Is that the curse?"

"Is what the curse?"

"Fucking."

Shaw snorted. "It's funny when you say that word. I've never heard you say it."

"I've said it plenty of times."

"Rebel. Rogue. *Scoundrel.*"

"All right. So maybe not just fucking. But...fucking...men?"

Shaw blinked at him. "What does that mean to you?" he said softly.

Chirrup, sang the frogs, chirrup, chirrup.

Heath shivered.

"You aren't cold, are you?"

"No. Just dirty."

Shaw laughed again. "We could take a dip, you and I, and just now."

"Skinny?"

"We've done it before."

Something huge and complicated reared itself up inside Heath's chest. *Words,* he thought desperately, *if only I had words—*

I'm strangling. Strangling here.

"All right," he said at last. "Why not?"

Shaw's bum flashed white in the darkness while he leaped from the bank and into the creek. Hooting, he and Heath flung water at each other, sank their toes into the slime at the bottom, and ducked each other over and over. The frogs scattered. A curlew screamed like a woman in fright. The grass parted to their left when something large hurried away, off to the west, where the sky still glowed orange like a dying furnace. Then it would be on its way to purple.

Tell me, Shaw. What does fucking a man mean?

Unanswered questions. Goddamn him.

He knows exactly *what it means.*

They paused for a moment, watching each other in the darkness. Or perhaps Shaw was watching the house a quarter of a mile down the road from them.

"I didn't love him," Shaw said, "if that's what you're worried about."

"Maybe."

"Well, I didn't." He snickered. "Or maybe I did."

"Shut up."

"Maybe in my limited, I'm-just-a-kid kind of way, maybe I did love him. I was twelve. He was fourteen. Maybe I only idolized him."

"He's married."

"That's what you do."

"That's not what *I* do."

"You can't marry me."

"Who says?"

"Heath, Jesus..." Shaw sounded afraid. "Heath, *Christ*, that isn't—I mean, we *can't*—" He clawed at the water and swam a few feet away from where Heath rested against the bank, long gray swords of grass stabbing at his back.

"What did you do with him?"

"You want me to tell you."

"Did you kiss him?"

"He never wanted to kiss."

"You've kissed men before."

"Yes."

Silence. The grass shivered on the bank above. Two yellow eyes flashed at them in the darkness, then vanished. Small. A cat. *One of the barn cats*, Heath thought, *watching us. Let it watch.* He treaded water lithely. *No. Shaw's the cat. Not me. Not me.*

Metal twisted inside him. Glass chewed at him. He wanted to sink into the water and never return.

"You should've been with me back in Boston," Shaw said at last. He moved closer now, Heath saw with some relief, though slowly, cautiously. The bit of moon floating over their heads caught Shaw's eyes and flashed silver back at Heath. "We would've had a jolly time, you and me."

"I belong here."

"You belong anywhere I go."

Pain. Metal tearing. Glass. *Pain.* "*Stop*," Heath groaned. "Please.

Stop saying things like that to me. Please. It hurts. It *hurts* me. Please stop."

Shaw, at his side now, cradling his chin in his hands, wet and dripping with the creek of Redwater. "Why?" he said, so tenderly. "Do you really want me to stop?"

"It hurts," Heath whispered.

"Things hurt."

"You know what I mean."

Closer now. "If only you'd've come with me that first time. I never should have left you here. You could've seen the world I saw. The places I went and the people—"

"Nouns," Heath whispered. "You're talking about nouns."

"Don't joke."

"We have to stay here."

"Why?"

"It's our place. Yours and mine now."

Shaw considered this. "Flora," he finally said. "And Lee."

"They don't matter."

"No. I guess not."

Closer, closer. Inches. Shaw's breath stank in Heath's face. It was sour with the last exhalation of the red wine they had drunk together, so quickly, a cheap bottle Shaw had materialized before dragging Heath out of the house and into the red-furnace dusk.

"Only we matter," Heath whispered. "We're the only two people in the whole world."

"Out here, in the grass."

"Just the hills, and they aren't so big—"

"Fences, far away houses—"

"No one lives in them."

"We can go where we want."

"Out here, just us—"

Body against body. Something brushed Heath's thigh, soft, smooth, but hard. His fingers found it, encircled it, and rubbed lightly at its tip. Shaw drew in a quick breath, and Heath brought it closer to him, pressed it against his own erection, which had been there all along, of course. Concealed by the water and the darkness.

And still, they did not kiss on the mouth.

Shaw leaned forward and dropped his forehead onto the place where Heath's shoulder met his collarbone. He wrapped his arms around Heath, who pressed them together even closer. They treaded water together, their legs dancing lazily. Cock to cock.

A sound. Someone crying out from the house. Aunt Lucy? Must have been. Lights blazing up. No lights in the house on the hill, though.

They clambered from the water, avoiding each other's gaze, white bodies flashing in the dark, covering their erections, shaking off the water, pulling at clothes, snickering a bit. Or Shaw did and Heath, or maybe Heath started to chuckle. It was all so ridiculous. Men's body parts were so *ridiculous*. But Aunt Lucy's voice was shrill, pierced the darkness, and hurried them along.

They left the wine bottle out in the prairie's night and drove the truck uneasily and swerving back to the Heights, where Aunt Lucy waited in the doorway, trembling.

"Where *were* you? We *needed* you. There's been an accident, and Flora is very hurt."

And behind Aunt Lucy came Lee and Don carrying Flora's limp body between them. Heath gasped to see how her head rolled so bonelessly and her eyes stared from beneath her lids, half-closed.

Aunt Lucy, in charge now, said sternly, "She's fallen down the attic stairs and needs a doctor. She needs a hospital. Heath, mind the house and the stock. We'll take her in the truck."

"She needs an ambulance," Shaw said, but everyone ignored him.

For a moment, and a moment only, Heath's eyes captured his, and they looked at each other somberly.

4

I didn't want Flora to come back to the house, but of course, she did. And of course, they all looked at me funny when I rode in the truck with her to town, even though I'm her husband and her man, and she's the only woman who ever loved me back. So I guess that gives me more reason than the rest.

I didn't want Shaw to come neither. That deluded son of a bitch. Perverted son of a whore.

I didn't say nothin' on the whole ride into town. To Sidney, the closest hospital, fifty miles down 201, mostly unpaved, but I drove close to ninety, and Flora moaned the whole way. Aunt Lucy tried to keep her still. Shaw stared at me without taking his goddamn ice eyes away the whole way, the *whole* way.

I never did nothin' to you, I wanted to tell him, but words always froze on my tongue whenever Shaw was around. Eyes like a goddamn Husky. Son of a bitch anyway.

He lies about me. Oh, he lies. He was always bad. That was why Dad sent him away. Because he knew. He is bad, and he brings badness out in other people.

Shaw brings out the badness in this house.

Why do you think *they* didn't come back 'til *he* did?

Him and that prairie man of his.

They are both *bad*. Full of filth. And dirty. And the man has a name that don't rightfully belong to him, but Dad gave it to him anyway because he was *weak*. They say I'm weak. They say, "Lee, you drink too damn much." Don tells me all the time, he says, "Lee, you're gonna drink y'self to death." So what? I won't. But so what?

They are bad, and they brought the worst out of the homeplace. Ah Christ, ah Jesus, but I love it here. I love the Heights. I love the house. I even love ol' Grammy's cabin on the hill. I love it all. By rights, it should be mine. But Shaw runs it. Goddamn it.

Runs it and ruins it.

They came back the same time he did.

No, not ghosts. They ain't ghosts. Not exactly.

I don't know what they are.

They come in the night into your room, and they sit on your bed and put their hands on you. Fingers in your mouth. Taste like dirt. Sometimes, they put 'em…They put 'em in *other* places. White faces and big staring eyes. Clown-faces, like, only their mouths are all dark and red, only not with paint. Don't make me say it. Aw, jeez. C'mon, please. Don't make me tell you what they do.

They put their hands on you.

They got long, cold fingers.

They *go* places on you.

I never could stop them.

They only came when Shaw was home.

Only then.

From the attic. From the basement. Hell, maybe even from the closets. Maybe they hide there all day. I think they hide in the walls. I think they're like rats. They scuttle around between the outside walls, and they watch us with their big eyes. They stare, and they wait for us to go to sleep so they can come out and come into our beds.

Flora saw one. So did the prairie man. Flora told me all about it. They both heard it stomping around upstairs. Shaw was out. That dumbass Reardon asshole come over.

What does he know about farmin'? Nothing. Religious, a super Christer, or maybe it's just the wife, but that is how he comes off. Holier-than-thou, don'tcha know? Better'n me, for sure. And us Lyons never did go to church. They talk about us in the town. They make up all kinds of wild stories. I heard we worship the devil. Sure. Like I'd know the devil if I ever saw him.

I would prefer the devil to *them*.

Then the Reardon fella came with some miserable excuse to see my brother, and Shaw was pleased as punch, Flora said, both of 'em grinning like egg-suckin' dogs. Couldn't *wait* to get away from the others and be alone, I bet. Then Flora sees one of them things walk past the kitchen, she says, while Shaw was talking to that Reardon fella. It just *gliiiiiided* right on by the kitchen door and down the hallway, she says, her eyes all wide and her face white as the moon. Round as the moon. Right down the hall and toward the basement door.

I told her to shut up, that there weren't no such things, but she says she saw it, and she says, worse, she hears them at night sometimes. This weird singing. Or grinding sounds. Like teeth gritting together. Grinding. One night, like something chewing in her ear. Like a cat sounds when it is chewing on meat. Like that, right in her ear. I never heard *that*, but a'course, I believe her. And a'course, I tell her she's full of bull-shit and needs to shut her goddamn mouth.

She tells me not to talk to her like that. Only I'm her husband, I says, and I'll talk to her any goddamn way I want to.

"You're a drunk and a liar and an asshole," and she hits me upside the head with my own mug of beer.

Can you believe that? She did it.

I said, "I hope them things get you and take you away with them."

"You wish they would." She grins at me. She grabs me and kisses me.

What the hell, and I kiss her back. What the hell? She is my woman. I am her man. I love her. She hurt me. I would never hurt her. I ain't built like that. Not with a woman. I would never hurt a woman. Never.

I put a baby in her.

I hope I did, is what I mean.

I hope the fall didn't hurt the baby.

She fell down the stairs.

I don't know if one of them *things* is what did it, if she had a bad fall, something scared her, or if them things is just like a...a...whaddaya-callit?...like a premonition. Like them banshees in Ireland. Like that.

That Shaw brought back to this place with his wicked deeds.

My Flora. My poor baby girl.

She will come back to the homeplace soon.

I will keep her safe from them things.

I can drink my PBR and still keep a watch out. Maybe I will watch all through the night. Maybe I can do that for my poor baby girl. Keep her safe. Keep us all safe.

From Shaw.

From his prairie man.

From them *things* in the walls.

5

Heath couldn't help himself. He had to skulk, to lurk outside the darkness of the farmhouse that lay a mile from the Heights. The Reardons, home of Nathan and Dolly and their baby. He had to follow Shaw, to know where he went, the paths he crossed through the tall prairie grass, over the hills, to the Reardon house, which would have been easier to drive to. But not as secret, Heath thought grimly, peering in the windows. Not as much of a *thrill*.

And what were they up to? Nothing so terrible, Heath decided, squinting in the darkness, barely visible through the glass if they happened to look up. His milky figure, his dark and narrowed eyes. Just sitting at the table, cracked cans of Schlitz before them, Nathan leaning, Shaw in a chair, legs spread wide, guffawing. Heath couldn't resist. He pressed his forehead to the glass, flattening it, and bulged his eyes *wider*. He could almost hear them.

Don't want to hear them.

A ridiculous lie.

You never came to me. You said you would, and I waited and waited until the dawn began to bleed, and you still never came to my room.

Jealousy bit and twisted inside him.

Nathan Reardon: not handsome exactly, or was he? What did Heath know of handsomeness?

They were near but not touching. And where was Nathan's wife? What was her name? Dolly? Where was she?

And the *baby*?

Close. But not touching.

Heath lowered his head. His forehead squeaked against the window.

Shaw threw back his head and roared with laughter. Nathan lowered his head and snickered.

Close. But not touching.

I wish him dead, Heath thought feverishly. *I wish him stuck full of pins and his mouth full of the black oily shitty bottom of the creek. I wish his eyes were cut by grass blades, the thick sharp kind. I wish.*

Who? Who do you wish that for?

Heath moaned.

You don't really know, do you?

Nathan Reardon's fingers danced lightly against Shaw's shoulder. Shaw looked up at him, his eyes full of light.

Heath pressed his ear against the glass.

"—back, but who knows for how long."

Shaw.

Nathan Reardon, looking.

"She's not *well*. Not since the fall."

"And she just...fell?"

"People fall sometimes."

"People at the Heights, you mean. Dingus."

Shaw roared with laughter again.

Nathan smiled lightly.

"Sorry. It's funny." Shaw turned away, and his next words were indistinguishable.

Heath ground his teeth together. Nathan sat in a chair beside him. So...close.

The other man spread his legs wide, placed his elbows on his knees, clasped his hands, and leaned in. "...she said about us."

"Us?"

"You and me."

"There is no..." Indistinguishable.

Goddamn it! Heath wanted to gnash his teeth and snarl and stomp about. Fury raced through him like lightning.

I am not an animal, goddamnit!

"Sure," Shaw said, all humor evaporated. "I know that."

"We're just—"

"I know."

"And we can't—"

"I *know*."

Close, close, close.

"But Dolly is gone," Nathan said, so low the rest of his words were drowned out.

Shaw's eyes widened. He stood up, gaping.

Something growled in the darkness.

Both men in the well-lit kitchen looked around frantically. Caught,

Heath thought jubilantly, even while his own fear rose and smote him hard. *Caught, caught, the bastards are caught!*

Red eyes glowed before him. The growling grew louder and more ferocious.

"The dogs," Nathan Reardon cried from inside the house. "They've caught—"

Dogs?

Plural?

Heath backed away. If he moved slowly, perhaps, perhaps they wouldn't take him down. If he proved to be no threat, maybe—

Two brutes emerged from the shadows behind the Reardon farmhouse. Massive, snarling. Didn't the Reardons keep Australian shepherds? These were...not those. Gleaming crimson eyes, blazing away, foam dripping from their gaping jaws and glowing as it fell—

Glowing?

"Get," Heath snarled back at them. They circled him, growling and fixing him with their impossible eyes. "Get on now!"

"Someone out there?" Nathan at the door.

Goddamn him.

"*I said get on now, dammit!*"

"Probably ghost dogs," Shaw called cheerfully from the safety of the kitchen.

They stood shoulder-high, and their heads were massive, the size of a horse's, maybe larger. They grinned at Heath. Their mouths stretched like taffy, pulling back and back, revealing more and more teeth. Long, yellow, curved. Going on down into the darkness of their throats.

"You aren't possible," Heath whispered, enraged.

One of the dogs snapped at him, lunging. He felt the passage of its air, the graveyard-wet stink of its breath filling his nose. The teeth made an almost delicate chipping noise when they clamped together inches from his windpipe. He stumbled backward, pinwheeling his arms.

"Who's there?" Nathan called gruffly. His voice deepened, grew rougher, arguably more masculine.

"Raccoons!" Shaw tittered.

One of the dogs sank its teeth into Heath's right shoulder. The other clamped down tightly onto the meat of his upper left arm. They shook their titanic heads at the same time. Blood flew in freshets.

Heath screamed.

He blinked upward, blearily. *My room*, he thought, dizzy. His head throbbed. His throat ached. He had been screaming.

Heath wanted water. He wore no shirt. No pants, no underdrawers. His forehead blazed. His skin seethed. Deserts bloomed on his tongue, urged by hag winds. Insects scurried over every inch of his flesh. Coyotes howled and buried their snouts into his skin. They gnawed. They chewed. They gored.

"Buffalo gals," he tried to sing, tried to sing, "won'tcha... won'tcha..."

Stop that.

Someone spoke. Who was it?

The sun flared up, hot, and vanished. Purple evening fell over him, blessedly cool without the sun's mad face glaring in at him.

Lie still.

Aunt Lucy. Someone moved through the shadows. Someone pressed a cool rag into his mouth. He sucked. Wine filled his mouth. Red, his favorite. Pinot noir. He swallowed it greedily.

Not Aunt Lucy. Taller than her, slimmer. Lithe. Moving quickly through the room.

You're going to be all right.

The old woman watched him from the corner, glaring at him with yellow cat eyes. She opened her mouth, empty of teeth, and squalled at him. He rolled away so he didn't have to look at her.

Don't look at her.

"I'm trying," he croaked. "She's won't stop staring—"

She was young and lovely, hips moving in a sinuous, snaking fashion. She crossed the room and stood over him.

A cool compress on his forehead.

More liquid. Water this time. In a glass? He sipped just as greedily. No, not water. Wine again.

"I warned you," she said in a voice of perfect stone. Her breasts heaved beneath the lovely yellow party dress. She raised a withered claw and shook it at him. Her eyes widened and glowed like coins. "Your love is the curse. The root of all that is evil."

"Not...true—"

Don't listen to her either.

"Can you hear her? I didn't think you could even see her—"

"Of course, he can hear me. Of course, he can see me." She sneered. "He always could."

Flora is dead.

Heath stirred. "What?" he cried. "What? How?"

She died, that's all. It was inevitable.

"There are beasts all through this house," the old woman croaked. "In the walls and the space between the walls and the spaces between the spaces—"

"My God," Heath groaned. "Do you *ever* shut up?"

"She saw the beast again. It came for her. It took her away."

"Flora dead—"

Not you, though. You are alive.

"How?" How indeed? The dogs. The giant dogs. His fingers wandered up his arm. He winced, anticipating the pain.

It never came.

Heath felt no pain.

The skin of his arm—the skin of his shoulder too—was unmarked and unblemished. No wounds. No pain.

"Why do I feel like this?"

The fever.

"The fever."

"The curse," the old woman proclaimed. "It's burning inside you now. You're lost."

"I wanted the curse."

The curse—

Struggling. Trying to rise. Swimming through water, dark green fathoms—

The old witch laughed. The form before him wavered. A hand reached for him, and Heath twitched away with a cry.

"The curse will force you together now for the rest of time. You're marked. You think those dogs came from the Reardon farm? Please. They're *ours*, which means they're *yours*. They belong to you. The two of you. Forever."

"Shaw," Heath whispered, and it *was* Shaw, oh God, Shaw bending over him, Shaw whispering furiously.

"You're safe. You're safe. I saved you. I drove them off, those monsters. Nathan saw them too, worse luck, but I beat them away with my bare hands and dragged you back here. And now you're safe." Kisses on the forehead. "Safe, my love." Kisses on the forehead and nose, raining kisses, until, finally, his mouth.

Shaw kissing his lips. Shaw's tongue on his tongue, around his tongue. Shaw pulling off his clothes. The old witch screaming, blackening, fading, and falling backward into nothing. Shaw's shirt dropping to the floor and his fingers flying over his belt. Heath tugging at the zipper on his dungarees. The dungarees dropping to the floor. No underwear, just Shaw. Shaw at last, sliding into the bed, kissing as he went, hot, forehead to forehead, mouths, down, down, together, pressing.

Heath arching and crying out. Shaw calling his name. Together, together, curse or no curse, together, together, and both stretching throughout the entirety of the house, over the prairie and the creek and up into the night sky. They owned it. It belonged to them. The whole of the Heights belonged to just they two.

"All cats," Shaw whispered, moving, Heath moving with him, crying out. So exquisite was the agony, so pure the pleasure. Shaw linked his fingers with Heath's. "All cats are gray in the dark. All cats, all cats, gray, gray in the dark—"

The dark.

Together, together.

Together, they opened the darkness.

PART TWO

FIVE

Autumn 1958

1

The fog curled around Heath's ankles while he walked along the place where the water licked forever at the concrete: Fort Point, the place he always went to stare and glare and think and glare and keep his hands crammed into the pockets of his long wool trench coat. He wore gloves, dove-gray, neatly folded at the cuff, but the cold was wet and pinching. The gloves alone did not protect his hands, which were chapped much of the year since he had left Montana and the Heights and Shaw and moved, impetuously, to San Francisco.

He went by the name Heathcliff Lyon—that was his full name, according to Earnest Lyon, who had, it turned out, left him a tidy yet significant sum of money upon his death, which Heath had used for moving expenses and to pay for an apartment and for school. It was what his professors had called him. Heathcliff. And his lovers. He was meeting one of them now.

Heath kicked his cordovan wingtip against the concrete and frowned. It would be an ugly little scene, he had no doubt. Roger had given him money as well, as had the others, four years of others, and he had stashed it all away until it had sprouted into a fortune. Also, he stole. Sometimes, he pickpocketed. Once or twice, he had actively mugged. Put the face of Lee on those bastards, all of them.

Seeing the face of Lee helped. Men, always men. He was bigger than them. That helped too.

The fog thickened. The sun had begun its descent fifteen minutes ago or before, and the temperature plummeted. Heath frowned. Why had he agreed to meet Roger here, after dark?

He won't beat me up, Heath mused. *Or would he? He wouldn't kill me. Or would he?*

It wasn't unheard of, murdering your rent boy. Roger was a big man, receding hairline, pink cheeks, bright eyes. Large hands that were usually gentle. He had never used them against Heath, certainly. But there was, Heath figured, that first time, and that one mattered the most.

Roger had inherited a shipbuilding firm from his father, and if he wasn't the wealthiest man in San Francisco, he was one of the top ten. Also, married. To a younger woman, Alma by name, though Heath had never met her.

Dark-haired and pretty in an anonymous kind of way—Heath had followed her downtown one day, into a flower shop, where he had watched her for nearly half an hour while she selected a single bouquet of carnations in a mighty spray of colors. She had been dressed lavishly, as befitted the wife of Roger Thornton. They even had a child. Heath despised it, and he had never laid eyes on it. He didn't love Roger, but he found himself prone to jealousy on occasion.

Which was ironic, considering what he planned to do now.

The fog, the fog, whirling and eddying. Someone, who knows how far of a distance away, began to whistle. The sound was flat, yet it carried effortlessly through the impenetrable gray skeins. It unnerved him. He shuddered.

Roger had discovered him in a painting class. Heath modeled. Nude modeling, which both thrilled and embarrassed him. What would Shaw have said? But he and Shaw weren't in communication. It was better that way. The advertisement which had seduced him offered a not truly terrible stipend for services rendered, and it wasn't like he posed for students at the school *he* attended. These were night classes at a community college, where he knew no one and wanted to know no one.

But Roger had been persistent. He had hounded Heath until they met in a darling little café Roger was fond of for espresso—Roger's idea —and back to Heath's little apartment to fuck—Heath's idea. Later, Roger bought Heath a guitar, expensive oil paints and watercolors, special paper and canvases, and even a typewriter. Together they discovered Heath was okay with music and writing, but he excelled at painting. And they learned together after Roger's night classes and from what Heath had gleaned while modeling.

Roger took Heath skiing in Aspen, and they lay together, kissing and suckling and nuzzling each other before the giant fireplace in the lodge Roger had rented.

Heath never discussed the other men who kept him from time to time, and Roger never asked. All Roger requested was that Heath attend regular checkups with Roger's particularly expensive personal physician.

Heath wasn't in love with Roger, and he suspected that Roger wasn't in love with him, but they shared *something*. A passion if nothing else. Roger was fascinated by Heath's tales of Montana, his life at the Heights, why he had left, what the old woman on the hill was like *really*. What had Earnest been like? Was the house haunted? Had he seen a ghost?

Heath never talked about Shaw.

He realized now he was shivering uncontrollably, so he removed his hands from his pockets, cupped them, and blew into the cup through the bottoms of his gloves. The warmth of his breath did little to spark any warmth in his fingers. Where *was* Roger?

The whistling continued.

Footsteps began, accompanying it. As the footsteps moved closer, so did the whistling.

Heath stopped blowing into his hands and listened.

He had grown and filled out, and now, at twenty-two, he stood well over six feet tall, with broad shoulders and a barrel chest, black eyes that flashed and glistened. His shining ebony hair could scarcely be controlled and instead tumbled over his forehead, no matter how often he attempted to push it back. Heath kept it cut short on the back and the sides, though a part of him hissed venomously every time he saw his barber. The thick, curling shag on the top and bangs was his concession to the ancestry he only dimly remembered.

Men grow their hair out. That's what we do. But he didn't.

Yet he enjoyed his intimidating qualities. He routinely lifted his chin, puffed out his chest, and let his arms swing boldly, revealing the muscles beneath the thin cotton shirts Roger supplied him. Why not? If he was powerful, why not allow himself to feel powerful?

He stood taller now, alone in the fog—alone, except for the whistler.

Who moved closer.

Whistling, whistling.

A not-recognizable tune.

Heath thought about the things he had seen at the Heights: the old lady, the dogs that had taken chunks out of him, except they hadn't and there had been no wounds, no scars, or any evidence the dogs had ever existed. *Except for Shaw. Shaw said he saw them.*

Better not to think of Shaw.

The occasional footsteps overhead when Heath knew no one else occupied the house. That eternal sense of being watched. Every moment. Out on the prairie, in the grove, in the attic, or in the base-ment of the house. Watched, watched, watched. Impossible eyes everywhere.

Heath kept up with Aunt Lucy, a phone call once a month or so. He always called from a booth in a drugstore down the street from his apartment. Heath didn't want her to have his phone number. He didn't even want her to know he was in San Francisco.

Heath asked her sometimes about the old lady on the hill and, once, the "other" old lady.

"I haven't seen her in a long while," was all Aunt Lucy would say.

The last time Heath had called—two days ago?—she had told him that Nathan Reardon had died. A particularly bad case of the flu. Heath tried not to feel anything. But the lizard-joy that reared its horned head inside him buzzed, chirped, and snarled with a feverish celebration, leaving him cold and weak. He wasn't still jealous, was he? Could that even be possible?

Had Nathan Reardon become a victim of the Heights? Had the curse reached out, even to him? Did that mean Shaw had developed more intricate feelings for him than he had claimed?

Whistling. Closer. The footsteps clicked. A woman? High heels? No, heavier than a woman. Much heavier.

He began to sweat.

A figure approached, wreathed in shreds of fog.

Heath's eyes widened.

Shaw passed by him, maintaining only a moment of eye contact. Shaw, his white-blue eyes gleaming, dressed nattily in a suit, with a dark navy tie, a long, tan coat, and a matching hat perched on his sandy hair. Shaw, aged four years, more or less.

Shaw offered him a half-smile, indicated no recognition, and passed a gaping Heath to disappear into the fog. He whistled again while he went, with one suspicious glance over his shoulder. He narrowed his eyes, turned his head away again, and vanished.

Heath heard his own panting close around him, pressed into his ears by the fog. The sound disgusted him. He tried to stop. His heart twisted in on itself. His lungs became wings and beat inside him, vying for escape.

Couldn't have been Shaw. Wasn't possible.

Heath wanted to turn and run. He wanted to catch the man. Seize him by the shoulders, spin him around, glare into his eyes, force him to admit he wasn't Shaw. Not my Cat. Who are you, to walk through the fog, whistling and wearing Shaw's face? *What* are you?

Sweat ran from his forehead and, burning, into his eye. He wiped it savagely away.

"That's not at all the sound to make, my boy."

Roger.

Heath straightened. He always adjusted his posture whenever Roger neared him. Roger, beaming, bare-headed, incongruously, dressed in tweed as natty as Shaw's ensemble. His stomach pressed laughingly, as it always did, against the vest of his suit. Heath loved to trace Roger's round, hairy belly with his tongue when they moved together passionately or with just the barest tip of his finger in the afterglow.

"I don't like it out here when it's like this."

Roger kissed him lightly on the mouth. "You're all tense. You mustn't be tense."

"Long day."

"I agree." Roger glanced around. "Can't see a damned thing. It was, I may remind you, your idea to meet here."

"I know."

"Don't be sullen."

"I'm not."

"You certainly sound sullen."

"I'm *not*."

Roger chuckled. Removed Heath's hat and ruffled, fondly, his hair and replaced the hat. Heath glowered. Roger treated him like a child. Hell, sometimes, Heath acted like a child *because* of the way Roger talked to him, touched him, commanded him. He knew that must be the reason. The only reason.

I did see Shaw just now. I did so.

Childish thinking. Sullen, like Roger said.

"We don't have to stay here," Roger said. "If you'd rather go somewhere...private."

"You said Alma was home tonight."

"She is, she is. But she won't mind if I go to the club. She won't have to know"—Roger chuckled—"that we have our own club, you and I."

"A room at the Plaza," Heath said dully.

"Your enthusiasm is contagious, my boy. We can go somewhere else, if you'd rather. We have the entire city at our disposal."

"I can't tonight."

Roger's eyes narrowed, became suspicious slits. He smiled beatifically. "Can't or won't?"

Heath stared at him, unblinking.

"Heathcliff, my darling dear, *you* summoned me here. I don't anticipate you're going to rob and murder me, but you might say *something*. You're making me quite nervous. More so than normal."

He *summoned* me. *Or...did he?*

Heath allowed himself a small half-smile. "*I* make *you* nervous?"

"Don't tease. You know you do."

"Roger, hey, listen—"

Roger raised a single, gloved palm. "I don't want to listen. And I don't have to. I shall take you now, as I had planned, to Ernie's for dinner because I know how much you adore it. And afterward, we'll visit the Plaza, and I'll leave you there. But I'll return for you in the morning, and we'll visit a haberdasher. Mmm, Roos Brothers, I think. And get you a brand-new suit because I think you need something fresh and vibrant. More color, Heathcliff. You don't think of half these things—"

"No," Heath said, surprised at how firmly the word emerged from his mouth. How it stopped Roger so easily.

Roger narrowed his eyes again, but this time, he didn't relax them. Not for a bit. Heath watched him steadily.

"You have something important to tell me, is that it?"

Heath refused to lower his eyes. Refused to look at the ground.

"It's bad news, is it?"

Heath refused to blink.

Roger smiled sadly. "Heathcliff, you are as cellophane to me. Don't you know that by now? You're leaving...erm, *me*. Is that the idea?"

"Yes," Heath said, "but not just you."

"I see. The entirety of the city. For greener, shall we say, pastures?"

"Something like that."

"Ever the mystery man. Back to Montana, then? This lover of yours? Erm, Shaw, was it?"

Heath's eyes widened, though he had told himself that Roger must not surprise him, or, if he did, Heath must evince no surprise.

Now Roger's smile grew cold. "Didn't think I knew your catalogue of secrets, did you? Darling boy, understand this and understand it well. What Roger Thornton wants, Roger Thornton always, *always* acquires."

The whistling sound of Roger's cane when it cut through the air surprised him. The white-jolt of pain slashing across his right cheekbone when the cane struck and tore at him surprised him even more. He stumbled, pressed his hands to the ground, clapped one to his cheek.

Ruined my gloves, he thought dimly while the blood gushed from the cut. *Roger never strikes me. He never has. He never has before. He never has before.* The words repeated themselves mechanically in

Heath's mind. *Never has before, never has before, never, never, never has before—*

"Do you think I'm a fool?" Roger whispered.

The man's face was white now, Heath saw blearily through the tears he wasn't aware he had shed. White with rage. His fleshy lips had vanished and become a solid white line which trembled, ever so gently. His free hand clenched and unclenched. The other gripped the handle of the cane, which was silver and shaped like a beagle. Roger was fond of beagles. He and Alma kept nearly fifteen of the beasts.

"Me? *Me*, a fool? Heathcliff, my darling dear, my sweetie little Heathcliff, let me assure you that I am, most sincerely, *not*." Roger blinked. His mouth opened wide. "Holy mother of god," he whispered and knelt at Heath's side. Heath tried to push him away while Roger also attempted, with one hand, to press the blood back into his face. "Heathcliff, my God, are you all right? Who *did* this to you?"

"Get...away," Heath moaned, attempting to stand. But his knees refused to support him, and he stuttered back down, barking both his shins on the cold concrete and shredding his trousers. "Get away from me."

"But I want to *help*!" Roger wailed.

"You," Heath snarled. "*You*...did this...*You*—"

Roger recoiled as if he had been struck himself. "No," he said breathlessly. "I? How could you ever imagine that *I*—"

Laughter rose out of the fog like moths, fluttering wings, delicate, evil. Delighted with its own wickedness.

Roger's face clouded, drew together, became furious and sharp. His eyes grew small and piggish. "I should beat you within an inch of your life, bucko."

Heath bared his teeth. "Please," he growled.

Roger threw back his head and bellowed laughter. He swung the cane again. It whistled through the air again, cracking when it struck—

———

That isn't what happened, is it?

You want me to think that your...your lover, whatever you wanna call him—Roger, sure, whatever, Roger. You want me to think he was possessed, in this moment of beating you with his cane, by some evil force, is that right?

You know I don't believe a goddamn word of it.

Ghosts, okay, sure. Maybe even witches. I put up with a lot so far, listening to your story. And the only reason I haven't left yet is because I know what I saw, man. I saw that face outside the window. I saw those eyes. They were goddamn yellow. Solid. Like a fuckin' cat. So, yeah, I'm not an idiot. I realize there's things we don't really know much about, that this world is a weird fuckin' place. This house is a weird fuckin' place, and it has always been a weird fuckin' place...But I think you want to paint yourself as the victim here, and I'm telling you, I ain't buying it.

I'm...I'm not buying it.

Heath.

That's what I told him, as I'm telling you.

But I looked closer at his hated, angry face when I said it. And, shit, I *saw* it. There was a scar, thin, old, cheese-white, running down the right side of his face, from the corner of his eye to the curve of his jaw, wiry now with white whiskers.

That shut me up some. I hadn't really said a word the entire time he had been talking.

Because I could feel the house listening too, focusing around me. *Coalescing.* That is a word I learned in school. Some force was coalescing...or a personality. It hummed. Something that could hear and watch, even if it weren't seen. I felt it.

And...I had seen that face outside my window, three stories off the ground.

Lockwood, you damned fool, I told myself. *You better listen. Just like the ghosts or the spirits or the house or whatever it all is, you'd better make like them and pay attention.*

This place has a mighty power, I reminded myself, when the wind rose to a hellish shriek outside. I cast an uneasy eye to the window, half-afraid of what I would see.

My Cat. Take any form. My Cat.

"So, he hit you," I said to Heath, and he nodded, all sullen.

"Hit me with the cane, but once," said Heath. "Thas all it took. I grabbed it from him 'fore he could swing again and busted it over my knee. But you better believe me, cousin. Roger Thornton never laid a hand on me before. Not once.

"There are forces in this world, boy. Learn that right now. Some want to help us. Some want to harm us. Some don't give two shits about us. But *this* place...it wants us. It wants to keep us here.

"And maybe its reach extends beyond even this house. This country. The farms and towns nearby. Maybe it has more power than we even ever dreamed. This Heights. Our curse. But...not the *only* curse."

Roger's eyes glared like yellow coins. His grin was huge and jostled with teeth, suddenly rotten and pitted and jagged. His voice, when he spoke, screeched. He sounded ghastly, inhuman.

"Poor boy, poor boy," he squealed. The flesh on his face roiled, as if *things* ran around beneath it. It bulged obscenely. "You'll do us proud, won't you? When you go back. When you go back."

Heath managed to clamber to his feet and stood swaying before Roger, who hopped and frisked about on all fours. His expensive coat flapped about him grotesquely.

"Roger," Heath whispered. "What's happened to you?"

"We'd like you to stay," the yellow-eyed thing spoke from Roger's mouth. "We surely would. We've taken the pleasure. Surely, we have. We've had our fun, sure. Now's the time for all, all, all good boys to say goodnight, Daddy. Goodnight, Moon. Goodnight, boy-son."

Heath's skin prickled into gooseflesh. "What's wrong with you?" he choked.

Roger paused, lifted one of his hands as if it were the paw of a cat, licked at it, and rubbed his face. He spat on the ground. What came from his mouth was black and squirmed and crawled on the concrete. He grinned his dark and bloody grin.

"I'm a very bad thing," Roger said. His voice bubbled. His throat sounded full of phlegm. "Very, very bad. I hurt my dolly. Do you know what happens to bad men who hurt their dollies?"

"Roger," Heath began, reaching for him, then pulled away with a cry when Roger threw back his head and slammed it against the concrete.

It made a sickening crack. When he lifted himself upright again, grinning still, blood streamed in black freshets from the dent Roger had created in his own forehead. The skin sloughed away as if it were wet paper. The blood glistened in the lights blinking dimly through the fog.

"I killed my Alma," Roger whispered. "I did it before I left the house. I broke her neck. Did I plan to do it? I think so, I think *so*. What was my plan for you, my beloved boy? Ask yourself *that*."

"No, Roger," Heath said. His face ached dully. Had the blood flow slowed? He wasn't sure. His head spun. His stomach turned over. He wouldn't vomit. He wouldn't. He must *not*.

"Yes, oh, yes. Broke her neck good and proper. Sometimes, a madness comes over people. Haven't you found that to be true? Sometimes, madness just *sweeps*—"

No. I can't tell it that way. The wind is badgering at me. The *house* is badgering at me. Tell the truth, they say. Tell the goddamn whoreson truth. Your eyes tell me you don't believe me, no matter what, cousin.

Goddamn. Goddamn.

You know I got my money somehow.

I got my money from a rich man out in California.

Told people I worked for him.

That much was true.

He did kill his wife. He broke her neck. I was gone, though. By the time that happened. Back to the homeplace. He loved me more than anyone he had ever had the pleasure of knowing, is what his note to me said. With the account number. With the amount inside it. A fortune. He had enough to share.

He killed hisself later, of course. Wouldn't even think of going to jail. Didn't want to get away with anything. Couldn't stand living the way he was. People are like that sometimes. They just get so tired. I get it. But I gotta keep on. That's part of the curse.

You're impatient, sure. Hell, I see it in your face. I'll get to it. I'll get it to it.

Roger did hit me with his stick.

I let him.

Roger did kill his wife.

I found out after I left.

The other part...why, that makes a better story, don't it?

Listen. I came back to the Heights with the money he gave me, and I took over the whole shebang, as was my right and privilege.

Maybe I dreamed the homeplace got into poor sweet stupid Roger and turned him evil and cold and yellow-eyed. Or maybe it really did happen that way. Or maybe both things can be true. But he's been dead these last thirty years, and there's not many anymore who remember him or would weep for him neither.

Too many sad, lonely men do their worst and pay the price for it. Don't I know that better than the rest?

So, I came back with my face cut and my pockets full of money. I had grown big and strong, and I found Lee sunk lower than low. I decided all by myself that I would be the one, *me. I* would do it.

Bring him to a place even lower than that one.

2

"Get out."

The house stank. How was it possible that it could smell so bad? Unwashed bodies, darkness, shit, and a vinegary, horribly *fungoid* odor that rushed out the door when Heath opened it.

Outside, the air was crisp, as only a mid-October Eastern Montana morning could be: hint of the grass, dying now, wet with melting frost, the earthy smell of the cows lowing somewhere nearby in one of the pastures, and the earth itself. And the leaves still clinging to the trees in the orchard, the metallic tang of the creek water. Heath hesitated to step over the threshold. But somewhere in the darkness, there was Lee, Lee's brat, and Shaw.

Shaw was here. Shaw had to be here.

It couldn't have been Shaw you saw in San Francisco.

More than once. More than that time in the fog. Again at a flower shop, and again at a department store, leaning against a wall with his arms folded, smiling directly into Heath's eyes. He had looked away, all nonchalance, as if they didn't know each other intimately.

I'm sorry, baby. I never should have gone away. I never should have left you or the homeplace.

Four years. An impossible set of days and weeks and months, somehow eternal in the feeling of its passage.

But Heath shivered. Though the sun shone over the graying prairie grass and glittered off the stones lining the road down from 201, the air gripped its crispness, jealous. Halloween approaching. Days shortening. Shadows stretching and trees turning to bones.

His eyes flickered up, involuntarily, to the house on the hill, but he couldn't see it from where he stood on the front porch of the Heights.

"I said, get out."

Lee's voice. Still recognizable. Despite the whine Heath perceived, despite the inhuman croaking sound, it was still Lee in there.

The outside lights flashed off his eyes, which were sunken, the whites faded and yellowed. He recoiled from the light, deeper into the house.

Heath took a breath and followed, closing the door behind him.

Shaw is here. Somewhere.

"You don't belong here."

"Sure. Sure, I do. I'm the owner now."

"The hell you say."

The floors needed sweeping. Carpets needed a good vacuuming. Or tearing out. When he passed the kitchen, Heath saw with a pang that the sink swelled full of dishes flecked with dried and rotting food particles. Pans, some still half-full, choked the stovetop.

The curtains had been pulled. The house was a veritable shadowland.

Shaw?

Cat?

The shadows parted, and something small and white emerged from them, from the place where it had been lurking in the living room. Something tottered forward, reaching.

Heath drew in a breath.

A little girl, four years old. Of course she was. Lee and Flora's daughter. She wore only a little slip of a rag that was, Heath perceived with dark horror, a diaper and did little to conceal her. She was stained with dark streaks across her chest, chin, and face. Her hands, likewise, dripped with darkness.

"Daddy," she said in a chiming, lisping voice. "See me, Daddy."

"No," Heath said.

"Yeah-yeah. Daddy home me see say."

The hair on the girl's head was so fine she appeared bald. Her eyes, big and brown, bulged. She grinned, showing no teeth. Only pink, smooth gums.

Something wriggled inside her mouth. Something squirmed in there and writhed.

She had been eating something alive.

Heath moaned.

A centipede—too big to be real, Heath thought, though obviously it *was*—wriggled from the girl's toothless mouth and dropped onto the floor, where it quickly danced on its thousands of clicking and clacking spiky little legs and disappeared. The girl giggled at the sight of the insect's retreat into the shadows of the living room.

"Abatha…" Lee spoke from the sweltering, stinking darkness of the room before which Heath paused. "Whyn't you go find your doggy?"

"Dogatha," the little girl said to Heath, drooling. She crammed her filthy fingers into her mouth and squealed with delight. The little girl turned, scampered past Heath, and disappeared down the hallway.

Head swimming, Heath ventured into the living room.

It was as he had expected. Heaps of paper plates smeared with a variety of foods, greases, and sauces lay scattered about the room in great, stinking heaps. A small black and white television played a grainy picture of what Heath figured was a man, but it might have been a giant rabbit as well. He wasn't certain. The TV offered the only light in the room. The big windows at Lee's back had been covered with thick wool horse blankets stapled to the wall.

Lee sat in an antique chair of emerald leather, now torn in places. He wore only his underwear. White and stained. Heath didn't look too closely.

"You don't own *shit*," Lee declared when Heath came closer.

"I do," Heath said, "though."

"Bull*shit*."

"You can say what you want. However you want to say it."

"You're always gonna be an asshole. You know that, asshole? The Heights belongs to *my* family."

Heath smiled, and his smile was thin, knife-sharp. "I am your family."

"Picked out of the trash—"

"You've said all this before," Heath replied wearily.

"Like some goddamn gypsy, some welp, *orphan*—"

"Nevertheless," Heath said smoothly, taking a step closer. "The Heights belongs to me. Aunt Lucy sold it. To *me*. Just last week. I have the deed. I have the deed right here and now." Wickedly, he added, "Would you care to see?"

"You lowlife. You *shit*. You're lower than that, even. You got nothing, and you know you do."

Heath revealed the deed. He'd had it all along, of course. Petty, perhaps, but wasn't he due some pettiness?

Lee squinted through the murk but deigned to rise from his throne. "That don't mean nothing."

"It does."

"Aunt Lucy would'a told me."

"She did tell you."

"I would'a *remembered*," Lee Lyon whined. "Listen, I would'a."

Something fell upstairs. Lee's eyes drifted to the ceiling before focusing on Heath again. He lifted the can of beer he held and wiped his lips around the hole in the top, slurping while he did so, watching Heath while he did so, unblinking while he did so.

Heath thought, *I am stone. I am stone. I am stone.*

Lee burped, a long and froggy sound. Something crashed upstairs. Lee smiled serenely.

"No," he said, his voice eerily calm. "I ain't gonna check on that."

"All right."

"Get out of my house."

"I'm going to let you stay here," Heath said. He made his voice as even and soothing as he could. Heath even knelt beside the smeared and encrusted chair, where Lee contracted his body, squirmed to move away from Heath, tried to sink into the cushions and vanish.

Lee's eyes widened. His mouth worked. His breath was beyond foul, stinking of rotting meat, as if he had been stuffing himself with slop that rose in his throat and flooded his mouth.

"I told you," Heath whispered in his ear. "I *told* you, Lee my love, my darling, my lamb...I told you that someday this would all be mine."

"Shut your fucking mouth," Lee whispered back.

"I *told* you. And it is. I own it all. And I'll keep you here because you must stay. And little Abatha too. And whoever else you keep, as it all falls down around you—"

"Aunt Lucy is gone," Lee whined. "She's gone to live with her sister on their farm. She's gone to live with Aunt Nell and Uncle Dean. They're Lindens. They ain't Lyons. They ain't like us. They don't never come here. They don't care about us. They don't never want to see us or come here or see us. They don't care. They *don't*—"

"Shut up," Heath said mildly. He rose and wiped his hands against his thighs.

Lee stared up at him with wide, terrified animal's eyes.

"Where's Grandma?" Heath asked.

Lee said nothing. He swallowed. His throat worked, and his Adam's apple vibrated beneath bare inches of blue skin.

"*Where's the old woman on the hill?*"

"Up there," Lee whispered. "She asks about you. She's strong. She's a horse. She used to come down every weekend or so, but since Aunt Lucy moved out—"

"Why did Aunt Lucy move out?"

Lee didn't blink.

"Where's Shaw?"

Lee threw his head back and cackled unexpectedly. He sounded like a witch.

Heath felt a grin work its way across his face, a hot grin stitching itself, stitching itself, growing wider and hotter.

Lee didn't see it. He screamed his laughter. "Oh! You! Would! Ask! That!" he shrieked. "Oh! You! Would!"

"Where is he?" Heath asked pleasantly. "Is he upstairs? Is he all right?"

Lee only laughed. He twitched and kicked in the chair. "Shaw!" he mewled in a kitten's voice. "Oh, my baby Shaw! Oh, oh!" And he roared his laughter.

"Tell me, Wesley."

"Call me whatever names you want," Lee said darkly. He made his voice high-pitched and squealing again. "Oh, Shaw! Oh, my love! Where are youuuuuuuuu?" He dissolved into laughter again.

Heath's grin grew another inch before he was even aware he had seized Lee by his giant jug-ears and hauled him to his feet, cutting him off mid-cackle. He goggled. Heath grabbed his tits and twisted them. Lee shrieked. Heath twisted harder until he felt one tear under his pressure.

Lee squirming, trying to free himself. Heath released his nipples, drew back his right arm, and backhanded Lee with such force that he flew back into his chair, toppling it. His legs, white in the darkness of the room, kicked at the air, reminding Heath of the centipede that had fallen from his little daughter's mouth. Christ, what an existence.

Heath was still grinning. He couldn't wipe it away. Heath thought of Roger. That night by the water. All alone in the fog. He thought of how he had seized Roger by the lapels of his fancy coat, his fancy fucking coat—he had given Heath a coat just like that one, fancy fuck— and how he had shaken him and shaken him. Roger had lashed out with the cane, cutting Heath's face open, and still he had shaken him like he was shaking Lee now.

Heath had lifted Lee by the shoulders, twin broomsticks covered with amphibian skin too slick and too hot, and shook him. Still Lee was screaming, and Heath screamed back at him, matching him shriek for shriek.

"Where is Shaw?" he roared. "What have you done to him?"

Giggling. The child's laughter, horrible. A wave of sickness passed over him. Heath dropped Lee onto the floor. The little girl, Abatha, stood in the doorway, watching them. A giant smile of pleasure wreathed her face, which was smeared with the shit she had been eating. Her own shit, Heath thought dazedly.

"Daddy does daze," she proclaimed, clapping her hands together. She dropped what she had been holding to do it.

Heath took a step toward her, and she beamed up at him, squealing with delight, and dropped to the floor to lift the thing so she could hold it tightly to her chest.

Heath's face twitched, tried to convulse, but he forced it back to stone.

A kitten. Little and white and dead. Its neck had been broken. Its eyes were gone. Empty black holes that stared. Its mouth gaped, and its tongue protruded. Abatha held it to her and cooed to it, licked at its white fur, grinning toothlessly up at Heath.

"My doggy," she said. "All my doggies, all."

"Yes," Heath said.

"Don't you talk to her," Lee sobbed from his place on the floor behind them.

"Daddy, doggy died," Abatha proclaimed solemnly.

"He's right here. He's fine."

"You died."

"No."

"Everyone, all do."

"I suppose, yes. You're a very pretty little girl. Do you know that?"

Abatha beamed. She lifted the dead kitten high above her head and performed a remarkably perfect pirouette.

"Don't, don't," Lee sobbed. "She's all I have left. She's all. Don't talk to her. Don't take her away from me."

Heath ignored him. He knelt to face the smeared and stinking creature before him. She watched him with wide-unblinking eyes and a guileless smile. The little girl licked absently at the kitten's face.

"I'm looking for someone," he said gently. "Do you know who I'm looking for?"

Abatha thought for a moment. Nodded.

"Good. That's good. Can you tell me his name?"

The little creature lowered her head. She put the head of the kitten in her mouth and sucked at it. Heath's stomach flipped, but he forced himself to smile. Her eyes flashed at him while she sucked and sucked, and he swore there was some wicked intelligence there. Heath thought of Roger. He thought of blood and eyes the color of coins.

"Uncle," she whispered at last.

"Uncle?"

"Uncle Oncle Ankle." The little girl spat the kitten's head from her mouth and hurled it away from her. She jumped. Her hands were fists she swung, and Heath fell backward onto his butt to avoid being struck. "Shit shame shape!" she howled. "Shame shred shop! Shop! Slop! Slop, slop, slop!"

"Slop," Heath whispered.

"Shit! Shit! Shit!"

"Shit."

Abatha paused. She reached for Heath with a hand that reeked of the dead kitten. Her fingers were stubby, the nails chewed away, though someone had attempted to paint them for her. A lovely coral pink. It took all the strength he possessed not to recoil when those awful fingers caressed his cheek.

"Where my doggy go?"

"You threw it away."

"Ah." She considered this. "Don't doggy. Doggy did. Doggy die."

"Yes."

She took him by the hand. Heath stood. Behind them, Lee howled his fury. Abatha led him to the door, opened it, and brought him out onto the porch steps. She pointed with her free hand at the hills that rose and fell like a woman's curves, lying on her side and waiting for a lover to come.

"Shaw," she said clearly. "Oncle Ankle. Shaman. Shay-man. Oncle. Out there."

"Shaw is out there? Where?"

"Call," she said. "Call him dead doggy. He come."

A chill rippled its way down Heath's back. No, he thought. Not Shaw. No.

Cat?

"Call," Abatha urged him. "Call, call. Howl. Hale."

The sun stretched its golden fingers across the hills, the coulees, and the creek. The frost sparkled, even while it melted away. No green anywhere, Heath thought dimly. Everything is dying.

"Shaw?" the soiled little thing beside him whispered. "Shaw?"

"Shaw?" Heath whispered.

"Shaw?" they said together. The sun chuckled and warmed the air, and the sky stretched over them, flawless and empty.

3

I heard him, of course, and came running. Isn't that what you would do?

I couldn't live at the Heights now. Not with the way Lee treated it. Not with Aunt Lucy abandoning us, abandoning *me*.

I told her, "Hey, listen…I'm used to being abandoned by now."

But she sniffed and rolled her eyes. "Don't be dramatic." She missed her sister, and they needed her more than I did. And anyway, the Heights wasn't a *good* place anymore. Maybe it had never been a good place.

What she *didn't* say was, "There are things in the walls, and soon, they'll get out." But I knew she was thinking it.

Hell, I was thinking it too.

Why did you leave me? I called out into the darkness one night a week or so before *he* returned to me. *Why did you go?*

"We can't be together," I told him.

"I need you," he told me.

"I will own this whole place one day," he told me. "When I do, I will come back, and we can be the way we deserve to be."

But I didn't know what that meant.

Why are you leaving? He never heard me. Aunt Lucy gave him some of the money Father left. Then he was gone. I didn't know where, and he didn't tell me. Bastard.

I went back to Boston for a while. Stayed with Jeanette. Her name was Johnny now. She had cut all her hair off and lived with a man named Bon and a woman named Sister Peaseblossom. They were happy as larks. I stayed with them for a week.

Depressing, man.

Johnny's happiness irritated me. No. More than simple irritation. It pissed me off. I told her I thought she was a dyke. She smiled and said that labels were meaningless. She was just a human being, and she loved who she loved. She wasn't a woman, and she wasn't a man.

I told her, "I don't know what you're talking about."

She smiled and said I would someday. Or not.

"Consciousness is coming for you," she told me and kissed me on the forehead, like Glinda the motherfucking Good Witch from the motherfucking *Wizard of Motherfucking Oz.*

I told her I had fucked her boyfriend. It was true; I had. It was awful. Worse, it was *boring.* He just *lay* there and took it. She said she had expected nothing more or nothing less. She refused to get angry. Even a little bit. I threw a tantrum. I was too old for tantrums, but I threw one.

Peaseblossom and Bon cleared out so Jeanette—sorry, *Johnny*—and I could have our fight. Except I was the only one fighting. Johnny kept smiling at me. Once, she touched my hair.

"Don't fucking touch me." I snarled and slapped her hand away.

"You never used language like that before," she said. Her voice was so soft and mellifluous that I threw my head back and shrieked.

"You're a fucking dyke, and you refuse to admit it," I told her.

"I am composed of bits of star and the heat of the sun," she told me, which was when I picked up the glass of whiskey I had been slamming and hurled it through the window.

After that, they all asked me to leave. They said they didn't feel safe around me. I didn't blame them. Johnny had the decency to at least look sad when she hugged me goodbye. I suppose she really meant it when she said she loved me.

"You don't love me," I told her. It was the last thing I ever did say to her.

I screwed around New York for a few weeks. I stayed in the biggest hotels the city boasted, ordered champagne and room service, and picked up a few boys I found in the Village. Thought, *I'm happy as a lark. I'm happy as a lark.* Only I wasn't. I thought of Heath and wondered where he was.

A policeman forced me to suck his cock on Christmas Eve and beat the fuck out of me after he finished in my mouth, of course. He left me unconscious and bleeding on the frozen street. After that, I got the hell out of the city. I will never go there again. Maybe not to the east coast at all. Rich, uptight snobs, all of them.

I came back to Montana and the Heights and tried to run the ranch the way I thought my father would have done. Nathan helped. Until he caught pneumonia the next winter and died. The sonofabitch. I was with him right up until almost the end, but I left at the last minute so Dolly, his wife, could take care of him. She wanted me to go anyway. Dolly hated me because she knew. She knew and she couldn't do anything to stop us because she didn't have the words.

And besides, who would believe it? Nathan was married. They had a kid. He wasn't like me, even if we did spend all our time together after Heath left. Even if we did what Heath and I did and kissed—finally—in his truck and fucked out in the tall grasses far from our houses, far from our farms. The only sound was the grasshoppers in the summer and the drone of a tractor somewhere down the road, or the cows lowing to each other, the excited snickering of someone's horse. Warmth. That is what I wanted. And Nathan was warm because Heath was gone, and I needed to be warm.

"I'm not queer, you know," Nathan told me one time.

I was going down on him, and he had just gone down on me. I could smell myself on his breath, so it seemed funny, and I laughed, which made him angry. Nathan angry was amusing. His face would scrunch up, like a little Pekinese Jeanette's dorm mother owned back in Boston—one of those terrible little dogs, you know, scrunching up his face like one of them. Sometimes, I thought it was cute.

We had known each other since we were born, and sometimes, I would think, *Nathan is like me*, and I would whisper, "I love Nathan Reardon." When we were eight, it was his idea to play "I'll show you mine if you show me yours" and his idea to play "Mommy and Daddy," only I was always the mommy until I told him I wanted to be the daddy. But then he didn't want to play anymore.

Nathan wanted a more ordinary world, I guess. A more—I hate to say the word "normal," but yes—a more normal life. Normal according to the thudding nimrods who populate the farmland and the little, little towns that are all they—all we—know. He wanted a wife, but he wanted me too, and I only wanted him.

Until Heath.

Goddamn you, Heath.

I walked out of the Heights at midnight the day after Heath left us. No, I didn't walk. I burst like a comet out of the door. Everyone else asleep, and I was on fire. I was full of fury and longing and a sadness that dug at me until it was a hole. And the hole ate at me until it grew bigger and bigger, and it filled me...And it filled me with *nothing*.

Only the nothing ached.

I have never felt an ache like that before or since. It *hurt*. It fucking goddamn *hurt*. I blew up. I raged. I kicked open the door, and I didn't care if I woke up Aunt Lucy or Lee or the baby. Not Flora, though. Flora was good and dead. But I kicked it open, and it hurt because my feet were bare, because I refused to wear the idiotic clodhopping boots *they* all wore. All the men: Lee, Don, and yes, even Heath. But because I refused and because I was a comet blazing away, my feet were bare, naked, and defenseless, but I kicked open the door anyway and roared a war-whoop.

Heath would call it a war-whoop.

I ran out, down the steps, and out onto the road, pounding down the hard-packed earth, shedding my clothing while I went. I jiggled out of my pajama bottoms and left them in the dust of the road, tore at my pajama shirt until the buttons popped like corn and scattered. I tore it off and threw it away, and it was just me, all white, a gleaming stitch in the dark, running and running.

And I thought, *Take me, prairie mine. Take me, open emptiness and your hills, your slick green grasses and the little orange and blue flowers that grow along the road. Take me because I am yours and I have been abandoned and I belong to no one else. Not Nathan Reardon, not the Heights, only to Heath and to you, to you.*

I left the road and made a sharp right turn, slugged through the creek so my legs darkened with the mud. "Take me, take me," I whispered while I ran.

Only the moon overhead spilled any kind of light, a kind of silver-blue effulgence, like fairy light. Heath left us on a warm afternoon in mid-June, so I was able to run without freezing in my silly nakedness, but I wanted to be pure and fresh for the country so the country would claim me and I wouldn't be alone anymore. And I would be warm. God, I needed to be *warm.*

I finally stopped, panting, maybe a mile from the house. The hills had risen around me, and I had come to a place where Redwater Creek had, probably millions of years ago, cut through one of the hillsides, leaving sand-rock formations to stud the hill some fifty feet to the place where Highway 201 ran mere feet away from the edge of the cliff.

Lee and I used to play out here when we were little. I brought Nathan out here once to play Magic Land, where we could cross the creek and enter a new world so we could be kings and rule over all the magical creatures who loved us. Nathan never wanted to play, but Heath did.

He helped me climb the steep hill, taking my hand and pulling me up onto the sand-rock ledges. Two came together at one point and created a little cave that was dangerous to access, but we did it regularly the summer we turned fifteen, too old to play games about magical lands, but we played them anyway. We stored sleeping bags, canteens of water, and packages of graham crackers in that little cave we were always careful not to tumble from. Otherwise, we would drop straight down, thirty, forty feet, and land on the hard bank of the creek.

"You are the king," Heath told me once, solemnly, "and I am the king."

I bowed and said, "Your majesty," and he bowed and said, "*Your* majesty," and kissed me on both my cheeks.

We laughed like goofy little kids. Heath liked my games.

So here I was, the only light from the moon overhead, and me, far from the house and alone. I was panting. I had been running. But my fury was far from expiated. I threw my head back and screamed at the night.

Something exploded from the water and, flapping, took to the sky, terrified by my outburst. A flock of four or five ducks. Scolding me, infuriated, they flew away to some less trifling section of the creek, where stupid humans didn't come to vent their rage.

"Take my skin," I screamed at the sky. "Take my heart and my eyes and my tongue! Take my worthless fucking cock because I won't need it anymore! I wouldn't know what to do with it anyway!"

I was panting. My head ached. I leaned over, put my hands on my knees.

"Tear my arms off," I whispered. "Tear off my legs. My face. My disgusting, shitting asshole. Take it all. I don't want it. Not me."

I sank into the grass. It was soft. It smelled sweet. It smelled right. The creek burbled delightedly at my side.

"Yes, yes," I whispered. "Yes, that's good. That's right. All this."

I am with you. I am one with you. I am earth. You are earth.

"Yes, that's right. Like that."

Look at the sky. Look at those stars.

I obeyed.

You've never seen a sky like the one hanging over Eastern Montana, I promise you. No lights, no smog, no pollution. An open wound overhead filled with twinkling fragments of bone. Millions of 'em. They don't call it "Big Sky Country" for nothing, I guess.

For a moment, I hated it.

Whoever had bidden me to look up there breathed, satisfied with my hatred.

You belong to us.

"I belong to you," I whispered. I clutched at the grass. I used it to bury myself deeper inside. I wanted to be a part of the earth. I needed to be inside it. I needed it.

You don't belong anywhere else.

"I am the stars," I said, staring upward. "I am the earth, and I am the stars, and I am the creek and the heat and the icy breath of winter. Here. I belong *here*, nowhere else."

Nowhere else.

"Will he come back?"

He will come back.

"I am not a patient person."

You'll have to be.

"I'm not a patient person!"

I pulled in agony at the grass. I whipped my head back and forth.

"I'm not, I'm not, I'm not!"

Stop whining. You are not a child.

Instantly, I held still. Tears burned my eyes. My chest heaved. A comet, I was a comet, and I *blazed.*

You can fuck this world. You know that, don't you?

"Yes," I whispered.

You can put your prick in anything you want. Anyone. You know that, don't you?

"Yes," I whispered. I didn't. A tear trickled from the corner of my right eye and vanished into the grass.

You can be part of the curse. You know that too?

"I don't want the curse."

You're a part of it.

"But I don't want it!"

The curse will keep you alive. Don't you want to be alive?

"I am alive."

Don't be sullen. Don't be an infant. We have no time for your infant behavior.

"I'm sorry."

The curse will keep you alive. Don't you want your lover to find you?

"I want my Heath."

And he wants you.

"I want to be with him forever."

I pulled at the grass. Cords stood out on my neck. My jaw clenched. My eyes closed, then *bulged* open, wide, wide, wide. The stars stared down at me, cold and aloof.

"Fuck you, stars," I said.

They laughed at me mirthlessly.

"I want to be with him forever!" I screamed at the sky.

No one answered.

There was no one there.

There had never been anyone there.

I lay where I had fallen, exhausted.

The creek tinkled beside me. Something heavy flew overhead.

I opened my eyes.

A white figure perched at the edge of one of the sand-stone cliffs, the highest one. Fifty feet above me. It was white and thin. Human. It put its hands on its hips and glared at me. I couldn't make out its features, but I knew it saw me. It lifted a hand and threw its head back, as if it were laughing at me. I heard no sound.

Then I was blasted by an intense cold, more than a wind. It was as if ice burrowed inside me, through my skin, my veins, into my blood and the marrow of my bones. I thrashed on the grass, trying to scream, but I was frozen, and I could make no sound. The cold stabbed at me. The cold flayed me. It pinned me to the ground. And it came from that figure overhead, the slim white *thing* that had found me and seen me and now tried to freeze me.

Maybe to death.

No, no, no, I tried to cry, but my throat was full of snow.

Heath, I tried to cry, but my tongue had frozen solid and was trapped between my teeth.

Laughter. A woman.

A stinking wind, thick with rot, invaded my nostrils and my mouth. Clung to my teeth and my frozen tongue.

I rolled over onto my stomach, gagging. The stench was unbearable.

A woman stood, reflected in the creek.

She was young, hair the same color as mine, intense eyes, wearing an old-fashioned yellow dress.

It was her laughter I heard.

The cold dissipated, as if it had never been, and was replaced by the warmth of the summer night. Frogs chirped again. Deer flies buzzed around me. One lighted on my bare shoulder and bit me. I cried out in pain and fury and smashed it to a red smear beneath my hand.

When I looked back at the creek, the woman was gone.

The white figure atop the cliff was gone as well.

Trembling, sure I would be unable to, I rose to my feet. My knees buckled, and I fell back into the grass, pressed myself up, gritting my teeth, grunting. At last, I stood, swaying, beside the creek.

Alone.

"Heath," I whispered. My eyes burned. I snuffled. I would not cry again. Not for him. Not for anyone. "Heath," I said again, and I tried as hard as I could to make it not be a sob. "Heath, Heath, Heath, please, please. Come home. Come home to me."

Now I lay in Eddie's arms, which was where I preferred to be most days. Technically, I lived at the farm four miles down the road, which belonged to my Aunt Nell—Lucy and my father's sister—and her husband Dean. They were the Lindens, and they wanted little to do with anyone living at the Heights. Their farm was smaller but arguably more successful. Their head of cattle was larger than ours, and Uncle Dean raised sheep *and* pigs while Aunt Nell took care of her chickens, which were good layers.

Aunt Lucy lived with them now, and technically, so did I. Really, I spent all my nights and days with Eddie Thrush, a bachelor—like me—though he was older, surlier, cared less about housekeeping since his father had passed away and left him the big two-story house sitting square in the middle of the country, with barely a road to reach it. He reminded me of Heath, though Eddie was prone to fits of self-pity that occurred more frequently these days. Eddie was almost fifty, and he whined about it with near constancy.

The lie we told was that we were cousins. I don't know if people believed us, and I didn't care. Nathan Reardon was dead, and his wife and child had moved to the big city of Billings, hundreds of miles away. The Palmers and Polly King and her brother, Linus, were our nearest neighbors, and we saw them two, maybe three times a year. And I was a Lyon. If I said Eddie and I were cousins, we were cousins.

Who slept in the same bed.

Who fucked nearly every night. Or we *had*, until recently.

Eddie wasn't like Nathan, but at the same time, he absolutely and a thousand percent *was*: He didn't like words like *queer* or *fag*, even though I did and used them as much as I possibly could until he would get mad and slap me or punch me in the gut to get me to shut up. Then I would disappear for a day or two. Drive my '57 Chrysler New Yorker —which I never ever should have bought but wanted to have, and so I had it—as far and as fast I could. It was seafoam aqua and the size of the entire state of Montana. It could fit all that sky inside if I wanted it to. I tried to keep it clean, but the dust from the roads scraped away at the paint, and when it rained or snowed, those same dusty roads became gumbo and threw great spats of brown across her body, so she looked streaked with shit.

But I would drive it to Burke or Sidney or Glasgow and find a bar, an Oasis or a Stockmans, and I would drink myself stupid. Usually, I would end up in a fight, which I loved. Some bruiser redneck in Wranglers and those fucking, *fucking* clodhopper cowboy boots I despised would call me a faggot. Then it was on. I would tear in to them, even if I didn't remember much about it later.

I had been helping Lee lift and arrange hay bales into stacks, unstack them, and replace them in the bed of one of our fleet of farm trucks to take out to the pasture on freezing cold winter mornings, chop away the bale strings, and push the frigid chunks of former summer out into the snowbanks, where the cows would greedily tear away at the hay until they had devoured it. Then we would do it all again the next morning. But I had built up some muscle by that time, so when those assholes wanted to start something, I was more than glad to throw it back at them. Surprised them too. Some of them knew who I was and would back off. Others weren't so fortunate. I would break their noses for their trouble. Make them swallow their teeth.

But I had amassed quite a reputation. And I never fought back when Eddie would wail on me. I let him. He needed to get it all out. Also, I loved him. Sometimes, you have to hurt the thing you love. Wasn't that the oldest of all the tales? It was certainly the motto of the Lyon family in Montana. As long as we had possessed the Heights, we loved only to cause and receive pain. Romantic. Vile. Disgusting. I ate it all up, though, so when Eddie would smack me in the mouth or blacken my eye, it only made me love him more.

You can call me sick if you want to. I'll accept it. I'll own it. But I love him, and he loves me too. I know he does. Eddie lets me live with him. He takes me to Billings and into North Dakota, to Bismarck, and buys me dinner and nice clothes, and he can be tender when we make love. It isn't all fucking, animal grunting, and clawing at each other. Sometimes, it's that way. Sometimes, it's making love, the way Heath and I used to do.

Don't think about Heath. Don't think about how you went out into the country the night he left and grafted yourself to the land once and for all. Don't think about idiot things like curses. Don't think about Boston or Jeanette or any of your other lovers. Think of your hair, which is golden, and your big blue eyes and how Eddie tells you how much he loves them, even if he doesn't ever, ever say he loves *you*. Think about the steak and eggs he makes you on Sunday mornings. Think about his big cock, which you never get tired of. It's like the best toy in the world. Think about how he will play the guitar for you on the porch some evenings, when it is just you two. He loves you. Even if he doesn't say it, he does. He *loves* you.

Shaw.

I lay in Eddie's arms.

I opened my eyes.

Cat. Cat-in-the-dark. Come back to me. Come back.

"Heath?" I whispered.

Eddie stirred. Groaned. He had come in from fixing broken barbed wire fencing since dawn, and we lay together. No sex, no kissing, even. Just our arms wrapped around each other. I was working on my novel, I told him, when he came in, but I would take time off for some loving. I had a typewriter and everything, all set up on the back porch. There was even a stove for the wintertime, when the wind howled and the drifts grew so high they reached the second-floor window some days. I would *clack* and *clack* away. A story no one would read. The story of me and Heath. Two men who loved each other. Who knew each other intimately.

Did people want to read stories like that? I didn't know. I really didn't care. I kept at it, imagining what Heath's childhood had been like before Dad brought him to the Heights. I invented an entire background: a drunken mother, an absent father, a whole passel of little siblings for him to take care of. And they all died in a fire. Only Heath survived. Some of the details came from the reality of what Heath had told me, the fragments of his past he claimed he could remember. I used it all shamelessly. I would tell him someday, I promised myself, if the sonofabitch ever came back.

"What are you saying?" Eddie whispered. His voice was harsh, full of phlegm.

He rolled over onto his stomach and released me, and I was up like a shot. Pulled on the cashmere sweater I had ordered for myself from a store in New York—aqua, the color of my car, the color of my eyes. A pair of white linen pants that were nearly see-through. Blue boat shoes, no socks.

It was October. The air practically sparked with the crispness of autumn, but I didn't care. Heath was back. Heath was here. Nearby. At the Heights?

I paused, listening.

Eddie watched me from the bed, wide-eyed. His dark hair, streaked with iron-gray, stood up in corkscrews. He hadn't shaved in days. His eyes were half-lidded and sleepy. He was confused. Didn't matter. So was I.

Heath is calling for me, I wanted to tell him, but he didn't know much about Heath, and anything I babbled about him would be meaningless. I didn't talk about Heath. Not with Eddie. No one else talked about him either. We didn't know where he had gone. Only Aunt Lucy spoke to him on occasion, though she didn't have to tell me and wouldn't anyway. I just *knew*.

Cat. Cat-in-the-dark. Cat-o-mine.

He was calling *me*.

He had returned to the Heights.

He was there now.

"Where are you going?" Eddie asked. He sat up. The quilt his mother had made him for his last birthday pooled around his waist.

I saw his gut. Fuck, I *loved* his gut. A round, hairy moon.

"To the Heights." I was nearly out the door.

"Now? Why?"

"I have to go."

"I can go with if you want to just—"

"No."

Eddie had never come to the Heights. I didn't want him to. I didn't want him to see how filthy it was now, how disgusting Lee had become, his revolting little daughter. My niece. Abatha Lyon. An abomination. The entire house reeked of decomposition. Vinegar. Shit. I couldn't expose Eddie to that.

I couldn't expose him to anything resembling a curse either.

"Will you be back for dinner?"

"Maybe."

"Supper?"

"Maybe. I don't know. Maybe not."

A line creased his forehead. His eyes narrowed. "Just fend for myself, will I?"

"You can. Eddie, I have to go."

"You don't need to sound like that. I let you go before."

"Thanks. Ever so much."

"Don't need *that* tone neither."

Did I love him because he was one of *them*? Those men I hated so much, the townies from Burke and the cowboys? Men who were unlike my father, though he had existed out here with his fortune and been very successful? Eddie wanted to rule me, and I didn't want to be ruled, but I let him think that he could. Was that the place where our love had bloomed? Like a crack in a dry boulder where some moisture falls and stays and a few flowers can creep into existence from time to time? Christ Jesus, was our love like *that*? Barren and dry like *that*?

Heath was back. All I could think of was Heath.

I had to get back to the Heights.

Eddie's fingers clutched at me. I heard him pleading. He had never begged like this before. He knew, he *knew,* something was wrong with me, but I was out the door, into my car, tires digging up clods of dust to hang like ghosts in the air behind me, down the country road, past hills with no color and trees that blazed, October and gorgeous, but I didn't care. Onto 201, nearly ran Ben King off the road, screaming at me, shaking his fist. I didn't care, *couldn't* care. Down, down 201, turned onto that old familiar road, and there below me was the Heights.

There below me was Heath.

My hands trembled so badly I nearly drove the car off the road.

I didn't.

I crossed the creek, and oh God, there he was, standing on the porch with that vile little creature beside him. She capered, giggled, and pulled at the hair she didn't have. Heath stood stock-still. I slammed the door of the car. I froze.

His eyes were dusty stones.

He didn't move.

"Go into the house," he finally said to the monster at his side.

She muttered some of her usual nonsense.

"Go on now," he said evenly. Heath didn't even look at her. He only had eyes for me.

I heard that song in my head. You know that song? Doo-bop-she-bop. Everyone out here listened to country, Patsy Cline and Johnny Cash, but not me. I liked The Flamingoes. I lived for The Shirelles and The Chiffons—*one fine day, oooooh, you're gonna want me, you're gonna want me, one fine day.* I was humming it, singing it, and Heath's mouth quirked into a grin with his surprised amusement. *One fine day, bop bop, are the stars out tonight, bop bop, I don't know if it's cloudy, bop, will you still love me tomorrow, will you still love me?*

His arms around me.

Crushing me.

His lips.

Crushing mine.

I crushed them back. I pulled at his hair. Oh God, his *hair.*

"I thought I'd never see you again," he whispered against my neck. Electricity, oh God, *running up and down my entire body.*

"I knew I'd see you. I never doubted it."

We drove. That is all I remember. My car left the road and bumped over the untrodden prairie. The sun burned over our heads and blinded me, but I didn't care. I blasted the radio, and Don Gibson warbled "Oh Lonesome Me," and I twisted the dial viciously.

"Let me," Heath said quietly. I had forgotten how quiet he could be.

My breathing slowed. I calmed.

He smiled at me.

Bump, bump, bump.

"*Poor little fool,*" Ricky Nelson crooned.

Heath took my hand. Incongruously, he leaned his head against my shoulder.

He didn't ask where we were going because he knew I didn't know.

Until I did.

I pulled over beside the creek. We stepped out of the car. The sand-rock cliffs reared over us. Our breath hung in the air like tattered bits of cotton. The sun would warm us. But we wouldn't need it to.

No white figure watched us from above, blasting us with jealousy and hatred. No ghost-woman in yellow swam in the red waters of the creek, with white fish arms and bulging eyes.

We looked at each other.

We grinned.

And came together inevitably.

4

The earth took them both, as it had before and would again, but they weren't thinking of death nor life. They were on fire, and the only way to quench the flames was to become as much a part of the earth as they could, and together.

Their fingers became the grass, stones their stomachs, which slapped together on occasion. The creek water spilled out of their eyes and their mouths, leaked from the tips of their cocks, which were chunks of sand-rock lying against each other and inside each other neatly, even though there was only the creek water splashing from their mouths to open the way, caves made of sand-rock too, teeth to nip, perfect little pearls of rock long ago washed away by the relentless gnawing of Redwater. Rough words, harsh words, soft purring.

"Cat, Cat, Cat," Heath growled at one point, nearing a climax Shaw denied him, flipping him over, pressing him into the earth and the sharp grasses that grew up around them, dead flowers falling from their hair, sweetgrass plumes emerging from one mouth and passing into the other.

Coming, then, the water and the air, at last, coming at last, pouring out of them and into the other. Sweetgrass and the chill of the air and the great thrumming in the land itself. *Feel it. Put your hand there. You can feel it.* Great thrumming. *Starts in the thighs and builds inside your ass and balls and explodes out of you.* The sunlight shining on the prairie, the grass growing from it. *Yes, yes, the power of growing things, bursting out of your cock and inside him or onto him so you can bathe it in it.* Together. Coming, coming, at last. After years. Too many years.

"I thought I saw you. In San Francisco."

"Is that where you were?"

"Yes."

"The whole time?"

"Yes."

"I could've found you."

"I thought I saw you. The other day, I thought that."

"It wasn't me."

"I think it was."

"How could I be?" Shaw laughed. "I'm here, aren't I?"

"The Heights."

"Reaching out?"

"You know it can."

Nodding.

"Take any form."

"Sure. Maybe I was there. Maybe it was me." Shaw nestled closer to Heath. Head on his chest.

Heath stroked his hair softly, as if he really were a giant cat. Shaw smiled. He wanted to purr. He nestled instead.

"I always believed you'd find me."

"Heath—" Guilt became a cramp. He rolled away, sat cross-legged, naked in the grass that was just grass again. The prairie was just the prairie. The sand-rocks just that. There was no magic. There were no curses. A shape was a shape, and you held it, and you never changed, not really. You were who you were. And what.

"Maybe," Heath mused, reaching for Shaw's hand, "*maybe* that's why I saw you. It was time. I knew it was time already, I really did, but I guess I needed to be *sure*."

"Heath, listen—"

"I'm a rich man now."

"Oh."

"I bought the Heights."

"Oh!" Shaw wanted to shoot up. The ground held him tightly instead. So maybe there was some weird magic in it after all.

"From Aunt Lucy. She sold it all to me. She wanted nothing to do with it."

"But I—"

"For us."

Shaw gaped.

"For you and me."

"Lee—"

"Will go wherever we tell him." Heath spoke patiently. Sparks danced in his eyes. "I told him once that it would be mine one day. All of it: the house, the property, the animals, the fields. And it is." He smiled. "He called me a nigger."

"I...know."

"Many, many times."

"I tried to—"

"Doesn't matter." Stroking Shaw's hair again.

Shaw closed his eyes. It felt so *good*. The guilt-cramp subsided.

"See what a prairie man can do? That's what I want to show him. See what I can do? See what I *did*?"

"And I—"

"I love you."

"I love you."

"Forever."

"Yes."

"So, the house is ours. And I'll send Lee wherever you want me to send him. To the cabin on the hill, maybe, to live with Granny."

"There's no room."

Heath's smile grew unpleasant. "That's their problem, isn't it?"

"Heath. Listen, Heath, I'm—"

Heath rolled over on top of him. He was hardening again. Shaw moaned in the back of his throat when Heath's erection brushed his own, which was growing up to meet it.

"We are the land, and the land is us," Heath whispered into Shaw's ear. "We are the house and the horses and the cattle, the birds, the lions and the bears, if there are any left. We are they and they are us. It's a magic spell. It's what Catherine Lyon told me long ago. We weave the magic so that we'll always be here."

"The devil—"

"No devil."

"There's evil here—"

"No evil."

Shaw closed his eyes and groaned. Heath spit roughly into his hand, wiped it on his cock, and slid it—slowly, fire, blazing, slowly, God, thank God for Eddie; thank God they had fucked only last night—slid it inside Shaw. He moaned again. They both did. Life. Fire. The magic Heath talked about—yes, there it was. They were all the same. Forever the same. Fuck the cowboys and their ignorant women if they didn't understand. Fuck their future spawn too. Fuck them all. Fuck even Eddie. This was now, and this was good, and it could go on and on forever. Just them.

The Heights loomed before them. Shaw drove the car slowly. Peaceably. Heath beside him, head lolling, eyes half closed, nearly asleep. Shaw smiled. The guilt returned, a horrible little rat-thing, and gnawed at his guts, which tingled unpleasantly.

Don't think about it. Heath was there. He had come home. Worry later. Worry about Eddie and Lee and Abatha and what Heath would do when he found out about Eddie.

Heath had lovers too. He told me.

The sun was descending, which meant it had to be after three. How was that possible? *We spent the whole day out there. Time is nothing. We are the earth and the water, the sand-rocks too. What do we care for time?*

Someone had parked a truck at the gate.

Shaw's guts turned to ice.

Big green farm truck. Viking.

Eddie's.

Shit. Fuck. Shit.

Heath stirred beside him. "'S the matter?" he murmured.

The front door of the house opened.

Eddie stepped out.

Lee hovered behind him. Grinning. Dressed in a stained wife-beater and faded jeans. Bare feet. Eddie wore his habitual costume: short-sleeved button-up shirt, dark blue Levis, his boots. A red ball cap slightly askew. His face was grim. His eyes thinned and flinty.

"You must be Heath," Eddie said.

Heath left the car at the same time Shaw did.

"I don't know you," Heath said. "But you know me. How's that?"

"I live by myself," Eddie said, "way out in the country. Name's Edgar Thrush. Folks call me Eddie."

"Eddie."

"Heath."

"Heath," Lee sneered behind the other man.

Seeing Heath and Eddie together for the first time, Shaw was dismayed to find between the two men a certain resemblance, particularly in their sizes, the swell of their chests, the width of their shoulders. Even their eyes were similar, though Heath's contained a wildness Shaw doubted anyone in their world exhibited or could ever exhibit. They both reminded him now of a pair of wolves glaring at each other, sniffing the air, sizing the other up.

Heath came up the stairs. Extended his hand.

Shaw held his breath.

"Pleased t'meetcha," he said.

Eddie took it. "Likewise," and shook it firmly.

They stared into the other's eyes.

"Kill each other," Lee Lyon said clearly. Behind him, in the shadows of the hallway, Abatha tittered.

Eddie snickered.

Heath frowned.

"Now why," Eddie said, turning to Lee, "*why* would we want to do something so stupid as kill each other? Ain't you got no sense?"

"Why should we kill each other?" Heath asked, his voice quiet.

Shaw swallowed.

"You're both freaks," Lee spat. "You both wanna fight for the hand of my faggot brother. I wanna see it happen, that's all."

Eddie and Heath looked at each other calmly.

"He doesn't talk about you," Eddie said at last.

"You neither," Heath replied.

Seconds unspooled.

Both men drew themselves up, made themselves appear even bigger.

Neither looked away. Neither blinked.

"Listen—" Shaw said, beginning to move at the same time Eddie said, "This is really pretty funny if you think about—" which was the same moment Heath seized him by the collar of his shirt and threw him off the porch onto the little hill leading to the twin granaries Lee and Mr. Lyon had built before his death.

"Goddamn it, Heath!" Shaw roared, but there was no stopping him.

Lee clapped his hands, stomped his feet, and hee-hawed evil laughter.

Eddie rolled down the little incline and stopped before he struck the thick wooden wall of the granary, which Lee had painted red. He sat up, blinking dazedly.

"Stop!" Shaw cried again, but Heath was already down the hill.

He kicked out, and his booted foot struck Eddie in the gut. The other man tried to gasp when all the wind left his body. Heath was already on him, snarling, his fists flashing and cutting the air. And Eddie's mouth. And his cheek. No, both his cheeks.

Somewhere, Shaw heard a woman's laughter. Lee's laughter blended with hers, low and animalistic, high and crystalline—the sound produced when a spook strikes a wine glass.

Eddie was slow, but he was strong. He wrapped both arms around Heath's legs and tore him to the ground. They rolled together, punching and kicking and growling.

Dogs, dogs, Shaw thought, furious and giddy at the same time. If he tried to wade in, he knew he would be dragged down with them, so he only watched, holding himself miserably, occasionally crying out their names in a futile effort to force them to stop.

And Lee laughed and laughed.

They sat together, the three of them, miserable and staring, in the kitchen at Eddie's farmhouse. The sun had set long ago. October darkness lay heavily, icily, over the prairie, the dirt roads, the houses and farms, which sat far apart from each other and which glowed as valiantly as they could through the pressing of the night. Coyotes howled, tentatively at first, then with more force. A dog barked somewhere in the hills. They listened to it, and no one said a word.

At last, a woman entered the kitchen. She wore jeans rolled up to her shins, and her feet were bare. The shirt she wore was pink and white gingham and hung down past her waist. Her hair was a light, mousy blond, where Eddie's was dark. She was significantly younger than he was but older than Heath, older than Shaw. In her late twenties, maybe early thirties. She put her hands on her hips and stood poised in the kitchen doorway.

"You idiot men," she spat at last. Annabelle Thrush, Eddie's sister. Plain but pretty in her plainness, Heath thought. "Always brawling. Goldarn pack of dogs—that's all you are."

"This my sister," Eddie muttered. His lip had split and swelled. Both his eyes gleamed sullenly from the thick black bruises encircling them.

He rather looked, Shaw thought, like a raccoon, and since he knew it wouldn't do to laugh at poor Eddie in this situation, he tried his best to keep his eyes on the kitchen table.

"My sister, Annabelle."

"I settled in before Eddie left for your place," and she nodded her head in Shaw's direction. "I know you. Shaw Lyon. I remember you from when you were just a little shaver."

"No," Shaw said, but she ignored him, smiling and glaring.

"Oh, sure. I babysat you once or twice while your Aunt Lucy and your daddy was at some farm convention in Missouri. You were too little to remember me. But *I* remember *you*. Sure, I do. You cried all the time. You put your hand through a window to spite me. Cut yourself all t'hell. Your mama, godresthersoul, she never let me come back again after that."

"I don't remember." Shaw sniffed.

"Now you..." Annabelle sat spread-legged, with her stomach pressed against the back of the chair like the farmhands liked to do, and leaned in close to Heath. "*You*, I'm not too sure about. You're the biggest bruiser of 'em all, I'm guessing."

Heath said nothing. Both his eyes were blackened, and his lip was split, his nose crusted with black blood, like pepper clinging below it.

"This is Heath," Shaw said. Some remaining slip of propriety made him add, "My brother."

"Adopted," Heath growled.

Eddie snickered.

"You shut the hell up right now." Heath moved as if to stand, his fists clenching again.

Annabelle planted her bare foot against Heath's chest and shoved him, surprised and blinking, back into his chair. "Hell no," she said. "Absolutely not."

"Never shoulda come here," Heath snarled.

"Oh, but you did, though," Annabelle said brightly. "So, let's make the most of it. I'm going to rustle up some dinner—I'm thinking chicken cacciatore, and I brung all the right ingredients from town with me, so *that's* all right. Heath, you look like a man who knows his way around a kitchen. You help me out."

All three men exchanged startled looks. Blinking, they rose from the table.

Annabelle leveled a finger at Shaw's chest, then Eddie's. "*You* two," she bugled, "are going to go work out whatever idiocy you gotta work out. Eddie, you go smoke on the porch. I don't stand for no smoking inside my house."

"It ain't your—"

"*Outside*," Annabelle thundered, pointing. Meekly, Shaw and Eddie slunk out of the room in time to hear Annabelle chirping to Heath,

"Now, you take that hammer there 'cause we're going to *pulverize* this chicken back to where it came from."

They escaped the house on a tide of her merry laughter.

5

Eddie's fingers trembled a bit while he lit his cigarette, inhaled, blew out a stream of smoke that was colored a pretty cerulean in the dim light of sunset, and handed it to Shaw. He took a puff, handed it back.

"This is crazy," Eddie said at last.

"You don't know crazy," Shaw muttered.

Eddie puffed. Turned helplessly to Shaw. "What happens next?" he asked.

"Hell if I know."

"You gotta have *some* idea."

"None of this can happen. We can't *tell* anyone. It isn't even sane to *fight*. And where the hell did your sister come from? What the hell does she think is *happening*?"

"We're friends," Eddie said quietly. "She thinks you're helping me take care of the farm. We're friends so we can get over our dads' deaths."

"That's idiotic." Shaw blinked.

"I don't know. Sometimes, I think it's true."

"The friend part or...?"

"Both, I guess."

"Idiotic," Shaw grumbled.

Eddie seemed, to Shaw, numb, faceless in the darkness. His head bowed. His hair was getting shaggy. He needed a haircut. Shaw had been cutting his hair for years. Would that continue? Depression in a black wave settled heavily, thoroughly, over him.

A coyote howled out in the darkness. Not too far away from the house. They were killers. Not much bigger than farm dogs, but a coyote would tear the throat from your sheep, your pigs, or maybe a new calf if the mother wasn't careful. They would eat your cats too. Dad used to shoot them. He had taken no pleasure in it, if Shaw recalled—those few times Shaw had been home to accompany his father on a coyote-hunting expedition.

He remembered one time specifically, long after sundown, nearing bedtime, when his father, eyes shining, had laid a gentle hand on his shoulder and said, "Come on, boy. Hop in the truck, and we'll see about a few things." And, just Dad and just Shaw—who must have been, what, nine or ten at the time?—they had pierced the thick prairie darkness with the sword-lights of the truck, bouncing over the hills of the back country, and Shaw had stuck his head out the window so he could whoop.

Dad never once said, "Don't do that. You'll scare the beasts away." In fact, if Shaw remembered correctly, Dad had howled along with him.

Had they found any coyotes that night? Shaw thought he had seen a slim, yellow-gray form slipping through the darkness, impaled by their headlights, but Dad had said, "Never mind. He's too pretty. Let's see if we can find something uglier." No, Shaw was fairly certain they hadn't killed anything that night, which was fine.

I would have cried, Shaw thought. *I would have bawled my eyes out and ruined everything, a nice jaunt through the darkness, just Dad and just me.*

Did that happen? Did it? Memory plays trick. Some things happen and some don't. Did it? Did it? Is there fucking, fucking, *meaning in anything?*

It howled again. The yard light that rose thirty feet in the air and shone like a sentinel created a wide circle of white light that would have exposed anything creeping through the hills toward the house. Shaw saw nothing.

He had often wondered, if he angled himself just right, if maybe he could see the lights of the Heights from here. But that was impossible. It was tucked so far down among its hills that no one could see it. Only from the road. Only from the turnoff.

We're even further back in the prairie than the homeplace, Shaw thought desolately, taking another drag off Eddie's cigarette. "We aren't *friends*," he said bitterly, spitting out the words and the smoke at the same time.

Eddie stared at him. "Whadda ya mean?"

"I love you."

Eddie dropped his eyes. His entire head. His chin rested against his chest. His breathing sounded wet. Frustration and disgust warred in Shaw's chest and veins and behind his forehead's plate of bone.

"Hey. Hey, *listen*." He dug his fingers into Eddie's shoulder. "I love you."

"No," Eddie whispered, "you don't."

"Shut up. You don't tell me how I feel. Listen. I love you."

"You don't. Not like that you don't. You can't. *We* can't. It ain't natural. It ain't—"

"*I love you.*"

"Stop saying that. It don't mean nothing." Eddie hauled himself off the porch step and stared out into the darkness beyond the yard light. "Christ. I want a beer."

"Me too."

"This can't happen."

"No."

"None of it." Eddie didn't turn. "We can't...We *don't*—" His shoulders surged with an emotion he didn't have the words to express. He glanced over his shoulder at Shaw, pinned him with his eyes, glared at him. "Don't go."

Shaw stood. "I haven't."

"Not yet. Not yet, you ain't." He sucked in air, which gurgled wetly inside him. "But you *will*."

"I'm here, aren't I?"

"*Now* you are."

Shaw took a step. Eddie flinched.

"Who says I'm going anywhere?"

"But you did." Eddie sucked in a breath. "You *did*. You left today. You went with *him*."

"I did."

"And you could do it again—"

"I could." Step.

"And maybe that bothers me." Eddie's hands clenched and became solid, like cinderblocks. "Maybe I don't know why it bothers me. But it does."

"I know why it bothers you." They stood beside each other in the darkness now, at the edge of the circle cast by the yard light's powerful beam.

"We never talk."

"Maybe we should."

"I don't got *words* for this," Eddie said miserably. He pressed his fists to the earth.

"I do."

"Don't say 'em."

"Whatever you want."

"Things can go on the same."

"Possibly."

"Don't you think? Even with Annabelle—I mean, she ain't here for long, I promise, and then...it can be just us again."

"Just the two of us."

Shaw blinked. Eddie's fists had relaxed. The fingers of his right hand had caught Shaw's own and now held them tightly. They left the circle of light, though it lay only inches behind them, and stood in the darkness. Eddie didn't look at Shaw. He aimed his face resolutely at the sky. At the prairie, where the coyote howled again. His brethren joined him.

Shaw remembered howling once with Heath into the big blue sky. Howling like beasts. *We were beasts. Yes, we were.* Long time ago. They were kids. Stupid. They weren't kids anymore.

You can't smash this. It's a life. You made it. It was your idea. You've been selfish and ruthless. Useless too. And weak. You don't like people to think you're weak, but you are. Ask Jeanette. Ask anyone who has ever tried to love you. Even Heath. You can stop being weak right now. See what happens.

Curses, Shaw whispered to himself.

No such thing.

The homeplace.

You don't have to go back. You have a life now. You have a man, and you have your novel, and maybe it can be real. Maybe it can. And you have a house that isn't all shadows and things that creep around at night. That come out of the walls and the shadows in the basement and the attic. A normal house. And Heath left you. Without a word. He did that. He did.

Be strong.

"Be strong," Shaw whispered.

Be useful for once in your miserable, silly life.

He squeezed Eddie's hand.

Eddie turned and seized him. Hugged him tightly. Pressed his face against Shaw's chest. It worked. Scalding wetness through the cashmere. *Let it. Let it. You're strong now. It doesn't matter. Who even knows what cashmere is out here anyway? Let it happen. Let it.*

He lowered his chin against Eddie's shaggy head. Let him sob silently. Let him quake. *Take it. Be strong.*

The door opened behind them.

Eddie leaped out of Shaw's arms and away, as if jolted by electricity.

Heath's shadow rested beside them. God, but he had gotten big. Shoulders so broad, chest, all bigger than Eddie—

No. Strong. You made this life. You did.

Eddie faced the prairie. Shaw turned back to the house.

"Dinner's ready," Heath said softly.

6

I saw him, oh, lots of times after that. When I would go into town and there he would be, milling around with a crowd of people. Barely standing out from them. How were there crowds of people like that in Burke or in Sidney or Miles City? But there he would be. I recognized his hair—same color as the mountain lions I always wanted to find when I was a stupid kid. I recognized the way he walked. He didn't walk like no one else here. I would catch a glimpse of him, and I would almost holler out his name, and then I would remember.

It couldn't *really* be Shaw. It was the Heights. It was the homeplace trying to tempt me. I would get the groceries I had been sent for, and I would ignore him—it, the thing—because I knew it was the same as what I had seen back in California, out there in the fog the night I left Roger for good. Nothing real. Even if other people could see him...*it*.

"Come find me," the Shaw-thing would call out, and I would ignore him because it was for my own good and for *his*.

People were scared of the Heights now. The people in Burke and the other surrounding towns. It had taken too many. It had taken one of the hired men and his girl and one of our own now. A Lyon. It had gotten greedy. The police couldn't find nothing. They weren't any good anyway. And Lee screamed and screamed, and when he wasn't screaming, he was talking nonsense. Or he was drunk.

I didn't drink.

Didn't seem safe.

So, nobody would listen to poor ol' Lee Lyon.

I seen to that.

If he ranted about the things in the walls, I let him rant.

No one would believe him.

Any more'n they would believe me.

But I knew *they* were real.

One night, I seen Catherine Lyon outside my window. She beckoned to me. I ignored her.

"Old witch," I grumbled. "Old bitch." I rolled over, put my pillow over my head, and squeezed my eyes tightly.

She touched me with her bony fingers the next second, and I bit back my scream because I wasn't going to give her the satisfaction.

Her face was a skull with bits of red and black flesh patched all over it. She laughed at me, and she beckoned. I crawled out of my bed and followed her, down the hallway, out the door, down the steps, and onto the road. She did a little dance there in the moonlight. like she was wont to do. I even joined her for a bit.

"Buffalo gals," I sang to her but softly, and she sang it back.

Her breath came wafting over me in a stinking sheet, and I let it because we understood each other now. The house was mine. The land was mine. I had it all.

"You don't either," she told me, doing her jig under the moon, lifting her petticoats and showing me the bare bones of her legs. Bits of her crumbled off, but she didn't stop dancing. Didn't stop grinning at me neither. "You don't have it all," she said, "and you won't until you bring *him* back to this place."

"Won't matter," I told her, sullen-like. "He won't come."

"You gotta make him," she says. Pert, just pert.

"He told me," I said, feeling those old tears I never let fall out of me just well up inside. "He *told* me…He told me he won't never come back here. I'm welcome to come visit him, and…and I can come out there to visit, to the Thrush place if I want. But he won't never come back here no more."

The sly old witch whirled around, waving her arms in the air.

And backhanded me.

Her bones cut my face right over what Roger had given me, the one that had been healing up. Now I knew it would leave a scar.

"Old bitch," I screamed at her, but I had fallen somehow.

She loomed over me, blocked the moon. Blocked the whole world. It was her in that stinking yellow dress, with bits of her flesh falling off and over me, like snow reeking of the grave. I didn't dare to open my mouth. It would get in there, and it would kill me when it did.

"We'll take and take and take," she said, her voice all cold. "We'll take 'til we can't take no more, and then we'll *still* take, you stupid sonofabitch. And you're one of us, so you'll take too. *Bring him back to this house.* Or the land. We're part of the land too. We don't care so much. We ain't particular. Give him to us. He's ours. Give him to us."

"No," I sobbed. "No, no, no." But no tears would come. Just the sobbing, foul wind from my gut.

"Yes."

What have you got to lose?

I had to keep him safe. My Shaw. I had to.

But the Heights was mine. The house, the land, even the ghosts. *Mine*, the way I always said it would be. I could stand on the road and look out at the prairie, and my chest would swell. I would feel so triumphant and big.

Big man. That was me. Big man, big house. With Lee inside, screaming and drinking, and his little girl shitting herself and running around until she didn't no more.

"This is all mine," I said to the land.

The land smiled and whispered back, *Give him to us. You must and you know you must. So do it.*

"No, no, no," I said, though I was tempted. I could drive to the Thrush farm and drag him. And would he fight me? No, I thought, he wouldn't. And put him in the truck, drive back to the homeplace, and carry him up the steps because I was so much bigger than he was. Or we could go hand in hand. I think Shaw would like that. But we would go up the steps and through the door, and we would rule it together, as I had always known was meant to be.

He's ours.

And I would lose him. I wasn't sure how. But that would happen. The house would take him, as it had taken the others.

You'll lose him anyway, you stupid sonofabitch.

Catherine Lyon. Laughing at me.

Your love is the curse, and through the curse, and only *the curse, will you be allowed to be together. Isn't that what you want?*

"Shut up, shut up, shut up."

Isn't it?

"Shut up!"

I stood out on the prairie the night before I decided.

"Shaw!" I screamed. Oh God. It hurt. Everything hurt. It built inside of me, a million hot galaxies, billions of suns and stars, all fire, fire, fire. Burning. I opened my mouth to let the fire out. "Shaw!" I screamed. "Let the fire take the prairie, the grass and the hills. Let it evaporate the creek and turn the frogs and turtles to instant ash. Let it all go. Shaw! Shaw! *Shaw!*

But.

But.

But he didn't come. This time, he didn't come home to me.

The next day, I visited the Thrush farm.

And asked Annabelle Thrush to marry me.

Six

Summer 1964

1

The darkness parted like veils before the vicious headlights of Heath's truck. All gauzy, purplish, dark blue. The lights cast crazy patterns on the gravel road while the truck bumped over the scoria and the rocks at a pace far too fast to be considered safe. But he had to race. It might even now be too late, but he couldn't give up. He *wouldn't*.

Annabelle had wanted to come. He had told her no. She had pouted, as she enjoyed pouting, then walloped him with the back of her hand. He had stared at her icily. At last, she had dropped her gaze.

"You treat me like a pig," she had said at last. Her eyes had welled with tears, which was unusual. Annabelle didn't normally cry. "You treat me like dirt. Like scum on the creek. You brung me out here and tied me to this place and turned me into pig slop."

Behind them, the sounds of scratching in the walls grew louder, then subsided. They both listened. Neither would admit to the other that they heard the little treble of giggles rise, almost out of earshot, but not quite, not *quite*. A child's laughter, surely. They pretended not to hear it, which was the pattern their lives had taken the last six years.

Annabelle's face had alternated between pale and puffy, like the Rice Krispies she so much enjoyed in the morning, sweetened with a spoon heavy with a sugar mound or three, and so thin that the skin stretched taut, like a cheese-white drum over her bones. Only her eyes remained the same: dark, ringed with circles. Her eyebrows had begun to fall out. So had her eyelashes. Her hair remained thick, lustrous, and a shining white-blond. She dyed it now. Heath loved her hair most. Everything else about her he found easy to ignore.

On this particular evening, her face was bloated, her eyes nearly lost inside the white swells of her cheeks.

"You made me this way!" she had shrieked once, hitting him with her hard little fists until he had roared and swept her away with the back of his arm. Annabelle danced out of his grip before he could strike her. "You won't touch me, you won't kiss me, you never love on me, and so I turned into *this*. It's because of you, you fink. All because of *you*!"

Tonight, her eyes had grown small and, yes, piggish.

After she had swatted him, she said, "Look, I care about him too."

But Heath was already pulling his boots back on and didn't look up to face her.

"I do!" she protested when he grabbed the truck keys and a flashlight.

There was no moon out. It was a hot night for July and still. Prairie fires from late June lightning strikes plagued all their neighbors, but not the Lyons. Not the Heights. No, the Heights was quite safe from fire. Safest place in the whole state, Heath figured. From fire, anyway.

Annabelle followed him to the door. "Let me go, let me go," she cried. "You don't know what happened, not *really*, and anyway, Eddie didn't say, did he? You shoulda let me talk to him. You shoulda let me—"

"Shut up," Heath growled. He didn't have time for this.

The last six years had been what he figured to be a necessary kind of hell. His wedding to Annabelle had been quick and to the point: the two of them and the justice of the peace over to Wolf Point. An old woman—an auntie, Heath figured—whom he thought he recognized from the Before Times—that is, the time before Earnest Lyon had spirited him back to the Heights, given him the name of his dead child, and stolen away forever his *true* name, and God help him, Heath knew he would never find *that* ever again—had goggled at him while he and Annabelle slid like shades from the pickup truck and forced themselves to walk all prim and proper up the steps of the Roosevelt County Courthouse.

Goggled, the old auntie did, squealed with laughter, pointed her fingers at him, and shook with the strength of her mirth. Heath had shot her a glare intended to silence her. Instead, she only laughed even more until she sank to the ground, where she held herself and rocked back and forth.

Old witch. What did she know? Heath and Annabelle would build a home at the Heights. He could share it with her. They would have children. Of course, they would have children. And Shaw would see. He would see what his choices had wrought.

"He'll see what he's forced me to do," Heath had growled from between gritted teeth the night he had called out into the empty prairie and no one had answered back.

So, they had been married. Annabelle hadn't the time to find a dress, but she didn't want one anyway, she claimed. She wore instead a pretty blue dress with green leaves all over that her mother had left to her. Annabelle had been living in Billings the last ten years or so, working as a secretary in a law firm.

Well, she was so tired of *that* nonsense, she said. She had jumped at any chance to get out. And Heath was handsome. Sullen and brooding, but handsome. That thick black hair! Like ink, but soft to the touch! And those eyes! Chips of coal, but soft and tender when he wanted them to be. The sonofabitch. The bastard.

So maybe she had fallen for him. Maybe she had ignored the things her brother said, the things she saw before her eyes—how Heath looked at Shaw and only Shaw, and how Shaw looked back. How Shaw and her brother were obviously lovers, whatever that meant. She didn't claim to understand, but then again, she didn't understand much about love herself when it came down to the mechanics or even her own experiences, which were nearly nothing—a single kiss goodnight from a Lambert football player back in high school, one night of heavy petting in the back seat of an Oldsmobile with some drunk she had met at a bar in downtown Billings. But it had never gone any further than that.

So, Shaw and Eddie were together—somehow—lived in the house where she had grown up, and shared the room that had belonged to her parents. *Oh* how that galled her, but she didn't dare to say anything. Shaw was terrifying in his own right. Feminine somehow but also sleek and ferocious when he wanted to be. He could tear you to pieces with his tongue and follow with his fists. She steered clear of him.

When Heath had asked her to marry him, to leave the Thrush farm and Billings and come live with him at the Heights, she hadn't even considered it. She had simply acted.

"Yes," she said. "Oh yes. Now."

He didn't have a ring. He didn't have *anything*. Heath had said he would buy her one; he never had. He said he would buy her whatever she wanted; sometimes that proved true. She should have known, she supposed, when they had driven the forty miles to Wolf Point, laughing and giggling like schoolgirls the whole way...She should have *known* he wouldn't love her the way she wanted to be loved. That is, at all. That is, to be acknowledged. That is, to feel him inside her.

She wanted to know him, and at first, after the justice of the peace pronounced them man and wife—Heath claimed to have no surname, so, bewildered, she remained Annabelle Thrush, as she had always been—they had driven back to the Heights, giggling again. So strange to hear that stream of little giggles. Girlish, really, coming out of that brawny, masculine man. They had driven back to the Heights and walked together, hand in hand, up the steps, through the front door, and into the shadows.

Heath had done much to clean up after Lee and his strange little daughter, but the house still felt as if it pressed on her. As if there were eyes watching. People inside the walls. She wondered often if there weren't. Hand in hand, they had gone up the steps, through the door, down the hall, and into the kitchen, where she insisted on making them steaks and French fried potatoes with a hint of garlic, minced onion, and a *pinch* of chili powder. After dinner, they had watched each other, suddenly awkward. Suddenly, the conversation dried up.

Annabelle had said, at last, "I suppose it's time, isn't it?"

Heath had placed both hands on the table and hauled himself up. "It is," he had said.

Hand in hand, they retired to his bedroom, which had, once, belonged to Earnest Lyon—the biggest bedroom in the Heights.

There the bed, neatly made, pillows cased in light blue and a quilt, Heath told her, put together by his Aunt Lucy before she had left the Heights to live at the Linden farm. It was blue and green and lovely, like the dress Annabelle wore, that she determinedly unbuttoned and stepped out of. Annabelle removed her bra and panties and stood before him, naked and breathing in deep gulps, but calm inside, ice inside, fire, ice again. She didn't drop her gaze.

He held hers back steadily, steadily. Unbuttoned his shirt. Removed it. His chest barely moved. Heath dropped the shirt on the bed. His eyes never left hers. She wanted to say something, but she didn't have the first clue what. Annabella traced circles around her nipples until they stood out, hard and purple in the chancy light of the bedroom—*their* bedroom now.

Heath took a step toward her. He was curious, she thought. He took one of her breasts lightly, gently, in his right hand. She moaned a little.

"No, don't stop," she had whispered. "Please. Don't be afraid of me."

He said nothing. Heath came to her. They stood, chest to chest. She kissed him. Cautiously, tenderly, he kissed her back. She slid her hand down the front of his jeans. What she found there sprang to life at her touch. *Good, good.* The kiss became heated. *Actual passion? Could it be possible?*

Heath stepped out of the jeans, kicked them aside. Barely broke the kiss to do it. It was early November. He had been back only a few weeks, but the house was cold. Heath told her he planned to replace the furnace soon. It had broken God knows when, and Lee had allowed it to remain broken. Outside, snow fell in streaks like white comets, slapping wetly against the glass of their bedroom window.

Heath and Annabelle lay together on the bed but gingerly, as if they both assumed the other was composed entirely of glass. Kissing, kissing. Heath was silent, but Annabelle made sounds. She purred. She groaned. His hands, so gentle, moved between her legs. Annabelle arched her back. She spread her legs to grant him access.

Good, yes, like that. Please, like that. Don't, don't stop. Never stop. She guided him inside her. *Now* he made sounds. Now he growled like a wolf. A great, dark wolf moving on top of her. *Oh, that hurt. Oh, that* hurt. She tried to tell him about the pain—searing, Jesus *Christ*, so big inside her—but she didn't think he understood. *It hurts, God. Please, help. Stop, it hurts. It* hurts—

Heath had understood. He moved off her and away. His face was flushed and miserable and confused. "Sorry," he mumbled. "Sorry, sorry." He tried to cover himself. His erection wilted, and his penis tried to turtle, the head to withdraw inside his foreskin.

She would have laughed if she hadn't thought it might scare him away even further. *And I'm the one who got stabbed in the puss,* she thought wryly. *Big strong men indeed.*

"No," she had said. "Come back, please. I...It's just...I haven't—"

"No," he replied. "No, me either."

"Oh."

"I didn't...didn't mean to—"

"No. Oh no, of course not."

They watched each other.

Heath dropped to the floor. It took her a moment to realize he was fumbling for his pants. "Oh no," she said again. "Please, you don't have to—"

"Sorry," he mumbled. "Sorry, sorry."

"Heath, please, come on—"

"I never...I shoulda realized...I shoulda *thought*—"

Annabelle slid from the bed and stood beside him. A trickle of blood snaked down her leg. She gritted her teeth, frowned at it, and turned away, praying he hadn't seen it.

"I'm okay," she said, using her best soothing tone, one she wasn't entirely well-versed in using. Annabelle had never felt especially maternal in her life. To be honest, she had never truly planned on having children. At this rate, she would never have any. "Heath, Heath, Heath," she sang, touching his damp hair, which was attempting to turn into curls. "Heath, Heath, it's okay. I'm okay. We're okay. We are, I promise. I swear, we're okay."

"Sorry," he muttered, unable to meet her eye. "So sorry."

"Come to bed," she whispered. "Please. It's our wedding night."

Heath had stared at her, his eyes wide and unblinking.

She touched his face lightly.

At last, he nodded.

This time, she gritted her teeth against the pain. But she said nothing. It was what her momma had said to do. Though, since all this time had passed, Annabelle had never really thought she would *do it*, what all her girlfriends had whispered and giggled about. *It*. She had never thought she would be one of them.

Annabelle wasn't prudish or priggish. She was scared, that was all. Annabelle had taken all those secretarial courses so she could have a job and an apartment in the city and support herself. She thought it entirely possible she would turn into a dried fig—an old maid, they were called, like her mother's sister, Loretta, who lived by herself somewhere in Virginia, all alone, all alone. A maiden lady. Annabelle hadn't ever really wanted to be a maiden lady.

And now, it seemed, she wouldn't ever be. Not ever again.

Bear the pain. That's what Momma had said. Put up with it. Put up with *them*. Men. Animals. They could be sweet and tender and love on you one second and turn cold and hard-handed and dirty, filthy, *foul* the next. Pressing at you. Pushing at you. It was okay to enjoy it, but they didn't expect you to. They might even be offended if you did. And Annabelle didn't think she could understand a man who wouldn't let her have her own pleasures. Apparently, they did. The bastards.

What did Heath want from her? What did he expect?

He couldn't tell her, or he wouldn't.

After that first time, they didn't again. Not for...not for a long, long time.

Even when she wanted to. Even when she tried to kiss him. He went to bed before she did or long after. Heath stayed up, pacing around the house. She heard him, heard his footsteps upstairs, going up and down, up and down, the door slamming. Annabelle heard the scratching in the walls, though she knew that was rats or mice, even though she put out traps and never caught anything. Even though she insisted on having a cat in the house—a great orange monster she named Jeremiah.

What crawled about inside their walls? Drove Jeremiah crazy. He could never find whatever it was. Annabelle was afraid to ask. Heath never mentioned it. But when they shared a bed, they usually slept in it. And he was up before dawn every morning, late autumn and winters, to feed the cows, and, spring and summer, to nurse the calves that needed nursing, to save them from spring snowstorms, from coyotes, to swath the wheat, bale it up, lift the bales, and stack them. The hired men, a gradual succession, they helped, of course, but Heath was in charge. The Heights belonged to Heath—the houses and the land—and he took his responsibility with the utmost seriousness.

He didn't apply the same care and consideration to his wife. To their marriage. Heath hardly ever looked at her. He certainly never *spoke* to her.

She couldn't go back to the Thrush farm. Annabelle couldn't bear to see her brother. To see Shaw. That first night, she began to accept the possibility that Heath was in love with Shaw. In love with her brother's lover. Oh, it made her head spin. Oh, it made her *ache*. Heartache was a real and terrifying condition, she had discovered.

I want a child, she decided a year or so after she had moved to the Heights. A year of nightmares, of feeling watched. Of running without thinking some nights, some mornings, before dawn, out into the hills behind the house, allowing the prairie to swallow her, and screaming out her anguish, words without sense that weren't words at all but only animal sounds. Her anguish. Her rage. Her face and body changed, seemingly, from month to month. Bloated and heavy one day and painfully thin and dry the next. She never knew which. Annabelle was lonely.

A child, she decided. Yes, yes, a *baby*. That was what the Heights needed. What *she* needed. Companionship. After that first year, there was no one in the house but them.

Lee: dead. Hanged himself in the red granary down the hill from the house one cold night in October, nearly a year after Annabelle had moved in. She had been the one to find him.

Abatha: disappeared. The house had taken her, Heath insisted, but he wouldn't explain what he meant by that or where she could possibly have gone. One morning, she just...wasn't there anymore.

Which, frankly, was a bit of a relief. The child didn't *grow*, and she wasn't right in the *head*. Whatever *that* meant around these parts. Annabelle felt like a great many of the farmers and the people in the surrounding towns weren't exactly as sane as she felt she deserved them to be. And Abatha had a disconcerting habit of putting any rotten thing she could lay her especially tiny hands on right into her mouth. Lee did nothing to stop her. Annabelle suspected Abatha knew more than she let on, or she saw things no one else did. Or could. Or wanted to.

It wasn't as if the Heights were *haunted*, exactly, Annabelle tried to explain to one of her girlfriends back in Billings, but when pressed, she found she was unable to express exactly what else this feeling—*feelings*, plural—could possibly be. Eyes watching. Sounds in the walls. The feeling that, if she sat up in bed in the middle of the night and looked out the window, someone—some*thing*—would be gazing back at her.

One morning, after a light dusting of snow had fallen, Annabelle opened the front door and found tracks on the front porch. They weren't human, not exactly, but they weren't an animal's either. Something with five clawed toes. Canine or maybe feline but big. Too big. And disturbingly...disturbingly *human*. She had brushed them away with her bare foot and put it out of her mind. Hadn't even mentioned it to Heath. What could he possibly say?

And then Abatha disappeared, and they never saw her again.

Well...that wasn't exactly true either, was it?

Annabelle was the last person to see her—before the child's disappearance, that is—but she never told anyone. Not Heath, not her brother. Certainly not Lee, who spent all day drinking steadily from an old brown bottle he claimed to have discovered in the basement.

"Belonged to my grandad," he told her, grinning with brown teeth. "And it ain't no business of yours, bitch."

After that, she left him alone.

Annabelle awoke one night to find her bed empty. That wasn't so unusual. Heath prowled about the house by night or took off in his truck and rammed the back roads. He never came home with evidence that he had been with anyone else, and for that, at least, she was grateful. What *was* unusual, she found, drawing in a breath to scream, was the little bald ghoul's face pressed up against her own. Grinning with pale pink gums. Her eyes glowing yellow with their own inner radiance.

Annabelle was frozen, flattening herself against the bed. The vile little creature spewed her foul breath over Annabelle's face, which poured in through her own open mouth, coating her teeth, her tongue, down her throat. A steady stream of giggles came from the little girl's mouth, mingled with unintelligible gabble that almost sounded like words.

With a disgusted cry of rage, Annabelle shoved the child as hard as she could. The girl flew backward, but she seemed to ride the air as she went and twisted, landing on her hands and feet like a cat. Her eyes glowed yellow, golden, like hot coins.

"Daddy deady drog doog dog," she snarled. "Coming, coming. Chasing racing pacing me. Can't catch the Gingerbread *Man*." Abatha spat something into her hand and flung it at Annabelle.

It struck her wetly between her breasts, and she recoiled, shrieking with rage, disgust, and fear. A mouse, dead and wet, the little girl had been gumming, all the while whispering and laughing only inches from Annabelle's face. Annabelle flung the horrible thing away with another shriek, much to Abatha's amusement.

"Catch catch can!" she yowled. "Find me finish! Can't catch me. I'm the Gingerbread Man."

"Get out of my room," Annabelle hissed.

"Catch me. They'll catch me," Abatha whined. "Catch catch and *kill*."

Annabelle heaved herself from the bed. Seized the little wretch by her arm. Oh, Jesus, Mary, and Joseph, she was *naked*. Her little body was streaked with filth. How had Annabelle lived in this house with these monstrous, degraded beings, this father and daughter? How did Heath allow it?

Because he enjoys it, Annabelle thought grimly, dragging the squalling creature across the room and toward the door. He wants to lord it over Lee, that he runs the roost, that this house is *his*. Not even ours. Just *his*. His castle. His kingdom.

She froze before the door. Abatha twisted and squealed in her grip.

It was closed.

It was locked.

From the *inside*.

"How—" Annabelle said. Her mouth snapped shut.

Abatha giggled wickedly, twisting, squirming.

"Hide hide hell," she pronounced. "Heave hell hit. Halve. I have to run, Gingerbread Man. I have to hide."

"Get out of here," Annabelle whispered.

"Catch kill keep," Abatha said cheerfully, then threw her head back and screamed. Her shrieks were piercing knives in Annabelle's ears, the center of her skull. "Help, help, help!" screamed the child. "Help hell hell hello help hello hell! Hell! *Hell*!"

"Sorry, sis," Annabelle hissed under her breath. She unlocked the door, threw it open, and with one fluid motion, hurled Abatha from the room and into the hallway without.

"No!" screamed the child. "Kill keep kill hell hello! Gingerbread me! *Gingerbread me!*"

"I don't know what that means," Annabelle said coolly, closing the door in the creature's face.

Abatha howled for a minute or two. Abruptly, the howls were cut off.

Silence.

The entire house pressed down around her.

Annabelle drew a breath.

Opened the door.

The hallway stood empty.

"Abatha?" Annabelle whispered. "You there?"

Nothing.

No moon. No light at all. Overhead, a floorboard creaked. And again.

"Abatha, come out now," Annabelle whispered. "I'm sorry. You... you scared me, that's all."

Nothing. Not even the board creaking.

Outside, an animal—large, by the sound of it—began to bay. Someone's dog? No one lived at the old Reardon farm. Maybe they'd had a dog that had run wild and bred...?

Sweat trickled down her forehead and the small of her back.

"Heath," she said in a calm, steady voice. "Heath, come here."

No answer.

Annabelle didn't want to leave the safety of her bedroom. But was it really safe? Abatha had entered somehow. *How?*

"I don't like this place," Annabelle whispered and tittered at the little-girl sound of her voice. She stopped tittering because she sounded crazy.

Annabelle wiped the sweat away from her forehead. A cool breeze blew down the hallway, strong enough that it stirred her hair. *What was happening?* A smell enveloped her, and she drew back, gagging.

Rot. Decomposition.

Arms wrapped around her. She struggled against them and fell backward, back into her bedroom. The arms were stronger than she was. The stench of death invaded her nostrils and her mouth. She clamped her lips shut and shook her head frantically back and forth. *No, no, no, no.*

With a wild yell, she burst free from the arms that held her and backed against the wall nearest the window. Laughter filled the air. It chimed, sweet and high and evil, lisping and ringing out wildly. Annabelle tried to scream, but that sickly sweet death-smell forced its way inside her again. She sank to her knees and crawled along the bare floorboards of the room she never truly shared with her husband.

Eddie. She would call Eddie. He would come and take her away from this place. *No, no. Can't call Eddie.* He had told her she had made her bed when she married Heath and that he would never come to this place again. Fine. She would crawl if she had to, down the hall, out the door, into the sticky night air. It was hot for early October, but she would take advantage of that. She would run in her nightdress if it came to that. Eddie would take her in. Eddie and—

No. Not him. Not Shaw Lyon. No, no. I refuse.

The laughter stopped.

Her head throbbed. She lowered it and moaned.

"I heard it," she whispered. "I did."

Heat pressed down all around her. Sweat poured down her back. Her thighs clung together. She rose, tottering, to her feet and fell onto the bed. Annabelle clutched handfuls of the quilt and thrashed while the heat grew more oppressive.

I'm on fire, she tried to say. *I'm burning* up, she tried to scream, but the air held nothing but wetness, and it filled her. Revolting. *Why didn't I help her?* she thought dimly. *Why did I let her go? This is all my fault. All, all, all my—*

It was over. As suddenly as it had begun.

Annabelle lay where she had fallen in the center of the bed, panting. Gradually, gradually, she released her hold on the quilt and sat up.

Silence. Deathly quiet. The house felt empty.

Where was Lee? Where was Heath?

I am alone. Alone with the dead.

Her teeth chattered. She covered her mouth to stop the sound. It didn't help.

Oh, Eddie. I'm so sorry. I'll come back to you. I'll pretend everything is normal. I'll even try to like...to like him, *if that's what you want, but please, please—*

A shadow fell over her.

She sat up, clutching the quilt so it covered her.

Heath stared at her. His face was stone. Empty eyes, like blank skies.

"It's late," he said.

"Abatha," she replied. "Abatha was here."

He frowned. Looked around. "She ain't here now."

"No. She...I...I made her leave."

"Good. She don't belong in here."

She doesn't belong anywhere now.

An impossible voice. Annabelle didn't even bother to look around. She knew she wouldn't see anyone anyway, and if she did—

Best not to think about that.

Heath had disrobed, stripped to his boxer shorts. He had taken to wearing them not too long after their wedding night. Before, he hadn't worn anything under his jeans. Now he wore these...these *things*, shapeless, revealing nothing.

He's hiding from me, she thought and felt a stab of sorrow intertwined with dark, venomous bitterness.

"I'm tired," he said. He slid into bed without looking at her. "G'night."

What about the mouse? Oh Jesus. The dead mouse Abatha had held in her mouth.

Annabelle scrambled out of bed.

"Jesus," Heath groaned.

She searched frantically, but it was gone. Annabelle thought she heard that wicked, wild laughter again, distantly, but Heath didn't move or react.

Well, I must be crazy now, sure. There was no mouse. Probably, there had been no Abatha. She giggled again. Clapped a hand over her mouth. No. She wouldn't give Heath the satisfaction of acting crazy. Or even *being* crazy. She would be strong. She would endure. Live in this house, haunted or not, live with this man, haunted or not. Nothing was real. Everything was real. There had been no Abatha, no mouse. Annabelle had been alone. No strange wind or wild laughter or dreadful stink. Only her husband. Only him. She wanted to laugh again.

No, no.

Annabelle slid back beneath the covers. Heath grumbled something and rolled over.

She lay flat on her back and stared at the ceiling. After a time, she smiled.

In the morning, Abatha was gone.

They searched, but, tell the truth and shame the devil, not terribly hard.

Annabelle saw her once after that. At the base of the stairs that led to the attic. Crouched there, grinning at her with a full set of teeth. Adult teeth, too big in her little girl mouth. Annabelle had been passing by that open door a few weeks after the little girl's disappearance, after she had found Lee's body swinging from a beam in the granary, and there Abatha had been, hunkering down there. Eyes blazing yellow. Grinning and rocking back and forth with that mouth full of terrible teeth, trying hard to contain her laughter.

"Abatha—" Annabelle had said, but no one was there.

I don't believe in ghosts.

But she believed in the things in the walls. The things that skittered and scampered. That clawed behind the plaster. She believed in them because everyone heard them. Polly King, visiting for coffee and a spice cake Heath had whipped up on a whim, heard the sounds and commented. Annabelle had said it must be mice, and Polly replied they'd better get it taken care of. Didn't sound like any mice *she'd* ever heard. Maybe rats. But it didn't even sound much like rats, did it? Annabelle said she didn't know.

The wall people.

Sometimes, she thought she heard voices. Conversations. Muffled, as if there were a whole crowd only inches away behind the paper and the paint. She came to think of them as the wall people: the things that occupied the spaces in the house she and Heath couldn't see.

And Abatha was one of them now.

"I want to go," Annabelle snarled now. "Please. Let me help you."

"No," Heath said shortly. He was already behind the wheel of the pickup. The heat of the July night fondled him, attempted to seduce him. He wouldn't think about the heat. Just the drive ahead.

The longest he had ever taken.

Annabelle screamed after him while he drove away, faster than was safe, surely, up the road leading to 201. She watched his taillights glowing at her like devil's eyes. He turned left and sped away, and she didn't see him anymore. But she heard him. The furious roar of his engine lingered on the sullen night air.

A hand enclosed her wrist. Annabelle tried not to scream. She failed.

"Sorry, sorry," the old woman said.

Jesus Christ. Birdie. The old lady in the homesteader shack on the hill above them. Annabelle had forgotten about her. It was easy to do. The old lady rarely came down, and it was Heath who did her shopping for her when she didn't feel able. Otherwise, she would take her little '45 Chevrolet into town for her groceries.

"Didn't mean to scare you," Birdie Lyon said now. "He's in an awful hurry."

"There's been an accident," Annabelle replied shortly.

"That so? Seems like there's always an accident out here, one way or another."

Annabelle dropped her gaze. She stared furiously at the grass beneath her bare feet.

"You come on up," Birdie said decisively. She still held Annabelle's arm in her surprisingly strong grip. "I can't sleep these hot nights. Or most nights, if I'm honest." She chuckled softly. "I got some coffee on. You have a cup."

Annabelle lifted her head. She still heard Heath's truck chewing up the road, speeding away from her. Toward Shaw. It had always been about Shaw, hadn't it? As if these last six years hadn't happened. Hadn't mattered at all.

She was surprised that the bitterness could still flower inside her chest. And the sadness. And the despair.

"Sure," she said, turning to smile at the old woman she had seen only a handful of times since she had moved to the Heights. "Sounds real nice."

"Birdie."

"Birdie," Annabelle said.

Arm in arm, the two women began the trek up the hill, Birdie leaning on Annabelle for support and Annabelle gladly supporting her.

In the distance, the sound of the engine stopped.

2

For Shaw Lyon, the six years had passed as they had for his brother: in a haze of wine—for Shaw preferred wine, the darker the better, while Lee found Lethe in the brown whiskey his friend Lester Pretty Weasel sold him for cheap. It gradually became a shroud, and he knitted it up around himself defiantly. He wasn't always drunk, but he told Eddie he did his best writing after a glass of wine. One to start the day, another with lunch, two more with dinner, another for the day's final writing session, and perhaps a glass of sherry before bed. No one in the country drank sherry. Shaw prided himself on his good taste.

Eddie left him to his own devices. He had developed an ache in his gut he never spoke of and Shaw never noticed. Claimed to never notice. Shaw worked on his book, which seemed endless. The pages stacked up and grew taller beside his typewriter in that little writing room of his, ream after ream of paper, which Eddie fetched dutifully from the general store in Burke. He told no one about his gut, and he saw no doctor.

Eddie loved Shaw ferociously. He could say it now as he approached sixty. Since he thought, *Death is coming. Death will be here soon. Why not say it?* No one bothered them. The whole of the country thought they really were cousins after all, and if anyone suspected otherwise, they were corrected. Or no one talked about it.

And there were no ghosts at the Thrush farm.

Just Shaw and just Eddie.

Eddie never saw his sister. Talked to her on the phone once a month, on her birthday, and on holidays. They wanted to have a baby, she told him, Heath's idea. Eddie had said, "That sounds nice," which pissed her off royally, but they never talked about anything real anyway, so what did it matter?

When Lee killed himself, they had all attended the funeral. No one seemed to know or care about Abatha's disappearance. Had she even been real? Eddie had never met her. Shaw rarely mentioned her.

But they slept together in Eddie's old bed, tightly pressed together and each basking in the other's warmth, and Eddie would say, "I love you, babe," and Shaw would reply, "I love you too," and Eddie would be satisfied.

But Shaw liked the drink.

It was only lately he had begun driving too.

Shaw grew obsessed with the backroads. "I want to see where they go" was all he would say. Sometimes, Eddie accompanied him, and they would drive for miles down those unpaved highways until they ended or met another. They would find an abandoned homesteader property and they would stop to wander around, sometimes entering the house, sometimes poking around outside.

Once, they had found the cemetery. "Grandview" proclaimed its wrought-iron gate. Of course, Eddie knew about it, but Shaw said he had never been. Which was funny, really, because his great-grandmother Catherine and her husband were buried there, miles from nowhere with only the wind for company, the grass, and the giant jackrabbits, which held dominion over the prairie.

Shaw had ordered Lee cremated and his ashes scattered in Redwater. He placed a stone next to their father's and mother's graves at the cemetery in Burke. Earnest Lyon had been clear with his wishes: His wife would not lie in Grandview, and neither would he. Neither would his children. The first Heathcliff Lyon's stone had been erected next to that of his mother, whom he had ungraciously killed on his way into the world.

"I want us to be buried here," Shaw proclaimed after he had parked the truck.

Eddie followed him into the little plot, which was maybe a hundred feet by a hundred feet, if not smaller. Homesteaders lay there, mostly. "1886," read one stone, "1905" another.

"Us?" Eddie asked, smiling slightly.

"Yeah, yeah. It's peaceful out here, don't you think? Real peaceful. And nice. It smells good." He had inhaled. "Sweetgrass. God, I love it."

"It's nice."

"Sure, it is! It's beautiful. God, the sky is so *big*. People don't realize that. No one in Boston did, for sure. They don't understand how the sky swallows all of us out here."

"Or the prairie."

Shaw considered this. "That too. It surely does, doesn't it?" He threw his arms into the air. "Take me!" he cried. He closed his eyes. Lifted his chin. Stood on his tip-toes. "Take me, take me! I'm yours!"

"Thought you were mine," Eddie said quietly and lit a smoke.

Shaw snatched it away from him and ground it out beneath his heel. "Not here," he snarled. "Christ. Show some respect."

"Sorry," Eddie said mildly. He was mild most times these days.

Shaw smiled at him beneficently. Kissed him. Eddie kissed him back. Shaw put his head on Eddie's chest.

"Put me here," he whispered. "I think I'll be lost otherwise."

"Whatever you want, babe."

"Both of us. Here forever. Just us."

"What about...*them*?" He smiled.

"They don't matter," Shaw scoffed. "No one else matters."

Eddie didn't want to speak Heath's name. He never wanted to say Heath's name again.

The Grandview discovery took place a year or so ago. Shaw's drinking intensified. Eddie let it happen. He couldn't fight it. He couldn't fight Shaw. Eddie had never been able to do that.

Tonight, he let him go. Off in his car, drunk as a lord, as Eddie's mama used to say. After the sun set at about nine-thirty. The hottest day of the summer so far. Shaw had insisted on more fans in the house in a mostly futile attempt to offer some respite. A bit of coolness. Eddie had acquiesced.

They weren't poor. Shaw had his daddy's money to live on, after all. But Eddie wanted to provide. He couldn't work as much anymore, was the problem. His gut ached all the time—a constant evil song he couldn't stop his body from singing.

So, he bought Shaw the fans, and he bought Shaw the wine, and he let him go out in his fancy, fancy car.

And he knew—he *knew*—the moment Shaw rolled that vast expanse of car off 201 and into a ditch.

Eddie felt it: the moment Shaw flew through the windshield and out into the humid night alive with the sound of summer insects, broken glass twinkling all around him like a galaxy of stars.

In his panic, Eddie had called Heath at the Heights, something he could never have foreseen himself doing. The pain in his gut nearly crippled him that day. He had tried to find Shaw himself, but he couldn't even leave the house. Eddie sank to his knees and cried, then crawled, crying still, to the phone. He prayed that Heath believed him.

Eddie didn't understand premonitions. He wasn't anyone they would ever call "psychic." Except that he had twinges from time to time. Feelings. Annabelle had them too. It was one of the reasons he worried about her all alone with Heath in that big, empty house.

But Heath already knew. "Where is he?" was the first thing he said when he answered the phone. Not, "H'lo," not, "Who is this?" Only, "Where is he?" followed by, "How long ago did he leave?"

Because we're connected, Eddie thought miserably. *We aren't like other people, and it's horrible. It's hell. But here we are. Strangers to the rest.*

I don't care about the others. I don't care about the people in town. Only Shaw.

"Save him," Eddie had said into the phone's dark green receiver, through teeth gritted with pain. "Go now. Save him. Please."

But Heath had already hung up.

Flying through the darkness. Pressing, sucking darkness. Wet with heat. Inside him, an animal ran around in his chest, with clawing, clinging toes.

I will not panic, Heath thought. *Everything is fine. It's just fine.*

He knew it wasn't.

Heath had seen Shaw go through the windshield just as Eddie Thrush had seen it: clear, crystalline in his vision. The glass filling the air, Shaw filling the air, the blood—

Find him. Now.

It was too late to take back the last six years. Goddamn it, why did he have to learn that lesson *now*?

It's all fine.

Dust in the road. An entire cloud blinding him, throwing his headlights back at him.

Heath slowed.

His heart pounded gallon after gallon of blood. It shrieked in his veins. The horrible rodent in his chest gnawed triumphantly.

The lights of Shaw's Chrysler continued to beam steadily into the night, despite the fact the car lay upside down in the ditch, its tires lifted to the heavens like the sad black feet of a murdered animal. The taillights glared red and sinister. The dust, still weaving through the heavy air, created strange, sinuous patterns, almost like people standing there and watching, here and then gone.

Heath leaped out of the truck, whispering, "No, no, no," under his breath.

The car was empty. He had known it would be. Smashed and snarled and the windshield empty of glass.

A sound.

A moan. Words? A name?

"Heath."

There he was. Thrown against the side of a hill in a tangle of broken limbs.

His face was streaked with blood.

Tears had cut the crimson.

His eyes were half-lidded and fluttering.

"You came," Shaw croaked. "My baby. My man."

"No, no, no," Heath said. He had to act despite the biting panic. Could he move him? He didn't dare to move him.

"You came for me. I knew you would."

"God, God—"

"No. Heath. My baby Heath. Why do you hate me?"

"I don't, Shaw. Please, I never did—"

"You deserve this," Shaw said wonderingly. His eyes were wide now. Empty. One of them had been cut down the center by a piece of window glass. "But so do I."

"No—"

"I've done wrong. So much wrong—"

"Shaw—"

"I'm dying for it."

"No!" Heath didn't care. He scooped him up.

Shaw moaned. His limbs were broken. His back was broken. Did he feel pain? It didn't matter.

The Heights. Take him to the homeplace. Get him in the house. Do it now.

Heath set him tenderly, so tenderly, into the passenger seat of the car. Shaw's head lolled. His skull was crushed on one side. Blood leaked out of a crack in his head and fouled that beautiful, delicate hair.

No, no, no. It wasn't too late. It couldn't be too late. It didn't dare to be.

"Forgive me," Shaw whispered, but Heath was already driving, squealing tires, sending up a spume of dust.

He flipped around and headed back down 201 toward the road that led to the Heights.

The drive to the homeplace was like passing through a woodcut engraving of hell. The faces of fiends and demons hung in the dust at his side, capered in the road, and vanished when Heath blew through them. Horned faces and lizard's faces, the faces of monsters with no names, animal-headed creatures, flames of emerald and azure flaring up around him. And as he approached the turn off 201 to the Heights, the specter of Catherine Lyon waited, ancient, hag-faced, snarling, drooling, and gesturing with long, bony fingers.

"I forgive you too, baby," Heath muttered, turning onto the road as Catherine Lyon faded away. "I'm dead. I'm dead without you. I'm a dead man. You'll murder me if you die, and I love you. I love my murderer, but not yours. How could I love yours?"

Shaw stirred on the seat. He groaned. His eyes fluttered, then opened wide. "No!" he shrieked. "Don't take me here! Not back here! No! No!"

"Be quiet!" Heath roared, but his words were meaningless.

"I don't want to die here! *Not here! No! No! Please!*"

Heath pulled up before the gate and the path to the front door, which gaped like an idiot's mouth. He left the truck running. Heath leaped from the door, flung open the passenger side, and seized Shaw, who screeched and kicked and frothed bloodily at the mouth.

From the hill above, the voices of two women floated down, but Heath ignored them.

"Please," Shaw sobbed, twisting in his arms, "for the love of God—"

Up the path.

Shaw's eyes rolled.

Up the steps.

His mouth juddered open.

The door gaped wide for him. Heath kicked at it anyway.

Into the house. Down on his knees. Bluster behind him. Annabelle crying out, the old woman whispering, maybe praying, and Heath, kneeling there over Shaw's twisted body.

His eyes fluttered. Blue. Almost white.

"Cat," Heath whispered.

"Gray," Shaw whispered a reply. He tried to lift his hand and could not.

Heath seized it and brought it to his face. Rubbed it against his lips.

"In. Dark," Shaw mumbled.

"Cat, I love you. I—"

No.

He was gone.

The body was a body. Empty. Dispossessed. The eyes half-closed. Blood stopped bubbling in a froth on his lips, on its way to drying.

Shaw was already cold.

Heath roared.

Behind him, Annabelle sobbed quietly.

Heath wished her dead. He wished black rot inside her, filthy, vile, into her guts and out her mouth. He wished her rotting and painful and dead.

Heath collapsed over Shaw's body.

Dead. He was dead. Gone. Cold. Dead.

A mad wailing behind him. Eddie Thrush. Oh Christ. Eddie Thrush, somehow, had made it to the Heights in the nick of time.

But Eddie didn't come forward. He didn't dare draw near. Not while Heath knelt beside Shaw's broken body.

Heath stroked his hair. Shaw's soft, sweet hair. His hands came away wet and red. Black in the dim light of the living room where he had dropped the body. The shadows pressed close around. Hundreds of feet shuffled. Someone cleared their throat.

Catherine Lyon stood at Heath's side, her head bowed in grief. Abatha capered at her feet, applauding and hissing her pleasure.

It isn't enough that they die here.

No.

It is true.

"He's dead," Heath whispered.

"Oh, Heath," Annabelle said.

Birdie murmured something comforting. Laid an arm around her shoulder.

"I'm so sorry," Annabelle said.

"He's *dead*," Heath repeated.

"Shaw," said Eddie Thrush. "Shaw. Can't. Be. Gone."

It isn't enough that they die here, we said.

"He's dead!" Heath roared, on his feet. A mad thing, a beast. So he would be a beast. So would Shaw. If that was the only way to have him, so be it.

"Look at his face," Eddie sobbed. "Smiling. Sweet smile."

"May he wake in torment!" Heath roared, and all present quailed, backed away from him.

Blackness flickered in his eyes and shone in his ebony hair. His fists, massive blocks, clenched until blood rained onto the hardwood floor, only inches from Shaw's face.

"Earnshaw Lyon," Heath roared, "may you not rest as long as I am living. You said I killed you—haunt me, then! The murdered haunt them that kill them. There are ghosts. There are ghosts *here*. Be one of them, or...or be whatever you want! Take any form, my Cat. Be with me always. Drive me mad! Only do not leave me in this...this *abyss*, where I cannot find you!

"*Take any form and be here always! That is my curse! That is my curse!*"

Heath fell to his knees. He sank to the floor. He banged his head against the boards until it split and his blood ran free, meeting with

Shaw's and mingling. It was all the same. It was all red. It was all the same. It was hot, even Shaw's, still hot. Combined now, mingled, and forever.

"Heath, no," Annabelle moaned.

"*'Tis done,*" Catherine Lyon proclaimed, and Abatha hissed. The hundreds of feet moved away. A hundred pairs of eyes glowing yellow faded back into the shadows and were gone.

"I cannot live without him!" Heath roared to the ceiling. His voice shook the entirety of the house, outside, and they all heard it.

The wind rose to a scream where there had been no wind before, shredding the thick, wet air, shredding the heat and cooling it, and the grass bent beneath its power. The trees in the arbor shook and lost their leaves, never to regain them, not ever. Doomed to be skeletal and white and bony for the rest of time. As long as the Heights stood. As long as the land held.

"Do you hear me! *I cannot live without my soul!*"

PART THREE

SEVEN

Fall and Winter 1966-1967

1

The fog came back—it always came back—but this time, it wended its way from northern California all the way to where Heath was and Annabelle, the baby, and the boy. It settled all around the homeplace, nowhere else in the surrounding area, in none of the towns. For months.

All through the late summer of 1966, when Heath returned with the boy, the latest, just after the baby was born, and then the fall and finally into winter. It was clear and crisp throughout the remaining countryside. At the Heights, the fog came close and pressed and stayed, was damp and unpleasant and secretive. And the baby cried.

Annabelle closed herself off and found less reason to speak. She saw the same ghosts Heath saw, but she ignored them steadfastly. Annabelle suckled her child, her little Hare, named thus because he was so dark and wild-looking, like the jackrabbits she had loved as a child and had chased and tried to catch but never could. Now she had.

But he cried; Christ Jesus, did he cry! And Heath left her alone with the hired men and the baby at the beginning of the summer, which was cool and wet at first, then aggressively, angrily hot. There were grasshoppers too, Lord, and they chewed the wheat crop, leaving nearly nothing behind. The cows would starve over the winter.

Heath didn't care. He had disappeared. For the second time. Would this round be any different, she wondered, exhausted, bouncing the baby against her shoulder and gazing from the front porch all the way up to 201. Did Heath really expect things would be better this time?

He must have, for he returned with the boy on the last day of August, and the fog came with them, as if announcing their presence. It snaked and foamed and looked for all the world like dark and thunderous ocean waves riled by a storm at sea. There, on the prairie. Impossibly, idiotically. But there it was.

It appeared, thick and foreboding clouds, just before dusk, when the headlights of Heath's old truck split through them and roared down the road toward the Heights. Annabelle stood on the porch with Hare, watching, her face expressionless. The wind came up with the fog and raised goose-pimples all up and down her bare arms while the temperature plummeted. The baby wailed. He thrashed furiously in her arms like a hooked fish.

The truck stopped at the gate. The doors opened. Heath emerged from the driver's seat.

Shaw from the passenger side.

She blinked, even though she had known what she would see.

Or...who.

This was the second time, after all, Heath had brought him back.

A boy, hopefully over eighteen—*please God, if there was a God, let him be over eighteen*—fair-haired, strong-jawed. Thin and lithe. Not Shaw. Couldn't possibly be Shaw. Shaw had been dead for over two years.

But this was the second boy Heath had brought to the homeplace after a significant absence.

Who bore more than just a strong resemblance to his dead lover.

Annabelle wanted to moan. How was this possible?

Whisperings in the hallway behind her. Constant whispering. She told herself she would grow accustomed to it someday. That day had yet to come. So, *they* were interested as well. She shook her head, sad and disgusted. Of course they were. After what they had done the last time, of *course,* they were interested.

The baby snuffled. He had cried himself out. For the moment. He twitched in her arms. Annabelle nearly dropped him. He was strong and growing stronger. She loved him with all her being.

Heath ambled up the walk with a big green duffle bag slung over one shoulder. The boy followed steadily with a dark blue suitcase in his hand. He swung it slightly. The boy didn't seem nervous or even a little afraid. She narrowed her eyes. The last boy—well, he had been a man, *really,* to be fair; he *had* been a man—had been timid. At first.

"We're back," Heath said inadequately. He leaned forward to kiss her on the cheek. Then the baby, who stirred uneasily at his father's touch.

"I see," Annabelle replied. She was proud of herself, keeping her voice level and even like she did. It was the little things these days she prized in herself.

"This is Rhys," Heath said.

"Reece," Annabelle repeated.

"Welsh," the boy said. "It's spelled funny. It don't matter."

"Doesn't," Heath corrected him gently.

"Doesn't," Rhys said sunnily, beaming. He took her free hand and pumped it up and down. "Sorry. I'm trying to be better," he said to Annabelle, looking adoringly at Heath. "*He's* helping me."

"How nice," Annabelle said. She looked down. Fog blew and eddied around her feet. She frowned. She had never seen such a phenomenon, not out here. Fog wasn't impossible, just unusual.

"It followed us the whole way," Rhys said. "The whoooooole drive. All the way from California."

"San Francisco," Annabelle said to Heath, who nodded tiredly.

"Makes me feel at home," Rhys said, grinning.

"Rhys is gonna help out around the house," Heath said. "He'll help with whatever you need. He'll help." He wouldn't meet her eyes. Not a surprise. "Because of the baby," he added clumsily.

"Yes," Annabelle said.

"I'm good at housekeeping," Rhys added.

"Yes," Annabelle said.

"He can stay in Lee's old room," Heath said.

"Bran's old room."

Heath froze. Rhys looked at him curiously. Annabelle permitted herself a tiny smile. Small victories. Little things. Bran—Branwell—had been the boy before this one.

The one who had disappeared.

"It's ready," Annabelle said, shifting the baby from one shoulder to the other. "I was expecting you."

"Groovy," Rhys said. "Thanks, Anna."

"Annabelle."

"Anna Banana."

Her gaze remained steady. Rhys smiled at her sweetly. He was nothing like Shaw...but at the same time, he *was*. How had Heath found him? *Another* one?

How was that even—

She wanted to sigh. Possible didn't mean much anymore. She had grown gaunt and starved-looking since Heath's latest disappearance. Her cheekbones protruded through the skin of her face, and her eyes were sunken and hollow. The baby ate and ate. Sometimes, she felt he was eating her. But she loved him still.

The fog wrapped around them like the tail of a cat. She shivered, thinking again of Shaw.

"Well," she said, more harshly, perhaps, than she intended. "Why don't we get you settled? Come in, Rhys."

By the following weekend, Rhys was gone.

Just...gone.

I didn't go after that. Not for a while. I stayed at the Heights. I could stand to be around Annabelle and the baby while Rhys was there. For that week, at least, it was all okay.

His hair was brown, so we're clear. When I found him. He would do whatever I said. I learned that right away. So, I asked him to dye it. He did, no problem.

Whatever you say, Heath baby, whatever you say.

We went walking away from the house the first day he was there. It was a hot morning, and the fog had stayed. The last bits of summer didn't do a goddamn thing to dispel it. Annabelle was with the baby. I didn't even think about her. I had Rhys.

He took my hand and held it real tight when we were about a quarter mile from the house and he thought for sure Annabelle couldn't see us. I said, I didn't care.

He said, "I care. She already hates me, I can tell. I never shoulda called her that name. I gotta live here. I don't need to make waves. I want to be with you." He stopped and kissed me.

It wasn't Shaw.

It wasn't close.

Not...yet.

The first one I brought back I had to hunt for. I went to San Francisco, of course, because I knew I had seen him before. I thought it had been Shaw in the fog the night Roger hit me with his cane, but it wasn't. I had only thought it was him...or his ghost. His doppelgänger, that is what the Germans called it. I knew now that it hadn't been Shaw. But...I thought that it *could* be.

Shaw could come back to me.

The more I thought about it, the more possible it sounded.

The first one, his name was Bran. Short for Branwell. I had to search and search for him. I started at Fort Point, where I had seen him that first time. In all that fog. I went back to the flower shop where I had seen him next, the art gallery, the cemetery.

That was where I found him. Laying flowers on a grave. A woman's grave. His wife, he told me when I approached him. He looked at me as if he had known me always. As if he wasn't at all surprised to see me. She had died having a baby. I gave him my condolences. He asked me why I was staring at him.

I told him, "You look like someone I know."

He searched my face. "He's dead, isn't he?" he said at last.

I nodded. He took this information in.

"Huh," was all he said. He asked if I wanted to get a cup of coffee.

I said, "Wine?"

"I don't drink wine."

"Maybe you haven't had the right vintage."

He laughed and said, "All right. Are you buying?"

I said I was.

We went to Ernie's and ended up having dinner. I hadn't been there since all those years ago, with Roger. It was the same: waiters in tuxes with tails, the wallpaper red as blood. The lights hurt my eyes. Bran asked if I was okay. I nodded and asked him about his wife.

They had only been married for a year when she died. He was on his third glass of wine—Merlot, the kind Shaw particularly enjoyed—when he confessed he had been about to divorce her, but before he could, she told him she was pregnant. He decided to stay with her for the sake of the kid. But they both died.

Bran told me he was sad but relieved at the same time. He asked me if I thought he was going to hell. I told him there was no hell. He laughed at that, asked me why I seemed so sad. *Melancholic* was the word he used. I liked it. It was a word Shaw would have used.

I told him I had lost someone too. He asked me her name. I hesitated, then told him I hadn't lost a woman. He digested this.

"I thought so."

I laughed. "What gave me away?"

"Nothing. I'm just psychic."

"So, you can tell the future?" I ordered us more wine.

"Sometimes. Sometimes, I can. I've been with men before. This is San Francisco. Love is everywhere, man. Everyone's loosening up. Look at me," he said. "I'm growing out my hair now. I'm gonna grow me a beard."

"Don't," I said. That stopped him. I remember blushing a little. "You should stay just the way you are. I like you this way."

"I like you the way you are."

And I remember thinking he was drunk, but he couldn't take his eyes off me.

Except, he said, "I wish you weren't so sad."

I fucked him brutally that night. In the hotel I had rented. He begged me for it.

"Hurt me," he kept saying. "Just hurt me."

I didn't want to. I couldn't help it. I had to hurt him.

He was crying and screaming and telling me, "Don't stop, don't stop, don't stop."

We walked by the bay. We went for drives in his car—big and old and the color of envy—into the hills, along the coast, up and down dizzying roads that threatened to crumble into the ocean. We ate at Ernie's every weekend for a month. I forgot about Annabelle. I forgot about baby Hare.

Bran kept his hair short at my insistence. He decided not to grow a beard. He told me I should talk more.

He said, "You just grunt."

"It all hurts, still. I'll always hurt, I think."

One night, while we lay next to each other, bare shoulder to bare shoulder, I leaned over and whispered in his ear.

"Shaw?" I said.

He muttered.

"Shaw?" I said again.

He rolled over, pressed his face into the pillow.

"Shaw," I said. "It's you. It's you."

He muttered something I couldn't understand.

Emerald light from the hotel's sign outside poured over us. We were swimming in deep green water. Our skin sweated green. It was like death.

"Shaw," I said, more insistently, and shook him.

His eyes blinked at me. He was still mostly asleep.

"Shaw, I see you. I know you're there."

"Shaw?" he muttered. "Shaw?"

"I see you." My mouth was only inches away from his neck. I could have been a vampire. Bite my way through his jugular. Find Shaw inside him that way.

But that was crazy. I wasn't crazy. The Heights was at work. There was the curse to consider. I wasn't crazy. Shaw was inside him somewhere.

"Come back with me," I told him. "There's nothing for you here. I can give you a life."

"In Montana?" he said. He laughed. It wasn't a pleasant laugh. "I'm a city boy. I don't know any other world."

I didn't let him go. I wouldn't let him look away from me. After a while, he didn't want to.

"We'll make our own world," I said. "It's possible for us to do that. Let me show you."

"There's nothing for you here," I told him again. "Nothing."

The fog appeared for us when we made the turn off 201, down that rambling road to the homeplace, but it didn't stay. Bran was a friend, I told Annabelle, an old friend of mine, and he would be staying with us for a time. She tried to fight me, but I won.

Annabelle saw the resemblance right away. She was not an idiot. She was so lonesome out there. I would feel guilty nights out in California, thinking about how alone she was. But I didn't—I *couldn't*—care. Not really. Because I owed it to Shaw to bring him back. He was lost. He was lonely too, goddammit. *He was lonely too!*

So, we cut Bran's hair, and we kept his face plum clean-shaven. I started introducing different kinds of clothes to him than he was maybe used to. He put up a fuss at first.

"You want me to look like *him*," he spat at me the night I brought him the white linen pants and blue-green turtleneck with the short sleeves.

"Be calm," I told him, soothing him like he was a shy horse about to turn skittish on me. "I brung you these nice clothes because I love you." And goddamn if I didn't see Shaw in his eyes, just a'peerin out at me. Grateful, even if Bran hisself wasn't necessarily so grateful.

It took him a day or so to put on the clothes. He said it was too hot for a shirt like that one, with a turtleneck like that. I told him the sleeves was short, weren't they, and it wasn't like he was out in the hot sun, toiling like the hired men were. Like I was supposed to be. Like Annabelle kept poking me to be. I told him how handsome he looked in them. He liked that, finally. I told him how much I liked his eyes. He enjoyed compliments, did my Branwell.

The old lady on the hill didn't care for him. She was Annabelle's only company, and we had her down for dinner most Sunday nights. She stared at Bran through her thick glasses that first night. He watched her back, all nervous. Nervous as a cat.

"Where you come from, boy?" she finally said, curling her lip.

Annabelle tried to hide a smile. We didn't have no Hare yet, and she was fat and pretty with her fatness. I guess it didn't matter how much she ate or didn't eat. Her body kept swingin' back and forth, back and forth, and the weight would come and it would go. It didn't really make no difference to me. But I thought she was pretty, and I told her so. She swatted me and told me to knock it off.

The old lady put a forkful of potatoes all mashed real fine into her mouth, and she just glared at Bran across the table.

"You tryin to look like a dead man, boy?" she finally asked, all shrill and hateful.

Bran looked down at his plate, then to me for help.

I said, "Shut your mouth, Granny."

She laughed wildly. "That how you speak to your elders?" She laughed at me. "How you speak to your wife's only friend?"

Annabelle said, "It's okay, Birdie," but I knew she was embarrassed.

"It's got to be said," says Birdie, standing, leaning over, and pointing one old chicken-bone finger in Bran's poor face. "I been up on that hill for seventy years, and I've seen all the terrible things that happen down here. I told myself I was safe up there, but I've never been safe. None of us has been safe. Not even you, young man. Pack your things and get," she told him.

Now she was only inches away from his face, which had turned white with terror.

"Go," she said, "while they still let you go."

"Goddammit it, Birdie," I roared. I slammed my hands against the table and stood up. "Goddammit, shut your goddamn fool mouth!"

Birdie blinked at me. She smiled. "You don't talk to me like that," she says, quiet.

"You old bitch," I told her.

Annabelle gasped and said my name. Bran stared down at the table.

"You old bitch," I said. "I'll talk to you any which way I feel. This house is *mine*."

"This house belongs to itself," she told me.

"This house is *mine*," I said, "and so is yours. So is yours, you old bitch. Remember it well."

Her hands trembled, and so did her face, so hard I thought it would break apart. We looked at each other inches away from the other, and neither of us spoke.

"I wash my hands of it," she said after that endless standoff. Birdie looked down at poor Bran, staring at the table. "You poor, stupid boy. You look just like him. But you aren't him." And she glared at me. "You aren't him at *all*," she said, spitting.

"Get out," I said. "Don't you ever come back to this house."

"Heath, no!" Annabelle cried, and now she stood too.

"If I see you down the hill ever again..." I told the old woman, and now I was spitting in her face. "If I ever see you in this house again, I'll fucking kill you."

She turned white, and her eyes bulged like eggs. Birdie made a thick sound in the back of her throat, and she stumbled out of the room and into the hall.

She turned once.

"They come to me now too," she said. I was sure she was speaking only to Bran. "They come into my bedroom, and they never used to, but now they do. They come slithering through the window like snakes. With their eyes all yellow and their faces green with death. They want to take me, but I fight them off. I'm strong. Are *you* strong?"

I thought she was talking to Bran, but she might have been talking to Annabelle.

Or to me.

"Get out!" I roared at her.

She glared at me, shook her head, and clucked her tongue but turned and went. We heard the door slam firm behind her.

"Heath, you fool," Annabelle said to me. She was crying.

Bran stared at the table.

"She can't talk to me like that in my own house," I told her. "You hear me, woman? Not in my own damned house she won't."

"She's my friend," Annabelle sobbed.

"Not no more."

She slapped me.

I...I don't remember if I slapped her back. I guess I musta. I didn't ever hit her. I love Annabelle. You gotta believe that I do. It is possible to love more than one person. You'll learn that for yourself, you live long enough. Most human beings got great big capacities for loving. You'll learn, boy. You'll learn.

I hope I didn't hit her. Christ, that was twenty-some year ago, and I still feel guilty. I guess maybe I did. I'm not a coward. Don't look at me like you think I'm a coward, or I'll put your lights out. I can still do that, and don't you forget it.

I love my Annabelle, and I love my Cat, and I loved Bran too. And Rhys. And...the other.

No. *Not* the other.

Shit.

I forbade Annabelle from ever seeing the old bitch on the hill again. She told me she would do as she pleased. She always had, and she wasn't about to stop now. I told her I would kill the old creature. I would wring her scrawny chicken neck. Annabelle said she would put a butcher knife in *my* neck in the middle of the night if I did that. Bran stared and stared at the table.

"Fine," I said at last. "You do what you want. Idiot woman. You will anyway."

"Damn straight I will," she told me.

We lay next to each other that night.

"Heath, I want a baby," she said.

"Hell no," I told her, or I started to. I remember I guess I didn't say anything.

"Heath," she said, kissing on me. "Heath, you do what you want otherwise. I don't care. But you give me a baby. You hear me?"

I told her I heard her.

She was tugging on me. Trying to get me hard. It wasn't working. She kept kissing on me.

"Fill me up," she said.

I remember that. Gives me chills to think on it.

"Fill me up. Fill me up," she kept saying.

I jumped out of bed and left the room, wearing just my shorts.

I heard her screaming for me down the hall.

I went out onto the porch to smoke.

Bran joined me.

"I'm going to stay," he told me after he took a puff off my cigarette.

I just looked at him. Like I was breaking up inside. Like the creek does in the spring. Big chunks of dark brown ice crashing up against other chunks and the water all roaring and angry underneath. The smoke filled me and made my head lighter. I wanted to kiss him. I sat there, watching him instead.

"Yeah?" was all I said.

"Yeah," he replied. His eyes were glowing. "You think I care what some old witch thinks about me? Hell no!"

Bran took my hand. He held it tightly. I squeezed his back.

"I want to stay here with you," he says to me. His eyes were full of the fever of the sunset. They looked almost red. I could see Shaw way back in there again, peering at me. Looking at me with love. I was so sure of it. "Please let me stay," Bran says.

I kissed him. "You ain't going," I says. "You just ain't."

"I'll wear the clothes. Do my hair. Shave my face. If you'll love me. Just love me."

I didn't say anything. I kissed him and kissed him again while the sun stabbed into the hills at the west.

I finally went back to my bed, hoping Annabelle would be asleep.

She wasn't.

She looked at me, starving like a wolf.

"Put a baby in me," she says. "Now, Heath. You do it *now*."

Our room was hot. She had closed the window so the cool night air couldn't flow in and refresh it at least a little. My head felt heavy from kissing Bran and the wine at dinner. I had insisted on wine at dinner. Red. I insisted that everyone drink it. I insisted. I forced them. I insisted.

The air in our room felt heavy, the way the world feels before a thunderstorm. Thick and wet.

Annabelle pulled off her cotton nightdress, lay back on the bed, and spread her legs. She never took her eyes off me.

My cock stirred in my shorts. She looked luscious lying there. Her little lamp at the side of the bed put out a thick orange glow. It was dark outside now. All Bran and I had done that night was kiss. I was stirred up. That was how I explain it. And the wine. I remembered Annabelle kept pouring the wine.

My dick was hard now. It stood out, this red soldier, poking through the slit in my shorts. Annabelle was touching herself. I had never seen a woman do that before. My head was swimming. I stumbled toward her, dropped my shorts, and stepped out of them. I lay with her. I slid into her.

We hadn't done it since our wedding night all those years ago. It felt different than it had with Bran and Shaw and the others. Shaw. *Don't think about Shaw.* I wasn't betraying him. He would forgive me. She was my wife. He would forgive me.

I loved her. She loved me too. I could feel it. She kept saying my name. Annabelle tried to scratch my back, but I kept saying, "Easy now. Easy, girl. Easy," kissing her between each word. She was nothing but soft. Her breasts were big pillows.

You been with a woman, boy? You know. It's different. I didn't think about how I preferred to be with a man. I thought about it later. And truth be told, I never been with a woman since. Just my Annabelle. And never again with her. Just that one last time. Moving in her. So soft. So *wet*. Moving in and moving with her. Her arms around me.

"Go slow," she said. "Please love me. Go slow."

So, I did.

I opened my eyes while I moved with her. There was a face in the closet. I didn't freeze. I didn't stop or let Annabelle know what I saw.

A face in the closet.

There, mixed in with her dresses.

A man's face? A woman's? I couldn't tell. Just the eyes there. Big and bright. Shining away. Watching us. I saw a mouth in the darkness. It smiled. Watching us and smiling. Full of teeth.

Long teeth.

I sped up. Our hips slapped together. I couldn't take my eyes away from it.

"Heath," she said. "Oh Heath...Oh my darling, my love."

Whoever—whatever—watched us from within the closet saw me seeing them and nodded approvingly.

"Heath," Annabelle kept saying, cooing in this breathy voice. "Oh Heath, my love, my love."

I closed my eyes and thought of Shaw.

3

Bran lasted nearly three months at the Heights before he vanished, leaving no trace. No advance notice, of course. Word spread in the nearby towns where the Lyon family had always selected their hired men. Three or four of them had disappeared by then as well. No remains. No word. Just empty beds left behind, and jeans, boots, a few flasks, some magazines tucked under mattresses.

Heath spent many nights curled up with Bran, like two cats intertwined. Almost every night following the one where he had fulfilled Annabelle's greatest wish, when, together, they had created the child who would be Hare. After that, Heath didn't come back to their bed.

He didn't tell Annabelle about the face in the closet, but he wondered if she hadn't seen it too and had just kept going, as he had. But it drove him from that room and into Bran's and Bran's arms, where he felt more truly comfortable.

The night before Bran's disappearance, Eddie Thrush ambled up the walk and knocked on the front door of the house.

It had been Heath's habit to have him over once or twice a month. It made Annabelle happy, and, contrary to everything he might have expected about himself—and his temper—Heath found that he enjoyed Eddie's company. He might even have considered what Shaw found attractive about the man.

It wasn't his physiognomy or his body, which had grown, Heath concluded, decidedly ape-like, decidedly hirsute. But after enduring more and more conversations with the man, Heath finally realized.

He reminded Shaw of me, he thought one night, freezing and standing stock-still in his bathroom, gazing at his reflection in the mirror in wonderment, gape-mouthed. *We're taciturn. We growl. We are dark of eye and hair. Or, at least, I am.* Eddie Thrush once was. But no longer. Since Shaw's death, his hair had silvered on its way toward solid white.

They played gin rummy some nights and pinochle on Christmas, or they sat on the porch and drank cans of beer together, talking amiably about the crops, the cows, and what the weather would do. And the grasshoppers. Lord, damn the grasshoppers to fucking hell. The fires that spread on some farms due to lightning strikes. The new family who had taken over the farm at the old Reardon place. Nice couple. Young. Eager. Maybe it was time to have another meet-up up't'the Hall.

Heath didn't always enjoy thinking about the Hall, but whatever had happened to him that snowy night he had tried to climb the hill to where the old lady's homesteader cabin brooded and watched had fallen so far back into the past it might as well have been a dream. A story someone else told him.

So, they all enjoyed a Halloween get-together at the Hall with that new family, Polly King and her brother, and the Ambersons down the road. Even Aunt Lucy and the Lindens came. Aunt Lucy brought her famous Depression-era chocolate cake that called for powdered eggs, though, as far as Heath knew, she used the eggs her sister's layers provided her. Heath brought chicken and dumplings, which he had worked on perfecting the last year or so. Others brought orange and black iced cookies and paper decorations shaped like bats and black cats.

There was even a dance. The new fella at the Reardon place played the fiddle like he could beat the devil, and they all stomped 'til the sweat poured down their foreheads. Their faces shone in the lights of the flame glowing from within the grinning pumpkins lining the dance floor.

It was one of the last good times Heath would remember. And he owed it to Eddie Thrush, who had helped him with the organization.

They never talked about Shaw. Not once.

Until the night Eddie came ambling up the walk and Bran answered the door.

———

Eddie didn't scream. What escaped his gaping mouth was a hissing sound, like air leaving a tire.

Bran stood there before him, silhouetted by the hall light, which glowed off his hair in a golden corona. His eyes, not as blue-white as Shaw's had been, were still bright. Bright enough to startle Eddie. To startle him into stumbling backward, to tumble down the steps and land square on his ass.

"Sorry, sorry," Bran said, jostling down the steps to help Eddie up, but the other man scrambled backward down the gravel path, panting and shaking his head. No, no, no. "I know, I know. I look like him, but I'm not. My name is Bran. Branwell, actually. So please don't be afraid. I've seen pictures. I know how much we look alike. I'm sorry—"

"Christ Jesus," Eddie moaned, his mouth slick with drool. "Oh my sweet Christ, you're even dressed like him."

"These clothes," Bran said, embarrassed, reaching out a hand to Eddie, "they weren't my idea. I like them, I mean. Sure, they're really nice, but it wasn't—"

Eddie swatted the man's hand away. "Don't touch me!" he screeched. In a higher, shriller voice, like a rabbit caught in a baler, "*Heath*!" he shrieked. "*Heath, goddamn you!*"

Heath appeared on the porch, rubbing his face. "Oh, Eddie," he said. "Jeez. I forgot. I forgot you haven't—"

Eddie bowed his head, drew his knees up to his face, encircled his legs with his arms, and rocked back and forth while he sobbed. "Shaw," he moaned. "Oh, Shaw. Oh no, no. Not like this. Not like—"

Heath skipped down the steps. Bran stepped aside miserably, holding himself. Annabelle appeared in the doorway, a hand on her expanding belly. In the Heights above them all, the lights went on. All of them. At once.

"Listen. *Listen.* My name is Bran. I came to...I'm a friend of Heath's, so I..."

"Jesus," Eddie muttered. He took Heath's hand and allowed him to pull him to his feet. "Holy Jesus. You asshole. You stupid *jerk*. How could you? How could you do this, Heath?"

"He's a friend of mine," Heath said steadily.

On the porch above them, Annabelle snickered to herself, but no one paid her any attention. After a moment, she turned, re-entered the house, and closed the door behind her.

"The clothes, Heath," Eddie said plaintively. His eyes searched Heath's. "Christ Jesus, even the *clothes*—"

"I know what it looks like," Bran volunteered, "but honestly—"

"Shut up," Heath said without looking at him.

Bran's mouth clapped shut. He looked furiously at the earth.

Somewhere, distantly, yet near enough that they all heard it clearly, a dog barked in the faraway hills. A big dog, by the sounds of it.

"I gotta go," Eddie muttered, shaking his head. "Too much. I gotta get out of this crazy house."

"Please don't go," Heath said.

Eddie stopped. Spun around, but slowly. Shuffled up the walk, one eye slitted shut, the other *bulging* and fixed on Bran. Bran stared back as if hypnotized, a rabbit before a cobra.

"Who are you?" Eddie said through gritted teeth. He aimed a finger at Bran and jabbed him in the chest. "Huh? You tell me that. Who are you? Huh?"

"Leave him alone, Eddie," Heath said tiredly.

"Huh?" Jab. "Huh? You tell me. Huh? Huh?"

"My name is Branwell," Bran said, drawing himself up. He shoved Eddie back with such force that the older man went tumbling backward again, ass over teakettle, as Heath described it to Annabelle later. "And you'd do well to listen to what Heath says. Leave. Me. *Alone.*"

"You can't be here," Eddie said, hefting himself off the ground and wiping the dust away. "You must know that. You must know who you are."

"My name is *Branwell*," he said. "I'm from Kansas originally. I moved to San Francisco because I found a job in advertising and my wife could be a secretary. That was before she died. Before she and our baby *both* died. So, you listen to me..."

Heath, startled, saw how Bran had clenched both his fists, held them aloft, and trembled with what Heath realized was pure fury.

"You listen to *me*, asshole. When I tell you my name is Bran, and I have never had another name in my whole *life*. I'm here for Heath. I understand that. I even understand why. But you better listen to him, asshole. Listen to him when he talks. *My name is Bran and no other.*" And he stood there, fists at the ready, eyes slitted, teeth bared.

"Who you really are," Eddie said. His eyes shone. He clutched at Bran's shirt. "Who you really are!"

"Come inside, Eddie," Heath said. "We can sort this out."

Eddie's eyes searched Bran's, which neglected to blink. They only stared, hard and blue marbles.

At last, Eddie dropped his. The life ran out of him. His spine drooped, his hands relaxed, and he stared dully at the ground. "All right," he whispered, lifting his gaze to the blazing windows of the house. "Go back in there? Yes. Sure. I can go in there. What could go wrong, hey?" He laughed. It was a broken and bitter sound. "What could possibly, *possibly,* go wrong with my life in that house? He wanted to keep me away, you know," Eddie said confidentially to Bran. "He told me, over and over and over and—"

"Eddie," Heath said gently, but he laid a firm hand on Eddie's shoulder.

The other man's mouth closed like a sudden trap. "Everything is fine and dandy, like Christmas candy," he murmured. Eddie cackled. "I didn't have your faith, Heath. I guess I should've."

"I'm Bran," Bran whispered fiercely.

"I guess I should've believed more than I did. Ah, well." Eddie shrugged his slumped shoulders. "Ah, ah. Well. Yes. Let's go inside your house. Let's play a game. I'll kiss my sister on the cheek and hug her and ask her how she feels, and she'll remind me about the day the baby comes. We can do that much, can't we?"

"Yes," Heath whispered. "All right." He looked helplessly at Bran.

Bran glowered back at him.

"One happy family," Eddie sang. "Oh boy. Yes, yes. One big old happy old family."

I don't blame Eddie for what happened to Bran. That would be ridiculous. Eddie never hurt a soul in his whole life. He loved me, and he always tried to do right by me. That's all.

I suppose I should have kept him away from the Heights. He told me, when Heath wasn't around, that Shaw tried to protect him. Shaw would never let him come here, he said. Men are such idiots.

That last night was astonishingly normal, even for us. Heath made dinner. I let him. I was tired all the time now. The baby was months away, but I felt him inside me. He sapped me. He drank me. Drank me *all up*. Isn't that awful? Mommy's little vampire. Heath would kill me if he heard me saying that, but it's true.

But I wanted him. I wanted my baby.

Such a normal night. Heath prepared *boeuf bourguignon*. None of us had ever had it before, except for Bran, once, back in San Francisco. It was delicious, of course. I remember telling Heath that he had really outdone himself. He smiled at me. He even kissed me. I'm sure he did. I'm sure I remember that.

"No one else is eating anything like this," Eddie said. "Not out *here*, not in *these* parts," and we all laughed.

It was good. It was really good.

But I saw him looking at Bran when he thought no one noticed.

I saw that look in his eyes.

I wanted to tell everyone, *No, Bran doesn't look like Shaw, not much, even though the clothes. Oh God, his clothes—*

He went into Burke, you know, sometimes. And they would stop on the street, and they would stare—

The people in town all hated us. Can you blame them? I can't blame them. We were killing their children, their brothers, fathers. *Killing them*.

Bran took it all in stride. He was proud of the way they stared. You know, he used to have a wife? I couldn't believe it. They can be anything they want, I guess. Turn into anything. Anyone. Look at what he did! Or what *they* did together, him and Heath. He had his Shaw back. Where do you suppose he spent all his nights? I quit caring. I told myself I quit caring. Our bed was too big and too hot. He spent all his nights upstairs in the attic, in Shaw's old room. The one at the end of the hall. It was Bran's now, of course.

I dreamed sometimes about leaving the Heights. Stealing Heath's truck and driving away. I wouldn't even tell Eddie where I had gone. It would be just me and the baby. Maybe we would go to California. Or Seattle. My mom's family had come from up there. It was far away. Far enough away to be safe, I figured.

I held on to that dream long after Bran and the others. Running away.

Somewhere far enough away to be safe.

And I would remember the fog that came creeping along highway 201, all the way from San Francisco, and I would know that I wouldn't be safe nowhere.

Once this place gets ahold of you, it has you, and there's no changing it.

Bran found out.

The *boeuf bourguignon* was delicious, and we played cribbage until past midnight, even though Heath had to get up to swath. Cut the hay. Bale it up. Field after field. I didn't care, didn't want to know. Eddie offered to help him from time to time. Heath always said no, but polite-like.

We was between hired men since the last one run off. I told everyone who'd listen to me that he'd run off, though they didn't believe me. Matilda Benson up t'the post office would stare at me like an icicle and smile like an icicle and nod her icicle head, and I wished her dead a thousand times, but I stuck to my story. We was between hired men, so Heath had to do the work himself.

Heath said he didn't mind. He was still young. Not even thirty. I thought him handsome. He was getting gray streaks at his temples. I loved them. I tried to ignore them. I let him work the fields. Bran helped too. I forgot about that. I get them all confused, you know. Ha. Can you blame me?

We played cribbage 'til late and drank red wine. I made up a bed for Eddie to stay the night. It would be the first time. He was too drunk to argue. I put him to bed. Bran and I passed each other in the hall on our way to our rooms. Heath didn't bother to hide the fact that they were going to bed together. What did it matter to me? I patted my stomach, my little lump, my heart, my heat, my vampire. Little Hare. I had already named him. Hop-along Hare. How I planned to love him.

I lay in bed for a long time, half-asleep. It was hot, I remember that. The room grew hotter. I didn't want to open the window. I was afraid to open the window. Someone was outside. If I looked, I would see them, and it would make me crazy. I would scream and run and hurt myself. I didn't want to hurt myself or the baby. Not little Hare. The heat pressed down on me. It was awful. It was thick and wet. It was like heavy blankets. I started thrashing. I kicked off the sheets. Didn't help.

"No, no," I said. "Please, no."

The doorknob turned.

I remembered waking up that long ago night to that horrible little child's face only inches from mine. I retched. I thought I would vomit.

"No," I said. "I will not soil myself or my bed. I will not. I will *not*."

The doorknob turned more wildly.

Had I locked the door?

Did it matter?

Something struck it. Hard. I didn't cry out. I was afraid, but I was smiling. I thought, *I am asleep. Nothing can hurt me in my dreams. I am safe in my bed, no matter how hot the room is. No matter what waits for me outside my door.*

The door buckled when whatever waited outside hit it again. And again.

The heat flowed around me. I left my bed and glided to the door as it opened. The lock had broken. I smiled at it like an idiot.

Bran stood before me.

He was smiling too.

We smiled at each other.

He moved as if underwater. I saw my reflection in the big round mirror sitting atop my vanity, the antique my mother gave to me that had belonged to her mother—one of the few possessions I brought with me to the Heights. I was moving slowly too. My hair floated on the thickness of the air.

We didn't say a word. Just smiled at each other.

Bran turned and left the room, and I followed him. My feet didn't touch the ground. Neither did his. We bobbed along. We floated down the hallway. Doors opened when we passed, and people saw us: a woman with a mouth too red and a little boy with carrot-top hair; an old, old, old woman with a screaming slash of a mouth and chicken-claw hands; and a girl with wide-wide eyes, a heartbreaking smile, and eyes black as sin. They nodded at us, and we nodded back, floating, until at last we came to the front door, which opened for us without our even having to touch it.

Such accommodation.

Our feet grazed the wooden boards of the porch while we settled, and we stood together, sucking at the night air. The heat was no better outside, but the sky over our heads was clear. It wept diamonds, I thought, though it must have been meteors. Red meteors tearing at the sky. Bloody tears. I thought, *This is fascinating. How lucky am I to be able to watch the sky rain down bloody tears?*

Bran turned to me. He didn't blink. His eyes were distant and very large. I thought, *He doesn't see me, not really.* But he put a finger to his lips.

Yes, yes, I thought. *I won't say a word.*

He moved slowly down the steps, but I stayed put.

I think I knew what was coming, even then.

I wondered why he wanted me to see it.

Bran moved down the hill and toward the grove. The trees were dead now and had been ever since Shaw's accident. You've seen 'em. They're horrible, thin, white, just skeletons. Creepy during every season. But that's where Bran headed.

Only, they didn't wait for him.

They came out of the trees as if they had always been there. Just watching. Waiting. Maybe they had been. I smiled to see them. They were naked, and their skin glowed, though there were all kinds of people coming for dear sweet Bran.

Some of them I thought I recognized. Abatha, of course, and old Catherine Lyon. *Her* I knew from pictures Birdie had shown me.

Bran waved to them, and I thought I heard his voice, welcoming them too. He opened his arms to them.

They ran. They rushed him.

They had long mouths and knives for teeth. They had glowing yellow eyes or black eyes or eyes that were dark and red as rubies.

They threw him to the ground and put those terrible mouths on him. They ripped at him. Shredded him.

To *bits*.

He screamed.

I know I heard *that*.

Bran screamed, but only once.

I moved down the steps to help him, but Lee was there, hanging by his neck. The old piece of stinking hemp he had used wasn't secured to a goddamn thing but went up and up into the sky, maybe forever. But there was Lee, and his face was green and puffy. His lips were all swole up. He looked like he did the day I found him, swinging from a beam in the granary down the hill.

Lee's eyes flew open. They were blank and glowed gold as coins.

He opened his mouth, and his teeth were sharp indeed.

Lee said my name.

He reached his puffy green hands out for me.

Behind him, I saw the mass of naked creatures, all down on their knees or spread prone on the grass. I couldn't see Bran anymore. They covered him. But their lips were black in the light of the moon, with strings of *something* stuck between their teeth. Abatha picked at hers with one long white finger. She saw me seeing her and waved at me cheerfully. I looked away, right into Lee's face. His smell washed over me. Vinegar and rot, and a lot of other odors, all terrible.

Then I *did* lose it, and I vomited.

And I kept vomiting.

Until I blacked out.

When I opened my eyes, it was morning, and the sun shone hot on my face. Made me wince. Hurt me. My head throbbed, and my mouth tasted like shit. I didn't like red wine the way Heath did. Or the way Shaw had, I guess. I felt real bitter about it in that moment, I can tell you.

I wobbled out of bed to close the curtains so I could sleep in near-darkness for a few more hours.

I stopped.

The door was closed.

But the lock was broken.

And I remembered how the lock came to be broken.

I shivered. I couldn't stop my shivering. My teeth chattered.

Footsteps over my head. In the attic. Moving slow at first, then running.

Running.

Down the attic steps.

I heard Heath bellowing. Calling out for Bran. I heard Eddie groaning, saying something whiny and quarrelsome. "Shut the hell up, you damned fool." Something like that.

But Heath only bellowed and bellowed some more. He sounded like one of his hellish cows.

He and Eddie spent the day searching. Driving out into the fields, into the back country. None of the vehicles were gone. Bran must have gone on foot.

I didn't tell Heath what I seen until later. Oh, years later. He beat me for it. I beat him back, and then we held each other and sobbed like children. This was years later, when we had given up any pretense of love. Only the pain of the fist or the back of the hand. Mine as well as his. Don't make it any better for either of us.

I gave birth to Hare, and I loved him as I knew I would. He was angry all the time, and he screamed all the time. I thought, *I understand you, tiny baby. I feel your pain and your rage, and I agree. I agree with everything you say.*

Then Heath disappeared for a good long while.

In the fall, he came back and brought home the next one, that boy with the weird-sounding name. Welsh, he said. I didn't really bother to learn it. Why would I? I can't even remember it now. I knew what was going to happen.

And I was right.

He lasted a few days before...whatever happened, happened again. Eddie didn't even get to meet him. I made sure of that. I told Eddie to stay the hell home, to keep far away from the Heights. I didn't want him back here. I didn't want what had happened to poor Bran to happen to my big brother. No, sir.

The new one looked even more like Shaw than Bran had, if that was possible, but I guess it was. Maybe that was why he went so fast. I don't know why *they* wanted him or Bran, or if I even saw what I thought I had.

There was no evidence in the grove the next day, after the dream I'd had, where Bran had come to me and then gone to meet *them*. No disturbance. No sign that a living person, a human being with thoughts and a past and feelings and a sense of devotion...No sign at all that a person like that, who would come into someone's home and sleep every night with the husband of the mistress of the house...Nope, not a sign that a person like *that* had been torn into shreds. Not a blade of grass destroyed or spattered or stained. No trace of my vomit, even.

So, when the new one disappeared, I thought, *Well, that's that, and Heath will have learned his lesson.*

Heath learns, all right, but he's a stubborn son of a bitch. You have to understand that about him. He knows what he wants, and he is determined to have it.

He's hungry.

Perhaps that's why he and this house are such good, good friends.

Eight

Spring 1967

1

The fog evaporated with Rhys and was replaced immediately by an early snowfall that came and stayed and stayed and then stayed a few months more. The temperature plummeted by Halloween into the low twenties, grew colder, negative numbers, below sixty by New Year's Day. The snow crystalized and turned hard and cutting, with sharp edges.

The baby suffered with croup and cried endless hours. Annabelle grew thinner and gaunter until, around Christmas, she inexplicably filled out. Her cheeks rounded and turned rosy, and her eyes sparkled. Her ass, which she privately hated and which had grown so bony of late, filled out and became soft and cushiony again. She smiled and laughed, even when Heath threw, with careful aim, a knife at her head one blizzardy Sunday afternoon.

The latest hired man had run off—really and truly run off, white-faced and gasping, jumped into his pickup after he came sprinting in from the pasture, where he had been feeding the cows alone. He leaped, white-faced and, yes, gasping, into his pickup and sped off at an unsafe rate of speed.

No one ever knew what he had seen, and no one ever learned what had scared him so badly that he left behind all his clothes and personals, though Heath had his suspicions as to what might have come crawling toward the hired man out of the frozen grass. Now Heath had to feed the cows all by his lonesome, and it made him cranky and prone to raging at the smallest inconvenience.

Annabelle had demanded he wipe his boots when he came in for lunch—they were befouled with the semi-frozen shit of the cows from the pasture—before allowing him entrance to the house she had just cleaned. Neglecting to follow her command, Heath stomped into the kitchen, seized a carving knife from the roast he had prepared the night before, which Annabelle had placed on the kitchen table as cold cuts for lunch, then spun and hurled the knife directly at her face. For Annabelle's part, she stood her ground, smiling coldly and unmoving, with her arms crossed over her chest.

The knife stuck in the wall only inches from her face. She continued to smile that glacial smile, turned, yanked the knife from the wall, wiped it calmly on the thigh of her jeans, and stabbed it once again into the roast. They never spoke of the incident again, and it was never repeated.

In late February, the temperatures enjoyed a brief and strange surge into the low fifties, roaring up from nearly sixty below. The snow tried to melt. The cows lowed. Heath and the two new hired men worried less about the mortality of the calves the cows attempted to deliver, and spring sang its vibrant siren's song all around the Heights.

Birdie Lyon died sometime during all that heat, though Annabelle didn't discover her body for at least a week afterward. She hadn't heard from the old woman in days, and so she went up the hill, tromping through the slop and the mud left in the melting snow's wake. After banging relentlessly on the brittle door—Birdie had grown deafer over the last year or so—Annabelle finally let herself into the cabin.

Birdie sat in her chair before the window, gazing out. Her eyes were wide, and her mouth gaped. The flesh of her face had already retracted and left her looking sallow and abandoned and monkeyish.

Annabelle, gasping, had retreated, stumbling a little, back toward the door she had left slightly ajar. She wondered what the old woman had seen while she sat gazing out her window.

Just a heart attack, she reassured herself. *You don't know what she saw, if anything.* But the deeper, wiser Annabelle within knew that something had passed by Birdie's window and stopped to gaze in at her, with pumpkin eyes and tombstone teeth, had undoubtedly said things to her, whispers and promises that forced the old lady's heart to stutter, misfire, and, finally, give out. Annabelle *knew*.

Heath claimed not to care. *Good riddance*, he said. *Let the house rot where it stands.*

But Annabelle would leave her lonely bed in the night, in the dark, and glide up the hill, the baby in her arms, and she would enter the little house, sit in Birdie's chair, and lie on her bed, read her books, hold the little figurines she collected. They glowed for her, every time, and warmed in her hands. Even little Hare grew calm and gaped in wonderment at the golden aura Birdie's figurines emitted at his mother's touch.

Annabelle didn't dare to bring them down to the Heights. She thought they were safe—her and Hare and all that Birdie had left behind—there in the homesteader cabin. Then winter came roaring back, gnashing its nasty icicle fangs and shredding claws of wind, a week or so after they buried Birdie in the Grandview Cemetery way out in the backcountry, not too far from the Hall.

It was so lonely, Annabelle thought to herself, crying when no one, not even Hare, was around. She insisted no one ever see her cry. It was so lonely for poor Birdie, who had been alone most of her life. It didn't seem fair that she should be so alone in death.

Unless—

—and the thought chilled Annabelle more than she had ever been chilled before—

Unless—

Unless Birdie is one of them *now.*

No, Annabelle would insist to herself. Not possible. Birdie had died peacefully.

Don't think about her face. Don't you dare think about that particular and oh-so-specific expression stamped on her, transforming her features into a grotesque death mask. Don't you dare. Don't you...

She had died *peacefully* in her cabin, where there had never been a single sign of the malignance that had infected the big house long and long ago. Maybe even before the house itself was built upon the land. Or maybe the malignance originated within the land itself.

Oh Jesus. If *that* was the case, maybe Birdie had never been safe. Maybe *none* of them were safe, and the Heights could reach out wherever it wanted to whomever it wanted, *whenever* it wanted. Annabelle would think this, sit in Birdie's chair, and look out the window into the darkness and try, *try*, not to see the white figures capering and dancing amid the bone-trees in the grove below.

"No," Annabelle whispered. "No, *no.*"

But there they were, and their dancing and capering refuted her denials. She held the baby tighter to her breast. He whimpered uneasily but didn't cry. Dancing, hand in hand—*how many hands did they have?*—arm in arm in arm in arm. Some slithered in the grass, and some rolled on their bellies. Some clambered up the trunks of the trees and held onto the bone-branches with their multitude of limbs.

Then, oh, and *then* they saw her, and she dropped her head and rose from the chair. Annabelle retreated into the dead woman's bedroom, but there were windows in that room too. *Oh no, no, no, no.* She heard the scratching at the windows, but she refused to look. Annabelle heard their whispers, their urgency, calling her, calling her. *Don't look, oh no, oh no.* And she sank to the floor.

Now the baby cried. *Oh no, Hare. Please don't. Hush, hush, my baby, hushabye. Don't you cry. All the pretty little, all the pretty little, all the pretty little horses—*

When the sun rose, they had gone, and Annabelle retreated down the hill, trudging through the new-fallen snow. She ignored the multitude of footprints.

And not all were human, were they? *Look close, dearest Annabelle. Look down and see. What appear to be pawprints and what appear to be hoofprints, but you've never seen hooves split like that. And is that a human footprint or that of a giant cat or both?*

Both.

And in some places, the snow was pressed all the way down to the dead gray grass beneath, and *those* indentations were almost ten feet across. *No, no, no.* She ignored them. Annabelle ignored them all. She changed the baby and fed the baby, and Heath came in from feeding the cows. He looked at her and said nothing but, "'Mornin.'"

Heath looked at the baby and poured himself a cup of coffee, and they sat together, looked at each other, and sipped their bitter coffee. No one said a word.

2

Heath had sent the hired men away, back to the little cabin they shared down by the corral, because they had all been up since two, trying to coax the latest calf into the world. They had succeeded, but the little beast had died before it could draw breath. It burst into the world in a flood of liquid and ribbons of flesh, possessing two heads, four great bulging eyes, and two tongues black as night, dangling heavily from its silent mouths.

Calving was always difficult, Heath said to the hired men, who had nodded, exhausted. He sent them back to the bunkhouse to sleep as long as they wanted.

Heath had gone out into the hills alone, driving the pickup he had used to fail to save Shaw—and don't think he didn't consider that fact every single time he wrapped his fingers around the steering wheel. He enjoyed, with his usual grimness shadowing his unshaven face, the bumps and jarring served to him by the uneven tilt of the hills, enjoyed the little rills and cuts that became coulees, which might topple the pickup over and over until he lay trapped beneath it, perhaps paralyzed, perhaps simply unwilling to leave the shattered wreck. Lying there to die slowly, miles away from anyone who might know where he had run off to. But none of that happened.

He drove for nearly an hour before he stopped, killed the ignition, slid off the seat, and stood, stretching and cracking his back, at the base of a tall hill he had never encountered before. Near the top of the hill, an abandoned house waited for him. The windows were shattered, long ago removed, and the only movement within came from a long strip of white curtain that remained in the window's frame, shredded and partially devoured by the endless roll of the seasons.

I've never seen this house before, Heath thought, staring, hands on his hips. The goddamn time change had stolen an hour when they all needed it most, though now the sun didn't begin its determined descent to the eager embrace of the western hills until nearly eight o'clock. Heath wasn't certain what time it was. But there was work to be done back at the Heights, calves to feed with bottles, the hired men to rouse, mother cows to reunite with their babies. Why was he wasting his time out here?

I own the Heights, he thought, staring at the house on the hill. *The Heights are mine. I can do with them as I please.*

Perhaps he would simply destroy the place.

Douse it with gasoline and throw a match.

Maybe not even warn Annabelle. Do it in the middle of some black, moonless night. Light it up and drive away. Lee was dead. Earnest was dead. Aunt Lucy never came around anymore. What was the *point*?

Heath glared at the house and ground his teeth together. *It's mine*, he thought. *All mine, and I even have an heir to leave it to, like I always said I would. And it don't mean a goddamn thing. Least of all to me.*

He had never admitted that to himself before.

Light it up. Burn it all down. Leave this godforsaken place and never look back.

"Shaw," he said. He hadn't meant to, but the word—the *name*—slipped out.

Of course, he couldn't burn down the Heights.

He had to wait, didn't he?

That was part of the curse as well.

There was a face in the window of the house way up there, staring down at him, watching.

Watching him.

That just wasn't possible.

Why am I here? How did I find this place?

The face up there was white. Dark holes for eyes. A hand crept like a dead spider turned to marble, reached from the window. Beckoned him. He was certain it did.

"No," Heath told it.

It was laughing at him. He could hear it.

None of this was possible.

He could accept that the Heights was...was...Was "haunted" the proper word? Were *they* the ghosts of dead people, those things in the walls, what Lee claimed had killed his Flora and what Heath had seen since the first day Earnest Lyon brought him from his old life to this one? Haunted?

Heath believed in curses. He had to, didn't he, if he wanted his Shaw back? *So, yes, give in.* He supposed he must believe in hauntings as well. Yes, sure, Heath could accept that the homeplace was *haunted*. But he was so far away now. Miles and miles. He wasn't even certain where in the backcountry he was. Somewhere near the Hall, perhaps, or maybe nearer to Polly King's place.

So many of these old homesteader houses were abandoned. The owners aged, couldn't farm the land any longer. Their children had no interest in taking the reins or had moved away long ago. The old places sat and rotted. Like this one. Just decomposing into nothing.

Almost nothing.

Except...someone is in there. Watching you.

Hallucination.

But what if it isn't?

What if...Yes, say it. You're thinking it. What if the entire prairie was haunted? Not just the Heights, but the *entirety* of these plains, hills, long grass blades, rocks, flowers, dust, bone—all of it, *fucking all of it?*

His forehead was beaded with icy sweat. Heath wiped it away with a grunt. More replaced it. He wiped them away too.

Shaw, come back to me.

Haunt me. I begged you to. Haunt me!

Shaw would come back. He had to keep trying. Heath had already seen him several times since that terrible night.

Shaw existed in the flash of gold which had dazzled him in the hair of a cowboy whose shoulder he had connected with back at a bar in

Wolf Point. He peered out at Heath with his typical winsomeness from the blue eyes of the gawky teenager bagging his groceries in Glasgow.

Heath was certain. Heath was positive. Bran and Rhys had been mistakes. That was why the house had taken them. Or maybe Shaw's jealousy was responsible and he couldn't abide these doppelgängers, these mealy-mouthed lookalikes. Perhaps in death, he became bent on the destruction he had only dreamed about in life, that he had confessed to Heath many a night he had dreamed about.

"But I was looking for you!" Heath would cry at night, writhing like a cat in heat in Shaw's old bed. A cat in heat, ha. That was funny. *I was looking for you, Cat! I saw you inside them!*

The curse had made Shaw jealous. Death had made him vindictive. That could be the only explanation. He was growing impatient with Heath's clumsy attempts to revive him in these other men, or maybe he enjoyed torturing Heath. That was possible.

Torture me, then, too.

Heath dug his hands into the thick shag of his hair.

No one peered at him from the window of the abandoned house.

He breathed a sigh of relief.

The door opened.

A figure emerged.

Tall, slim. He couldn't make out the features, but it was thin and pale. A tree that had learned to walk, that had grown sentient and then torn itself ruthlessly from the earth.

You!

It called for him.

You! Boy! Come up here!

We never should have taken this land, Heath thought, staring. *We never should have come here. We should have left it all, all, all alone.*

For the first time in years, Heath considered his origins. His *heritage*. His mother, whose face he had forgotten years ago, and his father, who he had never known. Mama was Sioux. That much he remembered. *The land was ours once*, he thought dismally, before the soldiers, before the reservation. *It was ours.*

Or maybe we belonged to it.

Don't make me tell you again, boy!

I have no name. Heath isn't my name. They took my name. They took my name, goddamn it. Goddamn them! Goddamn them all to burning hell for what they did to me!

Heath groaned. He felt wrapped in warmth, familiar, well-loved. The smell of sweetgrass rose all around him, invaded his nostrils, filled his lungs. A hand slid down the front of his jeans, and hot fingers encircled his penis. He jerked away, but the hand was insistent. Another hand stroked his hair. Another traced patterns on the small of his back. Another tickled that most private place between his buttocks. He groaned again—

Boy! Boy!

"No," he growled. He turned forcibly away, gripped the handle of the pickup, which was solid and real, and opened the door so he could slide into the driver's seat.

But the voice of the thing up there in that house on the hill—that impossible house, that impossible thing—that voice rang down to him, clarion-clear.

Fine. If that's how you want it, I'll come to you.

Boy.

He gripped the wheel and spun it savagely to the right. Heath roared away from that terrible house on the hill and the thing that had come creeping out of it to call just for him.

"There ain't no house like that out there," Joey Loomis, one of the new hired men, told Heath when he returned to the Heights and roused them so they could resume their duties. "I can show you, if you want, but I know these back roads like I know my own dick." And he snorted. Then sobered. "Sorry, sir."

Heath only stared at him stonily.

"We can go," Joey said, his smile dissolving completely. "We can drive around out there for a bit, try to find—"

"No," Heath said.

Joey watched him carefully, with some glint of fear in his eye. They never knew what kind of temper Mr. Heath would be in or what he would say, if he would use his words and the sharpness of his tongue to cut them down or if he would merely show them the back of his hand.

With Joey, as with others Joey knew, he had done both.

"No," Heath said again. "No, never mind. It's not important."

3

On occasional nights, Heath would drive away from the Heights and into Burke, the little town that waited some twenty miles down the winding, scoria-laden roads, to Stockman's, where he would sit alone at the bar. No one joined him, not ever. They only watched him from the corners of their eyes when he came through the door, exchanging troubled glances or, with growing rareness, some amusement if they were certain he wouldn't see it.

Heath's eyes were sharp, and he had been known to break the teeth of anyone he suspected of looking at him with any kind of scorn or, God help them, derision or even *mockery*. And after three whiskeys, he would take the guitar he brought with him and stand on the little stage—which was not much more than a six-by-six platform some nameless rancher had put together untold years before—with the guitar wrapped around him, and he would strum. He would sing, and everyone in the bar would stop to listen to his surprisingly pretty baritone, listen to him while he strummed and sang sad ballads like "El Paso" or "Walkin' After Midnight."

And, yes, though they would all be moved by the yearning they heard in his voice, in ways that burned or froze them, that they would talk about with their women or their men, with their heads on their flat pillows and the moon a frigid bone-eye peering in at them, listening to all, *all*, their confessions...Yes, though they were moved, all of them, moved beyond words, not a single man or woman in the entire place would talk to Heathcliff when his singing was complete and he packed up to return to the bar. No one dared.

The night that followed the afternoon when he had ventured out into the backcountry and found that not-so-empty house and its insistent, impossible occupant, Heath again visited Stockman's with his guitar. He sang ferociously to the thirty or so assembled patrons, never asking permission to ascend the stage, just *doing* it. Heath snarled out the lyrics to "Folsom Prison Blues" and "Blue Moon," and the audience clapped and hollered, though he never acknowledged their appreciation. He sang "Crazy" and followed it with "I Fall to Pieces."

They listened and breathed, and when he dropped the guitar and his head and sweat pattered from his brow and struck the little stage, no one clapped.

No one said a word.

Finally, Heath stepped onto the floor and tossed his wet bangs. They parted for him as if he were a shark and they stupid, staring fish, and they closed behind him when he sat at the bar and opened his mouth to order a shot of bourbon. He closed it again when he found one already waited for him. Glistening under the harsh lights, with the amber nectar within.

Heath stared at it, gape-mouthed, and glared.

"Take it," said the man next to him. "It's for you."

And the voice was too familiar to be real, but Heath glared and took the shot. He let it burn in his gullet and then set the empty glass delicately back onto the bar. Heath turned to see the face he already knew he would find.

Nose crinkled, mouth quirked with amusement. A shock of dark hair, nearly black in the chancy light of the bar. Not who he was expecting. Of course not. There would be no third time.

But the voice...

"Your voice," said the man.

"Yes." Heath couldn't look away from that face.

"When you were singing up there."

"Yes?"

"I liked it."

"Yes."

"Is that all you have to say?"

"Thanks, I suppose." The shot glass had filled again, miraculously.

The man at his side trilled merry laughter. "Aren't you thirsty? What are you waiting for?"

Heath took the shot, tossed it back, grimaced, and set it back on the bar just as delicately as the first time.

The man leaned in closer. His eyes sparkled with mischief. "I've never heard Patsy Cline sound quite like *that* before."

"Yeah."

"Like you were dying inside. Like *she* was dying. All over again."

"Yeah."

"And her pain had to come out of you. Roaring out of you, I guess."

"I guess."

"*They* liked it too." The man jerked his shaggy head in the direction of the other patrons. "Don't worry. They aren't paying any attention to *us*."

Heath smiled grimly. "Us?"

The man extended his hand. "Scott. Friends call me Scotty."

"Scott." Heath took it.

"And you?"

"Don't you know?"

Scotty shook his head, smiling slyly. "I'm new here. Or passing through. I haven't decided yet."

"Heath."

"Heath."

Heath leaned against the bar. Raised a hand. The bartender whose name Heath had never bothered to learn glowered but set another shot before him. Heath raised two fingers. The bartender shook his head.

Heath bared his teeth, leaned both elbows against the bar, and held his two fingers higher. The bartender rolled his eyes but set a second shot beside the first. Heath handed one to Scotty and took the other for himself. They clinked them together.

"Just passing through?" Heath asked, smiling a little. "*Here*?"

"My family lived here once. Long time ago. My mother spoke about it often."

"Here. Burke?" He might have said "hell" or "vomit" or "Lee."

"Oh, yes." Scotty's eyes were dark, like his hair.

For a moment, Heath trembled. He placed a hand against his forehead. The lights in the bar flared up, went out. The faces of the assembled patrons glared green, then electric blue. Their voices grated and squealed. The acrid smell of burning hair filled his nostrils. Heath refused to utter a sound, not even a moan. He shook his head.

Then the lights were just the lights again. The patrons continued to ignore him, and the only thing he smelled was the clash and tang of whiskey and beer, the unwashed floor, and his own sweat. Scotty watched him, his eyes slitted with concern.

"Everything okay? For a second, you looked—"

"I'm fine."

Scotty relaxed, and Heath allowed himself to drink the other man in, as delicious as the shots he had provided. Early twenties. One perfect dark curl fell languidly over his forehead—a suggestive comma. He wore a simple T-shirt, white, but with a blue stripe across the chest, which hugged him and revealed a hint of his nipples beneath the fabric.

Heath's cheeks flushed.

Scotty's jeans hugged him as well. Very well. Oh God.

Heath wished for another shot. His head swam. No more. Too much. So tight. Christ. He wasn't at all like Shaw...but would Shaw have ever chosen to wear a shirt like that one, jeans like those? Dark blue loafers, no socks. Oh, Shaw would. Of course he would. The cuffs of the jeans were even rolled up slightly past Scotty's ankles. Heath was certain he would.

No one else in the bar looked at all like him. The men kept their hair trimmed and neat, and all of them wore Wranglers and the plaid cotton shirts with the pearl-button snaps Shaw had so despised.

No, Scotty didn't look like Shaw, and sure, maybe he sounded like him, a little. Admit it, he wasn't at all like Shaw...but at the same time, he *was* like him. Heath knew it. He felt it.

Take any form.

He didn't want to hope.

It was stupid to hope.

"I'm still looking for a place to stay," Scotty said. He drummed his fingers along the bar. Long fingers. White. Slim. Nearly pointed.

Heath blinked. Not possible. The two in the middle were the same length, he would swear it.

"Right now, I've got this godawful room at what I guess you'd call a hotel...?"

Heath did not reply. It seemed safer.

"Calling it a rattrap is an insult to rats. But I dunno if I wanna stick around anyway. This place has bad vibes."

"Bad vibes?"

"You don't feel it?" Scotty shivered exaggeratedly. "The people too. I've seen friendlier folks at an execution."

"You been to many executions?"

"Oh, sure. Hundreds. Millions. And everyone there looked just like *them*." His face darkened. His brow furrowed. He leaned closer. "Except for you."

"You don't know me."

"I suppose I don't."

"Maybe I like executions."

Scotty snorted laughter. "Hell, maybe you do. Everyone's gotta like *something*, right? And everyone's got the right to like...what they like."

"Not always."

"Now you just wanna argue." Scotty grinned sunnily.

There was nothing of Shaw in him. Nothing at all. Best to go. Pick up the guitar before one of these hillbilly pigfuckers stepped on it and crushed it to splinters. Best not to order a beer. Yet that's exactly what he found himself doing, hillbilly pigfuckers be damned.

"Hillbilly pigfuckers! Man, that's good. That's grand. Wicked crazy hyperbole. I'm impressed."

Heath paused mid-swig. The beer was disgusting. He swallowed half the pint glass anyway. Wiped the back of his mouth. Hell. Had he spoken aloud?

The air grew thick with smoke. The kid—not a kid, a man, early twenties, surely—the man, Scott, Scotty to his friends, held a joint. He grinned. Handed it to Heath.

Don't take it. Don't put it in your mouth. Hell, don't inhale! But he was. He already had.

Because this isn't real. It isn't real, so it don't matter.

His head felt like a balloon, light and barely tethered. Soon it would float away.

A grin stretched hot across his face, like a cut.

An answering grin zig-zagged across Scotty's.

They grinned at each other, just a couple'a grinners.

"You can't smoke that in here," the bartender said.

"The fuck you say," Heath replied.

Or Scotty did. He didn't bother to look at the little man, squat, bald, a monkey, just a fucking monkey.

"And you can't call me names. We've talked about this before, Heath."

Shit. He was saying things out loud, and he wasn't even aware of it.

Scotty blew a cloud of cerulean smoke that hung like a lovely blanket over their heads.

"You think you can do whatever you want. You think you can come in here—"

Heath wasn't even aware that his fist was going to cut the air until it did, cut the space between him and the bartender into half, then a quarter, then less than that, unaware his fist was going to connect with the bartender's nose and mash his lips up against his teeth, that one of the teeth was going to give way. Scotty was *laughing*—

They jumped him, four or five of the cowboys who had been leaning against the bar, seemingly paying him no mind.

Scotty said into his ear, just before they did, "Let's get the hell out of here. Whadda ya say?"

But the bastard pigfuckers jumped Heath while the bartender squalled, "Mess him up! He broke my goddamn nose. He broke my *teeth*. Teach the bastard a lesson. Mess him *up*!" And they wailed on him, fists like iron bars, arms thick or lean but muscled nevertheless from the endless work with the cows, the steers, the calves, fencing, riding tractors, fixing tractors, endless work. But endless work made them strong, and so they wailed on him and at least one of them hissed, "Fucking *faggot*," into his ear.

Heath roared like a bear, but it wasn't enough. At last, Scotty had him by the hand and *yanked* him from the bar. They tumbled together out into the street, and somehow, they were both laughing and laughing and laughing.

"You don't have to go back there, you know," Scotty said at last. "You're bleeding."

"Of course, I'm bleeding," Heath growled, bloodied and drunk, swaying there on the crumbling street corner outside the fucking Stockman's. "Of course, I am. Pigs beat the shit out of me, didn't they?"

"You think it was my fault."

"I know it was."

"So what if it was?"

Heath considered this. His head hurt. They had cut his lip with one of their punches. Probably someone wearing a ring. He had never worn a ring. Why would he? He and Shaw had never been married. Impossible to fathom marriage, *real* marriage, then, impossible to even begin to imagine. Wasn't it?

Why was it?

"I loved him," Heath whispered.

"I know."

"Shut the fuck up."

"Let's get out of here."

"There's no 'let's,' you hear me, boy? There isn't any 'us.'" He threw his head back and howled, a wolf's sound, full of desolation. "*I don't know you, and you don't know me!*"

"I could."

Heath lowered his head, blinked his surprise. Had the other man really said that?

He was staring at him with those large dark eyes.

None of this is real. I know it isn't. There's no one here like...like me, not anymore. There was only Shaw.

Those eyes. Scotty had taken a step closer. Behind them, through the door to Stockman's they had left half-open when they had tumbled out into the fragrant April evening, someone had plugged a quarter into the jukebox. Grace Slick began to snarl "Somebody to Love."

Heath's stomach churned. Her voice wasn't human. She sounded feline, a cat wailing words that were intended to be English but weren't, couldn't possibly be.

Don't think of cats. Heath couldn't help himself. Her feline snarl squalled on and on. A guitar wailed. Where was his guitar? Fuck. Misery descended over him, pulling self-pity with it. Fuck all it.

Scotty was reaching for him.

"Come on," he said quietly. "Easy as hell, man."

Heath slapped his hand away.

Covered his face.

And ran.

Heath woke when the sun rose, sprawled in Shaw's narrow bed, in Shaw's little room. His head throbbed like a rotten tooth. He groaned. He was naked somehow. That was unusual. Normally, he slept in his shorts at least. Many nights he fell asleep fully clothed, boots and all.

He dressed, wincing at the thin sunlight marking him through Shaw's window, and clomped heavily down the stairs. The baby goggled at him. Annabelle set before him a plate heaped full of fluffy eggs and deer sausage from the animal she had shot herself last fall. They had skinned, gutted, and cut it up together, turning the poor beast into steaks and fat links of sausage. Heath muttered his gratitude to her and tucked in.

She watched him expressionlessly, then turned to the window over the sink that looked out at the granaries on the hill below.

"I think one of your hired men's run off," she said at last. Her tone was even, expressionless. It was like that all the time now. Except when she spoke to the baby. She loved the baby. She didn't love Heath. He wondered why that stabbed at him.

Heath speared a piece of sausage and crammed it into his mouth.

"Doubt it."

"I seen Matt this morning. He says Joey didn't come back last night. Says his bed ain't been slept in."

Heath grunted. "Maybe he found himself a woman."

"Maybe." She turned to the baby and fussed gently with him, wiping away the little bit of egg fouling his mouth and chin.

Hare gazed adoringly at his father and hurled his spoon at him. It struck Heath's forehead before he could duck. Pain flowered. Red, everything was red. Annabelle screaming. His hands around the baby's throat—

Heath opened his eyes. No. Just the pain. Annabelle watched him warily. She was a mother bear, a thick, vengeful creature with hidden claws she would reveal if Heath demonstrated any desire to hurt her offspring. He didn't want to hurt her offspring. *Their* offspring. Shit. He didn't really care either way.

"Sorry," Annabelle said at last. "He's going through a phase."

"Yup," Heath said. The pain stabbed him behind the eyes. Not just from the goddamn spoon either. Christ, he had promised himself he wouldn't drink like that, not in the towns, anyway. It wasn't safe. Had they thrown him out of Stock's? *Again*? Jesus fuck.

Come on. Easy as hell, man.

He opened his eyes wide. That voice. Heath knew that voice. Yes, yes, they had thrown him out, and he hadn't been alone.

Easy as hell.

And those eyes—

"I been trying to get ahold of Eddie," Annabelle said, bouncing the baby on her knee. "He isn't answering his phone. Thought you might want to head over there later today. See if he's around."

"Why don't you?"

"I could go with you."

Heath took a heavy swig of his coffee. Too bitter. Annabelle made shitty coffee. "Make it your own damn self," she would say, and he would drink it anyway. Heath finished it off. Set the mug down. Glared at the baby, who glared back. Heath winked at him. The baby, astonished, sprayed delighted laughter.

Heath hauled himself up from the table. "All right," he said while the pain stomped and roared its own delight behind his eyes.

The Thrush place felt deserted. They both knew it the moment they pulled into the dooryard. Eddie's truck was parked by the gate as it always was. His dog, a Golden Retriever named Bruce, came bounding from around the house to greet them, barking joyously.

Eddie kept no more chickens or horses or pigs. He had been living off Shaw's money for years now. That was all right. Heath was fine with that. Sure, he was. Why wouldn't he be? Eddie was old now. His hair gone white, his eyes milky and dead-looking. Annabelle would smack him whenever he described Eddie's eyes that way, but it was true. Eddie might as well have been dead.

Hare twisted in Annabelle's arms. He made a thick, gabbling sound indicating his displeasure. Annabelle shushed him. She looked to Heath. He nodded. They opened the doors of the truck and stepped onto the hard-packed earth of the road.

Bruce had ceased to bark. He panted instead and gazed at them both adoringly. Heath patted his head. Bruce grinned and bounded away, back behind the house.

The wind sniffed at them, found them wanting, moved away, moaning.

"It's so quiet," Annabelle whispered.

Heath swallowed. He didn't want to agree with her. But it was, though. Besides the moaning of the wind, which had been especially pissy this spring, the entire Thrush farm held its eerie quiet tightly. Possessively. Heath began to sweat despite the light licking of the wind.

Annabelle shuffled Hare from one arm to the other. With her free hand, she took Heath's and clutched it tightly. Each observed the fear in the other's eyes and relaxed slightly. Annabelle squeezed Heath's hand. He squeezed it back.

They looked at the Thrush house.

Nothing moved in the windows. The door hung open, though, slightly ajar.

"The door," Annabelle said. Her voice trembled only slightly.

Heath squeezed her hand again.

Together they moved through the gate. Together they moved toward the house.

The wind sighed, already in some kind of terrible mourning.

A sob hitched in Annabelle's chest and died.

They moved slowly, carefully, toward the house.

He won't be in there, Heath thought concretely. *Eddie will be gone, and the house will be deserted. We'll never find him, and we'll never learn*

*what happened to him or where he went. And we'll have to sell the farm
and the house, and Annabelle will be crazy with grief. And she'll never let
it go, and she'll always wonder. And she'll always blame me a little or
a lot—*

The front door opened all the way.

They froze, both gaping.

Hare sneezed; Hare growled.

A man appeared there, a shirtless man, a man with damp hair, a man
wiping that hair, dark, thick, luxurious, with one of Eddie's plain white
towels. A man grinning sunnily at them, as if he recognized them.

Fuck, hell, he did.

"Mornin'!" chirped the dark-haired man Heath recognized from his
time at the Stockman's in Burke last night. "You must be Annabelle!
And little Hare!"

Annabelle, too startled for words, could only gulp, then gape before
forcing her mouth to close. She looked at Heath, confused. Her eyes
pleaded with him.

"Sorry," the dark-haired stranger said, grinning his familiar grin.
"Just got out of the shower. We heard you pull up. Why, you're a sight
for sore eyes, as they say. And mine are pretty sore after all that whiskey
last night. Whoo!" His grin widened. He wrapped the towel around his
neck.

Both Annabelle and Heath stared at his chest, which was dark, with
scraggles of hair as black as that atop his head. His nipples were small,
hard nubs colored a delicate coral. His abdominal muscles stood out but
subtly, and both Heath and Annabelle traced that trail of black hair
dusting his muscles down and down, to the place where his bellybutton
met his sky-blue chinos.

They realized how they stared, and their eyes snapped back up, first
toward each other, then toward the stranger.

He knows we're staring, Heath thought distantly. *He knows, and he
loves it.*

The man juddered out his hand, as he had at Stock's last night, only
this time in Annabelle's direction. "I met your husband last night.
Heath, wasn't it? Yes, Heath. I thought so. I'm Scott. Friends call me
Scotty. And you're Eddie's sister."

"Annabelle," she said slowly, dazedly. She looked once more toward Heath for some kind of guidance, but he had none to offer her. Instead, she took Scotty's hand.

He shook it, firmly and eagerly.

Behind them, Eddie appeared in the doorway. He was dressed, though his hair was also wet. And his feet were bare. Heath stared. He had never seen Eddie's bare feet before. They seemed small and white and defenseless. He had crammed his hands into the pockets of his own chinos, which were a dark, forest green. Eddie looked miserable. He said nothing. Just stood there.

"Eddie and I met up last night when I was on my way back to that awful hotel I was telling you about," Scott said, smiling, smiling. He slung the towel around his shoulders and laid his hands solidly on his hips. "He offered me a place to stay as an alternative, and I took him up on it. Kindness of strangers, and all that."

"Strangers," Annabelle said politely.

"I'm looking for a job, is the thing," Scotty said. "I want to maybe stay around here. For a while, anyway. I got nowhere else to go." Smiling, sunnily, smiling.

Annabelle stared furiously at the ground.

Eddie hitched up his pants. Cleared his throat.

Hare said, clearly and distinctly, "Hell. Hell fuck hell."

No one laughed.

Heath cleared his own throat.

"Well," he said. "Well. We had a hired man, see. Mighta run off this morning—"

Scotty's eyes gleamed.

Eddie opened his mouth, perhaps to protest. No one knew what he had been prepared to say. He closed it immediately with an audible snap.

The next day, they found Eddie dead in his bed. Alone. And staring.

As if he had seen the very devil.

· · ·

4

The stranger moved into the bunkhouse with Matt—the single remaining hired man now that Joey had run off—who looked at Scott-Friends-Call-Me-Scotty with the same contempt Heath recognized because he had seen it all his life, only aimed at him. It had been stamped for certain on the faces of the people in Stockman's that night they had thrown him out.

I know what you are, that face said. *Faggot.*

But Matt didn't say anything. He knew better. Besides, he had heard about Rhys and Bran. He knew this one wouldn't last either.

He's real. He's real, he's real, he's real.

Heath found himself repeating that mantra several times a day.

They buried Eddie in the Grandview Cemetery. Beside Shaw. Heath had considered fighting this. In the end, he let it go. Heart attack, was what the doc from Sidney determined. Not unexpected. Annabelle sobbed endlessly. Their father had died of a heart attack when he was right around Eddie's age.

"It isn't uncommon," said the doc, "not around here. These men work themselves too hard for years. And, why, finally, *finally,* somethin's gotta give. Somethin' always gives."

The doc had seen Eddie's face. Seen the expression marring it. Twisting it into a purple, pop-eyed grimace. Heath knew no heart attack had contorted Eddie Thrush's face into an expression as grotesque as *that.*

"Something is scaring your sheep," Scotty said at the end of his first week on the job.

Heath was certain he would square up to look ridiculous in his work clothes, but he didn't. *He looks just like the rest of us*, Heath thought wonderingly: the Wranglers, the flat-toed boots, scuffed and obviously well-used, the plaid cotton shirt with the pearl snaps, sleeves rolled up to his elbows. The cowboy hat. Much like Heath's own. It made him seem human—of course, he was human—more real—of course, he was *real* —and less like...Well, *more* like everyone else.

Matt relaxed around him, gradually, gradually. They joshed together, ribbed each other, working down in the grease together fixing the tractor, flat on their backs, patching fences after an agitated cow, chasing her new-born calf, tore a section of it in the north pasture to pieces, scratching the hell out of herself on the barbed wire in the process. And working with the sheep—a new project Heath tried at Annabelle's request.

"Something new. A diversion," was how she had put it. "And I know sheep're hard, but that'll be part of the fun."

Though what Annabelle knew about fun, Heath couldn't guess. So naturally, Heath thought sourly, *naturally* it was the sheep Scotty now approached him about.

"They're all in what my mother would call a tizzy," he said, smiling slightly.

"Any missing?"

"Not so you'd notice, no."

"Sheep are sensitive."

"Oh, yeah. I've heard that."

"You ever worked with sheep before?"

"Thousands of times. Millions." That same odd little smile flickered across Scotty's face.

He sounds like one of us, Heath thought. *He looks like one of us. He didn't before. I swear it.*

"So, you know."

"Oh, yeah. Sure, I do. Sure."

Now he was grinning.

No one was around.

They stood by themselves, both leaning against the ancient wooden posts Earnest Lyon's grandfather had erected when he had homesteaded this land not quite a hundred years ago. They stood. Watching each other. Scotty hadn't shaved in a few days. The stubble looked like pepper scattered over his cheeks and chin.

"You want to find it," he said, grinning, "whatever it is, and kill it before it tears through your livestock. Anything that leaves a footprint like *this*—" And he gestured for the first time, and for the first time, Heath saw what Scotty pointed out, and his eyes narrowed, and his teeth gritted together. "—really isn't anything to joke about. Sheep being so sensitive and all."

A pawprint. Indented deeply into the mud. Five inches wide at least. Round. A cat print.

Heath remembered the tawny streak of yellow he had seen when Mr. Lyon first brought him to this place.

Devil cat. Puma. A beast, Heath-my-boy. Swallow you whole.

He could hear Catherine Lyon chiming her wicked laughter.

"He's a big ol' boy too," Scotty said. He knelt beside the track. "He's just playing with our little sheepies now. But he'll be back. Probably tonight. Probably take one or two with him."

"You know mountain lions too."

Scotty looked up. His eyes sparkled in the light of the morning sun. "Oh, yes," he said. "Of course, I do. I know *lots* of things. Heath."

Heath lay that night in his single bed in Shaw's old room and stared at the ceiling.

"I murdered you," he muttered. With one hand he clenched a handful of the sheets.

Outside, something began to wail in the night. Something screamed like a woman in pain. His hand bore down on the sheet.

"I murdered you, and I accept that. Sent you into that abyss. Couldn't follow you there. I know. I know."

The thing outside grew closer, its screams louder. Heath writhed on the bed, twisting the sheets.

"I murdered you! I begged for you to torment me. I begged you!"

The thing outside *shrieked*. Heath sat up in bed and shrieked with it. Downstairs, he heard the scrambling of feet. The wailing of the baby. Goddamn it.

"Torment me!" he roared. "Bastard, you bastard, torment me, then! I deserve it! *I deserve it!*"

The thing screamed its pain and its triumph as if in agreement.

Three dead sheep in the morning. One missing. The dead ones disemboweled. It had snowed in the night, a pretty spring frosting, and the snow was spattered with splashes of bright crimson. Like berries. And all around were the footprints of the beast, the great cat.

Scotty wasn't smiling any longer. He shivered at the lick of the wind against his thick blue chore coat—Wrangler, like his jeans. Scotty glared at the dead bodies, sucked his teeth, and shook his head.

He was blond this morning.

Suddenly.

Heath stared.

Had he always been blond?

No. You know he wasn't. He dyed his hair.

"What a goddamn waste," Scotty said. He turned away with his blond head bowed.

"No," Annabelle said quietly. "He wasn't always blond. You know better, baby. You got eyes."

"Yeah."

"He musta dyed it. Like you said."

"Sure."

"Nothing else is possible."

"Okay."

"We live in the world of real things, Heath."

Did she really believe that? All around them, the Heights shifted and sighed.

"Shaw is gone."

Heath turned to her. He bared his teeth. She bared hers back.

"You have to accept that, baby. Shaw is *gone*." Her chest hitched, but her eyes remained hard and flinty. "Just like Eddie is gone. People *go*, Heath. They leave us. And they don't come back. Not ever."

He didn't have to explain to her. She didn't believe her own words.

"Curses aren't real. Ghosts aren't *real*."

He relaxed. They watched each other. The snow outside had melted, and the sun rode above them like a blazing eye. It left dappled patterns on the floor of the kitchen, where they sat and ate their noontime meal.

"I have to accept things as they are," she said at last, carefully and quietly.

Hare sat in his highchair. He stared dreamily at the ceiling, waving at an unseen passerby.

"That includes Scotty's hair color. You should too, baby. I don't know what else to tell you other than that. Accept things as the way they are."

"What we can see."

"Yes."

I do that, he wanted to say. Instead, he pushed his plate away and rose. Donned his hat and work coat. "I got a cat to hunt."

Annabelle relaxed a little, spooned some baby food—strained carrots, which Hare loved—past the baby's lips. He gurgled with pleasure and promptly spit them back up. Heath closed his eyes.

Yes. Accept what you see. This is life. This is your life. You made it this way.

"Kill it," she said, "and kill it fast. Before it takes any more of the things that are *ours*."

He stared at her. She cleaned the spit-up from the baby's chin and leaned forward. Kissed his forehead.

"Shit," said Hare, smiling. "Shit hell damn."

Heath took his rifle from its place in the hallway. Checked to see if it was loaded. It was. He would have to watch that before Hare learned to walk. A baby in the house was dangerous.

"Yes," he said, surprising himself by leaning over and kissing Annabelle's lips. She kissed him back and looked at him for any signs, he supposed, of wildness.

"Shit," she said, smiling, and kissed him again. Her eyes sparkled. "Shit hell damn."

Scotty sat beside Heath on the passenger seat of the truck. He stared straight ahead, with eyes so clear and crystalline they were more than blue, nearly white. Heath refused to look at them. Refused to admit they had changed. They bumped their way through the back country with no road to guide them. Only the hills and the coulees.

The rifle across Scotty's lap waited for his command.

"You want to bag this cat, boss," Scotty had said, catching Heath while he prepared to jump into the truck. "I'll come with you. Let's find it. I want it dead too. You don't know how bad."

He'll admit it now, Heath thought. *He'll tell me who he is. Or who he's pretending to be. Oh God, I don't know which it is! I could ask. I should ask. But I can't.*

Scotty's fingers rested lightly over the rifle's stock.

Christ, he could kill me now if he wanted to.

Why should he want to kill me?

There is no reason.

He could be a thing, *like* them. *Like the other things you've seen all your life. A part of the Heights. If he's one of* them, *or something from* outside, *he could absolutely want to kill you. Eat you. Take you with him. It. Out into the darkness.*

Or—

"Take any form!" he had shrieked while Shaw's life had fled his twisted body. "Take any form, my Cat."

It was too much to hope. After Bran, after Rhys. It would be too cruel to hope.

I didn't find him, Heath thought when Scotty turned his head to gaze pensively out the passenger side window. *That's the difference, maybe. I didn't go in search of him. He* came to me.

He wasn't watching the passing countryside, Heath realized with a shock.

He was watching Heath's reflection in the window glass.

And he was smiling. Again.

The sky over their heads was broad and without a single streak of cloud. The temperature had risen into the high sixties. They had left their coats behind in the cab of the truck, and now they wiped sweat beads from their foreheads. Heath held the rifle. The blond man with the ice-blue eyes tromped along faithfully behind him.

They had stopped because they had found prints. Big ones, shaped like an M, with two lobes on the front and three on the back. Puma tracks. Mr. Lyon had pointed them out to Heath before, long ago. The ground was soft from the melted snow, and the tracks stood out starkly.

"We don't know much about each other," Scotty offered from behind him.

Maybe he hoped Heath would stop and face him. Heath didn't know. What the hell. But he didn't. Wouldn't give Scotty the satisfaction, even if that was what he did want.

Heath grunted instead. Kept walking. More tracks.

"I'm sure you think...Hell, I don't know what you think. About me, I mean. But I want you to know. If we're going to—if *I'm* going to work with you. For you. I'm from Kansas."

Heath grunted again. Bran had been from Kansas.

"You're from around here, right? Matt told me. He said you're from the reservation originally."

A shadow fell over them. Heath didn't stop moving, but he looked up. A cloud had covered the sun. Cold, unpleasant and sudden, pinched at him.

"You ever go back?"

Heath grunted again. Scotty said nothing. He was waiting for a response, Heath realized.

"No," he said shortly.

"How'd you wind up here?"

"Adopted."

"I'm adopted too."

Now Heath *was* surprised. He glanced over his shoulder.

Scotty smiled. Fresh grass, new and green, crushed under their feet. The smell filled Heath's nostrils. Betokened summertime. The sun returned. The smell intensified. The tracks were gone.

"My mom adopted a whole mess of us. But I don't really know

them much, my brothers and sisters. They're all older than me anyway. I'm the baby. But I don't know them, and I don't really want to. Makes me feel really silly. Stupid, I guess, that I always felt so alone growing up, even though the house was always full of people. You know how that is?"

Heath said nothing.

"Stupid, like I said. That's why I left. I tried college. It didn't really take. I didn't know what I wanted. Hell. I guess I still don't know that."

Heath said nothing. There, where the grass was thinner, was another track. Good.

"I was hitchhiking. Just had my pack. I got picked up a lot. I aimed for Montana, though."

"You had family here." Heath surprised himself.

"In Burke. Long time ago. They aren't there anymore. I don't know anyone. I met Eddie because he remembered them. My aunt. My cousins. I mean, they're no one to me, not really, but Eddie, he remembered them. Aw, man. Poor Eddie. Seems stupid to feel as bad as I do. I mean, I hardly knew him. And he was a nice guy. He was sure nice to me. But I knew he wasn't doing well that first night. I could see it in his eyes. I read his horoscope for him."

Heath sighed. Shook his head. Idiocies. The man spoke in riddles. None of it could be real, or all of it could be. Heath sighed again. He was tired. So tired.

"It's a thing I do. I taught myself. I read his cards too. The tarot, you know? You know?"

"No," Heath growled.

"They tell the future. My older sister taught me about *that*. I saw right away that Eddie didn't have much time left. Poor old guy. He sure was nice to me."

I'll bet he was.

"Aw, jeez. Look."

Heath stopped.

Scotty knelt. The corpse of a rabbit—shredded fur, tendons, large black eyes staring blankly—lay on its side before them. The grass was flattened all around it. There was no blood.

"It's so quiet," Scotty whispered.

It was. No birds sang. Not even the wind whispered, as it always seemed to whisper out here. No tractors ground away at the land in the distance. No car chewed at the scoria that comprised the roads.

Heath felt his stomach drop.

"Look what we have here," said Scotty.

Ahead of them was the house, the one perched on the top of its hill like a growth. The one Heath had found by accident before he had gone into town to play his guitar. The night he had met Scotty. Impossible night; impossible house.

It rose from the prairie grass like a figure in a dusty gray cape, empty window frames black and staring. The wood that was its skin had lost any paint it might have possessed long ago. No, Heath thought numbly, the boards weren't like a cape or a giant coat at all. They were more like ribs. Bones, but dusty-looking and colorless.

The puma's tracks headed in just that direction.

Heath whipped his head back to Scotty, who was smiling. But only slightly. Of course he was.

"I'll bet no one lives there," he said.

"I'll bet you're right."

Scotty's fingers danced lightly over Heath's shoulder. Heath flinched back. Scotty tittered.

"We have to go in there, you know."

"Do we?"

"That's where *it* is."

"Is it?"

"You know it. You see the tracks."

"You want to go in there?"

"I figure we have to. We gotta find this thing and kill it."

"Kill it."

"It'll only cause more destruction. Kill more sheep. Or cows. Or worse."

"Is there worse?"

"You know there can be."

"Ah." Heath nodded sagely. His eyes flicked up to the house on the hill.

The door stood open. Something waited inside. Something had made the house its home.

They moved up the hill, Heath in the lead.

"I saw you in San Francisco once," the blond man behind him sang, "and I waited for you to find me, and then you did. And I thought, I can stay. I can stay. Inside him, I can stay. He'll keep me safe. So, I followed you. Through the fog and in the grass and the stones and even the spiders and the atoms in the air. I followed you, followed you. I came along for you, my Heath, just for you."

Heath gritted his teeth. *I don't hear this*, he thought. *I do hear this.*

The house above them gaped wide its mouth. Something moved across the threshold. Something flickered. Tawny? Yellow? Something flicked its yellow tail, beckoning them.

"I followed you, and I waited. And I lived inside, oh, so many people, mostly men. Vile, hideous men. I waited in them, and I waited for you, Heath. My Heath, my sweet—"

The voice bubbled as if the throat of the speaker had filled with phlegm.

I won't turn around. I won't turn around. I won't. And Heath didn't. His hands clenched convulsively around the rifle and bore down on it instead.

Now the voice rose in pitch, soaring upward, no longer human but something high and shrieking. And it said, "I came all this way to find you, and we will be together for forever and forever and forever!"

All semblance of humanity was gone. Just the shriek of the wind over the prairie, the lonely sounds they had learned to live with, that would haunt them long after they slept or tried to leave this particular world behind. Forever and forever.

"Look at me. Turn and look at me, my Heath."

Heath stood before the door of the house. Something moved inside. Something made a rumbling sound—a growl? Something clicked and clattered along the ancient dusty floorboards.

The thing behind him panted. Wheezed. Thick, bubbling sounds rattled in its throat and in its chest. Heath felt its breath on his neck. It stank like the creek.

"I love you, Heath," it said at last. "I came back for you, like you told me to. I love you Heath. I came back. I came back like you wanted me to. I love you, Heath. I love you. Heath. *I love you, Heath. I love you, Heath. I love you—*"

"*You're not him!*" Heath roared.

Spun around.

Aimed the rifle.

And pulled the trigger.

5

The old man was asleep. Heath snored with his mouth gaping. And Christ, he wasn't *really* all *that* old, was he? Late forties? Early fifties? Though the little he claimed to know about his own origins, including his age, astounded me. His chin was covered with a bristle of tiny white hairs. His Adam's apple bobbed. His hair was a solid white. Like a fright wig.

How had he aged so much? He wasn't much older than my father, probably younger than my father. How had he *aged* so damned much in such a short amount of time?

Oh, sweet, stupid Lock. You know the answer to that.

I couldn't wake him. Didn't want to. Even though I needed— *needed*—the rest of the story. His story, and Annabelle's, and Shaw's.

But I left him. My questions were unanswered. I sat and spoke with Annabelle instead, for a while. She had stories too. She backed his up, which I didn't expect.

"Oh, yeah," she said.

She was old too, God help her. Her face was all webbed with wrinkles, her eyes faded like yellowed old sheets. But not *yellow*. Not like those eyes I had seen outside my window.

"I don't know about *that*," she said, when I told her about what I had seen out there in the darkness. Annabelle scrunched her face when she thought so she looked like a rotting apple. "But I do know we seen things out at this place, year after year, night after night, that shock us.

Yes, that's the right word: We are *shocked*. And you best be careful, boy." She said that to me. "This place has a power, and it has a *reach*. Might be it'll reach for *you*."

I listened to her, then I went to a different room since the one they meant me to occupy had a broken window. That sniffing December wind was coming in strong.

The next morning, Heath refused to see me—Hare said he was out. He had gone out. Didn't I know nothing about farms?

Christ, fuck, but you're dumb," he said.

And so I took my horse and rode back to Gramma and Grandpa's. Aunt Lucy was waiting for me. She truly was old by now, near eighty, maybe nearer ninety. But she was still sharp. Most of those farm women are, you know.

She didn't warn me off or tell me to stay away from the Heights, like I expected her to. Aunt Lucy only smiled a little.

"It's a secret place," she said. "What'd you see?"

I told her. She nodded as if she had expected to hear exactly that.

"You should treasure that, Lock." She never called me "boy," like they did at the Heights, or "cousin," like Heath did. Aunt Lucy called me always and forever by my very own name. "You should treasure what you've seen out there. It's proof, isn't it, that there is more to this earth than we know. That maybe there's more to death than we know. Don't you think?"

I agreed with her. I called her "ma'am," as I had always done.

"Funny places out here. Hardly ever been people. Even the Indians. Hardly ever did much with the land. They were wiser than we are, I guess. We tried too hard to make the land what we wanted it to be, make it do what we wanted it to do. The land doesn't care about us, and sometimes, I like to think it fights back. That would explain a lot, wouldn't it?"

I acquiesced as to, "Yes, ma'am, I think it would."

She nodded as if satisfied. "Why don't you take a nap, Lock?" she said. "I think you had a long night."

I went into Burke the next day. It had shrunk, Grandma claimed, over the last thirty years or so. There wasn't much of anything left: a main street, a few churches, a school. A library that was really just a box painted turquoise, like they wanted it to be pretty. For something, *anything* to be pretty. The road that ran through town and up to the highway—paved, not like the ones in the country that led you to places like the Heights— that road was shit. Torn apart. Potholes. Sidewalk crumbling.

But there were people in the café—The Farmer's Kitchen, they called it—and the street was lined with vehicles. Pickups, mostly. Those ubiquitous farmers, in town for a late breakfast, an early lunch, or a cup of coffee they could drink while they bullshitted with their friends.

I entered the café. I hadn't been in there since I was a little grasshopper, all scrub brush hair and long legs and knees and elbows. I would go with Grandma when she had errands to run in town.

Three tables were occupied by old men who sat with old women. A young, fat farmer with a face like a walrus perched upon a stool at the counter, where a thin dishrag girl leaned with both her elbows planted firmly on the yellow Formica and laughed and sneered and tittered at what the walrus-man had to say. She wore an apron, and she was pretty in a vague sort of way.

I don't know if I found her attractive. Heath's story had me wondering exactly what "attractive" meant—to me, at least—and if I could really possibly and truly stay with one woman for the rest of my life. Not the first time a man has ever thought that way, for sure, but it had really never occurred to me. Not until Heath's story last night.

The girl saw me and stopped laughing, stopped smiling, and looked at me with flat, reflectionless eyes. The walrus-man grinned at me from beneath his bushy mustache. Sweat ran down his forehead. He lifted his coffee cup, took a healthy swig, and grinned at me again. He didn't say a word. No one did. But they all stared.

"Mornin'," I said at last, fitting my friendliest smile onto my face. It felt false and exhausted. I don't know exactly what I thought I was doing. I am still not sure what I thought I could prove by this little expedition.

My mama had told me once I was too nostalgic. This interaction occurred when I was seven or eight. Maybe younger. But it stuck with me.

Too nostalgic.

Probably the reason why I had nearly gotten myself killed last night, taking my poor old Sasha down to the homeplace. Probably why I wanted to spend the night at the Heights. My childhood had swarmed around me at Grandma and Grandpa Linden's. It always did. But the Heights...

Had I even ever really been there before? I must have. It made me crazy to think that I still wasn't certain, even after Heath's story. Even after my night in that bed. The things I had seen and heard. I still wasn't at all sure. Goddamn memory after all.

"Mornin'," I said, and after a beat of silence, the girl exchanged a look with the heavyset farmer before her, who made no movement, did not do a thing to change the expression on his face.

Finally, she trained her gaze back on me. "Mornin'," she said at last. "Coffee?"

I said yes.

She poured me a cup. Old and yellow. Chipped. Someone had attempted to paint a daisy on it, but the daisy appeared forlorn and wilted, as tired as the girl who had handed it to me.

I sipped at the coffee. It was revolting. Weak. Like hot water. I smiled as pleasantly as I could. Asked for cream.

The farmer snorted. The girl disappeared into the kitchen and returned with a half-gallon carton of skim milk, which she handed to me. It didn't do much to improve the coffee's flavor. Now it tasted like hot water with milk-water in it.

"Delicious," I said, smiling my horribly insincere smile, and the farmer snorted again. Shook his enormous head. I ignored him.

The couples at the tables behind me whispered. I looked at them. They didn't stop. The café felt hot. The heat becoming oppressive. I was sweating like the farmer. I sipped at my coffee. I sipped.

"Why don't you get out of here?" the walrus-farmer said at last, and his voice was pleasant.

His smile the same. There was a light in his eyes, though. Like a dog's eyes. A kind of craziness. I thought of the dog that had come for me in the grove last night. His eyes were its eyes.

"Why don't you just get the hell out?"

"Just drinking coffee," I said. Was I shocked? I felt shocked. People in my world didn't talk to other people this way.

College boy, college boy. Think you're better'n us?

The girl stared at me with her flat gaze. I realized they knew who I was. Knew who I was and hated me for it. But why? They didn't *really* know me. My hand trembled. It knocked up against the coffee cup. Tipped it over. The white-gray liquid spilled over the counter. The girl cried out. The farmer shook his head.

"You people," he growled. He was no longer smiling. "You goddamn people from out *there*. Always causing trouble. Can't you just leave us alone? Have to ruin *everything*. Can't leave *nothing* nice."

"I don't know what you're talking about." To the girl, I said, "Can I help? Is there a rag?"

"No, no," she said, clearly flustered. She fluttered her hands about beneath the counter for several long seconds before she finally materialized a towel stained with filth. The girl scrubbed furiously at the coffee spill.

"I'm really sorry," I said.

"Fuckin faggots," the farmer observed. "All a bunch of goddamn queer-ass faggot mother*fuckers*."

"Steve," the girl said mildly, still scrubbing.

I began to grin. Something inside me started to blaze a bit. I thought of Heath, who I kind of hated, and his story. I thought of Earnshaw Lyon, now long dead but still beloved. Still goddamn loved. Someone should love me like that someday. Set out a curse to keep me in the world. Love was a curse, or it *could* be. It could hold and tear and claw and *hurt* but still keep you. Keep you *here*.

Yes, yes. I grinned at the man.

"Yeah, Steve," I said, grinning, grinning. "You better watch your mouth. Steve."

He stood. His belly, sheathed in red flannel and straining against it, was its own planet. His unshaven face swelled before me. Reddish-brown hairs marched in little armies all over the immensity of his throat.

"You better watch *your* mouth. Son."

"I'm not your son." Rage was pulsing behind my eyes. It lifted the corners of my mouth even further. I had never known rage like this before. I liked it, God help me. There was a well opened inside me, and I wanted that hot crimson water. *Give it to me. Give it all to me.* Shaw Lyon had died for love, and this motherfucker, *this* beast of a man—he dared to talk like that? "You dare?" I said. "To use those words? With *me*?" Didn't he know who I was?

He knew. He knew.

"Steve, c'mon," the girl whined.

"Shut up," Steve said. He didn't take his eyes off me.

Silence fell over the café. They were all watching, the bastards. Watching, like they had always done where my family was concerned. Filthy bastards.

"We take a lot from you people." Steve stepped toward me, light and graceful for such a big, clumsy-looking man. His fists were the size of hams. He clenched them. He was as full of rage as I was.

Well, I thought, grinning, *We'll see about* that.

"Sure, we have. Taken a whole *helluva* lot. We don't gotta, you know."

I thought about the missing ranch hands. If Heath was to be believed, how many were there? How many had gone missing? I felt cold. My grin faded.

"Get outta here," the girl whispered. "Please."

Her eyes were flint. Jesus. I paused. They hated me. *Hated* me.

I thought of Heath. I thought of Shaw. And Eddie Thrush. Three goddamn queer-ass faggot motherfuckers in that same place, that same time. Waiting for each other. Their whole lives spent waiting to collide. No wonder these people were afraid of my family. The places we lived. No wonder. They didn't know. They had no idea what real love was like.

For the first time, I thought I understood Heath.

My grin resurfaced. Hotter than before.

The old couples were staring at me with that same flat hate I saw in the eyes of the girl behind the counter, etched in the folds of fat on farmer Steve's walrus face. I hated them right back. I wished them dead, with dark tendrils of cancerous rot burning up inside their guts and their throats and their eyes and their *brains*. I wished and I wished, and I felt that red fire blazing behind my eyes. In my teeth.

I thought of Annabelle. Her warning.

This place has a power, and it has a reach. *Might be it'll reach for* you.

Oh, how I did not care.

I carried a little knife. Most men in this part of the country did.

It appeared in my hand as if I had conjured it there. Maybe I had.

I flicked open the blade. It was as sharp as my mouth. As the teeth in my mouth.

Steve's eyes narrowed. His face turned to milk. The girl behind the counter moaned. The old people at the tables rustled at each other, like stalks of wheat in the field at the Heights. The beautiful Heights. Lost now in the drifts of snow that had accumulated overnight, but it would return. And I would return to it. As soon as I finished my business here.

"I didn't think so," I said to Steve. I waved the knife in the air before him. I jabbed. I laughed. My eyes blazed. I imagined his guts in my hand. Pink ropes. Full of shit.

Oh, Steve. I would enjoy cutting into you. Worrying you with my teeth.

"Get out," the girl sobbed. "Please, please."

"Get out, mister," an old woman quavered at me from her place at the table. I saw her husband had covered her chicken-claw hand with his own withered paw. "Please. Leave us in peace."

"Leave us alone," echoed another couple behind them.

I narrowed my eyes.

I held the knife extended before me and lifted the glass case protecting a stand of donuts. It was smeared with something gray. I didn't care. I lifted it, grabbed one of the donuts, crammed it into my mouth, and chewed it into crumbs. They sprayed out of my mouth and onto the counter in thick, wet gobs. It was delicious.

I grinned at the girl behind the counter with my donutty mouth. She looked away. Steve made a grab at me. I laughed. I shook my head. Crumbs flew. I laughed until I roared, until I was sobbing with laughter. And, shaking my head and my little knife, I left that ridiculous place with its ridiculous people and their terrible, ridiculous worldviews. And I climbed into my pickup, and I sped away from that terrible town, and I laughed the entire way.

All the way back to the Heights.

Where I would hear the rest of the rest of Heath's story.

I would.

And then we would see what I would do with it.

6

Heath pulled the trigger, and the gun exploded with fire and power. It was familiar and good, but there was no one standing before him for it to shoot. There was no one behind him when he whirled around. There was no one down the hill, in the coulee where the dead rabbit lay. Just the lithe moan of the wind and the open door of the house. But the sounds inside, the growling and the clicking of claws, the air sliced by a furious tail, those had all ceased as well. He heard the wind. Only the wind.

Heath brushed icy sweat off his forehead. He slitted his eyes. "Scotty?" he called.

Only the wind. No response.

The sky rushed over him, speeding chunks of grim and gray.

Heath inhaled. Oh, the sweet smells of spring. A robin hopped in the grass nearby.

Something on the hill across from this dreadful house moved unseen through the sheaves, parting the swell of green, shivering it, and freezing the air around it.

Heath froze too. He stared.

It was moving away from him, though, up the hill, up, until it was over and gone. Whatever it had been. Birds sang, and the sun emerged through the sheath of dark cloud. Heath breathed again.

I am alone, he thought.

He knew that, when he turned around again, the house behind him would also be gone.

Heath turned.

The house remained. Tall and proud, even though it hadn't been inhabited for decades at the very least. Colorless, pawed by the wind and clawed at by the rain and snow. He could go inside if he wanted to.

Yes, boy. Yes, dear. Yes, love, come inside.

He stood in the doorless doorway.

Come, come, come to me, boy. It's what I wanted all along.

He traced the doorframe with one trembling finger.

Inside, something growled, a delicate purring sound, like the tearing of fabric.

Heath's nerve broke, and he ran back down the hill to the truck.

He stood with Annabelle in the kitchen. Annabelle held the baby, who watched what they watched with great and mounting interest. Heath laid an arm around Annabelle's waist. He drew her closer to him. She allowed herself to be drawn.

Silently, they watched—

—as Scotty, the new hired man, with his hair dark again and his eyes black voids, wriggled and writhed across the lawn, down the little hill to the granaries. His arms remained affixed to his sides. His legs were ramrod straight, and his toes inside his cowboy boots were pointed. He squirmed, and he writhed, and he humped at the ground.

Once, he turned his head impossibly to gaze at them, man and wife and child, posed together in the window. Whatever he saw, whatever he thought of them, it made him grin. His teeth were too long, Heath thought wearily.

"His teeth are wrong," Annabelle murmured, and Heath muttered his own acquiescence.

Scotty—or whatever his name really was—resumed writhing his way down the hill. He stopped. He lowered his head so that the crown met the new grass. He began to shake it. Faster and faster, fury that crescendoed until dark chunks of earth flew up around him in a spray. His body squirmed and writhed.

Annabelle cried out in disgust and pressed her face against Heath's shoulder. Hare sobbed. Heath watched, fascinated. The man—thing, whatever he was—burrowed and burrowed until, at last, only the toes of his boots pointed out of the hole he had made. Finally, even those disappeared. Only the hole remained.

Annabelle looked. Her face was stony. "Them things," she said. "We gotta live with *them* goddamn *things* if we stay out here. I don't know if I can, Heath."

"Where else would we go?" Heath asked.

Oh, but there were answers. Thrush farm, for one. It had sat deserted since Eddie's death. Or they could move into town. Or Billings. Or anywhere they wanted. They had money.

She looked at him bleakly.

"Hell," Hare remarked. "Here."

They looked at each other. Then back out the window to the hole where the worm-man-thing had disappeared.

Heath filled it in before dusk.

7

I made my way back up the hill for the last time. The clouds were thin and scummy that day, just dead gray. The sun burned through them while I climbed. I had left Annabelle and the baby behind.

I thought I knew where Scotty had gone after he had disappeared into the ground. Where they all *really* lived. Well, I guess *lived* isn't exactly the right word, is it? Where they *existed*. I'd seen it all before.

So, I climbed. It took too long. The hill wasn't that high. The grass grew thicker along its hide because it was spring grass and new and alive, and the trees off to my right remained dead but twined all around each other like they was great chums. They writhed around each other like Scotty had writhed his way into the ground. It made my stomach twist to look at them, so I looked away. I kept my eyes on the homesteader cabin. Empty since Birdie's death. Or not.

Two things can be true.

The door opened as I climbed. Catherine Lyon emerged, lifted one bare arm to the top of the doorframe, and stroked it gently with the tips of her fingers. She crooked the other arm and laid her hand on her hip, which she jutted out at a saucy angle. Catherine beamed at me.

"Welllll," she drawled, "if'n it ain't my gentleman caller."

"You gotta sic off your monsters," I told her.

She sniffed. "Don't know what you mean."

"We can't keep living this way."

"I think you can. I think you'll live." And she sneered at me. "Any old way you *can*. So long as you *live*."

"I'll burn it down," I said, holding high the gas can I had lugged up the hill. With my free hand, I demonstrated the Zippo Bran had brought with him and left behind with everything else.

The flame flickered in Catherine Lyon's eyes. She watched it as if hypnotized.

"No," she said at last, in that rich, raspy voice of hers. "You won't."

"Try me."

"You'll die too."

"Not sure I'm really livin' right now."

"No," she purred, "but...isn't *he*?"

I stared. Released my thumb. The flame disappeared.

"Thought so," she smirked. "You don't really know *where* your lover's gotten off to—"

—and the music from the fiddle, which exploded at the touch of the man who stabbed the bow again and again at the air around him, sounded like bliss in my ear. Heat swam all around us while we stomped our feet against the wooden floorboards, so new and fresh they oozed pine sap.

We hollered and swore, grabbed the women by the waists, hauled them up, and tossed them. They landed prettily and jigged away, clapping and roaring, and returned to seize our shoulders, our biceps. They flung us away from them. We chanted, we chanted, we chanted. The animal-headed gods and goddesses of the prairie shrieked, squealed, growled, and sighed, champing teeth and beaks and tusks.

And I thought, *I am home, I am home, I am home—*

"Yes, home." Catherine Lyon sighed, then sang, "Buffalo Gals, wont'cha come out tonight—"

"Come out tonight." I joined her.

"Come out tonight! Buffalo Gals, won'tcha come out tonight." We sang together, harmonizing beautifully. "And dance by the light of the—"

—moonlight shone down through a tear in the sky's shroud, and the wind roared. The snow pierced me, as it always had and always would, and, groping, I thought, *I need to reach the cabin. There's a clue there. Something wonderful waits for me there. Something that will help me, now and forever—*

"Don't ever leave me," Shaw said exquisitely, laying his head against my chest.

I sang out with the joy of it, of his flesh and his hair against me, we two together in the grass in the deepest heart of the prairie. The creek gurgled behind us, and the sun delighted in the west, turning purple all the heavens.

Something heavy and awkward croaked over our heads. It soared near, too near to us—

—and I groaned when the tip of my spade bit again into the earth. I looked around, shocked, silvered by the moonlight overhead. I dug, and what I dug was at the grave of my beloved. "Earnshaw Lyon" proclaimed the tombstone.

Goddamn Edgar Thrush anyway, burying my boy out here in the greedy maw of the prairie, in that damned Grandview Cemetery. And I had to be certain, didn't I? I had to know, didn't I? I had to know if Shaw was really interred there, if his body remained there, and what the condition was. I had to know, and my shovel bit, and my shovel gouged. I cried out in ecstasy when it scratched and squealed against the lid of Shaw's coffin—

"You'll have him again in your arms," Catherine told me wickedly. "And if his body feels cold, why, it's just the winter wind snuffled at him. And if his eyes remain closed, it's just that he sleeps. He slumbers. He waits for your kiss, you, a prince in a dark fairy tale—"

—and I reached out my hand, and someone reached for me, eagerly, greedily—

"Heath! Heath, *no!*"

Annabelle. Screaming. Somewhere near.

I drew back my hand and heard a cheated snarl. I felt the air parted by five claws.

Somewhere, Catherine Lyon was laughing. Only inches from my face rested the twisted countenance of the man I had known as Scotty, his hair dark again, his eyes dark too and seething with hatred for me. Hatred and...something else.

I don't want to dwell too keenly on what that something else might have been.

I found I was standing outside the cabin. Scotty loomed over me, covered from the top of his head to the tip of his boots in black, crawling earth. He bared teeth green with moss, long, tombstone teeth, like all of *them* seemed to possess. His face bulged and worked as if something moved beneath it. Worms, I thought, but I also thought I saw the shape of fingers pressing up under his cheekbones and beneath one eye.

I didn't know what he was, and I still don't. If he was a part of the Heights or something older, from the land. That's what I suspect. There are gods and goddesses—I know; I've seen. And there are their *things*. I don't know why they own them or how, but they do, just as I know the thing that called itself Scotty wanted me. Or all of us. Maybe I should've let him take me. Spared the others. Spared the last twenty years.

His mouth opened, and a cheated, snarling gabble emerged. No language I understood. Nothing human-sounding, for sure. As if a razor had learned to talk, or a chainsaw. Buzzing and roaring at the same time.

He reached for me. His fingers were long and pointed. The middle and the index finger were the same length. They ended in ragged, earth-clotted nails.

He froze at the same moment a hideous roaring filled the entire world. I heard Annabelle screaming, but her shrieks were drowned out by that sudden and terrible roar.

We all turned, the three of us—me, Annabelle, and the Scotty-thing. Turned to look at the big sandstone rock that must've attracted Catherine and her husband when they set out to build their home together here. The first, the truest Heights.

A mountain lion stood tall and proud atop the rock. Biggest damn lion I ever saw. Head like a boulder and golden eyes glaring at us.

No, not at us.

At *Scotty*.

It roared again; it *screamed*. Awful sound rending the air. Its teeth were perfectly shaped, pointed, beautiful, and glaringly white in the light of the sun tearing at us, sharp as the lion's own yellow claws. Its paws were massive, and it used them to scratch at us, at Scotty, at the sky.

Scotty screamed. Then he screamed again. The lion roared, drowning out his screams like it had drowned out Annabelle's.

"You dare not," Scotty hissed at it. "You terrible, bad, bad thing. You go back. You aren't wanted here. You dare not. You dare not. *You dare not—*"

It leaped.

I seized Annabelle and threw both of us to the ground. The lion sailed over our heads, roaring as it went. Its paws met Scotty's chest and took him, howling, down to the ground.

It pinned him.

Stared into his eyes.

Scotty twisted and writhed beneath it. Maybe he was attempting to go to ground again. I don't know.

The lion's eyes were yellow lamps.

"Stupid thing. Stupid boy," snarled Scotty.

It opened wide its mouth.

"He doesn't want you. He never did. He wants me. He wants us. He wants—"

And plunged its fangs into Scotty's chest.

His mouth gaped open, but no sound came from it. His eyes grew wide and wider until I thought they would burst.

The lion worried at the wound it created.

"*No,*" the Scotty-thing said breathlessly.

While the lion tore his heart out.

Scotty howled as it did, as the lion devoured its prize, using those teeth to rend and to tear, shredding the beating heart to a pulp and gulping it down eagerly.

"Bastard." Annabelle spat in Scotty's direction.

The lion returned to its meal and used those lovely fangs to tear at Scotty's throat, then to peel his face from his skull, which it proceeded to eat as well.

And all the time, the Scotty-thing's body jived and jittered, and his pointed, endless fingers tried to dig at the earth.

Until the lion snapped them off, one by one, like tree branches.

And then it ate those as well.

Hare welcomed us home with a long, trumpeting snarl. We clung to each other, my Annabelle and I, laughing and weeping together. We stumbled through the front door. Well, the one to the side of the house.

Didn't know I could weep. I found out.

"The lion," Annabelle wheezed, giggling. "The lion, Heath—"

He had clawed a few more times at the twitching body beneath his paws, then rose, bowed regally toward us, fixed me with his amber, evil eyes. Then he turned, flicked his tail, and vanished up the hillside, over the hillside, back to wherever marauding mountain lions go when there are no mountains to shelter them. He had done his job. He had killed the usurper.

Only, he wasn't really a mountain lion, was he?

Annabelle and I knew what he was.

But we never said. We never spoke of it. We never talked about it again, to be honest.

We retreated, together, into a kind of silence. I say "kind" because we spoke to each other. We spoke to Hare. He grew larger and darker and meaner, and we loved him. We still do. He's so much like the both of us in little ways and big ways.

We don't leave the Heights if we don't have to.

Those eyes. Those evil, beautiful eyes.

You saw them tonight. Not the same eyes. Not a mountain lion. He was a hound at first, wasn't he? He can take any form. I gave him that. That was my gift. His gift is existence. No matter what it is. Or looks like.

You made me believe it all again. For the last twenty years, I've been alone. There's been nothing: no signs, no whispers, no footsteps, no lion appearing on top of a massive rock. There's been no word, and we've all been paralyzed. Don't you get it?

Twenty years. Alone in this place for twenty. Motherfucking. *Years*.

But now you're here! You've come! You brought him with you somehow, Lockwood. I don't know how you did, but you did. And the most wonderful thing is—

Excuse me.

The most wonderful thing is that I don't need to grieve anymore, you see? It's wonderful. It's *wonderful*. Because death isn't the end. Not here. I still don't know what comes after, and I guess I don't care because I know, I *know* that Shaw is out there. You saw him. He spoke to you.

Oh my God. I didn't even ask.

What did he say? *What did he say to you?*

Ah. Oh. Yes. That makes all the sense in the world.

It's a curse. Not a miracle, I suppose, or even real magic. Just a curse. Welded together with whatever makes the Heights the way it is. Whatever makes all this country around here—the prairie, the long grass, the hiss and whine of the wind—whatever animates it all, makes it what *it* is. I guess...I guess I forgot that.

I could go out there. Right now. In this howling storm. I could go to Grandview, and I could dig up his grave. And either he would be resting inside, all perfect and beautiful, or the coffin would be empty. And I'd be sure, certain at last, that he was out there somewhere.

Out there. Where I could find him.

Twenty years, Lock. *Twenty years.*

Lock?

You aren't there. You aren't listening. Where are you, Lock?

Oh. It's you.

You aren't Lock.

I don't know you.

Listen, I swear I don't know you.

I'll beat you until your brains come out. I'll eat your ribs and break them and suck out the marrow, I swear I will! Stay away from me. I'll smash you until you're *pulp*!

Shaw? Let me go. Shaw? Let me go, I said! Shaw, are you there? I see you! Come in! I invite you in. I always did. I always have! Come in! Come in! Earnshaw Lyon, I bid you *come in to me!*

No.

Goddamn it, no.

I'm alone. You aren't there. No one is there. I'm alone. All alone.

Like I've always been.

But—

It doesn't have to be that way, does it?

That's what *this*—all of this—means.

It means I don't have to be alone.

So.

I'll come.

Yes.

I'm coming.

Shaw?

My Shaw.

I'll come to you, then.

I'm coming.

I will.

I will.

I will.

Epilogue

October 2025

1

I let time inside me, the way we all do. I resisted it, though, the way some of us do. I have never understood people who wanted to just go forward, then keep moving forward. I was—I have always been —perfectly content to just be. Unchanging.

But, hell, I let it in eventually—time, like I said. After I left Montana. Again. Studied law this time. In California. My parents swore they would disown me if I went out there, but I did. And I loved it. Turns out, I have got the ocean inside me too, or once I saw it, breathed it in, I made a place for it inside myself that was, honestly, maybe always there. Tides and waves. Not like the prairie at all.

I met a girl at school, a strange girl with one eye, but what a beautiful eye it was! Name of Zila. Lovely. Tall. Smart. From North Dakota, Bismarck, so she knew the same things about the wind and the snow and the prairie that I did.

She told me all the different ways she had lost the eye. A bird darted by one day while she walked along the beach, pulled it out, and flew away with it, back out over the ocean. She had lost it in a poker game played against an evil, beautiful, jealous cousin. She used it as a marble, rolled it away, and called for it, but it never came back to her. A thousand more just like that, strange, maybe stranger.

I was charmed by her in an instant. Soon after, I loved her. God, I did. Resisting all others, the girls, all those college girls. It was only her. Up until last year, when cancer finally took her, my strange, sweet Zil.

We lived in Sacramento. I thought that was far enough away to be safe. Eventually, I stopped thinking of things like safety. Eventually, I decided I didn't even really know what that meant. Until I would wake, sweating, a scream still kicking around in my mouth, seeing those yellow eyes outside the window, glaring back at me across four decades. Hearing that voice, pleading with me.

Let me in. I'm so cold. Let me in. Stay, Lock. No, he never said. None of the ghosts ever did. *Stay with us, forever and forever, Lock, Lockwood, Lockwood Linden.* My name. My very own name. Except now I am thinking maybe they did. And they have been, all along.

It has been twenty years, he said to me, that boy outside the window at the Heights, pleading. I haven't been inside in twenty years. I have been out here all that time. I am alone. Please, please. Let me in. Please. I am so cold.

I am so alone.

I can't find him. I need to find him.

He did this to me. I need to find him. Will you help me? He did this.

Sometimes, the scream would echo through the room, and I would wake to hear it. My face and torso would already run slick with sweat.

And Zil would soothe me, pet me, and rain little kisses on me. Never ask me what I dreamed that had scared me so bad.

I couldn't tell her.

I never did.

I decided I didn't believe in curses. I thought, *I'll never go back there. Why would I? There's no reason.*

My mom called me when Annabelle died. Years after Heath. Maybe ten? Fifteen? We didn't talk much about it. She said she thought I would like to know. She called when Aunt Lucy died too. Thought I would like to know. I didn't come home for the funerals. I hadn't attended Heath's. Why would I bother with any of the others?

I was the one who found him, of course.

I had come back from Burke with murder on my mind after my... experience with the locals at the Farmer's Kitchen in town. Steve, the walrus-farmer, and the limp dishrag girl.

Why murder? Christ, I don't know. Not much of an answer. It scared me, that feeling, for years and years after I ran away from Montana. Knowing that I was capable of it. Or knowing that *it* could reach inside me. Or *them*. Make me feel certain ways. Think certain things. Violence. Heat. Desire. I don't know. I wanted it all *out*.

I remember thinking, all that long drive, *I will murder Heath*. Doesn't he deserve it, after all this time?

But turns out, I didn't have to murder him.

He was already dead.

Lying on that bed in Shaw's old room. His hands were claws drawn all up on his chest. His eyes were fierce, like a rabid dog's. His teeth were bared in the way you might expect.

Forty years is a long time. Was I really on my way back to the Heights that grim December day to stab my knife into Heath until he was dead? I had gouged out all his stories, his feeling, *his* desire, or mine, or ours? Until I had found the truth somewhere deep inside him, way down under all that bile and thundering rage?

The truth inside me too, maybe?

Stabbing, gouging, tearing, and digging.

The ghost of Catherine Lyon.

The ghost of Earnshaw Lyon.

The things in the walls and the ceiling and those that crept and burrowed in the earth beneath the Heights.

The disappearances. The hired men. Had those even happened? Had they been *real*?

Would tearing Heath into pieces so I could peer into his guts and his veins and his blood offer me any true insight at all?

I didn't kill him. I wouldn't have, even if he hadn't been dead already by the time I made it back. The madness I could feel, the things that grinned and capered with my mouth and my hands...I fought with all of it just before I reached the turn to 201, only a few miles away from the Heights, when I pulled my truck over to the side of the road.

I turned my brain off. All my thoughts. I didn't think. I was afraid to. Afraid I would lose my nerve. But whisper, whisper went the voices.

There was a boy that time, little Lock, a pretty boy at camp with dark hair and wanting eyes, and you and he. Then there was that boy in junior high, and you spent the night at his house. He offered you his bed, or you asked to snuggle next to him. And you let him, and he let you. And then, that time in college. Oh, what a cliché. But you were both very drunk, even though maybe you weren't drunk at all. And he came back to your dorm because you invited him back to your dorm, and then. Oh, and then *you—*

Bone. Cracking of bone. Rib, spine. *Snap.* Hiss of blood—

What do you love, Lock? Or who?

Eyes glaring at me. Red-rimmed, throbbing with veins, with blood. Crimson eyes. Animal lips, all drawn back, revealing the teeth, the sharp glint of the teeth—

My teeth. My face. Glaring at me from the rearview mirror.

I smothered the scream before it could escape my mouth, then I opened the door. I drew my arm back and hurled my knife as far as it would go. It flew, somersaulting through the air, over and over, the same thing, the same thing over and over, until it vanished into a coulee in a sugary puff of snow. I wanted to go after it, but I held myself back. Forced myself into the pickup. I almost drove past the turn to the Heights, but I needed to see Heath.

Closure, they call it now. Yes, I still needed that.

Love is complicated, I would tell him. *Desire* is complicated. We can't control it! I would scream this at him. *There are more things in heaven and earth!* I might scream that. I planned to. College boy. Better'n the rest of us. I would say those things. I would.

No one greeted me at the door. I didn't hear any further whispers. I didn't see any ghosts. Annabelle and Hare were nowhere to be found.

I knew that I was attracted to women. Listen, I had always been. I had loved girls in high school, in college. A brilliant bear of a woman named Emily, when we worked together at a pizza place just off campus. It was to Emily I had almost proposed. But, she told me, she wasn't the marrying kind.

I had never even looked at another guy, not at the urinal, not in the locker room at the gym. I didn't notice them. I swore to myself I didn't *care*. There was nothing in me like that. Nothing in me like Heath's story.

I'm nothing like you, Heath.

Desire is complicated.

Attraction is complicated.

My hand clenched again over the handle of the knife I no longer possessed.

I had to tell him. He had insinuated it, hadn't he? As good as said it out loud. *Sure, little Lock, little boy. Of course, you love women, and you can, and you should. But there's more to you, and I feel it. I know it,* and so do you.

So do you, he had said to me.

He was wrong.

"I am *nothing* like you, Heath," I growled.

I had to tell him.

I headed to that room in the attic. I knew where I would find him.

And I was right.

The bedding was soaked. The window shattered. Snow, currently in the act of melting before my startled eyes, snow in vanishing clumps everywhere.

He glared at me. Wide eyes, bulging. Glared. Right through me.

Grinning. Those yellow teeth. Tombstone teeth. That was how he had described the teeth in the mouth of that man who had called himself Scotty.

But his teeth were just the same.

His chest did not rise, nor did it fall.

I knew instantly that he was dead.

I stepped into the room. Moved toward him. His corpse, what-was-Heath but would never be again.

You're like me, Lock. More than you know.

I tried to close his eyes. Pressed and pressed.

His eyelids refused to lower.

For a moment, I was certain I felt his flesh crawl beneath my fingertips. I jumped back, shuddering.

He was grinning, I thought, shivering and moaning. Why?

Grinning at death, I told myself.

Or whoever—whatever—he had seen before death took him.

You're just like me. Just like me.

Something moved within that room.

I jumped back.

Something behind him. Something I couldn't see. *Something in the wall.*

It slithered. It smothered a laugh.

It knocked, but just once.

Nearly sobbing, I hurried away to find Annabelle or Hare. Or maybe just to leave the godforsaken place. And forever.

Which is what I did, essentially.

Until yesterday.

2

It is fall now. Gorgeous autumn. The grass is tall and yellow. Snow has yet to claim the plains. The wind is gentle. The skies are still clear. That sprawling, somehow vacuous blue.

I drove my Honda CRV down Highway 201. It is the same. Grandma and Grandpa Linden are gone. Aunt Lucy is gone. Most of the people out here are gone, I suspect. I wonder about the old Reardon place, but that isn't part of my mission.

Forty years is a long time.

Memory is a tricky thing. As complicated as desire, as love, as attraction. There are layers upon layers and hidden things, and sacred things.

But there was the turn-off of Highway 201. I took it. Aimed myself down that vanishing road.

I saw immediately, even a mile away, that the house was gone.

I forced back the gasp that wanted to flee my mouth.

My hands gripped the wheel of the car until my knuckles turned white.

They tremble a lot these days, those hands do. I don't consider myself an old man, not yet, but I am certainly not *young*. I think about Heath, that last time I saw him. Jesus, he could have only been, what, in his late forties? And he seemed *ancient*. My hair is a bit thinner. It is streaked with gray, but I am not *old*. I know I'm not. Not like Heath was. I know I'm not.

I followed the twists and bends in the road. Crossed Redwater Creek. Pulled up before the fence, which guarded nothing anymore. There wasn't even a pit in the ground to signal where the basement had been. There was just...nothing.

Instinctively, my eyes flickered to the top of the hill.

The homesteader cabin was gone as well.

"By God," I whispered.

Heath's makeshift fence, with the pallet for a gate and a horseshoe for the latch, had disappeared too. Only the barbed wire remained. No way over it.

I had worn city clothes, stupidly: a pair of light blue chinos, wingtips, a blue windbreaker. I snagged the coat on the barbed wire when I tried to part it with my hands so I could crawl through. Just a little tear. Nothing significant. But I would take it away with me, goddamn it. Unless I left the coat here.

Anyway, it didn't stop me, a little thing like that. Morbid, I suppose, but I wanted to walk around where the house had stood. I couldn't believe it was gone. I still can't. Tore my coat a bit, even snagged my pants. But listen, they were only things. Impermanent. Still, I was pissed at myself for catching them like that. I could have been more careful.

I should have known.

I walked up the slight incline to where the porch had been. The orchard remained. I flinched, thinking of the dog I had seen. Or whatever it had been. Just a dog, surely. Forty years is a long time, and I told myself that there were only dogs in the world and nothing else. The big white dog that had come for me out of those trees.

There was no sign of it now, of course. The trees were all dead, and the grass growing secretly around them was shaggy and thick. Crisped into yellow death as well by the blazing heat of the summer sun.

The earth where the house had reared itself, high and mighty, was flat. Nothing grew there. Just dead earth. A large square. I tapped it gingerly with my toe. I don't know what I expected. Nothing, I suppose.

Some sound?

I turned. The wind through the trees. I didn't feel watched. I told myself I didn't. Who could watch me? No one lived here anymore. They couldn't. The granaries remained. Could someone hide in there, maybe even live in there, squatting, at least during the heat of the summer months? Surely not *after* that. Could someone hunker down there now, watching me with wide, frightened eyes?

Or...maybe not frightened.

A bird flew over my head. Big. It screamed down at me, or it laughed. *Wasting your time*, it said. *You're wasting all your time, Lockwood Linden.*

There was no house left to haunt out here. Not anymore.

So why did I feel this way?

Something moved in the trees. Something passed through them. I watched it. Grass rustled. I heard it. My mouth dried up. My hands clenched into fists. I saw it. I know I saw it. Something, something moving about in that bright autumn sunlight.

An animal. A rabbit. Coyote. Dog. Maybe even a puma, like Heath said he had seen. It wasn't necessarily impossible.

Moving, moving.

Toward me.

I backed away, licking my lips.

Then: the buzz of a motor.

I turned. Shaded my eyes and glanced quickly over my shoulder, back at the rows of trees, but I saw nothing, so I turned more carefully back to the road. But I would keep my eyes on the trees as well.

Someone coming. A truck. It had turned off 201 and made its way down the winding road to that place where the Heights had ruled for so long. Coming to me.

I waited. I moved away from the tree rows so that the thing there couldn't get me and take me away with it. These are crazy thoughts. I acknowledge that. There are only animals in this world and nothing else.

Big old farm truck, like all the others out here. Hard to tell the year. Even the decade. 70s? 60s? It growled and grunted while it worried the road. While it bounced down and down toward me. I couldn't see the driver behind the glass. Until I did.

A woman, older than me. White hair, like a drift of cotton blowing atop her head but cut short, into waves to frame her face, which was a mass of crisscross lines cut deeply into her skin. A thick, strong-looking woman. She smiled at me when she left the truck and moved with quick authority up the path.

"Took you long enough," she called. Her voice was merry and slightly raucous.

"Do we know each other?"

She only chuckled. "From photos."

"We're family." There was something familiar about her face, the curve of her cheek, the shape of her eyes.

She laid hands on her hips. Glanced around. "I thought you'd come long before now."

"The house is gone."

"For years now." She chuckled. "It was my idea."

"You—"

"So sorry. You're Lockwood Linden."

I nodded impatiently. I was too old for patience, dammit.

"We're cousins. You guessed that."

I nodded again, with a bit more patience. But just a bit.

"I own the land now."

"But the homesteader cabin—"

"Fire hazard. All of it. Even the house." Some of the levity faded from her voice. Her eyes, inscrutable behind her thick glasses, narrowed, I could tell. "Especially the house."

"How'd you know I was here?"

"I live there." She jerked her head in the direction of the Reardon farm. "I was putting up plastic on the windows, gettin' 'em ready for winter, don'tcha know. And I saw your fancy car there bumpin' down the road. This road. And I says to myself, why, that has to be Lockwood Linden, come home after all this time."

"What about Hare?"

"What about him?"

"He didn't inherit all this after his mama passed?"

"He did."

I was growing tired of that little smile tickling her colorless lips, whoever she was. Weathered, I guessed, by life out here.

"He didn't want it, as it turns out. Signed it all over to me. I did what I thought was best."

"You—"

She pivoted back to where the house had rested. Closed her eyes, lifted her chin. Exulted, it seemed. "I like it better," she said. "Actually, much better, without either of them houses. Don't you think?"

I didn't know what to say to that. Did I?

"But the history," I said finally. My hands tugged uselessly at the air. "All the memories—"

She chuckled again, but I thought there was little humor in it. "Oh, is *that* what you call it?"

"What would you call it?"

"Gonna write you a book, Lockwood Linden?" She dropped her head and gazed at me.

I thought there was something flat and hateful behind the coke-bottle-thickness of those glasses. But it could have been my imagination.

"Write it all down? The *history*? Heath's stories?" She shook her head and, shockingly, spat into the grass. "Don't know why you would."

"People forget. Then it's like it never happened."

"Never should have happened."

I stared. I didn't like this woman.

"Why did you come back?" she asked.

"I wanted to see it again."

"Why?"

"I don't know you."

"You've heard of me."

"If you're family—"

"If? You don't believe me?" She tittered. "That isn't very nice."

"I feel disconnected." I heard the frustrated snarl in my voice. I had already crammed my hands sullenly, like a child, into the pockets of my poor, snagged windbreaker. I glowered at her. "I left Montana a long time ago, and I haven't been back for a long time."

"Nothing changes out here."

"I see that."

"*We* don't change. We like it that way."

Movement in the trees. Something flickering? An animal.

She stared at me steadily, refusing to acknowledge anything besides me. "You probably shouldn't stay. There isn't much to see, not *really*."

"I suppose."

"Hunters come out here sometimes. They liked to stay in the house. Until they didn't."

She smiled, revealing her teeth for the first time. Big, horsey teeth. Startlingly white. I wondered if they were false. I thought not.

"It's not easy to be a woman out here, all on her own. But I manage. I thought I might manage a bit more easily if those two damned houses was burned down."

"And the earth salted."

She started a bit. I thought her mask of conviviality had slipped. If it had, she righted it immediately. She grinned at me slyly.

"Superstitions," she said. "Don't hold with them myself."

"I did. Once."

"Time changes things."

"It all gets distorted."

"I understand. So did Hare. He lives outside Poplar now. Last I heard, around this past Christmastime, he got hisself so drunk he drove his pickup into a moving train. Smashed the pickup all to heck, but Hare was fine. Not even a scratch. Not sure about the train. Well. God watches out for drunks and little children. That's what I always heard."

"He didn't want the homeplace at all?"

"The homeplace!" She smiled. A genuine smile. It changed her face. Gave her an air of youth, of warmth, that had been lacking until that moment. "No one calls it that anymore."

"What do they call it?"

"Nothing." Her smile vanished. "No one talks about it at all. It doesn't exist, see."

"Right." So, they believed it. Everyone out here, maybe even in the town, they believed it all.

She moved back toward her pickup. Paused for a moment. Glanced over her shoulder. "I don't know as I should leave you here alone."

"I'll be all right."

"Will you? Well. I suppose you know best. You men, you always do." She shook her white head sagely.

"I didn't catch your name," I called when she pulled open the door to her truck.

"Abby," she said. "Your cousin."

"Didn't know I had a cousin Abby."

"I'm a Lyon." She giggled gently. "Oh, I've always loved that name. Means I get to call myself a lion all the time."

"Abby Lyon."

"Yes. Wesley was my father. My whole name is Abatha."

The wind traced patterns on my forehead. My stomach filled with sparks that jumped and burned.

Abatha Lyon.

No. Not possible.

According to Heath—

"According to Heath," she said, smiling but unpleasantly now, revealing those terrible horsey teeth. "According to *Heath*, I disappeared. The Heights ate me all up, I suppose is what he told you. No wonder you got that look on your face. Like the devil done tweaked your private bits."

"Annabelle said—" I cleared my throat. I felt like a fool. Embarrassment thudded behind my eyes. "Annabelle said so too."

"Perhaps they just wished that I'd disappeared."

My head felt full of flies. Buzzing. Clacking. Rubbing their awful little hands against my memories, both of what I had seen and what I had been told.

What did you see? What were you told?

"My father died. It wasn't pretty, from all I've heard. I don't even remember him. Well, maybe a tiny glimmer now and again. But I don't trust glimmers like that. And anyway, they didn't want me, Heath and his wife. I was not exactly a normal little girl." She chuckled ruefully. "So, when Aunt Lucy came to visit one day, I went with her."

"To live with Uncle Dean and Aunt Nell."

"Yes. And I never came back. Heath had...a temper."

"To put it mildly."

"I couldn't be around him. Not in that house. I bounced around after high school. Went east. Came back from time to time. I never seen a ghost, but I remember how that house could make you feel. Like you were living inside of Heath. His mind, maybe. The whole house vibrated with his feelings. Even as a little girl, I couldn't abide that."

"No. I don't think I could've either."

"I never seen a ghost, like I said. Don't believe in 'em. But I couldn't stand the idea that those houses would sit out here, all by theirselves, and be so full of all those awful feelings. And those memories."

"Ghosts," I said, more to myself than to her.

Abatha Lyon. Standing before me. Looking at me with those inscrutable eyes.

"Never seen one. Don't believe in 'em. I wouldn't either, if I were you." Staring at me, staring at me.

My head swam. The air around me smelled pleasant, crisp with October's descending temperatures. I smelled the creek. I smelled the grass of the prairie.

Oh, the prairie. Sprawling out in front of us. Did a house *really* matter? If the land had a mind of its own—its own memories, say—did anything *we* do or could ever hope to do *really* make any kind of difference at all?

"They all sleep quietly," Abby Lyon said to me in an even voice, just above a whisper. "Heath and Annabelle. My father and mother. And... Uncle Shaw. Quiet, they are, in the quiet ground."

"Quiet."

"It *is* quiet. You must believe that. For your own peace of mind. Even if they lie in Grandview. *That* awful place. They lie quiet. I promise you."

The wind laughed in my ear. Something rustled the yellow grass, which rubbed like cats against the shins of the dead white trees of the orchard. Something splashed in the creek water. Someone whispered behind me. Someone wept.

My head swam. I brushed my fingertips against my forehead. It didn't help.

Someone cried out for help. Someone begged. Someone vowed revenge. Jealousy and hatred, wild, wild jealousy. Bitter bile burned my throat and filled my mouth. Became the iron of the creek. Then the slime of its mud.

"For your own peace of mind," Abby said, stern now. "Come on, Lock. It'll be a drive back to town, to your hotel. The days are shorter than ever now."

"How'd you know about my hotel?"

"Where else would you stay? You don't have family here anymore. No one knows you. The Heights are gone." Gentler now: "Let them be gone."

Whispering. Pleading. Snarling and vowing. Oh, such foul vengeance.

Let me in. Please. I'm so alone.

"Lock."

I need him. I can't find him. Help me find him.

Help.

Come with me.

"How do you do it?" I asked.

"Do what?"

"Live. Out here."

"Oh!" She waved a dismissive hand at me.

Was it a young woman's hand? A headache thudded behind my eyes and gripped at the back of my neck, where my skull met my spine. I couldn't see her clearly. The sun, westering now, blinded me.

"Never you mind. I get along. You have to, out here. Especially, as I said, if you're a woman. It's hard."

"Yes."

"Hard for people like Uncle Shaw. Like Heath. Hard for women too. But we find our strengths, don't we? Probably you wouldn't know."

"Probably not." And I didn't. I swore that I did not. I wished for my Zila, for her hand in mine.

"*You* never had to. We have to find them, or we don't matter anymore. The land would take us. Or throw us away. You have to be friendly with loneliness. You have to breathe the wind and listen to it. You can't be afraid."

I whispered, "I don't know how to do that."

"Then you should run far away," Abatha said kindly, laying a strong hand on my arm and squeezing it. "Go. This isn't the place for you."

I am afraid, I said, or tried to say.

She watched me expectantly. A young woman, I swore she was.

Finally, I nodded. Exhaustion came crashing down all around me.

"Believe they're gone," Abatha said. "It's...safer that way."

I paused, my hand on the latch of the driver's door of my car. "Safer?"

But the old lady was already seated in her truck. It roared to life. She grinned at me with those big, white teeth. Her glasses caught the sunlight so I couldn't see her eyes. Only circles of fire, red and gold.

You can't be afraid.

Oh, but I was.

I looked to stare at the base of the hill, troubled, where nothing crouched. It was as if the Heights had never been. Nothing waited. Nothing grew.

Let me in, the voices pleaded. Or *take me with you*, perhaps. I wasn't sure. I didn't want to *be* sure.

Let us in, maybe.

Or...

Let us out.

I climbed behind the wheel of my car, too modern to ever belong comfortably in this place.

Abatha Lyon led me up the road to 201. The homeplace waited behind us. Maybe, it thought, maybe we would change our minds. Maybe we would turn around. Maybe we would stay. And forever.

I left that little, disappearing road. Aimed my car at town.

I didn't look back.

3

Nearly one month later and fifteen hundred miles away:

I opened my eyes early this morning, All Hallow's Eve, and looked out my window.

Heath, finally, peering in at me. His face was white as marble and scarred all over with wildness. It twitched feverishly.

Sweetgrass. The iron of the creek. The whisper, the moan *of the prairie wind.*

A man stood at his side.

They were hand in hand.

It has a reach. Maybe it'll reach for you.

I opened my mouth. Closed it. What could I possibly say to them? To myself?

They lifted their free hands. Pawed at my window, both of them.

Their eyes glowed solidly in at me, flashing in the dim light like golden coins. Urgency there. I felt their pressing—against the window glass, against the world. This reality. My life. Their hands. Pressing.

And my hands.

Pressing.

My hands were already reaching out for them. Heath and Shaw. Shaw and Heath. Reaching. Reaching.

To open that window.

Maybe I did that. Maybe I only wanted to. Maybe the window opened itself. Maybe *they* opened it.

Because it opened.

They did it. I did it.

It opened.

They came in, or I went out, or both of those things.

Doesn't matter. I went with them. I did.

Maybe I *begged* them to take me.

I am with them now.

Aren't I? Where am I? Where am I? *Who am I now?*
Memory, goddamn evil, *evil* memory.
Plays tricks.

Acknowledgments

To my mother, who picked, with effortless precision, most of the horror, both novel and film, that inspired me as a child. And you gave me a giant typewriter for Christmas when I was seven, so that helped too.

To both my parents, who survived living in the actual Heights for over twenty years. The ghosts should be afraid of *you*.

To Lyndsey, for giving me this opportunity.

To Debra, because you listen and I listen and then we laugh and laugh and laugh.

To Gwendolyn, for your friendship and for all our writer talks on porches, both front and back.

To La Doty, who always offers me a place in her shoppe as well as her heart.

And, as always, to my husband Ryan. Your support means all the worlds to me.

ABOUT THE AUTHOR

Laramie Dean grew up during a drought on the wind-swept plains of Eastern Montana, which helped him fashion his writing style—what he refers to as "Montana Gothic." After earning his Doctorate in Playwriting from Southern Illinois University Carbondale, Laramie became the director of theatre at Hellgate High School in Missoula, Montana, where he lives with his husband. He is the author of several plays which have been performed around the world, as well as co-author of a playwriting primer, and of *Black Forest*, his first novel. Find him on Instagram at @bylaramiedean and check out his website at bylaramiedean.com.

Black Forest

Kīrīnyaga, 1635

There was no escape. Nowhere to run or to hide.

The beasts were faster than him, one with the forest, with the soil and trees. They knew the lay of every stone, every inch of the undergrowth twining its wiry arms around him, as if trying to ensnare him.

Father Fernão Abreu crashed through the bushes and forced his thoughts away from the hopelessness of his efforts, toward the diminishing trail under his feet. Prayer would be of no help here. That much he had known even before he had followed the caravan of Arab traders into the high country, away from Mombasa and the protective walls of Forte Jesus. Far from the infidel settlements along the golden coast, deep into the savage heart of this new world. Before he had beheld the great mountain's snow-capped peaks rising from the verdant valleys, inhabited by beasts so strange that the very sight of them stilled his breath.

In doing so, he had broken his covenant with God, turning his back on his vows, on more than twenty years spent as a member of the Jesuit order, and he had done so gladly, with grace and lightness in his heart. Because Providence itself had brought him here to reveal the secret hidden away in this wilderness untrammeled by man. To cast off the veil from one of the Creator's miracles and bring it out into the world.

Or so Father Abreu had fooled himself into thinking. Blinded by hubris, enchanted by the siren song of the wild. He had strayed from the righteous path, too far from any light that could guide him back. Now there was only one way left open to him.

Up. Higher up the crags, into open terrain. Away from the demons pacing him through the trees.

Boughs and saplings snapped back, scoring the skin of his hands and face. His pursuers sounded closer, growls and yips and the excited scratching of paws on stony ground. Father Abreu's lungs struggled with the thin air of the mountain he scrambled upward. He had once believed these peaks hid angels—an entire lost city of them, waiting to be discovered. Even in this extreme of panic and despair, the depth of his error filled the priest's heart with bitter bile.

Evil. Older than the mountain itself, shrewd and knowing. Changing faces appearing between towering trees. A bark carried across the rocks, a sound pregnant with bloodlust and savage anticipation but with a hint of mockery in it. The beasts must have realized they would be upon him soon.

Save your servant, Lord. Do not forsake him now.

Father Abreu would never get off the mountain alive, but hope still burned in his breast, a guttering candle in the encroaching dark night within him. Perhaps he could avoid being consumed by the demons. Sacrifice his body to save his immortal soul.

Most importantly, the secret of the mountain would perish with him. Without the final piece of the map inside his robe, no one would find the way through the steep cliffs. No human eyes would ever gaze upon the mountain's hidden horrors. Father Abreu had sinned unforgivably, and he asked no mercy for himself. But as he ran, breathless, his lips moved without ceasing, imploring God to show mercy to the world.

Another shriek echoed behind him, reminding him of the laughter of madmen at the Hospital Real de Todos os Santos, which used to set his teeth on edge in his novitiate days. It was immediately responded to by another further up the narrow gully.

Meu Deus. They had already cut him off and were waiting for him. Toying with him. They couldn't leave their mountain lair, not in this weak, undernourished state. Not without taking on the appearance of men. But they were cunning and patient, and they knew—

The priest reached under his collar. Felt the leatherbound journal in a specially made pocket, next to the waterskin slapping at his side. His final volume, a confession of his waywardness, his grand, self-important delusion. Two other tomes were on their way back to Mombasa with the Saracen trader al-Busaidi and his soldiers. Meaningless now, without the third to expose the author's folly. He could only pray they would be dismissed as fantasies or the hallucinations of a fevered mind.

Because the creatures knew, or at least suspected, what Father Abreu hid under his robe.

Any single one of them could have overtaken him easily, torn him limb from limb. Great teeth sinking into his flesh, ripping bloody chunks with a jerk of its powerful neck. Unlike its natural enemies, the lion and the jaguar, the hyena simply ate its prey. Devoured pieces of it until it died. Sometimes, that could take a long time, and it wasn't only his meat these monsters were after. They were penning him in, herding him from a distance.

No sooner had he thought this than he spotted one at the top of the dry gully, as if it materialized from the scrubby bushes.

It didn't look like a hyena, not this time, although there was still a trace of the animal to its form: a stooping of the shoulders, a bend in the mighty hindquarters, like it was about to lope on all fours. Like it was shedding the beast from itself in increments.

The closest resemblance was to a human being, although one unusually tall and thin, with disproportionately long arms. Except no man or woman created by the Lord had skin as black as onyx or fingers tipped by long, razor-sharp claws.

Or a terrible skull-like head crowned by thick horns. It must have circled the rock promontory while Father Abreu had been busy evading its brothers.

Their eyes locked briefly across the distance. Human eyes and the glowing, sulfurous orbs of a spawn of Hell. Caught in a game older than both of them, older than time itself.

Father Abreu broke the gaze first. Not because his nerve had failed, but to study the escarpment rising above him. A wall of rock seemingly as smooth as glass. But Abreu was a seasoned mountaineer, and his trained eye quickly picked out a route among the protrusions, hand- and footholds where others would see only abraded stone.

Up. Because up was the one direction the demons couldn't follow. Because these cliffs were what kept them inside their ancient prison. Or at least, that was what he chose to believe. Not much to go on, but the theory was all he had now, his last reprieve from complete despair.

The priest didn't turn when a second beast crashed through the brush not twenty paces behind him. Turning would take precious seconds, and horror might drain a fraction of the strength from his muscles and sinews. Vigor he would need to survive the next few minutes. He sank his hands into the rock and hoisted himself upward.

Several feet up the rock wall, the scrub erupted with snarling and barks. He looked down and saw two of the hyenas leap up clumsily, trying to reach him with their great foaming jaws, front paws scrabbling on stone. One of them vented a howl of frustration, then dropped and raced back up the trail, followed closely by its companion.

Father Abreu paused on the rocks, gasping, every muscle quivering with the effort of keeping himself aloft. The demon further up the gully was motionless for another moment, staring directly at him. Hate and rage pulsed from it like a physical force. Then it, too, was gone, racing through the trees to join the others.

The priest closed his eyes, offering his gratitude to God. He was not tricked into thinking the demons had given up. Forbearance was not in their nature. They would probably circle round until they found another way up the escarpment. But that would buy him minutes, *precious* minutes, and that would be enough.

With fresh resolve, Fernão Abreu continued his climb.

Rock fragments crumbled under his hands, but he kept his eyes fixed firmly upward, concentrating on the next protrusion, on the skillful shifting of his weight from his hands to his feet. In spite of himself, he felt a flutter of treacherous ambition.

Maybe the beasts would not be able to follow him. Maybe there was a way to escape the mountain, to survive. If the Lord shone His benevolence upon His unworthy servant, Fernão Abreu would swear a bloody vengeance upon this desecrated land. He would return to the mountain with fire and sword and cleanse it of the demons. Soak its very soil with enemy blood. If God—

His hands found the ledge, and he pulled himself upward in one convulsive heave, elbows first, dragging the rest of his body along until he lay atop the escarpment, gasping and trembling, too exhausted to stand. Below him, the forest was a green inferno, the shadow cast by the cliffs already swallowing much of the cauldron-like hollow. Ragged sunlight broke through the clouds and caressed his face like a blessing.

Father Abreu rolled to his knees, raising his arms toward the heavens. Around him, from horizon to horizon, the many peaks of Kĭrĭnyaga thrust into the sky like spear points. Some of them white with snow, but most were gray and windswept, like the rock upon which he knelt.

For a second, he was alone here, alone and one with his Creator. A sudden calm, a sense of his own insignificance before infinity, balmed his tortured soul. The terror fell from him like a cloak, his horror and suffering melting under the scalding gaze of the sun.

Then he heard them.

The padding of heavy paws on rough stone. The clicking of claws and strong, sharp, yellow teeth. A grunt of triumph, or resentment, escaping from jaws that only hours ago had shaped human speech. A living blasphemy, a mockery of life crafted in God's image.

The many-faced ones.

All seven of them were there, and they were circling him slowly, making sure there was no route of escape. Two of them were on all fours, in the shape of hyenas, but their eyes betrayed them, something old and crafty in their gaze. The other four hunched over, ungainly, caught midway in their transformation. Keeping their distance. Watching. Calculating.

Almost without thinking, Fernão Abreu reached for the crucifix that was no longer around his neck. He had discovered a different truth in the wilderness. One before which the relics and rituals of his faith turned out to be powerless, a futile delusion. Yet he still *believed*, maybe more than ever before.

Whatever had birthed these demons had to have an equal, opposing force that kept the world in balance. Otherwise, existence had no purpose, no meaning. It was no more than a cruel joke and the universe a hollow gourd rattling with the dead cinders of stars.

The priest slipped free his journal and the waterskin inside which he had inscribed the map. He clutched them like weapons and turned to face as many opponents as he could.

In another lifetime, before he had taken his vows, his prowess with the dagger and rapier had been a thing of legend on the hot, dirty quaysides from Porto to Barcelona. Quick feet and hands and even quicker wits weaving a dance of death: flashes of silver in the lamplight, red stains blossoming on white cotton.

Against these agents of Hell, he carried no cutting or stabbing weapons, but he was not unarmed either. At his side was the sword of the Spirit, the sturdy breastplate of faith covering his chest. The killer instinct in his brain, the one he had suppressed over the years but was forever part of him, was wide awake again, calculating angles and momentum, picking out weak spots in defenses. He would only get one try.

Faith against tooth, divine grace against rending talons.

He sprang at the two hyenas, and they jerked back in surprise, wheeling on him almost immediately, powerful jaws clacking. But their teeth met only empty air. Father Abreu feinted in the opposite direction, then ran directly at the nearest of the manlike creatures.

It hissed, its leathery face contorted with hate, and swiped at him with a clawed hand, but it was off balance, and the priest tumbled past it, evading its grasp, rolling along the stony ground. Then he was in the open, heading for the golden glow of the day, toward the end of the ridge.

The hyenas were coming for him, but he was fast, too fast, a small, weightless dove in the all-seeing eye of the Lord. Over the opposite edge of the cliff, the valley opened its green arms, beckoning, until it was easy to ignore the hundreds of feet lying between him and the treetops. God was always watching, and He would understand. He would forgive this final, ultimate sin.

Eyes full of the sun, Fernão Abreu, child of God and His lapsed servant, closed his eyes and felt the earth vanish under his feet, his soul traveling in the opposite direction from his mortal coil.

Upward...to Heaven.

Want to find out what happens next? Purchase your copy on Amazon.

The water—gleaming, shiny, and black in the faint moonlight—chills her skin despite the warm, humid air. Her toes push further into the sediment, squishing past weeds and over a sharp rock or piece of glass, sending a spasm of pain up her right leg.

I wonder if I'm bleeding? she thinks, aware it no longer matters. She trudges forward while the lake swallows her thighs, billowing out her dress and creating the illusion of a swollen midriff. Hot tears trickle from her eyes, and a moan erupts from her lungs. She gulps air between sobs.

These will be her last breaths.

She doesn't struggle; resistance is futile. When the water rises past her nose, she squeezes her eyes closed, as if for protection. She holds her breath until she can't any *longer, assaulted by the burn, and draws in the cold, murky water. Thrashing, she tries to push up those few inches to the surface, to the air, to life.*

Regret floods her consciousness when the water invades her lungs.

How could I let this happen? *she wonders, picturing the stern but loving face of her father, the gentle smile of her mother, the mischievous grin of her little cousin missing his two front teeth.*

And she sees his *face, as well. Of course she does.*

She wants to live, yet her limbs are numb, devoid of the strength survival will take.

She surrenders to the nothingness.

Want to find out what happens next? Purchase your copy on Amazon.

Tight as a drum. The phrase rattled through Tyler's head every time he looked at the girl's tan thighs and her high, rounded apple-cheeks. What was her name again? Madison? Mackenzie? It didn't matter. Tyler had taken one look at her striding across the gas station parking lot in a barely there tank top and short shorts, looking fit for a mudflap, and instantly forgot what Mitchell had said to call her. Whatever name she went by—Melissa or Marjorie, Miss Northwest Arkansas, even—she was there for him. That was all Tyler needed to know.

He opened the truck door and pulled the front seat forward so she could climb in, savoring her scent when she brushed past. Mitch had told him the girl was "so fresh outta school, you can still smell the textbooks," but Mitch was wrong. It wasn't the smell of textbooks wafting off her but the sweet tang of early morning, post-shower sweat and cloying drugstore perfume. The mosquitos were going to love her. Tyler, on the other hand, only planned to screw her.

"We got one more in the back, so you're gonna have to scootch," he said.

The girl nodded and slid over to the farthest corner of the bench seat, where she would be catty-corner to Tyler in the front and he would be able to look at her with a slight turn of his head.

"Little help, maybe?" Althea, Mitch's girlfriend, lurched across the parking lot. She was carrying a couple of heavy plastic sacks of ice, one in each hand, with her arms raised to keep the frosty bags from hitting her bare legs. She reached a patch of mottled shade and nearly disappeared for a second in her camo shirt, green cargo shorts, and hiking boots.

Tyler pulled a wad of mucus up into his sinuses with a gagging snort and spat it onto the ground, all the while congratulating himself for leaving his own woman at home. Not that Jaelynn had needed much convincing on that front. She never went further south than Neosho.

"You got this," Tyler said to Althea, making no move to assist.

Althea reached the vehicle and tossed the ice up to Mitch, who stood in the truck bed, straddling a large cooler box. He ripped open the bags and let the contents shower like hail stones over an army of beer bottles, then he replaced the cooler lid and hopped down. Mitch gave the quad trailer's hitch a reassuring kick and yanked the straps on the dirt bike once before climbing in behind the steering wheel. The truck peeled out of the parking lot in a storm of pea gravel and dust.

Tyler twisted around in his seat to grin at the girl. She returned the smile, revealing—dear Lord—dimples and granny-smith green eyes.

"Thanks for lettin' me tag along."

"You get out into the woods often?" Tyler asked, shouting to make himself heard over the road noise coming in through the four open windows.

"It gets old 'round here when you're local," the girl yelled back. "You seen one tree and a couple of show-caves crammed with tourists, and you seen enough. You guys come down outta Kansas City or St. Louis? Your profile didn't say where you're from."

"Bolivar," Mitchell replied.

"Oh, sure." The girl's pretty smile sagged. "That ain't so far, then." She stared out the window, fiddling with a heart-shaped charm hanging on a slim metal chain around her neck. It had begun to turn green where her fingers played over the gold finish. She crossed her long legs, bumping her shin against the center console inches from where Tyler's elbow rested.

Tight as a drum, he thought, glancing down at the bronzed swell of her calf. Mitchell nudged him.

In the back seat, directly behind Tyler, Althea leaned to the side, trying to make out Mitch's face. Wrinkles high on his cheekbones—faint crow's feet—he was grinning behind his wraparound shades, enjoying his friend's potential conquest —enjoying it a mite too much maybe. They had left the stench of Missouri's turkey farms and industrial hog lots behind an hour or so earlier, and the air was fresh and clean, albeit thin with a sour, metallic taste.

"Jaelynn have to work this weekend?" Althea asked Tyler.

"Something like that," Tyler mumbled, staring hard at the road ahead. "Camping's not her thing, and she hates riding bitch on the quad."

"Didn't she grow up around here, though? Like, exactly 'round here?" Althea stretched her leg to the base of Tyler's seat and pressed her boot against his seatbelt.

The strap pulled tighter against his neck, and Tyler shifted uncomfortably.

"Seems weird she wouldn't want to swing on by for a visit if she still has people down this way," she continued.

"You get a job I don't know about, Thea? You with fuckin' CNN now? Put away the goddamn waterboard!" Mitchell glared at her in the rearview mirror. "I think we need some tunes to get this party started."

The truck swerved toward the center of the road while Mitch examined his phone, searching his playlists for the right song and finding it seconds before the last tire exited their lane. He righted the car and thumped the steering wheel with the meaty part of his palm when a guitar began to wail and Axl Rose welcomed them all to the jungle, promising them fun and games.

"We're in the jungle now, baby," Mitch crowed, taking a hard right off the cracked black asphalt of the main highway and onto a narrow dirt road which dropped into the dense foliage of the mountainside. "Back to nature. Howl with me," he instructed Tyler before letting out a long, ululating cry.

"Dumb ass." Tyler shook his head. "This song is older than your mother."

The young girl laughed and undid her ponytail, freeing her long blond hair. It whipped around her face and caught in her heavily mascaraed eyelashes. Even Althea pulled her foot back from under Tyler's seat and relaxed.

A bead of condensation slid down the slender neck of Tyler's beer bottle. He caught it on his tongue and licked it off, then finished the beer in one final swig, flinging the bottle away. It hit the trunk of a tree and shattered with a sharp crash. Across from him, her narrow rear perched on the seat of Tyler's ATV, the girl grinned and tossed her own bottle in the same direction. It fell short and landed with a soft thud in a clump of moss.

"You wanna look for the others now?" she asked.

"Naw." Tyler shook his head. His brain rotated a dizzy half-turn in his skull.

They had lost Mitch halfway along the trail, when he shot upward on a path too narrow for the quad. Tyler had been forced to head down, following switchback after switchback until he and his companion reached the very bottom of the gorge. Now they were alone in the hollow of the mountain, a deep cradle sunk in the center of the hill.

Jutting stone cliffs rose above them on four sides, and all around, emerald foliage heaved in the afternoon heat. Plant-life burgeoned from the forest floor, like green lava streaming out of a volcanic cauldron, and surged upward to form a canopy, trapping the warmth and turning the basin into a stifling, tropical pot. The sultry atmosphere made Tyler's head spin and set his ears ringing. There was tangible electricity in the air, and not all of it was emanating off Madison... McKenzie...whoever-she-was sitting across from him.

"Hear that?" he asked, leaning forward suddenly and throwing his body off-balance. Tyler caught himself with an elbow on his knee.

"Hear what? The bike? It's your friend's, I think. It was up there across from us maybe fifteen minutes ago. That way." The girl pointed over Tyler's shoulder to a high tree-lined ridge, then frowned, unsure. "Maybe it's over there?" She pointed at a second ridge which ran perpendicular to the first.

A hawk screamed, its shrill cry ricocheting at them from multiple directions.

"I can't tell." Defeat crept into the girl's voice. "Everything gets mixed up out here, with the cliffs and all. That's why I don't come here. I hate these woods. Something about 'em feels like they want to swallow you up."

"I didn't mean the bike," Tyler snapped. "I meant the buzzing." A cloud of irritation settled over him, making him forget the girl's apple-green eyes and the smell of her smooth skin.

The girl shook her head. "You sure the buzz ain't from that six pack you just sucked down?"

Tyler held up his hand. "Shut up and listen."

High-pitched enough to set it apart from the quad's motor, a whirring hum had followed him and the girl ever since they split off from Mitchell and Althea, but Tyler couldn't determine its source. There were no power lines nearby. No cell towers. The place was a wasteland.

The closest town was a two-bit hole at the top of the mountain called Oracle Springs, where they had stopped for ice and beer and to pick up the girl. It was the town where Tyler's girlfriend, Jaelynn, had been born, and she had told Tyler a few stories about growing up all the way out there in Nothingsville, AR. No streetlamps. No radio signal. TV reception so bad you couldn't even get a single network station without connecting to cable. It sounded like hell on earth to Tyler.

"C'mon." Tyler staggered to his feet and gestured for the girl to follow. They left the quad behind and, for thirty minutes—maybe more—tramped through the forest.

Years of fallen, decaying leaves slid over one another like dull satin under the pair's feet and gave off the stodgy, throat-tickling scent of autumn, even though spring wasn't half burned through yet. The couple ducked and dodged low-hanging tree limbs and thick spiderwebs and swatted at clouds of insects congregating in the shade. They plodded through marshy creek beds.

Tyler took the lead, determined to find the source of the noise, and the confused girl scurried behind to keep up. They stopped only when they ran smack into a sheer wall of rock on the far edge of a deep pond.

"End of the road, seems like." The girl giggled nervously. "Should we head back?"

Tyler craned his head up to where the towering rock met the sky and vines snaked down over the top, forming an uneven fringe. Pale, mint-colored moss clung to the underside of minor outcroppings, but the cliff was mostly a smooth plane of honed, gray granite which reflected darkly in the water before it. A narrow crevice ran down the center of the vertical rock exposure, widening at the bottom to form a slender, pyramid-shaped doorway into the mountain. It looked like the opening to an ancient temple hidden in a jungle.

"Let's check it out." Tyler grabbed the girl's hand and pulled her toward the opening.

"I don't know." She hung back, resisting Tyler's dogged attempts to drag her forward. "Some caves around here are no good. Folks go missing in 'em, they say."

"*Who* says?"

"Old timers."

"Do I look like an old timer to you?" Tyler scowled, and the girl wilted under the weight of his glare. "Don't be stupid. You got me with you, so there's nothing to worry about." He held out his hand, and the girl took it, finally allowing him to lead her through the angular opening.

A robust thermal weight struck the pair when they stepped inside. Before them was an undulating, ribbon-like path of slippery, sweating rock leading into a deep, tunnel-like cave. A sheet of light cut through the gloom from a gash in the rock overhead, illuminating the tapered corridor as far as the eye could see, which wasn't that far at all. The stone walls of the cave had formed in waves and hair pin turns and, every five to ten feet, turned back on themselves, rendering a full assessment of the cave's depth impossible.

"How deep into the hill d'you think it goes?" the girl asked in a whisper.

"Don't know," Tyler said.

"What if we get lost?"

"Nowhere to get lost. It's a single path. C'mon."

Tyler pulled her deeper into the conch-like cave, tugging her along when her pace slackened. Humidity formed clouds of fat water molecules which caught the light streaming down onto the couple's shoulders. Despite all the moisture, however, little to no moss or algae grew on the walls. They glistened, slick and barren, fading from deep charcoal to the color of warm sand and then to that of a ripe peach as the trail wound on.

"We been walkin' for ages," the girl said after a while. Her small voice still managed to echo in the hard space. "Let's head back."

"Not yet. I think we're close to it."

"Close to *what*?"

"The goddamn buzz! It's coming from down here."

Down here. They were headed down, descending while they made their way toward whatever lay ahead.

At the entrance of the cave, the path had been level and, for the first few hundred meters, possessed the merest intimation of grade. But as it progressed, the path grew steeper, and each step had carried the pair lower. The roof of the cave yawned away, and the sunlight receded. No longer cascading down in a brilliant sheet, it trickled over them in unreliable glints and flickering patches until it finally abandoned them altogether.

Undeterred by the darkness, Tyler unhooked a small flashlight from his belt.

"I want to head back," the girl said. "I wanna go *now*."

Tyler's light moved around the cavern. The warm sunset oranges and terra cotta tones of the stone had deepened further and were now rich and rusty, the color of raw flesh. In the wavering light, they throbbed like something living. The space had the air of something soft and yielding. Like an organ. Like a beating heart or a womb.

The flashlight died.

It went out without so much as a blink. Tyler and the girl were alone in the dark. Their ragged breath beat against the walls—those deep red, living walls, invisible now in the gloom—and the girl tugged at his hand.

"Let's go. We can find our way back, even without the light. Sure we could." Her voice was hoarse and tremulous. "Like you said, it's one path. Only one way back."

"No." Tyler's reply was a Neanderthal's grunt made less abrupt by a slight echo. He shook off the girl's hand and took a step further down the path, remarkably sure of himself in the darkness.

One step, then another, and a light appeared around a bend. Tyler moved toward the glow, and the girl followed. The narrow passage took one final twist before ending in a wide-open inner chamber. Tyler stumbled out of the dark and was momentarily blinded.

High above the floor, in the stone roof of the cave, was a skylight—a grass-rimmed oculus large enough to light the chamber and set the ruddy walls aglow. It illuminated a pool of Aegean blue at the far end of the stone rotunda. A slope, like the funnel of a spiral wishing well, led to a deep central point in the water which peered up at them like a black pupil within a bright blue iris.

Tyler approached the pool and leaned over to assess its depth. Close up, the water was so clear that the trough appeared to be filled with nothing at all. Staring into it gave him vertigo.

"What's wrong with those fish?" The girl leaned over Tyler's shoulder, breathing into his ear, her smell no longer sweet to his senses. A school of silvery white minnows swam toward them, rushing this way and that in blind unison. Where they should have had eyes, there was nothing but pale scales, smooth and undisturbed from nose to gill. "Where're their eyeballs at?"

"Animals living in pure darkness don't need eyes," Tyler answered. If the girl had known him better, she might have wondered at the unnatural evenness of his voice.

"But it ain't dark in here." She pointed to the hole in the ceiling while still watching the fish in horrified fascination.

"No, it ain't," Tyler agreed, looking around the cave.

A few feet away, on the lip of a stone outcropping, a white salamander perched, motionless. It, too, lacked eyes. A membrane of thin bluish skin stretched taut over the round organs, which twitched and quivered underneath.

Tight as a drum.

Someone—or some*thing*—repeated Tyler's words to him. The buzzing noise grew louder, and a ripple formed on the surface of the water. A small V-like wake which matched the shape of the cave's entrance grew wider as it cut through the water. It raced toward Tyler and the girl.

The buzzing in Tyler's head stopped, and for a moment, he thought he heard someone laugh. Tyler laughed too, and he kept on laughing even when the girl, Madison...or McKenzie, or whatever...began to scream.

Want to find out what happens next? Purchase your copy on Amazon.

"Piece of shit," Charlie whispered to the empty sink.

The disposal made a hiss before going completely dead. The stench of rancid chicken began to loom over the small kitchen—a good reason to go off on those bitches in the office when he dropped off his monthly ransom tomorrow.

Last week had marked ten years to the day since Charlie first picked up his keys, walked through the door of his final home, and fell to his knees, crying himself to sleep in his empty apartment. Once he awoke, there was still a glimmer of hope he would recover. But that glimmer went pitch-black when the days poured into months and months poured into years of solitude.

Charlie shuffled back to the sofa and plopped down on the long end of the sectional. Minnesota kicked another field goal, putting the game just about out of reach. Another commercial replaced the game, and the old man sighed.

The lives of his twin boys, Cole and Christopher, had been cut short just a week after their twenty-second birthdays a decade ago, when Cole's little sports car hit a patch of black ice. The silver two-seater was sent on a death spiral into a massive oak tree. Cole died on impact. Christopher lost his right arm when the first responders cut him from the wreckage but held on for two days before Elizabeth made the call to send him to his brother.

Charlie never forgave his wife for that, nor God, who had placed the giant oak in their path.

He had always been a bit of a hard-ass, but the tragedy turned him into a raging monster. Elizabeth tried everything to hold them together. The last straw for Charlie had been the day she placed adoption papers in front of him. For the still-grieving father, just the consistent tall glasses of bourbon tainted with a splash of soda would ever replace his boys.

She left, only to return and take possession of their house after the divorce. The sugar plant Charlie had given his life to had allowed their fearless leader three months to mourn, then another six before they realized they needed to cut him loose.

After thirty years of dedication, Charlie left the factory with a decent pension and a cheap watch. Elizabeth took half the pension. She let him keep the watch.

A chilly breeze filtered over him from the sliding glass he had left slightly ajar. After letting loose a gigantic burp, Charlie swung his legs over the bottom cushion, then staggered over to the door and fumbled through the long slats covering his window.

A rustling sound came from behind one of the bushes sitting to the left of his patio.

"Who the fuck is out here? I'll kick your damn ass!"

No response to his threatening inquisition. Only the sound of the frigid Susquehanna flowing with fervor toward the Chesapeake.

Small clouds formed from his heavy breathing and disappeared past the sad man. Charlie turned to close the rusted door—a feeble attempt to shut out the miserable world for another night.

Two large hands pushed him backward with force.

In a flash, a hooded figure, mask resembling an evil pumpkin, had him pinned to the carpet, his knees on Charlie's upper biceps, rendering the old man helpless.

Charlie attempted to scream, but the large intruder caught his jaw, effectively cutting off any sound. The man held Charlie's mouth open and shoved several pills down his throat.

A vinegary flavor exploded along Charlie's tongue. A minute later, with his unwanted guest still hovering over him, Charlie's breathing stopped. Small drops of foam erupted from his mouth and coated his cracked, blue lips.

Satisfied his host was now dead, the hooded figure positioned the old man in a reclined position on the worn sofa. He poured a splash of soda over his victim's lips and placed a few more pills on the wooden table sitting next to the sofa.

Once the carpet and door track were wiped clean with a solvent-filled rag, the masked figure took a moment to look over his work. A grin broke out from behind his orange mask. The long road of preparation was finished.

His reign of terror had begun.

Want to find out what happens next? Purchase your copy on Amazon.

The drive back to his funeral home was peaceful. Angie slept in the cradle of her mother's stiff arms, still covered with the traveling blanket. The rain slowed to a drizzle.

There was a sense of something accomplished in the silent car. A fate fulfilled. But Stillman's fate remained a mystery to him. He struggled with his tight throat when he pulled into his driveway.

Stillman stopped the car, killed the engine, and slowly plied his daughter from her mother's embrace. Angie cried out only once, at the first break of connection. He wrapped her tightly in the blanket, held her closely to him, and breathed deeply of the rich caramel scent from the top of her small head.

"Let's go, Angie baby. Pop has work to do."

Stillman turned on all the lights in the house. He had left the heater running, and the rooms felt comfortable. Stillman placed his daughter on the couch in a nest of her mother's clothes, where the smell of her still lived. He kissed her before descending to the basement.

Stillman didn't know how much time he had. At any moment, his daughter might need him. That thought made him miss a step and nearly fall.

He remembered what Doloris had said in the car, just after her first labor pain.

She will know me, Stillman. She will feel me. While you do your work, she will be safe. Take your time. Be your usual methodical self. Trust me.

His embalming studio was immaculate. Everything had been prepped for his final act of devotion.

Embalm.

Embrace.

Perhaps those two words had always meant the same thing.

All the rivers of life needed to be run dry for the illusion of life to flow freely. That was the credo of his practice. The credo of all the painters of the past who had prepared the dead. And like poplar board or canvas, his bodies must be prepped to receive the tentative lies he would suffer upon them.

Stillman was a portraitist. Arterial injection of the common carotid, with the tandem drainage of the lesser jugular, was his gesso. Glutaraldehyde, formaldehyde, and methanol, in proprietary percentages, were his crude underpainting. But the illusion of life, he rendered with his fingers and thumbs.

Doloris had wanted none of his old master techniques. She would force his hand into the abstract of the post modernists. Into realms past mere likeness. And over the threshold of taste into the spiritually functional. Her request had repulsed him. Made him feel unworthy of all his accumulated craft.

She had always admired the way he prepared his dead. Why had she insisted on this grotesque configuration for herself? State laws would be leveled. His embalmer's license imperiled. And for what? Love, dummy. To suit her, he would have to work without his usual aesthetic light. This would be an act of love. Like making love. In the dark.

To arrest her decay, Stillman had brewed something which wouldn't make her seem lifelike. Or pliant. From the organic mother of vinegar, infused with cinnabar and the crushed resin of myrrh, along with several desiccating tinctures, he injected her delicate arteries. She would not seem a kiss away from awakening. Doloris would stiffen like the ancient pharaohs. Gloss over and shine.

But first, he needed to extract and refrigerate what was left of her breast milk. Then he could begin her new form. The final loving vessel she would be become.

He emptied her peritoneal cavity of her omentum, her splenic, hepatic—all the now useless Latin of her. Stillman removed the muscle and flesh from her middle. And with her open thoracic cavity clean and heavily salted, he began laying the soft and fragrant stuffs in her hollow. Dove down, as he had been instructed. But heartier stuffs too. Goose and owl down. Duck and hawk and hummingbird. All the avian down he had begun collecting from nests and tree limbs when she was in her eighth month.

And then the flower petals. He had much to choose from. All those funeral wreaths and bouquets he had gathered after the services ended in his upstairs chapel. Those floral show ponies put to pasture after only a few quiet hours of a single day. Carnations and roses and lilies and lilacs—all dried and only slightly dusty smelling.

When her ventral cavity was comfortably packed, he assembled the false breast, which would nourish his daughter. Stillman removed the baffle from an old transfusion pump so the sloshing of the mechanism might sound like a heartbeat. He clamped it to a feed tank. The delivery hose he ran between her deflated breasts.

God, those breasts on their wedding night...Revealed like soft moons with a part of her baby blue night gown.

The breast milk he diluted with formula to prolong it. And with a rubber nipple attached to the end of the tube, he stopped and regarded his work.

It would still smell of her before it cured. But also, of everything she had loved. Spice and incense. All of nature's daily airs perfumed by once-living things. A woody cradle of bone and preserved skin. Eyes sown shut. Ears and mouth forever closed. But *her*. The her she had been willing to become for Angie.

At least her hair would be the same. Stillman brushed it until it shined. He put down the hairbrush and ran his fingers through it. She had always worn it loose before bed. Shining like this, before she slipped under the covers with him.

He mounted the basement stairs, found his daughter curled in sleep where he had left her, lifted her, descended again, and placed sleeping Angie inside it. It would take months to fully harden. But the dead flesh already smelled like Doloris's sewing room. Nothing an infant would fear.

Stillman made sure she could find the nipple when she awoke. He patted his daughter's belly while she squirreled herself into the soft bed.

Doloris Mudstill Ayers had no funeral. Her fate was well known and endorsed by all her female relatives. Who, in turn, explained to all their partners why such a ceremony could not occur. They knew Doloris's real final resting place. And it was not the dry, lunar lagoon of her namesake. That was all. She was still among the Mudstills.

Only Stillman felt her absence.

Want to find out what happens next? Purchase your copy on Amazon.

A tiny sliver of gold filigree shines on the eastern horizon while Andrew and I make our way out of Houston. After the red-eye from Los Angeles deplaned, we picked up a rental car resembling a tin can and are now rattling down the highway toward Oleander.

"I hope you know where we're going." Andrew stares out the window at the flat green fields flying past. The suburbs have faded into the rearview. "Because I've never been to the South before. Texas counts as the South, right? South with a capital 'S,' I mean."

"Maybe, but Oleander isn't too far from the Louisiana border. I suppose that makes it the South with a capital 'S.'"

"Cows!" Andrew raises his phone to snap a picture of several sleepy heifers grazing under a lonesome black oak.

I ignore the farm animals and my husband, choosing to let the car fill with silence. We don't speak again until we are hours from the airport. A large green road sign appears.

"I think that's our exit," I say, about half a second before the virtual navigator on Andrew's phone advises me to get into the right-hand lane. My stomach does a funny little flip. The marker should be a relief. We're not lost in the Godforsaken countryside. But all I feel is a tightening sensation in my gut. "I need this trip like I need a hole in my head."

"What's that?"

"Nothing. It's just that this whole thing throws a wrench in my plans. I was going to look for a new job this week."

"You were?" Andrew sounds doubtful.

"You don't think I was?"

He bites his tongue before speaking. Andrew contemplates his response so hard, steam is almost coming off the top of his head. "I'm sure you were *planning* to look for something," he says finally.

It's a careful answer—cautious and safe, like Andrew himself. What he likely wants to add but doesn't is that *planning* and *doing* are two different things.

I know that. Of course, I hadn't *planned* to get caught in the ladies' room, popping pain meds I stole from a coworker at the journal where I worked. I hadn't *planned* to fail an HR-ordered drug test. Hadn't *planned* to get fired from the only job I ever loved. And I certainly hadn't *planned* to have to fly to the middle of nowhere for the funeral of a man I have not spoken to since before I hit puberty.

I obey the GPS's commands and steer the rental car up the off-ramp and onto a smaller road running perpendicular to the interstate. Pockmarked with deep holes and fissures, the sad ribbon of asphalt creeps past worn-out farms and stretches of uninhabited wetlands. There are abandoned pick-up trucks and other junkers resting up to their door handles in marshes, like mammoths caught in tar pits. Andrew lets his phone rest on his lap.

"It's not how I imagined it would look," he says when we reach a town as dismal as the road in.

A wasteland of empty buildings and desolate parking lots make up the city center. I stop at a red light and correct him.

"This isn't Oleander. It's Magnolia—the next town over. We have to drive through in order to get around the swamp. It's funny, though. Magnolia always seemed like the better town back when I was a kid. They had a movie theatre at least...and a mall. Not that my dad ever took me there." I point across the road.

On the far side of the intersection sits a dilapidated galleria. It's abandoned apart from two men, who pace the sidewalk in front of the entrance to the parking garage. They wear bulky windbreakers despite the heat of the morning and keep their hands shoved in their pockets. It's not hard to guess what they might be concealing in there. A user knows a dealer when they see one.

At the next intersection, the highway narrows, and a block beyond that, the town of Magnolia fades into a blur of overgrown brush and litter. The road forks, and a white finger post sign with three arrows appears.

"Someone scratched out the 'M' in Magnolia and replaced it with an 'F.' It says *Fagnolia*," Andrew notes.

"Bible-thumpers. Plenty of 'em out here." As if to underscore my point, I turn the rental car south, following the arrow that says "Oleander," and drive straight into an Old Testament-sized swarm of locusts.

The insects pelt the windshield like green hail, leaving behind vivid yellow smears. The thoroughfare tapers into the measliest sliver, and a marshy wilderness springs up along the road. Vines overwhelm the crumbling pavement, which has, bit by bit, eroded at the edges and disappeared into the conquering landscape.

There's a sign rising out of a bed of tall sawgrass which reads, "Welcome to Oleander," and seconds later, the town emerges like a mirage—or something straight out of the Twilight Zone, maybe because it is almost as though the little rental car has gone through a time warp and taken us back seventy years.

Oleander still lacks a mall: mega, mini, or outlet. There are no high-rises or designer coffee shops, no sushi houses or chain restaurants. Nothing that speaks of commercialism or the modern age.

Narrow shops and tidy storefronts line the street, like antique books packed neatly on a shelf, and every window box has an array of brightly colored flowers. The lawn of the square in front of the tiny town hall is about as weed free as one can get, and there's not a single loose shutter or crumbling brick I can see.

"It's nicer than I expected," I say, frowning. "Nicer than I remember." Not that I remember much.

"You could put this place in a snow globe." Andrew raises his phone and once more begins snapping pictures while we pass a shop for quilters and an ice cream parlor.

"Except it doesn't snow here." I'm being pedantic, but the town, as charming as it is, brings me no joy, though I can't explain why. Anyone else would be impressed with its Mayberry-esque qualities.

"You know what I mean," Andrew says. "It's quaint, like something from a painting. See that sign? Tully's Mercantile and General Store? Who even knows what mercantile is these days?"

Oleander's tiny business district yields quickly enough, and before long, sweet little cottages and stately farmhouses begin to spring up along the road. They line quiet avenues and cul de sacs, absurdly delicate and organized, with their freshly painted siding and gingerbread trim amidst the chaos of the marshy woods. It is as if, a hundred years ago, someone shook loose all the finest Victorian homes from the Sears Roebuck catalogue and sprinkled them down into a steaming jungle of palmetto and alligator weed.

Children skip rope on their driveways, and a group of ten or twelve boys and girls zigzag over a lawn in pursuit of a muddy soccer ball. Their shrieks and laughter penetrate the quiet confines of the rental car.

Amongst the wild, romping horde, a child stands apart from the rest. He's a statue with his back to the road, staring into the woods. A breeze ruffles his ivory curls when the children sweep past him, paying little attention as they dodge clotheslines and each other.

I crane my head, trying to get a better look at him. The boy turns slowly as we pass, offering a fleeting glimpse of his face, which is stained dark with what appears to be...

Blood.

"Picket fence! Picket fence!" Andrew cries out. "Watch out for the fence!"

I jerk the steering wheel, correcting our course before we slam into the obstacle.

"I see it. I see it. Jesus." My heart beats fast, and I am sweating despite the blasting AC. My hands tremble on the steering wheel. I glance over my shoulder, searching for the child, but he appears to have vanished.

Or joined his friends behind one of the houses, I allow, conceding this is the more likely option. The houses thin out, and the pavement abandons us, morphing into rust-colored clay.

Without warning, the lane curves sharply, and the bayou, a verdant emerald smear, appears like a serpent emerging from its den, slithering along the road's edge. The imperious oaks fall away, and the misshapen cypress rise from the banks. Their wide bases, swollen with water, give them the look of old-fashioned ladies in full skirts, with narrow corseted middles, strolling atop the Salvinia-covered surface.

"Oh, wow," Andrew says, mesmerized by the twisting channel. "I don't think I've ever seen water that color." He gawks at a heron near the swamp's edge but rips his eyes away long enough to notice a single-story cottage on the opposite side of the road. The place is almost entirely hidden behind a large garden of wildflowers. "Is that it? Is that Sapling Cove?" he asks excitedly.

"No. *Cypress* Cove is at the end of the road, where it dead ends. That must be Emma Lee Yarborough's place. She's the one who called me. I think she said she's Curt's nearest neighbor."

"Looks like she's been there a while. That's one hell of a garden. Did your dad ever mention her?"

"I told you," I remind Andrew irritably, "Curtis and I didn't speak."

"I know, but you had to have heard from him now and then. He must have visited after you went to live with your aunt."

"You assume he was a decent parent because *you* have decent parents, but the last I saw of Curtis Brightwood was his outline through the back window of his truck as he peeled out of the parking lot of the boarding school he dumped me at when I was twelve years old."

"Shit."

"Yeah, he was a shit, all right." I take the car around another curve in the road, and the house on Cypress Cove materializes incongruously out of the vegetal anarchy. "We're here," I say darkly.

Want to find out what happens next? Purchase your copy on Amazon.

By 11:15 p.m. on October 23, 2018, Alfie Turner, six years old and almost a big boy, had been in bed for hours. For the first sixty minutes, he had mostly thought about how much he missed his nightlight. For the rest of the time he had focused on the noises. Sounds that had begun to slither and creep, out from beneath his bed.

In recent weeks, especially since his father had taken the nightlight away, Alfie had endured many nights like this, lying awake for hours, holding his breath and listening, keeping his tiny limbs as stiff as boards. He would strain his ears for clues, sifting with care through distant sounds—the muffled conversations from far below, the tiny specks of noise outside, a dog barking perhaps, the sea-surf hiss of a passing car.

And below it all, clinging to the edge like mist to the shore, the hush.

A deliberate, conscious quiet. An almost-silence in which he could hear his own heartbeat, the patter of the rain, the wail of the wind chewing past the brickwork. In it he could feel, as weight within the space, that awful, pregnant stillness made by things which like to wait in the dark.

On nights like these, beneath the thin armor of his bedsheets, Alfie would swelter and listen but never dare to lift them. Somehow he knew, as all children know, that to lift the sheets was dangerous. To reveal a hand, an ankle, or even a toe was to invite some grip of terrible strength to close like a vise around it and drag him bodily, kicking and screaming, from the bed and into ever-waiting jaws.

So, he didn't. No matter what.

Instead, he clung to them, pulling the sheets over his head and cowering below. Every inch of skin covered by this fragile cloak shielding and holding him, disguising his body and the scent of his meat, from whatever unseen thing lurked beyond that veil.

Now, though, from out of that hush and out of that dark, a real sound began to slink and creep.

At first, it was barely there. An indistinct whisper, a suggestion of something just on the brink of audible. It was muffled, like the voice of someone speaking through a thick pane of glass. Almost imperceptible.

Almost, but not quite.

For as muted as it might have been, the fact remained the sound *was* there, and Alfie thought, *If the sound is there, then so is the thing that made it.*

The sound came once more. Louder now, or closer?

Alfie tried again to ignore it. With his eyes screwed shut, his breathing shallow, he attempted with all his might to convince himself it wasn't real. Over and over, he told himself he was imagining it. What he thought he heard was nothing but a dream, a sound only really existing in his head.

But it wasn't. Whatever that sound was, wherever it was coming from, and whatever horrible thing was making it, it was *not* in his head.

It was in his room.

"Go away, go away," Alfie muttered quietly, his breath hot and damp. The air beneath the sheet became more stifling. He wished again for his nightlight.

Oh God, please, the nightlight.

It was still there, plugged into the wall but switched off with iron finality by his father, who had insisted that keeping it on would make him "grow up a pansy." Nevertheless, the sound came again, this time accompanied by a long liquid hiss and the tacky half-slap of feet on the hardwood floor.

Alfie couldn't help but turn toward it.

He looked, even through the opaque wall of sheets, to where the nightlight's pinkish hue had been before, hoping, wishing, for its soft, comforting glow. There was nothing. Only darkness hung, massive and total. Shadows and footsteps.

Big boys, his father had told him, were not afraid of the dark. They didn't believe in monsters, and they didn't need a nightlight. Alfie wanted to be a big boy, to be brave and strong like his daddy, to work on cars, stay up late, and drink dirty beer. Big boys never had to worry about monsters in the cupboard. Alfie wanted to, but he couldn't.

So, instead he pretended. If anyone asked him, a jovial uncle or a scowling father, whether he was scared of the dark, he would simply lie. He'd puff out his chest as if he was the Hulk and laugh at the idea. As for monsters, he'd have told them there was no such thing. Only babies believed in things like that and he wasn't a baby. He was a big boy. And yet, though he would never have admitted it, for him, the dark still held onto its horrors.

Until his nightlight was taken away, the greatest terror in his daily existence had been the stretch between the bottom of the stairs and the living room. Many times, when his parents had called him from his room, he would descend the stairs, only to shrink in fear when he saw the hall light was off, the switch for which was on the other side of the passage.

Though the distance between the bottom step and the safety of the living room was only around ten paces on short legs, that stretch, that massive expanse, seemed like acres. A hideous, perilous sprint taken through the pitch-black over a terrain populated by untold terrors. Legions of long-toothed beasts formed from an amalgam of half-seen images. Creatures lurking, biding their time, waiting for the perfect moment to jump out and snatch him up. Dragging him away to be devoured and never seen again.

He hated that run, but he could tell no one. It was his private hell.

His parents would never understand.

Once in the safety of the living room, Alfie would put on an act. Though his heart still pounded in his chest, Alfie would walk to the sofa or dining table calmly, with an air of nonchalance, concealing from his oblivious family—and especially from his daddy—the terror he had experienced only moments earlier.

A terror, which of course, he would never have owned up to having experienced at all.

Now that same reluctance, that same fear of looking weak, of never being considered a big boy, stopped him from calling out. From screaming to his parents and asking them, *begging* them, to turn the nightlight back on. Instead he spoke, low and quiet, to the sound in his room.

"What do you want?" he whispered.

"To eat you," came the reply.

Want to find out what happens next? Purchase your copy on Amazon.

Flames roar against a clear night sky littered with stars. The stray sparks take to the darkness like fireflies. It would be beautiful in a way, if there weren't three bodies burning inside.

By morning, the flames will have eaten them, along with the house. The truth just has a way of consuming beautiful things.

It is almost poetic. But it shouldn't be so easy to erase someone's entire life like that. To have all those memories, all that history, reduced to a smoldering pile of ash.

Like it never existed.

This place was supposed to be a fresh beginning for my family. A chance to start over with the one I loved, who loved me, even though they were never very good at it. Everything felt so safe. For a moment, nothing in the world could touch us. But I was terribly wrong.

I *wasn't* safe.

And I don't know that I ever was. I am reminded of this with each crash and pop sounding from within the furnace of my former life.

A detective in a crisp white shirt approaches me in the ambulance, pulling me from my thoughts. When I notice him, I instinctively pull my son closer to my side.

We met before, when he first arrived on scene. The detective is a boulder of a man, stone-faced and hardened in a way only someone who has confronted real evil would understand. You have to build a wall around yourself to keep it from getting inside. I know that now.

"Ma'am." His timbre is even, and he scribbles something down on a small pad.

With one hand, I wipe the tears from my eyes and grip my son's shoulder with the other, preparing for more interrogation. I understand, of course. He is just doing his job. But that doesn't stop me from feeling like I am going to choke on my words if I have to relive this awful night...again.

"You doing okay?" he asks.

Relief floods my body. What a gentleman. He is just inquiring about my well-being. I open my mouth to answer, but he isn't speaking to me at all.

The detective is focused on Bodhi.

"He's still in shock," I offer in a shaky voice when Bodhi doesn't answer. "He hasn't spoken since the fire started."

"That's understandable. You've been through a lot tonight, buddy." His voice is soft. Kind. Not the emotionless hard-ass who grilled me for almost an hour while my entire life was burning to the ground. He even offers Bodhi a smile which reaches his eyes.

Bodhi doesn't return it. He doesn't react at all.

When the detective turns to me, his tone stiffens. "Did EMS complete their evaluation?"

"They did. Just a few scratches and some bruises. We're so lucky." I give Bodhi a kiss on the top of his head.

The detective nods, studying my son and me for a moment.

"Any idea when I can get him out of here, Detective? He doesn't need to keep seeing this."

The detective looks at me for a moment longer than I think necessary, then back to Bodhi. His shoulders relax, and an expression of sympathy washes over him.

"We've got your statement. We can put you up in a hotel if you don't have other accommodations."

"That's very kind of you, truly, but we'll be all right. We've got some family I can call to help."

"I understand. I'll need an address and phone number…in case we have any more questions." He hands me a notepad without waiting for me to agree, and I take his pen without hesitation.

I can't let him know I am lying.

We have no other family. That bitch made sure of that. All Bodhi has is me. I have to be strong for him. For my son.

All I want to do right now is get this place as far in my rearview as I can. So I scribble a random address from the next town over, one which will take a while for him to verify, and I make up a phone number. The detective gazes down at it for a moment before raising his eyes to mine.

I don't like the way he is watching me. Like he is trying to find some reason to make us stay. To question me further. But I have told him everything I can. What else does he want?

"We'll be in touch, Ms. Cole," the detective finally says, releasing the vise on my gut. Luckily, the detective didn't notice it. With one last gentle glance at Bodhi, he turns and walks back to his SUV.

"Come on, kid. Let's get you out of here," I say.

Bodhi doesn't look at me, even as I strap him into the back seat of the Altima. When I close the door, he rests his forehead on the window and stares off into the crackling dark. He stays like that, unmoving, while we pass through the awful iron gates surrounding our quiet little community.

I am not who he wants. If he had been given the chance, if things could have been different, it wouldn't be me sitting in the driver's seat. But for now, I will have to do.

Bodhi just needs time. He will understand how much I love him. That everything I had to do, I did for him. To keep him safe.

Safe from *her*.

Want to find out what happens next? Purchase your copy on Amazon.

From a dim afternoon sky cluttered with gray storm clouds, a steady rain fell.

It filled the flooded, sewer-choked lanes of Springfield Drive, where, from a second-floor bedroom window in a nondescript suburban house, a solitary boy watched.

Eleven-year-old Bobby Fisher frowned while he closed the curtains. The power had gone off five days ago and hadn't returned yet. Deep shadows bathed the room. He thumbed the rubber end of a flashlight balanced across his lap. A narrow beam of light shone on a pair of white plaster casts covering both of his legs, which were propped upright in the supports of a wheelchair. Each wrapping bore the scribbled signatures of his friends.

Bobby missed them terribly.

He considered how long they had been gone.

Bobby pressed his lips together in a tight line of concentration and spun away from the window. A jolt halted his movement.

With a groan, he reached down and undid the wheel brakes. He had spent the last four agonizing weeks confined to the chair but still hadn't gotten used to it. The unfortunate accident had occurred just before his friends all left on that big yellow school bus bound for summer camp. The same summer camp he was supposed to have attended too. Of course, that was before he had taken a little trip down a flight of stairs and a couple of fractured tibias put a kibosh on any chance of those plans happening.

The wobbly circle of light from the bouncing flashlight on his lap guided him through the darkness. He crossed the room and brought the wheelchair parallel to the bed. Then he set both palms on the armrests and pushed his rump up out of the seat. With a mighty heave, he pivoted his body and launched it onto the mattress, landing in a clumsy roll that made the box springs squeak.

He let out a low wail of anguish when his right leg, the side he landed on, throbbed with a sharp skewer of pain. Bobby winced, then elbowed himself into a sitting position, with his shoulder blades flush against the wooden headboard.

He sighed. Big beads of sweat pricked his forehead. With effort, he managed to wedge a soft pillow between his back and the hard wood. Then he sat and listened. Listened for any sounds the commotion of his maneuver might have provoked from the rooms below. The opening of a door, the clatter of a kitchen chair being pushed away, the initial creak of investigating footsteps ascending the stairs.

Bobby couldn't say exactly what it was he strained his ears to catch. But he heard nothing. Only the gentle pitter-patter of rain tapping against the window like many imploring fingers pleading to be let in.

Despite the humid summer air, an icicle of fear lanced his heart, and an involuntary shudder tingled his spine. He wondered what he dreaded more: the uneasy silence filling the entire house or the possibility of an answering noise.

Not for the first time that afternoon, he found himself thinking about Dylan.

Out of anyone, he missed his older brother the most.

Only two grades higher, Dylan had gone with the rest of his friends to summer camp four weeks ago, leaving Bobby stranded and forlorn, in a practically childless town, to while away the dreary hours convalescing in the lonely limitations of his room.

He wished Dylan were beside him. Bobby felt so miserable and empty without his presence. Dylan would know how to buck his spirits up. At the very least, he would know how to make him laugh. Dylan always knew how to make Bobby laugh, even if the joke was at his expense.

"I'll try to have a nice trip without you so long as you promise not to take any more *trips* while I'm gone," Dylan had teased before sprinting out the front door, joining the crowd of whooping kids on the bus that had borne him away.

But even when Dylan turned to go, Bobby had recognized the look of genuine regret that flashed for an instant behind his brother's pale blue eyes.

Bobby blinked bitter tears from his own eyes and swiveled his torso, holding the flashlight pinched between his knees. He threw an automatic glance over his shoulder at the closed bedroom door before prying up a corner of the mattress.

Crammed beneath the folds lay a disorganized pile of magazines. Plastered on their wrinkled covers were pictures of naked women with their boobs out. Hand-me-downs from Dylan, the only other person who knew where Bobby stored his secret stash. However, what Bobby currently sought was nothing pornographic. Brushing aside the nudie mags, he retrieved a small book.

He let the mattress flop back into place. Bobby tucked the flashlight in the crook of his armpit, arranged the book comfortably on his lap, and traced the tip of an index finger across the decorative leather cover. The word "Diary" was embossed in gold lettering.

Bobby had initially ridiculed the idea of keeping a diary when he received the journal as a birthday gift from his mom the previous year. *Only girls do things like that*, he had scoffed. Now, imprisoned in his own room with only a window to link him to the outside world, it had become the sole companion to whom he could confide his thoughts.

Perhaps he would let Dylan read it when he returned. Then again, perhaps not.

Ever since the storm that had thrown a shadow over Strawis Bay and the ensuing series of events, which had painted Bobby's imagination with black shades of doubt, he had observed—or thought he had—many curious things. Bobby wondered if all the suspicions and conclusions he had harbored during the preceding days were simply a delusion fabricated by his solitary and underactive mind.

He undid the elastic strap binding the book shut and opened it to the first blank page. While he flipped through his past entries, a terrible tapestry knitted itself before his eyes. Amidst a growing dread, his skepticism vanished.

A pencil lay in the crease between pages. He grasped it, pressed its dull lead tip against the paper, and jotted down today's date. *Aug 11.*

Then he paused, the pencil hovering above the first available line, his brow furrowed in intense focus. Bobby deliberated on where to begin.

He started.

Five days now without power. I hope it comes back soon.

The beam of the flashlight gave a flickering blink. When the light returned, he continued.

Flashlight batteries running low from constant use. The thought of them dying frightens me. I've grown afraid of the dark, and I don't feel like a baby for saying it. Though, I'm sure Dylan would laugh at me and call me one. But he doesn't know what I know.

Bobby paused again, rereading what he had written. On second thought, he erased and revised the last sentence—*what I think I know.*

When he found his flow, the words came to him with greater ease. Bobby wrote quickly, almost impatiently, seldom breaking, covering the lined composition page with the scarcely legible scrawl of an eleven-year-old boy.

Mom or Dad didn't bring me any breakfast this morning or any lunch at noon. In fact, I haven't heard a single peep from them all day, even when I called out to get their attention. Downstairs has been quiet ever since Mr. and Mrs. Beekman from across the street visited yesterday evening after sunset.

It's strange they'd visit at all, let alone so late. They've never been to our house before. I can't even recall my parents ever speaking to them, except for that one time when Dad borrowed Mr. Beekman's lawnmower.

I was watching from my bedroom window. Since I've been laid up, there's been nothing to do but watch. It was raining pretty hard, and they both carried large black umbrellas above their heads. Opening the window, I overheard Mr. Beekman's deep voice asking to be invited in and Dad's surprised voice granting permission.

I must have dozed off in my wheelchair after that, for the sound of the front door closing again woke me. I don't know how long I slept. When I looked back out the window, Mr. and Mrs. Beekman were recrossing the street with their umbrellas raised.

Engaged in his work, Bobby didn't become aware of the faint sound until it was repeated.

A rough grating, like wood scraping against wood, reached his ears. He glanced up uneasily. His vision wandered to the rain-spattered window. The sky had turned pitch black. A full moon hid behind billowing clouds.

It's only the wind rattling the loose pane in its frame, he told himself. However, the wind didn't open doors, especially ones within the house.

From below, the basement door creaked shut.

Bobby's breath caught. "Mom?" he whimpered. "Dad?"

Two sets of footsteps navigated the space between the basement door and kitchen. Bobby followed them along the floor with his flashlight. The trembling beam traced a line across the carpet with the route they took. Through the hall, across the living room, and stopping at the landing of the stairwell, where he thought he detected muffled voices.

A paralyzing fear held Bobby as immobile as the two casts binding his legs. There could be no mistaking the familiar tread of his parents' feet, but it struck Bobby that there was something different about the steps he didn't like. Something furtive.

The hairs on the nape of his neck stood up. Impulsively, he snatched the blanket stuffed under his knees and drew it to his chin. The flashlight on his lap rolled off the bed and hit the carpet with a dull *thud* that seemed awfully loud.

At that moment, the footsteps mounted the stairs and began climbing. Bobby's paralysis broke. His pupils desperately searched the room for something to aid him. His sight landed on his bandaged legs bearing the names of his friends.

Larger than the others and displayed with prominence in a spot purposely reserved was Dylan's name, followed by the humorous quip *Break a leg!*

Thump! Thump! Thump! Thump!

The footfalls hastened, approaching in a heavy two-step stride.

Each stomp brought Bobby's heart that much higher in his throat. The fallen flashlight lit the opposite wall. From the shine reflecting off the white paint, Bobby flipped to a new page in his diary and penned a last hurried message.

Dylan,

Don't trust anybody! Not even—

His pulse racing, Bobby finished his warning and restored the book to its place under the mattress, alongside the smutty magazines. The doorknob jingled and turned.

Bobby spun and faced the open door.

Two tall figures crowded the frame. Two figures who *weren't* his parents.

The figures were dark, with red eyes and white teeth.

Bobby let out a jagged scream.

The figures advanced, and their shadows cloaked the wall in darkness.

The flashlight fizzled out, as if shielding its eyes from a particularly unpleasant scene.

Want to find out what happens next? Purchase your copy on Amazon.

9 781967 163816